MURDER

FOR THE

MODERN

GIRL

KENDALL KULPER

HOLIDAY HOUSE   NEW YORK

Library of Congress Cataloging-in-Publication Data
Names: Kulper, Kendall, author.
Title: Murder for the modern girl / Kendall Kulper.
Description: First edition. | New York : Holiday House, [2022] | Audience: Ages 14–18
Audience: Grades 10–12 | Summary: In 1928 Chicago, eighteen-year-old Ruby, daughter
of the state attorney, uses her ability to read minds as a vigilante to hunt out murderers
and kill them even if they have not yet committed the crime; Guy works in the morgue,
and wants to understand the human body, because maybe then he will learn how it is
that he is able to shapeshift into other people—something Ruby plans to use because
someone is out to get her father and she is pretty sure it is the police, not the gangsters.
Identifiers: LCCN 2021037949 | ISBN 9780823449729 (hardcover)
Subjects: LCSH: Telepathy—Juvenile fiction. | Shapeshifting—Juvenile fiction.
Murder—Investigation—Juvenile fiction. | Vigilantes—Juvenile fiction.
Conspiracies—Juvenile fiction. | Fathers and daughters—Juvenile fiction. | Nineteen
twenties—Juvenile fiction. | Chicago (Ill.)—History—Juvenile fiction. | CYAC:
Telepathy—Fiction. | Shapeshifting—Fiction. | Murder—Fiction. | Vigilantes—Fiction.
Conspiracies—Fiction. | Fathers and daughters—Fiction. | Chicago (Ill.)—History—
20th century—Fiction. | LCGFT: Historical fiction.
Classification: LCC PZ7.K9490164 Mu 2022 | DDC 813.6 [Fic]—dc23
LC record available at https://lccn.loc.gov/2021037949

❖

For Iris and Flora, my girls. Stick together.
You're stronger as a group.

❖

ONE
RUBY

Golly, good murder took ages! *Two hours* I'd been sitting at this horrible excuse for a bar. At this rate, by the time I got out of here, all the best parties would be over!

Across the room, one Francis G. Mather, married, (wretched) father to five, sat with his arms around two women wearing enough paint to redecorate Tribune Tower. I'd watched them drink Smoke and toast to the end of 1927, *Good riddance what a damned awful year!*, and now I was ab-so-tive-ly determined Francis Mather would not see the start of 1928.

In front of me sat my own smudgy glass, half full on account I wasn't draining it the traditional way but in secret sips-and-spits into the flask I kept snuggled in my décolletage. Though Papa'd lectured me and my sisters for hours about the Dangers of Alcohol in All Its Forms, I didn't have to be the daughter of the Cook County state's attorney to know how colossally idiotic it would be to drink a full glass of Smoke. Glittery speakeasies might manage to sneak some legit booze past the jaws of Prohibition, but here in Back of the Yards, where they hadn't been able to get a drop of the real stuff since 1919, they had to make do with homemade rotgut. Might as well go outside and siphon out some gasoline from the nearest automobile—it'd be quicker, and cheaper, and have the same effect. But even if the bartender had offered me a beautiful flute of fizzy golden Champagne, chilled and freshly popped, I'd still pass it up. Drinking fiddled with the reception.

As Francis Mather launched into another chapter of *Horses I Have Known, Bets I Have Made,* I had to prop myself up to keep from wilting. I had places to be and people expecting me and, underneath this shabby pink coat, a party frock that was practically required by law to set heads turning. In my pocket, a postage-stamp-sized paper sachet of arsenic waited to be dropped into Francis Mather's almost-equally-poisonous cocktail. It would be so easy to slip it in and walk away...

But I had rules.

TIPS AND TRICKS FOR A SUCCESSFUL MURDER:

1. Locate the target.

Fellows like Francis Mather weren't hard to come by. *Good-for-nothing drunk bum bad husband worse father* rang through minds from Hyde Park to Uptown more often than the chorus of "My Blue Heaven." But as much as I would have liked to take the business end of my hairpin to every deadbeat in the city, the ones who earned a visit from me had to have something truly evil in mind. In this case, three trips to the hospital for Mrs. Mather within a year—illnesses that only seemed to get worse, like terrible rehearsals for something even more awful—followed by a visit from the life insurance man got people talking. And worrying. And whispering. And that got my attention.

2. Determine appropriate response.

Well, did I have to kill them? No, not always. "Ruby, the law can be a powerful weapon for justice," Papa taught me, and I believed him. But I did find it highly suspicious—not to mention highly annoying—that it seemed to be a helluva lot more powerful for a certain kind of (male) person. Still, if the situation called for it, I'd pass tips on to the law. Always anonymously, of course, because as far as anyone knew, I was just a barely eighteen girl in the city, glamming around parties, only interested in fast cars and fast boys.

As for Mrs. Mather, maybe I could have convinced her to try for a divorce, and maybe the right cop or the right lawyer could have believed her, but Francis Mather had a cousin on the force who was happy to look the other way, and too much resting on a large insurance policy in Mrs. Mather's name.

Someday I'd be that right lawyer, and I'd take all the Mrs. Mathers in the world and use the law to pos-i-lute-ly skewer anyone who tried to hurt them. But, golly, I'd only just graduated high school and law school was years away and by that time, Mrs. Mather would be dead. I'd take my chances with the arsenic.

3. Wait for the starting pistol.

The most important part. How could you possibly be sure a person intended to do real, terrible harm? How could you snip someone out of existence for a crime they had, technically, yet to commit? How could you be sure of someone's mind?

But I am always sure.

Ever since I was a kid in knee socks, other people's thoughts have bobbed through the air like pretty baubles floating in a stream. I simply had to reach in and pluck them out. Worries and wonders and idle passing fancies—somehow, like a supernatural radio antenna, I could hear them all, and the older I got, the easier it became. I went deeper, under the surface for those bright flashy fishies, and even all the way down to the mucky bottom, where I could sometimes pry up the deepest, heaviest rocks. I learned to recognize different kinds of minds and what they told me about the person they belonged to. Honest, open people had minds as smooth and clear as a millpond. People who kept secrets had minds walled up tight, riddled with hidden whirlpools that tried to pull me down.

Killers had a particular kind of mind, too. Icy cold. Oily slick.

At this point, Francis Mather'd spent the better part of two hours fantasizing about the freedom and money that would come with his wife's death—never mind the five mouths relying on him—while also looking forward to a little privacy with his two companions. He was a scummy man. A bad father. A worse husband. But not a real murderer. Not yet.

And so, I sat, waiting, drumming my fingers against the bar and spitting out burning mouthfuls of Smoke into my pocket flask.

"Another one?" The bartender—and I'd use that word with a whole Christmas basket's worth of generosity—reached for my half-empty glass.

The *real* Ruby Newhouse probably would have snapped at his hand with her purse, flashed a dazzlingly gorgeous smile, and said something like "The last man who tried to jimmy my dregs lost his whole arm." But I wasn't myself tonight. My red hair was tucked up into a messy black wig and topped with a pitiful pancake hat the color of old putty. I kept my shabby coat bundled over my best deep-blue silk dress (and underneath that, my best black satin knickers, the grown-up ones my mother would hang me for if she ever discovered them). With no makeup and a pair of specs nicked from Papa's upstairs office, I was a regular Mrs. Grundy and 100 percent guaranteed no one'd give me more than a fish-eye glance—except for the bartender, annoyed at the sluggish pace of my drinking.

"Not done yet," I snapped, snatching my glass away, and, with the patience of a person who worked for tips, he gave me a stiff smile while mentally picturing my gruesome disembowelment.

"And what're we gonna *do* once we get there?" one of Francis Mather's girls giggled. He leaned in, whispered something that made her snort with laughter. Her thoughts came out mushy and muddled and drowned in Smoke, but I could read him loud and clear:

...tonight. Or tomorrow. Tonight's better. Get the money by the end of the week. Rat poison. Sneak it into her hot cocoa. They won't find her until the morning. Tonight or tomorrow. Tonight's better...

Starting pistol, and we're *off.*

"Hey! Bartender! Top 'er up," I said, and the bartender narrowed his eyes at me but sloppily filled my glass. Once I had my Smoke, I slipped a hand into my pocket for the paper sachet and slid back off my stool, the soles of my scuffy shoes sticking to heavens-knew-what on the floor. I stumbled a little, cursing, swaying, making my way to an empty table on the other side of the room. Just as I passed Francis Mather's table, my foot caught the ankle of companion number one and my glass of liquor went flying, hair to hemline, down the front of companion number two.

"Watch yer bony feet!" I shouted, while Number Two let out a screech like a cat and jumped up.

"My *dress*! You *ruined* my *dress*!"

"Blame her and those Clydesdale stompers!"

"I'll call *you* a Clydesdale!"

"Girls! *Girls!*"

They both came at me, with Francis Mather laughing fit to bust. The bartender whipped out between us, more worried about what three hellcats could do to his collection of glassware than what we'd do to each other, so I brayed, "I'm leaving, *I'm leavin'!* You can have this stinkin' hole!" before retreating out to the street.

Number Two wanted to go after me but she got one bite from the Chicago winter wind into her wet dress and lost her nerve. I was gone in a twenty-cent flash, sideways to a hidden alley where I'd hid my favorite kitten heels and my mother's tarnished makeup compact.

Ten minutes later, I'd traded the scuffy shoes, oily wig, and sad putty pancake hat for a smear of kohl over my eyes and a Cupid's pout on my lips. After giving my red curls a good fluff, I stepped back into the street, my heels snapping on the pavement.

I didn't need to stick around to see the end. *Acute alcohol poisoning* would be the official report, and no one would fuss with an autopsy; come morning, the county coroner would find his office hopping with revelers laid out from the 1928 Special. Hell, at the rate Mather'd been drinking, maybe the arsenic wasn't even necessary—quite literally overkill—but I didn't bother with chance. In my experience, the wicked tended to be inordinately luckier than the innocent.

Which was exactly what made this work so satisfying.

As I tucked my favorite pin into my curls and made a beeline for the taxi stand on Ashland, I felt the weight of Francis Mather lift from the world, turning everything lighter and brighter—including me. I couldn't help dancing down the sidewalk, knowing I looked perfect for tonight's party: fresh and pretty and glowing with a mysterious kind of *something* that would send the fellas gathering like moths to a candle. I grinned.

Honestly, murder worked better than mascara.

TWO
GUY

"We're almost done here, sir. Are you all right?" I asked, looking up from my notes to where Mr. Roger Carrell lay stretched out under the pale lights. "I'll get you tucked away in just a minute."

Roger Carrell didn't answer, which was to be expected, as he was dead.

People underestimated the dead as conversationalists. You couldn't disappoint a dead person, or incorrectly guess what they wanted you to say. Living people had brains swimming in chemicals, electric pulses shooting through their bodies like fireworks. They kept their intentions hidden inside their skulls.

But the dead—the dead were open books.

Take Mr. Carrell, for example. Four days ago, before Mr. Carrell arrived at the Cook County Morgue, when his elegant nervous and circulatory system still hummed along in perfect order, he worked in a smelting factory in West Town. He had several inches and a good hundred pounds on me, with thick, solid muscles developed over decades of labor. I knew with absolute certainty that, had we ever met,

I wouldn't have had the courage to look him in the eye. Never mind speaking to him—no "hello" or "good morning" or any of the nice, normal things I practiced daily before the mirror.

Here, though, dead and cold in the white-plastered windowless basement of the morgue, his blood already drained and his rib cage cracked open from the autopsy this afternoon, Mr. Carrell looked almost…friendly.

"And now," I said to his corpse, and I reached for the section knife. "I'll need to—"

From somewhere upstairs, the soft, sighing whine of a floorboard made me go as still as Mr. Carrell, my eyes frozen to the ceiling above. This late—near midnight, and on New Year's Eve—the morgue should have been deserted. I didn't move again until I counted three minutes of silence.

I wasn't supposed to be here.

Well, that wasn't quite accurate. Guy Rosewood could be here, now, in this autopsy room, but with a mop and a bucket, not a bone saw and a dead body.

"This ain't a place for weak stomachs, got it, Rosewood?" Three months ago, on my first day as the janitor for the Cook County Morgue, my boss at the main hospital had escorted me across the medical campus courtyard to the small graystone morgue building and directly down to the autopsy room below.

"You gotta be sick, you do it outside. The doctors don't want you muckin' up their nice copper basins."

That might've been a test. He had a big grin on his face as he pushed open the door to the autopsy room—which was…ah…freshly used.

But as soon as I saw the bright lights, the neat rows of instruments, the walls papered with large hand-tinted diagrams of body musculature and the skeletal system and the beautiful, treelike branches of nerves, I smiled. This was exactly where I wanted to be, for two important reasons.

First, I needed to learn how bodies worked, and the dead made good teachers.

Second, I needed to learn how *my* body worked, and there was only one teacher for that.

I always knew my body was…unusual, but after years combing through medical journals looking for answers, I'd found nothing. Until I discovered a single paper, a theory based on an observation, no more than a page long and titled "A Proposal Regarding Cellular Metamorphosis in Humans." I couldn't've been more shocked than if I'd turned the page to see my own picture printed there. I needed to meet the man who had written that paper, which, it turned out, had gotten him fired from his prestigious university job, forcing him to find work as a medical examiner in the Cook County Morgue. I saw him on that first day: Dr. Gregory C. Keene, a bald man with a pair of hawkish eyes and a permanent scowl, barking at me to *MOVE. NOW!* while I stared at him in amazement.

I jumped aside and my boss frowned. "Don't talk to the doctors," he said, unnecessarily. It was clear that even if Guy Rosewood opened his mouth, no one in the morgue, and certainly not Dr. Keene, would ever bother to listen. Except, of course, the dead.

"Hello, Dr. Keene," I practiced, leaning over Roger Carrell's chest cavity. "Good morning, Dr. Keene. Yes, Dr. Keene, I *am* the janitor, but I have something important to say." I cleared my throat, stood up straighter. "I have something *extremely* important to *bring to your attention*." I glanced at Mr. Carrell. "Was that too much?"

Even dead, Mr. Carrell seemed politely embarrassed for me. I sighed and went back to his autopsy report, written up earlier that afternoon by the chief medical examiner, Dr. Chase. The reports taught me how to examine the bodies, how to decipher the hidden signs inside blood and organs and bone to create an image of the living person: How did they die? How did they live?

But tonight, I spread my notes out next to Dr. Chase's and frowned.

The official cause of death read *acute pneumonia,* something so mundane it wouldn't even usually merit an autopsy, except the family—here I paused to decipher a note tacked to the report—insisted Mr. Carrell had complained of joint pain before collapsing four nights ago. They kicked up enough of a fuss that the coroner asked Dr. Chase to take another look, and he had, this afternoon, confirming the pneumonia.

But...

I'd seen pneumonia before, strangled-looking lungs crisscrossed by spiderweb patterns of bacteria. When I pulled Mr. Carrell from his drawer and took a look inside...brownish lungs, shriveled and small and covered with a fine amberlike sheen. A smoker? No—his medical report firmly noted *The deceased did not smoke.* So, what then? If not pneumonia, what had killed him?

A secret. Roger Carrell had a secret, and that I understood.

I had a secret, too.

To everyone—my boss, my landlady, the other employees at the morgue—I was Guy Rosewood. Early twenties, tall and thin with hair so light it was almost colorless and a face designed to be completely forgettable. Guy didn't talk much and lived alone in a boardinghouse on the West Side. And only three months ago, he didn't exist.

I touched one of Guy Rosewood's pasty fingers to Roger Carrell's tanned, rough hand and watched as my skin shifted color, grew darker like a piece of bread set to toast. My fingers shortened, thickened, curly dark hair sprouted from the knuckles, and when I made a fist, it looked just the same as the one resting on the marble slab.

It made my skin itch, wearing another disguise. By now I was used to Guy Rosewood's face and body, as comfortable as a broken-in pair of boots. He made it easy for me to hide and slip into places unnoticed. He swept, and he mopped, and he made regular visits to the medical library on the second floor, where he read every book, paper, and scientific report he could get his hands on.

Reports like Dr. Harrison Martland's early findings on the effects of beryllium poisoning on metalworkers.

I flipped through my notebook until I got to the page listing Dr. Martland's observations.

Heavy, discolored lungs

Swollen feet and ankles

Skin irritation

Roger Carrell, a smelter from West Town, worked in a metal factory, melting down and shaping and grinding, breathing in millions of tiny particles of an especially adaptive element that made metals stronger, sturdier, more resistant to heat and shock—and settled like termites into lungs.

It would take a chemical analysis to be sure, but I felt confident the medical report was wrong. Roger Carrell hadn't died from pneumonia but from acute beryllium poisoning.

"Gotcha," I said, smiling—and then my smile faded.

If I'd been a doctor or a medical examiner or a coroner or a coroner's assistant, I could have made a formal request to amend the death certificate. Another autopsy. An inquiry. But now, Roger Carrell would go underground with his secret.

I picked up the medical examiner's report. It wasn't too late. I could simply…change it.

And what would happen then? The coroner would call the chief medical examiner into his office and ask questions, and then the medical examiner would demand to know who on his staff had changed the report. Maybe one of them would get fired. Maybe they'd suspect someone was performing after-hours autopsies. What if they hired a new night watchman? Installed locks on the body drawers? Brought in the police…

I shuddered.

Guy couldn't—*I* couldn't—have trouble with the police.

But what about the truth? Didn't Roger Carrell's family deserve to know what had happened to him? Didn't his fellow smelters deserve to know what had killed the man they'd worked beside? What was the point of filling my head with all this science if I ignored it as soon as it got inconvenient?

I picked up a pencil and a scrap of paper and scrawled out *signs of beryllium poisoning, further analysis necessary,* but before I could do anything with it, I heard another sharp squeal, this time right overhead. Footsteps.

I looked around the room, at my papers, the dirty instruments on their tray, the *dead body* in front of me, and dread flooded my veins. I couldn't be caught here. *Guy* couldn't be caught here. GET OUT.

Bag—books—coat—clean the table—put away the body—

I still looked like Guy Rosewood, but panic made it harder to keep the disguise in place. One of those pale limbs jerked out of control, sending a tray full of instruments crashing to the floor.

Wincing, I looked up at the ceiling. The footsteps paused, and then I heard them make their way rapidly to the stairs. I went every bit as bloodless and cold as the bodies in their drawers.

Maybe I could come up with some excuse for why Guy—

Squeak of the stairwell door opening, thud of my heartbeat in my chest, footsteps down the hall, and I was going to be caught, fired, arrested, *found out*!

BOOM—the door burst open, I spun to face the sink—

"What on earth is happening in here!" a man yelled.

Take a breath, take a breath. My back to the door, I stared down at my hands, at the sink.

"You!" he shouted, and I recognized the voice: a lowly clerk, new on staff. "You're not supposed to be in here! Hello! I'm talking to you!"

Slowly, my hands balled together to keep from shaking out of my skin, I turned toward the man and watched as his narrowed eyes went wide as eggs.

"D-Dr. *Keene*?"

I stared at him.

Back straight, chin up, scowl, breathe, breathe, breathe.

"And what are *you* doing here?" I asked, and—*thank the heavens*—Dr. Keene's deep, gruff voice rolled out.

The man gulped.

"I'm so sorry, sir. I had to get something at my desk and I heard a noise. I thought maybe—sir? Are you all right?"

Breathe, breathe, BREATHE.

I stood behind Mr. Carrell on the autopsy table, which I gripped so hard it made my bones ache. My skin burned, itched, and a tremble worked through my hands and feet.

"Y-yes."

Don't say too much. Breathe. DON'T LOSE CONTROL.

He blinked at me—although, of course, it wasn't me. Not the real me, not even Guy Rosewood, but instead the first face and body I could think of: Dr. Gregory C. Keene, the very reason I'd arrived at this morgue.

"I...I heard a noise and I thought an animal had gotten in, or... But I see you're...working? Is that..." He looked over at the body, the identification tag. "Oh."

I could see the questions in his face. Dr. Keene was one of several medical examiners. What was he doing in the morgue near midnight, with a body that had already been autopsied?

"Was...there something wrong?" He took a step forward, and I panicked.

"Beryllium poisoning!" I blurted out, and when he glanced down at the note I'd written, I felt Dr. Keene's features go soft as taffy. A strangled gasp of panic fought its way through me, and I just managed to spin back around to the sink and turn on a jet of icy water.

"T-type that up, will you?" I was losing it. Dr. Keene didn't stutter. "Get it into the r-report."

A pause. "Did Dr. Chase—"

"Do you think I'd do anything without Dr. Chase's say-so?" I shouted, out of desperation, to be honest, but luckily Dr. Keene was famous for his yelling. I didn't hear anything behind me and the cold water didn't help to keep my disguise; under the stream, I could see my fingers stretch and shrink and shiver. "Get to it! I don't want to spend my whole evening here!"

"Oh, yes, sir!" he responded quickly, and a moment later I heard the sound of his footsteps, the door closing behind him.

The second I was alone I slid down to the floor, swallowing great, galloping breaths of air. Everything swam in front of my eyes, and I dropped my head into my hands, feeling Dr. Keene's hollow cheeks and large nose and furrowed brow. In an instant, it all fell apart, and suddenly I was me again—the *real* me, eighteen, straight nose, square chin—before I realized what had happened and yanked on Guy Rosewood's pale, rabbity, forgettable features.

The shivers came over me like a fever, hot and cold, and I let out a shuddering sigh.

I had to be more careful. I had to get better control!

It'd taken a long time to come up with this face, and I really did not want to lose it.

THREE
RUBY

"Roo! Where've you been? We were about to send a search party!" Tommy Gibson appeared like a freckly-faced vision, fingers throttling the necks of half a dozen sweating bottles of Champagne. He had his shirtsleeves rolled up—I was that late—and his eyes shone bright, and when he leaned in to land a kiss on my cheek, it felt sticky and hot.

"Car troubles! Had to promise my firstborn to get a cab." I yanked off my shabby coat and looked around the entrance hall of the Gibson mansion—an absolute *treasure* done up in white and black and pink marble—for a place to leave it.

"Oh, toss that anywhere." Tommy jerked his head at the piles of minks and ermines and foxes lounging around the hall like a snoozing menagerie.

"Bundle up, darling," I said, draping my coat over the shoulders of a marble nymph in the corner.

"You should—oh damn, bottle's slipping! Listen, head on in. Got some lemonade stored for you in the back!" Tommy, rebalancing the

Champagne with a loud *clunk,* threw me a heart-fluttering wink before sailing off toward the glass-covered veranda.

Oooh, I went ab-so-tive-ly *mad* for the Gibsons' parties. They were simply the best—the most adorable boys and the swingingest music and the deepest liquor stores and *no chaperones* except for their uncles, who were hopeless.

Stepping through to one of the drawing rooms, I felt like Jane Porter exploring a jungle. The Gibson mansion was a dream of limestone whipped into delicate froths, and on the inside, all dark wood paneling and brocade curtains and crystal chandeliers dripping light through the steamy air. Beautiful, dangerous animals, decked out in feathers and diamonds and glitter and gold, draped across the pedigreed furniture. A thousand candles hung suspended from the ceiling and walls like a whole universe of burning suns, and my ears vibrated with wonderful music: from the cat's yowl of a trumpet somewhere in the dining room to the *pat-pat-pat* of my own thudding heart.

The party'd already turned sideways, the boys' jackets gone and shirtsleeves rolled up and the girls laughing hard on a bubbly wave of Champagne. I couldn't go two inches before I felt another hand on my arm or my waist or another kiss on my cheek and just as I thought I'd *never* make it through the party, I heard like a foghorn, "Ruby! Over here!"

From a corner sofa in the back of the picture gallery, my best sweetest friend, Maggie—*"Margaret Stowe, heiress, expert sailor, engaged"* in the papers—stretched an arm high into the air and waved me over. Oh, Maggie was *just* the berries! A bearcat always decked out in the latest, and I loved her to pieces, not because she was the first to adopt me or even because she was the *filthiest* of filthy rich but because—

What's Roo wearing? Damn, I'm overdressed.

"Damn," she said, giving me a kiss on the cheek. "I'm overdressed."

—she had the rarest and most charming quirk of saying exactly what she was thinking.

"Don't be a loon," I said. "I'd cross hot coals barefoot for those duds." She was dressed to the nines in shocking pink with so many ruffles she looked like a gorgeously exploded flower shop. "I am capital-d DONE with this blue silk—I've worn it out half a dozen times already and *look*—I had to stitch the pearls back on after Sherman Fitzpatrick yanked them off trying to dip me at the Elks' Ball. I have to bully Papa into letting me get something new."

"Ohh, I'll buy you something! You need a birthday present—"

"What are you talking about? Those books were a smashing present." I bent down and turned my cheek for a kiss from Maggie's fiancé, J.P., before saying hello to Georgie Gibson, currently occupying the other end of the sofa.

"*Law* books! That you asked for! Hardly an appropriate gift for an eighteenth birthday."

"Eighteenth birthdays call for *in*appropriate gifts." This from Warren Maxwell, sitting on the windowsill with his wing tips balanced on the edge of the sofa and eyes *very much* on me. Wasn't that interesting, because usually Warren hardly gave me more than a nod but tonight…

Ruby blue dress Clara watching? Ruby blue dress that'll work well

Oh lovely, he was trying to make his latest ex-fling jealous.

"Get her a little sports car, Maggie. Red—to match the hair," Warren suggested.

"*Oooh*, that's a good—"

"You're forgetting I don't know how to drive," I said, and J.P. snorted out a laugh.

"So? That never stopped Maggie."

"No cars," I said, and since there wasn't an inch left on the sofa, I dropped onto the nearby lap of Georgie Gibson, damn Warren and his plans. "Your brother promised me lemonade."

"No Champagne? Not even tonight?" J.P. asked. "You know, Prohibition didn't outlaw the *drinking*, just the *paying*. And I don't intend on giving Georgie a single cent."

Maggie swatted him. "Ruby doesn't drink. She's a good girl."

"But not *too* good," Warren said, lifting an eyebrow, and I gave him my best just-what-in-the-hell-are-you-up-to look.

"Lemonade, coming up," Georgie said, trying hard to act nonchalant about the feel of my silk on his lap—poor kid, his mind had gone haywire—and he raised a hand for a nearby waiter. I smiled at him and felt him blush from forehead to ankles before he quickly thought, *Gotta change the subject gotta get my mind off*—"Ehm, hey, Roo—I heard about your pop's party next week."

"Party?" Maggie asked, swiveling around to look at me. "What party? Why wasn't I invited?"

"Not my party, darling," I said. "The mayor's decided Papa's done such a smashing job as state's attorney, he deserves a little shindig."

J.P. let out a snort. "I'd never in a million have guessed a sopping-wet mayor like Tommy Gun McGuire would go for your father, Mr. Law."

I shrugged. Papa had worked his way up through the state's attorney's office before finally throwing his hat into the ring the last election cycle. He ran on a reform platform—lots of opportunity for that in a city like Chicago—which made Mayor McGuire nervous until he realized Papa didn't intend to take him out. In fact, to the mayor's surprise and delight, it turned out people actually *liked* it when Papa went after corrupt business owners and racketeers; thanks to Papa, the mayor had enjoyed some much-needed positive press.

"He's said it's a party celebrating Papa's work but I guarantee he'll take credit for the whole thing. I'm not even going."

"You should!" Maggie said. "Wouldn't it be good for your career, knowing all those people?"

"Oh," I said with a sigh, "maybe. I'd have to survive the small talk, though."

"What's that?" J.P. asked. "Career? You know you can't make a living out of charades, Roo."

"Ruby's going to be the best woman lawyer in the world," Maggie said, and J.P. rolled his eyes.

"A rarefied bunch, that."

"Then she'll be the best *lawyer* in the world, period."

"Sure she will," J.P. said, smiling at us, and through his thoughts I could see he saw us as adorable, but dangerous, like a pair of puppies tussling over a bomb.

Oh please, I wanted to tell him, *I know you had to donate practically the whole library of Alexandria before Harvard would graduate you.* But instead I gave him a smile that showed all my teeth.

"Don't worry, darling," I said, "when the muckrakers hire me to dismantle your family's empire, I'll save your yacht."

Maggie barked out a laugh. "Too generous! Wring 'im for every cent, Roo," she said, leaning in to fluff up J.P.'s slicked-back hair.

"I think it's brilliant," Warren said, but when I raised an eyebrow and sifted through his thoughts, I learned that what he *really* thought was brilliant was how I managed to fill out my silk dress—which was accurate, of course. I looked *amazing* in this dress. "A girl should have more hobbies than golfing and tennis."

"And shopping," added J.P.

"And dancing," said Georgie.

"Which reminds me," I said, sliding off Georgie's lap. "Too much gabbing over drinks and not enough fun. You fellows better ask us to dance or we'll head straight for the sad little bachelor birds making eyes and never look back."

"*Just* what I've been saying for the last hour," Maggie said. She jumped to her feet and yanked J.P. off to the thumping blare of the trumpet. Georgie—who really did look downright adorable—glanced up with a hopeful mind, but just as he opened his mouth, Warren leaned over.

"You're dancing with me, right, doll?" he asked, and before I even got annoyed, he had me in his arms on the dance floor, where he pulled me up against that fan-*tastically*-fitted tuxedo of his and whispered the kinds of things that gave him such a delightfully horrible reputation.

I stuck with Warren for three dances and then pushed him away to give Georgie a shot, but he blew it by treading my feet to pieces. No loss—turned out he was really moony for someone's Iowan cousin—and then I snatched up his brother Tommy as he passed through the ballroom, rosy-cheeked from their father's best gin. Finally, I gave a few charity dances to the hopeful birds hanging on the side of the ballroom—*two* of whom spent their allotted three minutes struggling to keep up with any kind of conversation, so distracted were they about the state of things underneath my dress—before my poor feet revolted.

The party had slid into that comfortable, drowsy time of the night…the cream puffs speared by discarded cigarette butts, the girls no longer bothering to pull up the straps that slid from their flushed shoulders. Thoughts drifted up like soap bubbles, lazy and beautiful:

…*love this song…*

…*want a kiss…*

…*one more minute…*

…*right there…*

Gamely, the band kept swinging, playing the kind of music that had couples swaying together, dreamy and smiling, while two or three bolder Jacks suggested disappearing to the house's various famous dark corners.

Warren made another appearance, asking if I'd like a private driving lesson, and I laughed and checked the time and decided I'd stayed at the party long enough and might as well get myself a ride home.

"I'm going to say my goodbyes. Get me my coat, will you? It's the only one that isn't a fur."

I left Warren standing at the edge of the reception room, thinking about how I looked while I walked away. I wasn't an idiot; I knew those thoughts would last about as long as the hothouse flowers already wilting in the drawing rooms. There was nothing more obvious than a fellow with a girl on his hands. As for anything serious, dating or engagements or even marriage—oh please! The daughter of the Cook County state's attorney was a lot of fun at dances and parties, but these boys married heiresses.

And honestly? Fine by me. Steady beaux seemed like a lot of work, and being married was no fun at all, just a load of babies and bad dresses. How was I supposed to be a crusading lady lawyer out for blood with a husband nagging me? I'd take a lifetime of one-night adorable Warrens, thank you very much.

First, though, I wanted to give my Maggie a kiss good night. I wandered through the house searching for her flashy frock and had just reached the dining room when I heard it:

These Gibson boys sure know how to keep the liquor flowing, but I don't care how well stocked they say their cellars are. They've got a bootlegger on retainer just like every other blueblood in this city…

I spun around, looking for the mind behind the thoughts, sharp and shrewd and clear as a lighthouse, and landed on a woman standing in the shadow of the grand staircase. She was an absolute *fright* in a lime-green frock, baggy and uncomfortable, judging by the way she kept picking at it. As she peered around the party with narrow-eyed scorn, I pegged her as someone's chaperone aunt, but then she peeked into her bulging black handbag and I caught the tiniest glimpse of a camera.

Ooooh, who let in a damned reporter?

Honestly, they were worse than cockroaches, these gate-crashers, looking for stories to fill tomorrow's gossip pages—although, if the best she could drum up was a halfhearted accusation against the Gibsons' hospitality, she needed a better angle.

And she needed to know her shortcuts. With the camera at her side, I was sure she meant to pop into the smoking room—a favorite place for couples—so I dashed sideways through the main hall, snatching up someone's top-shelf Scotch along the way and arriving at the door of the smoking room just as she did.

"What's that?" I said, spinning like someone had called my name, and for the second time that night, I tossed a full glass of liquor all over a very surprised woman.

"Oh, no!" I turned to the reporter, my hand fluttering like a distressed bird. "Oh, *gosh*, you're soaked!"

She spat out a mouthful of Scotch, her cheeks red, eyes wide, mind stuttering swear words like a vulgar typewriter.

"Golly, I'm sorry!" I set my glass down before taking the reporter by the shoulder. "Let's get you mopped up! There should be something in the washroom, fix you right up."

"No—I don't—"

"I insist. Here—Darwin!" I waved over the Gibsons' long-suffering but discreet butler. "Darwin, this lady needs a change. Would you mind terribly tracking something down for her?"

"I really—"

"We'll be in the green washroom upstairs, thank you, Darwin," I said, and as I steered the reporter away I leaned back toward him, my voice low and quick. "First, let the boys know we've got a newshawk in the chicken coop, will you?"

Darwin gave me a slight nod, and out of habit I reached for his thoughts, only to find them completely obscured as though behind a wall of ice. I never could figure out why I had trouble reading certain minds. Some people just seemed to have an innate ability to tuck away their thoughts.

Meanwhile, the reporter's thoughts flew at me as fast and fierce as daggers: *Stupid idiot flapper!* She tried to wriggle away, but I could be ruthless with inane, positive chatter, and in an eye blink I had her out of the main hall, up the stairs, and dripping on the marble floor of the guest room bath.

"Gosh, it soaked all the way through, didn't it?" I grabbed a stack of small white towels and dabbed at the reporter's horrible frock, giving her a quick once-over.

She needed to stop scowling, and that cloche hat of hers was a *disaster*, honestly, no one wore that style anymore, but in the bright lights of the washroom I could see she was younger than I'd first guessed, and prettier, too, once you subtracted the menace from her eyes. The gown, however—obviously expensive and the wrong color for her—couldn't be anything but hideous. And—*whoops*—borrowed. *Double whoops*—from a girl this reporter lady was sweet on.

"Try rinsing it with a bit of white vinegar," I said, with a stab of guilt. I didn't want to ruin the frock of some innocent girl, in spite of my feelings on reporters. "Let it dry and if there are any wrinkles, keep it hanging while you take a bath. The steam should get those right out."

"Don't think I asked," said the reporter, and she tossed the sodden towel into the sink. "Now why don't you put an egg in your shoe and—"

"I'm Ruby. What's your name?" I gave my brightest smile as I stuck out my hand. I didn't really think the reporter would give her name, of course, but sometimes if I sprang a question on someone, they answered the truth in their mind before coming up with a lie. This woman, however, went stiff…

"Ruby Newhouse!" she exclaimed, and she let out a laugh. "Well, well! Baptized with Scotch by Jeb Newhouse's baby girl! How in the hell did the state's attorney ever let you out to a cathouse party like this? Lemme guess: you told him you were off to Bible study."

"Oh, don't be a gas! If you'd ever seen the boys' private stock, you'd know every drop here was perfectly legal. Papa doesn't give a wooden nickel about my friends enjoying some of their stash."

"That wasn't what I meant, kid," the reporter said, turning to look back into the mirror. "I meant I'm surprised he even let you leave the house, given his rogue's gallery of enemies."

Well, that just made me laugh. "I know the boys serve some kicky coffin varnish, but I doubt you'll find any gangsters here. Or what? D'you think Herman Coward's hiding in the butler's pantry?"

"Coward?" Now it was the reporter's turn to laugh. "Kid, Coward's small potatoes. Your pops has got more important things to worry about across the river."

Across the river? Her mind filled with the big square marble temple that was Chicago City Hall. But that didn't make any sense, either. Mayor McGuire had a crush on Papa these days—wasn't that what the gala was about?

"What are you saying? Papa's got no troubles with City Hall."

The reporter stopped scrubbing her frock to look at me, a surprised smile on her face.

"You don't know?"

"Don't know what?" I asked. I dove through her thoughts, which moved quick as lightning bugs, flashes of faces and rumors and gossip: *Newhouse targeting police administration threats plot attack—*

KNOCK KNOCK

I jumped a mile—I'd forgotten all about Darwin! I threw open the door to see him standing with a plain blue dress in his arms. "For the lady."

"Finally," the reporter said, snapping the garment from his hands and herding me out the door with an uncharitable shove.

Before I could open my mouth to protest, the door slammed shut, and Darwin cleared his throat. "Masters George and Thomas thank you for your assistance," he said, with a slight nod. "The lady will be escorted out in a moment."

"Oh. Smashing," I said, distracted as I reached back to the reporter's mind, but she had already moved on....*told Gail I shoulda just worn my own duds but I had to let her convince me to wear one of hers and damn, how am I gonna explain this to her?*

Shoot. I dashed down to the main hall, hoping Warren hadn't given up.

Threats? Attacks? A plot against Papa?

He'd debated running for state's attorney at first. Enemies came with the office furniture—you couldn't promise to root out corruption in this city without ruffling a few feathers, and that was without considering the never-ending war going on in Chicago's criminal underbelly. The day he accepted the position, he sat me down with my younger sisters and warned us about what to do should we be cornered. Or threatened. Or shot. ("Scream" had been the sum of his advice. Later, I pulled the girls aside and taught them how to aim for a fellow's various soft spots.)

I couldn't stop thinking, though, about one word that had appeared in the reporter's mind: *police.*

It was something of an open secret that Chicago's resident mob boss, Herman Coward, more or less ran the police department. And for a reform-minded state's attorney, taking back control of the police had to be high on the priority list. It was enough to make some higher-ups in the police department nervous—Coward's bribes offered a nice cushion to their civil servant salaries—but so far Papa hadn't made any moves against them.

As for City Hall and the mayor, why would that reporter think Papa had anything to fear? Wasn't the mayor throwing Papa a big bash?

But maybe it was for show...Or a *trap*?

It gave me a creepy-crawly feeling that, minutes later, tucked into the backseat of a candy-colored, purring sports car, not even Warren Maxwell's expert hands could shoo away.

"You sure you're all right, doll?" Warren asked, again, pausing to smooth back his hair. I slid the strap of my dress over my shoulder and gave him a kiss on the nose.

"Sorry, Warren, I think that party did me in. Maybe you'd better get me home before I turn into a pumpkin."

He let out a sigh, but he had the decency to help me into the front of the car, and twenty minutes later we roared to a stop on Lake Park Avenue, a few blocks from my house, just as I'd instructed. Heaven knows I didn't need another patch on my tattered reputation.

"I'll call you," he said, which was such a lie, but a sweet one.

"'Night," I said, stepping out of the car, and made for my family's beautiful little three-story graystone.

The cold wind burned my flushed cheeks. I tried to think about Warren's lips on my collarbone or Georgie Gibson's adorable tuxedo or even my sweet Maggie promising me a birthday present, but the only thing I could think about was that reporter.

Newhouse police threats plot attack...

Maybe it was nothing. Maybe she hadn't heard right. Maybe she just wanted to rattle me...

Oh well. No point thinking about it now. I wanted my bed and then an absurdly big breakfast, no matter what time I woke up. *Then* I'd figure out what it all meant.

Yawning, I climbed the steps of the graystone and unlocked the door before slipping inside. I kicked off my kitten heels, my toes giving a joyous wiggle of freedom. I would have left them there in the entry-way except we had a bear of a housekeeper, and I wanted to avoid the mental ranting about *lazy miss* and *spoiled ways* and *what is wrong with this horrible generation???*

Letting out a sigh, I bent down to pick them up, just as a splatter of bullets exploded through the windows, sending a million shards of glass sparkling through the air like rain.

FOUR
GUY

"Oh, Mr. Rosewood, you're back! Out trimming the town, were you?" My landlady, Mrs. Coyne, stood up from her green patterned sofa, glass of gin sloshing in her hand and phonograph hopping on the side table. Oh, damn. Usually this late at night I could sneak in undetected, but I forgot she'd be up celebrating the New Year.

"Um, good evening. Just home from, um, work. I'll let you—"

"Work! You've gotta have one drink at least!" she said, and judging from the conjunctiva redness in her eyes and signs of ataxia as she stumbled to the side table, I'd say she'd had more than one. She pushed a glass into my hand and uncorked a cloudy bottle with her teeth. "There you are, have a drop! This is the good stuff, you know, got it from a fella"—here she paused to wink at me—"real and sealed straight from Britain! None of that bathtub swill."

"Oh, but it's easy to reseal bottles, you know," I said, "you just steam off the label and repaste it, and you can fill it with anything you want! We're always getting bodies in the morgue poisoned by—oh."

She had that look on her face. The one that said *What the hell is he talking about?* I could feel the silence fill the air, so I gave her an awkward smile and lifted my glass.

"Eh, um, bottoms up," I said, and I took a tiny sip, sputtering as the liquid hit my throat. But it must've satisfied Mrs. Coyne, because she smiled and patted my back.

"There you go! Now we're social! You know, I never see you, Mr. Rosewood, you workin' those late hours, and come to think of it I never have any mail for you. Haven't forwarded your people your new address? Where is it you're from again?"

"I, um, Michigan."

"Michigan? I thought it was Minnesota."

I gulped and took another swig of my drink—a mistake. I coughed so hard my eyes watered. "Oh, right, um, Minnesota."

"Still got any family out there? Get back often?"

"Um. No."

"Which one? Don't get back there or haven't got family there?"

"I…um…"

"What about here in the city? Any friends? You can't blame me for being curious, with you missing supper every evening! Haven't got a girl you're sneaking off to visit, have—*ugh!*"

The very thought that I had some secret girlfriend made me spit out my mouthful of gin. Mrs. Coyne, a disgusted frown on her face, groped for something to mop herself up.

"S-sorry!" I said, setting the glass on the table. "I'll just—sorry! Happy New Year!"

"Wait!" she called as I whipped up the stairs. "Don't keep food in your room! I've been hearing rats!"

My footsteps thudded down the hall as I half walked, half ran to my door, my cheeks pink. My hands fumbled with the key in the lock but eventually I got the door open, stumbled inside, and slammed it shut. I couldn't stand the scratchy, itching, prickling feeling under my skin one second longer: I tore off my hat, my scarf, my coat, my shirt, and finally, my face.

Nails on the floor, softly clicking, a weight against my leg, and I put down my hand and felt warm fluff and a wet, scratchy tongue.

How did I end up with this little white dog? A few weeks ago, I'd found him on the street, where he convinced me to give him the last of my crumbly cheese and then followed me back here. He was just supposed to come in for a minute to stay warm, and now here we were. Every day, I smuggled him in and out of the boardinghouse in my coat. Before we came back inside I'd say to him, "Are you sure you want to stay? You'll have to sleep in the closet and hide from Mrs. Coyne or she'll turn you into sausages."

Now he ran his nose along my shoes and pants, taking in my day in loud snuffs.

"Hi," I said, my voice soft, and I startled. I'd forgotten I was just me.

With the lights off, I kicked aside my clothes before stumbling in sock feet to the washroom—private, which cost me an extra dollar a week. I turned the faucet and let loose a firehose of icy water before bending down to wash my face. My real face.

I hadn't seen this face in some time. It came to me in pieces.

Brown eyes.

Dark hair.

High cheekbones.

Narrow nose.

I hated it.

I kept the lights off.

Blind, I searched for the towel slung over a pipe sticking out from the washroom wall and patted myself dry. By the time I snapped on the light, I was back to being Guy Rosewood: older, paler, plainer. In the corner, the dog spun on top of my discarded shirt before settling into a heap to watch.

I was tired. The run-in at the autopsy, Mrs. Coyne's drink—I'd talked more in the last three hours than I had in the last three months—but I had work to do.

Time to practice.

I fished a notebook from its hidden spot behind the toilet and stared into the mirror at Guy's gray eyes.

In truth, what I could do wasn't so amazing. Cephalopods—octopuses—had special cells on the surface of their skin that could change color second by second: red, white, gray, brown, black. They could control texture, too, going spiky or bumpy or smooth. I'd even heard reports of octopuses that used their long limbs to mimic clumps of seaweed! *Seaweed!*

But forget about ocean depths. Pound for pound, I'd say the best transformation on the planet happened in gardens and parks across the world. *Lepidoptera*, the common butterfly, which metamorphized from branch-crawling larva to chrysalis to winged adult. How did it do it? How did something disintegrate into goo, rearrange itself, burst out bigger and lighter and more colorful? How did something with no brain hold on to the memory of its past life?

It was harder for mammals to change their looks, relying on tiny melanocytes, cells that sat in the basal layer of the epidermis like a billion tubes of paint. Usually, they kept to the same palette, but every now and then those little artists would go mad, splattering the skin with fireworks of freckles or bleaching whole sections or failing to show up altogether, leaving a person pinkish pale.

And then, there was...me.

What was it that let me change so quickly, so effortlessly, faster than a caterpillar and better than an octopus and brighter than any other mammal on the planet?

Whatever was inside me, it was unpredictable. But if I could study it, understand it, then I could control it.

In the mirror, Guy Rosewood frowned before, slowly, his nose began to swell, stretching like Pinocchio's, growing blocky and beaky. I turned to study my profile, pushing it out until I felt a tight pinch; then I let out a breath, and the nose shrank back to its original size.

Ears next. Stretch, hang, wobble, pull in tight as a flower bud.

Fingers: spiderlike, stunted, huge and muscular.

My shoulders inflated, straining the seams of Guy's grubby undershirt. I grew ropey muscles, then wasted away. Added a few inches of height, which I checked against the pencil marks scratched onto the doorpost (an increase of one-eighth inch!), and then shrank down (*Minimum height remains four feet, six inches*).

Colors next. Golden to russet to brown to an inky, deep, purplish black, and then back again, growing paler and more bloodless until I could have doubled as one of the corpses in the morgue.

My skin burned, and I took a break to splash water over my face.

Finally, I closed my eyes and thought of the people I'd seen that day: the older woman, pushing a rickety baby carriage across a busy street. The thin man with reddish-brown skin so stretched and dry it made me think of preserved meat. The young girl with the elaborate braids and perfectly smooth, round, pink cheeks.

I opened my eyes and watched the faces appear in the mirror: older woman, thin man, young girl. Everyone wore Guy's faded, scrubby undershirt. I couldn't do clothes, which meant I only went outside as a man—I didn't have the money for a woman's wardrobe.

The hardest part was how to get the details just right. To stretch my skin into papery wrinkles, delicate and thin, and then turn hard, cracked, dry. And *braids*. I could get the hair, the texture, the color, but my hairstyles came out sloppy. I needed to study more fashion magazines. Then there was the little girl's height—the older I got, the harder it was to make myself small.

I finished by pulling on the body of the teamster who boarded next door to me, huge and bald and bulky. I mugged in the mirror before turning around to the dog and giving him a toothy growl. He ignored it. No matter what I looked like, I never fooled the little dog. I guessed he could smell me out, which was fine. He couldn't tattle.

"Hello!" I said into the mirror. "Hello, how are you? Well, I'm fine, how are you?"

It was always easier, talking to my reflection, same as it was easier to wear these masks alone.

Back to Guy Rosewood again. I gave myself a salute and then wiped the sweat from my forehead. It felt good tonight! That didn't always happen. When I was tired or distracted, it could be a mess, the faces soft and lumpy like clay and patchy-colored, but I had to practice.

Practice. Study. Control.

I already knew certain things.

I could only shift into another human form.

I could not produce any fantastical colors, no rainbow skin or purple hair.

It was easier for my body to grow bigger than to grow smaller, easier to grow fatter than to grow thinner.

I could not grow or shrink by a magnitude greater than one foot, nine inches.

I could not produce extra body parts, but I could give myself scars, mutilations, and even, with some concentration, missing limbs.

It was harder to copy a real face, but it looked better when I did.

I preferred to wear a man's body rather than a woman's.

My true face and body aged even when I did not wear them for months. Or years.

But I didn't know why.

And I didn't know why I lost control sometimes...

Guy's face went fuzzy in the mirror, itching and burning, and I squeezed my eyes shut, dropped my head into my hands, and felt my features shift:

Blue eyes

Dark hair

High cheekbones

Straight nose

Like mine but different. Just as I started to feel light-headed, Guy snapped back into place, leaving me breathing hard over the sink.

"Hold on," I told myself. "You'll figure this out."

I flipped through my notebook to the dog-eared paper folded in the back: "A Proposal Regarding Cellular Metamorphosis in Humans," by Dr. Gregory C. Keene.

I looked up into the mirror, and this time, my hand resting on Dr. Keene's paper, on my meticulous notes, I could feel the weight of all that knowledge settle into me like an anchor. Dr. Keene was a scientist. The only scientist who believed that someone like me could exist. If I just showed him the right data, in the right way…maybe he could teach me how to control these transformations.

First, though, I had to figure out how to open my mouth in his presence.

"Hello," I said, lifting Guy Rosewood's chin. "Dr. Keene, I have some questions for you."

FIVE
RUBY

"You would think they'd have the decency to spare my rosebushes." Mama, clad in her house robe and a pair of faded slippers, frowned at the bullet-riddled plants on our front lawn.

"I could have done without the rhododendrons," she said in her scandalized Southern drawl. "We've got too many anyway. But my *roses*…" Mama clucked her tongue. "What will we ever do for color? Barbarians."

"They were aiming at *me*, Mama," I reminded her, and she let out a little *tsk*.

"You, darling! But you're far too young to be murdered by some gunslinger. Don't you think so?"

The police officer assigned to the mess outside 5151 South Dorchester Avenue did not have an answer for that. His mind pulsed with a whopper of a hangover, and all he cared about was getting off our front lawn as soon as possible.

"Hm. We'll find the men responsible, ma'am," he said, and Mama let out a sniff.

"Oh, but we know who's responsible for this, don't we? Why doesn't Commissioner Walsh grow a backbone and tell that Herman Coward to—"

"*Mama.*" I gave her shoulder a firm squeeze and steered her back to the house. "You look chilled to the bone. Let's get you inside for a cup of tea."

Like a butterfly fluttering from flower to flower, Mama's mind turned to thoughts of tea, breakfast, and a new audience to whom she could spread her gardening woes, and she drifted back inside. I adored my mother, really, but she tended to toss lit cigarettes into sawmills without a single care.

"I'm going to check the street again," the officer told me, warily, a brittle rind of annoyance cast over his thoughts at the mention of Herman Coward.

No one could prove the connection between the police, led by Commissioner Liam Walsh, and the head of Chicago's criminal underbelly, Herman Coward, but the working theory went something like this: Coward made a lot of money doing illegal things, and the police made a lot of money looking the other way. Most people, Mama excluded, had enough sense of self-preservation not to wave that around in an officer's face.

But even though last night's shooting could practically have spelled out *Courtesy of Herman Coward* in bullet holes, something about it didn't feel quite right. For months, Papa had been circling around Herman Coward and his crimes, but he hadn't made any statements to the press about investigating gangsters. I hadn't even caught a wisp of anything like that in his mind. Jumping straight to an attack on our home seemed a bit much, even for Coward, and I couldn't help but think about that reporter at the Gibsons' party last night: *"Your pops has got more important things to worry about across the river."*

Right now, Papa was busy with another officer on the opposite side of the yard. He had his *I am listening to you intently* face on, which, coupled with his round glasses and round face and round button nose, made him look disarmingly friendly and polite, and masked the absolute *machine* in his brain. Sharp angles, neat lines, carefully organized thoughts—I just loved being inside his head. It was the first mind I ever mastered, and it still took my breath away how beautifully he managed to fit together the puzzles he met. It made me so proud I almost wished I could boast about it.

If I had to guess, at the moment he was thinking about thirty different matters, from the state of our shattered windows to how to keep the implications of this story out of the newspapers, but as I walked closer, I got a surprise: the thing that worried him most was the blue-uniformed man before him.

"...going to want to do something about this," the cop was saying, gesturing at the house with something like genuine concern, which confused me, because when I dipped into his narrow mind I found it sludgy with disgust. He hated Papa—hated the reforms he was trying to bring to the city, hated the attention it brought to the police department—which should have meant he was firmly in Coward's pocket, but the next thing he said was "You can't let Coward get away with this."

A corrupt cop, in Chicago, suggesting the state's attorney actually *go after Herman Coward???* Good lord, call up the Field Museum, they were going to want to stuff him and put him on display!

Papa weathered his disbelief better than I did, the expression on his face icing into a grimace while his mind held a single thought: *Get him out of here.*

That was my cue; I walked up to them, shivering.

"Hullo, Papa," I interrupted, and as he glanced at me, I felt his mind flood with relief. "Almost done here? *Brrr-rrr!* I'm an icicle!" I still wore the velvet coat but underneath, my blue silk did nothing to keep me warm.

I slipped my arm around his and he patted my hand. "Yes, Ruby, just a moment. Thank you for your assistance," Papa said to the officer. "But I don't think we need to make a fuss about it."

"You sure?" the cop asked, something like panic in his mind, and when I pried in deeper, I found a memory, a conversation with his superior before he came out to our house: *"Pin it all on Coward. He's lost our protection."*

Did that mean—was this a setup? The police wanted Papa to think Coward had attacked him? But why? And who was really behind the shooting? I glanced at Papa, wondering how I could fill him in, when I realized he was already ahead of me: the cop's comment hadn't illuminated anything new so much as confirmed some suspicions about Coward's relationship with the force.

"I mean, I'm just sayin'," the cop continued, "if Herman Coward almost murdered my pretty little daughter, I'd—"

"Herman Coward!" I said, laughing, and I raised my voice loud enough for the neighbors to hear. "That wasn't Herman Coward last night!"

Papa, well used to my antics, kept quiet, but the police officer gave me an unsure look. "Wh-what's that?"

"Not unless Coward makes a practice of singing 'Auld Lang Syne' out on hits," I said. "I could hear them, just after I stepped inside. Who-ever shot at the house, they were soused up on celebratory drinks and making a jolly ruckus. Probably thought they were shooting straight into the air."

This gummed up the officer's thinking. He blinked at me, his mind wondering where to go next, but Papa swooped in first.

"That settles it. I'll put out a statement through my office that this was nothing more than careless New Year's revelry. Thank you again, Officer, for your assistance, and if you could kindly ask the crowd to step back a bit, thank you." Smoothly, Papa put an arm around me and turned us both to the house, leaving the officer on the lawn.

Inside, I slid out of my coat and picked my way carefully past Mrs. Ritter, the housekeeper, and her dustpan of glass shards. Her mind was a thundercloud of grievances, ranging from the ache in her back to the rising cost of a bag of flour. In the front living room, Mama held court before my little sisters, cup of tea raised like a sword of justice.

"It's simply a disaster," she said with a sigh. "I'll have to start plan-ning for spring immediately."

"I think you should plant orchids." Henrietta, twelve years old, sat draped across the floor with our fat, orange, squashy-faced cat simi-larly boneless in her lap.

"Don't be a goose, orchids are hothouse flowers, hardly suitable for this zone."

"When will we get new windows in?" This from Henrietta's twin, Genevieve, who shivered in her thickest winter coat as she toed a stray piece of glass.

"I'll call right away," said Papa, hanging his own coat by the door. "You can go on ahead to breakfast without me."

The girls exchanged glances before they dove for the dining room, Mr. Hubert the cat landing on the floor with a soft *thump* and mew of protest. Mama swanned up the stairs to her bedroom, where she always took her morning tea, while Mrs. Ritter dropped another shard into the dustpan and pushed herself to her feet, thinking of the unfairness of having to make breakfast at a time like this.

"Coming, Ruby?" Henrietta asked as she reached the dining room. "I'm not saving you a thing, even if you did almost get bumped off last night."

"What is that ridiculous language?" I asked. "Those flick magazines of yours should go right in the woodstove. I'll be there in a minute and *if you eat all the flapjacks* I'll never tell you about the Gibsons' party."

Henrietta rolled her eyes—honestly, the girls would turn into little urchins someday without me—but I couldn't pay her any mind. Papa had already retreated up the stairs to his office, his thoughts swollen with worries and plans, and I didn't want to miss a thing.

Would Papa have scolded me if he knew what I could do? Probably. He had a narrow view on ethics, believing if you gave an inch here or there, you might as well be personally culpable for the inevitable downfall of society. I'd like to say I couldn't help my ability, no more than I could help overhearing gossip on the trolley car, but...It didn't work *quite* like that. I could sense thoughts, especially idle thoughts, like a kind of constant buzz, but anything more serious required concentration. Sometimes I heard secret things that I was sure people wouldn't want me to know—like Genevieve's worries she wasn't as pretty as Hen, or Mrs. Ritter the housekeeper's money troubles. I couldn't stop myself from peeping in like that, and it made me feel rotten, but I tried to be good about it, I really did. I tried to help when I could, like today, creeping up to Papa's closed office door and catching the tail end of a telephone conversation.

"Yes, Albert, thanks," Papa said, before I heard the clank of the receiver falling back into place. Well, no surprise there. Albert Rollins was my father's private secretary, a whiz-kid lawyer and an ace social climber—he had an absurd number of connections for someone who'd barely cracked his thirties. Papa trusted him, but all that ambition made me suspicious. I scoured his mind raw the first few times I met him, until finally, I had to agree. Loyal as a dog and devoted to Papa, Albert made an excellent confidant, in spite of—or, probably, because of—his simply soul-crushing boringness.

Small sounds of movement, Papa opening drawers, his mind a whir: *move quickly, secure evidence, mayor's gala, Albert's private protection, contact Coward—*

CONTACT COWARD! Since when did Papa have a line of communication with Chicago's most notorious gangster? That was it, I couldn't help it...I lifted a hand and knocked.

For half a moment, Papa wondered who could be at the door before deciding that, of course, it was his eldest daughter, checking up on him. He sighed, but I would say with a certain fondness, and then he opened the door.

"I suppose you want to come in," he said, but he hadn't gotten the words out before I'd sailed into the study and straight for one of the stiff leather armchairs in the corner.

"Well, the police are useless," I said. "Albert's sending bodyguards?"

It had been years since Papa had wondered *How did she know that?* He had resigned himself to assuming I had stunning perception, which led him to say things like "Ruby has a lawyer's talent for observation better than anyone I know." It made me feel proud, if also a little guilty.

"Yes. And he says they aren't in Herman Coward's pocket, if men like that even exist anymore."

"Does that matter?" I asked. "You're not convinced Coward was behind this."

"I'm not sure."

"Oh, horsefeathers. It's the kind of thing that *looks* like the work of a gangster like Coward, but it feels all wrong."

In spite of everything, I felt Papa's mind prick with interest and a bit of pride. "How so?" he asked, and I crossed my arms over my chest and thought a moment.

"Coward doesn't miss, for one. And he doesn't go after young girls. Besides, he'd have to be a damned—sorry, *darn*—fool to dust up the state's attorney. He knows that'd kick off a war, and I'm guessing he'd only go that route once he'd exhausted all other options. The real question is: Why would that police officer pin the blame on him?"

Papa kept his mouth shut and his hands tight on the back of his chair, an internal debate zipping through his mind—*She's too young she'll figure it out don't put her in danger she's already in danger*—before nodding at the door behind me.

"Close it."

I did, jumping into his mind, and *hoo boy,* I found the bushy moustache and scowling red face of the Chicago police commissioner, Liam Walsh.

"For the last several months, I've been looking into the police department. Quietly," Papa added, to my raised eyebrows. *I'll say*—he'd managed to keep it hidden even from me.

"It's clear there's been some level of obstruction of justice going on, along with bribery and extortion. I assumed it had to do with Coward's operations, but I was mistaken."

"Don't tell me Commissioner Walsh is an upstanding, law-abiding citizen."

Papa grimaced. "Not quite. I had been working under the assumption that Coward and Walsh were partners. Perhaps that's how the relationship began, but I believe now they're closer to business rivals."

"Business rivals..." I said, trailing off, as Papa's mind filled with a short, colorful list of criminal activity: bootlegging, gambling, prostitution, murder. My skin started to prickle with that same kind of heat I felt when I uncovered a particularly bad mind; my senses went sharp as a tack.

"A mobster who cannot count on the collusion of the police is in a vulnerable position," Papa continued. "Coward knows this, and he knows his options are limited. I offered him a deal."

"A *deal*? You want to work with Herman Coward?!"

"There's something rotten in City Hall. Bigger than what Coward's doing," Papa said. Even though he didn't know specifics, I could feel his suspicions. He imagined it all as a black web, a seeping, creeping disease, touching hundreds, thousands of lives, and under the protection of the very people who were supposed to stop it.

"So, Commissioner Walsh is running his own criminal organization? Just cut out the middleman, huh?"

But Papa shook his head. "I don't think Walsh is at the top. He's taking orders from someone extremely powerful and extremely discreet. It's difficult to find out more information without tipping him off. I've begun to collect evidence, names, people who are likely involved, but until I know who's running things, and how, there's no point in going after the rank and file. Coward may be a criminal, but criminals know crime, and he's desperate enough to consider assisting us. I thought we were close, but then he cut off communication, and now..."

The officer's smug face appeared in Papa's mind, and he frowned.

"News of the deal leaked," I said. "Now, this mysterious well-connected ringleader knows you're investigating him, and that Coward might rat him out. Oops, sorry, Papa, I know you hate that word. Coward's *assisting in the investigation of a crime.* So—what? The mystery man sent a few of Chicago's finest out last night to savage Mama's greenery?"

"I'm not sure. Maybe he wanted to frame Coward for a crime. Maybe he wanted me to believe Coward reneged on our deal. Most likely? He wants to scare me off the investigation."

I laughed. "Good thing you don't scare easily."

There was a tug of worry in Papa's mind as his frown deepened, and when I took a closer listen, I almost fell out of the chair.

"You're not thinking of resigning!"

He lifted up his hands, helpless. "My darling, I never imagined..." His mind flashed back to earlier this morning, the shots, my screams, running downstairs to see me crumpled on the floor, his world rending in two for a moment before I popped up, my face very white, bits of glass glittering in my hair, my voice shrill: "I'm *fine*, really, *fine!*"

And I understood, I did. What if it hadn't been me? What if Genevieve had gotten up wanting some book from the library? Or Henrietta had heard me coming home and had run out to meet me? What if this was just the beginning?

But still...I walked the streets at night listening for terrible minds. There were so many out there: killers, monsters, abusers, men who discarded women with no more care than tossing out a spent cigarette. They did what they did because they knew they wouldn't get caught, or if they did get caught, they wouldn't get in trouble. If people like Papa didn't do something, who would?

"You can't give up now, Papa. Last night proved that you're getting closer. *And* I'm coming with you to the mayor's gala next week."

"The gala! Absolutely not. Why would you think I'm still going?"

"Everyone who's anyone will be at that party, including, almost certainly, the person who ordered last night's shooting. I bet he'll be pretty annoyed to attend a party celebrating the very fella trying to take him down. It's your chance to get a closer look at the City Hall muckety-mucks and give the most suspicious ones a good grilling."

A flash of pride like a sudden burst of sunshine lit up Papa's mind.

"Argued like a lawyer!" And then he realized what he'd said and winced. "Oh, no."

"Oh, yes."

"You aren't coming with me, it's too dangerous." After a moment's staring contest, he sighed. "Make a case."

"But you just said—!"

"A *stronger* case."

I let out a *harrumph* and purposely did not peek into Papa's brain to try to figure out the most persuasive arguments, which I considered cheating.

"You need someone you can trust. Not only men brought in by Albert. And you need someone with excellent perception, which just happens to be my best quality."

"I—"

"And, most importantly, I'll be there now, no matter what. So, you can arrive with me on your arm, or you can feign surprise when I step out of the cab. Well? I rest my case."

"Ruby—" Papa started, as *Tell her no convince her this is serious lock her in her bedroom* flashed through his mind. But he knew when he'd been beat, if not by the first two points, then by the last. I would sprout wings if that was what it took to get to that gala.

He shook his head, and I waited for him to lecture me about *safety* and *don't take risks* and *remember our lives are in danger,* but when I peeked into his mind, I got such a surprise, I almost laughed.

"Please," he said. "*Please* be on your best behavior."

"Papa. I'm always on my best behavior."

"This is a big event. Everyone from City Hall will be there. With their wives. Do you understand? No slang, no slouching, no...sass."

"Sass?"

"You know what I mean. Make a good impression."

I leaned in and kissed his forehead. "You don't have anything to worry about," I said, and I stood up to head out and do battle with Hen for the flapjacks. As I reached the door, I spun around with a smile.

"You *do* know this means I'll need a new dress."

ʃIX
GUY

The first of the year is the most important day! Whatever you sow today, you reap for all the days following. So be careful, boy.

The morgue was a hive of activity, coroners rushing out to or back from examining dead bodies, their clerks hopping to answer phones and fill out death certificates from last night's rowdy celebrations. Everyone ignored me while I made my way through offices, emptying the wastebaskets, tidying up the supply closet, and as I worked, I heard those words over and over in my head, just like every other New Year's Day. When I was little, the words felt full of possibility. Now, I just heard a warning.

Whatever you sow today . . .

Sighing, I stepped out into the hallway and tumbled the dirty linen from the latest autopsy into my laundry cart. All right, so I wasn't unearthing any biological discoveries or analyzing my cellular structure, but I was getting closer. Maybe this time next year, I'd be in a lab somewhere, researching my—

"No!"

I went still.

From an open side office just down the hall, the voice continued. "You expect me to drop everything and run off—" There was a murmur of someone responding, and then the louder voice again: "Damn it, fine! Give me the damn address."

A moment later, a harried-looking clerk rushed out. It was the one who found me last night, although of course he didn't recognize me and pushed past without so much as a glance. There was another shouted swear from the office, followed quickly by a huge crash. I jumped and headed toward the noise, nearly colliding with a man—red-faced, bald, with sharp, darting eyes and a coat half hanging from one arm.

"Oh! I'm sor—" It was Dr. Keene. The author of "A Proposal Regarding Cellular Metamorphosis in Humans." I tried to speak, but the sounds that came out of me whimpered and died on the vine.

"Kaufman!" he shouted. "KAUFMAN! Where is—oh damn it, the blasted holiday! *I need an assistant!*"

Quickly, I dropped my eyes to the floor, my heart racing, and ducked inside the office to clear up the papers that had fallen. Then I felt a hand on my shoulder, jerking me around.

"You!"

Me?

"Yes, you! Name!"

Stomach in shoes, I could only blink as Dr. Keene scowled at me.

"N-n-*name*?" I asked, and he rolled his eyes.

"Oh, damn it all. Don't you speak English? Just my damned luck."

"Eng-glish, s-s-sir?"

"Know how to write, do you? Big, bold, clear lettering? Right— come on!" He threw his coat over his other arm, whirling around for the stairs, but when I didn't move, he spun back, shouting, "Get! Get! I don't have all day to wait around!"

A twitch sprang through each of my limbs, and I hurried after him, following him up the stairs—which he took two at a time. We were through the bustle of the main floor and out the door, when, shivering and confused, I wished I had thought to bring my coat. Moving quickly, Dr. Keene made his way down the granite steps of the morgue and out toward the street, where a plain black car stood idling.

"S-sir?" I didn't know what made my teeth chatter worse: the cold or the doctor himself. "S-something I c-can help with?"

"Bodies!" he said, throwing open the door of the car. "Too many damn bodies!"

I scurried around for the other door but paused once the words sank in. "Sir?"

"New Year's Eve might as well come with a public warning. People take it as an opportunity to drink themselves to death or fall off roof ledges or drop into the river!" the doctor half said, half shouted over the roof of the car. "All morning the phone's been ringing Handel's *Messiah* with cops asking for coroners and now they cleaned the shop plumb out! I was just fetching a liver when that rat of a clerk told me to go take a look at some corpse in Back of the Yards. Tried telling him I haven't been out in the field in years and it's illegal to boot, but he said I *owed* him! For what, I'd like to know!"

"Owe—owed him, sir?" My heart caught in my throat as I remembered telling the clerk to amend the autopsy report with my note on beryllium poisoning, while wearing Dr. Keene's face.

Oops.

"My damned assistant begged the day off!" Dr. Keene continued.

"You'll have to do, and you'd better not be squeamish. When you see that dead body, I don't want to see your breakfast." The doctor slid into the car and slammed the door shut.

I hurried to open my own door, and as soon as I yanked it closed behind me, Dr. Keene waved at the driver. "Back of the Yards, come on now, I've got to get to my liver." He pulled out a sheath of papers from his case.

"Yes, sir, Dr. Keene," the driver said. The car bucked forward and it finally hit me: I was alone with Dr. Keene.

Dr. Gregory C. Keene.

The reason I got on a train to Chicago and created Guy Rosewood and applied for this job. I gulped and looked out the window, hoping that the rumbling motion of the car hid how much I practically vibrated. Dr. Keene! *Dr. Keene!* I was boxed up and alone with the man who might hold the answers to my questions.

Oh.

Uh-oh.

I could feel it.

Rising up inside me.

Not my breakfast, no—worse.

Enthusiasm.

"Yourpaperaboutcellularmetamorphosischangedmylife!" I blurted out, and then I winced. Dr. Keene looked at me like I actually had thrown up all over the car.

"What? What's that? Speak up!"

I attempted to get my tongue and brain in the same county.

"I said, um, sir, I, uh, read your paper. About cellular metamorphosis. Theorizing a new kind of cellular form. Tricoloroforms."

"Tricoloroforms! My paper!"

"Y-yes, sir. Your reasonings were…incredible."

"I know they're incredible! I wrote them. Fat lot of good it did me. Kicked out of the university and lost my funding. Idiots." He narrowed his eyes at the back of the driver's seat, as if mentally throttling every one of his former colleagues, and then turned that gaze to me. It was a startling experience. "And how in the hell did *you* read it? Don't I see you mopping the floors??"

"Well…I'm…"

"Never mind," Dr. Keene said, waving a distracted hand and returning to his reports. "So, you read my paper. It's all just theoretical. Couldn't find any real-life proof tricoloroforms exist."

"But it's not," I said quickly. "Or, I mean, you're right. They exist. Tricoloroforms."

Dr. Keene turned sharply and gave me a look of such fierce scrutiny that I wondered if I might crumble to dust.

"There was…a boy. Where I grew up. He…he could change."

"Change *how*?"

"Just like you theorized. Skin color. Shape. Size. Eyes. Hair. He could alter his entire body, at will, in a matter of seconds."

"Where's this boy now?"

"He…" I didn't know how to answer that question.

train whistle

bright light

screaming

"…died. There was an accident. He didn't survive."

"Mm-*hmm*. Parents?"

"P-Parents?"

"*Yes.* Did he have any kin?"

"Oh. Um. No siblings. Mother died in childbirth. Father—"

Wait—wait! Stop—wait!

"—passed. Same accident."

Dr. Keene looked at me flatly over the top of his papers, unimpressed.

"But he was—I mean, he could—The way you described the tricolo-roforms was exactly—"

"Have you ever done scientific research?" Dr. Keene didn't even wait for me to shake my head. "You need a proper lab, and labs are expensive. Chemicals. Equipment. Assistants. Time to *do* the damn science you're trying to do. You only get money when someone with money cares about the work. And no one cares about tricoloroforms. So, as much as I appreciate your stammering flattery, I will have to ask you to kindly shut up about the research that killed my career. Actually, if you wouldn't mind shutting up until we're back at... Actually, just shut it for the rest of the day."

"But, sir, I—"

"No, no," Dr. Keene said, as if he were scolding a naughty pup. "I said *quiet.* You think you're the first to bring me one of these stories? And whenever I'm gullible enough to investigate, it's always the same thing: *Oh, he's dead now, oh, he could do it last week I swear.* I don't want to hear anymore. Shut it. Yes? Thank you." And he turned back to his papers.

The car slowed to a stop outside a dingy brown building, unremark-able except for a few people gathered outside. Shaking, I stepped from the car as a police officer in a blue uniform put his hands out to keep the crowd at bay, and instinctively, I shrank back, my eyes wide with fear.

I couldn't move, pinned under the officer's suspicious glare, until Dr. Keene breezed by.

"Step lively, assistant, hep, hep!" he said, passing me a pen and notebook. I ducked my head and followed on Dr. Keene's heels, down the stairs and into a dark basement with sticky floors and a stale odor. I blinked as my eyes adjusted to the light and looked around the room: in the corner, two more police officers watched me—I gulped and wiped my sweaty palms on my pants, double-checking they were still Guy Rosewood's—while a body lay slumped on a bench in front of a small wooden table. Three glasses sat on the table, which even from a distance looked grimy with dirt and spilled liquor. A mismatched collection of tables and chairs filled the rest of the room, one side of which was lined with empty shelves and a bar—no doubt the owner had cleared out the illegal alcohol before calling the cops.

"Name?" Dr. Keene strode over to the officers and slid his glasses over his nose as he peered down at the body.

"Uhh…Mather. Fra…What's the first name? Can't read Mullaney's handwriting for shit."

"Francis," the other officer replied. "Francis G. Mather."

"Have you contacted his people yet?"

"Yeah, we rang up his cousin—he's with the Eighteenth Precinct. Mather's wife's laid up in the county hospital. She's got poor health."

"Recent?"

"Been there a week."

"And any companions last night?"

"Two. Female," I said without thinking, and every face in the room swiveled toward me. Even Francis G. Mather seemed to wonder who this joker was.

"I believe I told you to *shut it*," Dr. Keene hissed, and I winced and looked down at my notebook. A moment later, though, Dr. Keene let out a small *hm*. "Three glasses… Was he with anyone?"

"He was a family man, I said." This from the other police officer, who'd taken off his hat to show a mop of such red hair, it almost looked like he'd set it on fire. "He didn't need to be runnin' round with a coupla cats."

Dr. Keene said nothing, and I said nothing, watching him peer down at the glasses.

"Lipstick," he said, pointing at them. "Two different shades." He gave me a curious glance.

"You're bringing your own detectives out here?" the red-haired officer asked Dr. Keene, while the bald one gave me a look that suggested *detective* wasn't the word he would use.

Dr. Keene ignored him, turning back to his examination of the body. While the officers glared at me, I clutched my pencil, struggling to keep up with Dr. Keene's barked assessments, but something nagged at me. Dr. Keene and the officers kept talking about how much he'd had to drink, how this bar'd been cited before for serving Smoke, a deadly cocktail of water and industrial alcohol, which packed all the punch and ten times the poison of regular ethyl alcohol.

I didn't doubt that Francis G. Mather had had plenty to drink last night, but there was something else I noticed about his glass…

"…to examine the posterior—hello? Are you paying attention?"

I hurried to scrawl down what Dr. Keene had said. "S-Sorry, sir!"

"Got another observation to share?" the redheaded officer asked, and I expected Dr. Keene to pay him no mind, but instead he caught me eyeing the glass and raised an eyebrow.

"Well?" Dr. Keene asked.

Eyes down. Head down. Say nothing. Don't attract attention.

But...I couldn't deny the facts.

"I only...Well...The glass, sir. It looks like there's something inside."

One of the officers let out a sniff of annoyance. "Cigarette ash."

"Then where's the butt?" I shot back, and then I swallowed. "I mean...I don't think so."

Carefully, Dr. Keene leaned over the table, squinting into the glass. He reached into his pocket and removed a pair of fine cotton gloves and, after slipping one over his right hand, picked up the glass and raised it to the pub's grubby lights. At the bottom of the glass, a ring of grayish-white crystals glittered.

"Well, well. What do we have here?" Dr. Keene murmured, and then he set the glass back down on the table. "Take note! Postmortem signs on body consistent with alcohol poisoning but—excuse me? Are you writing this down?"

"Y-yes, sir," I said, and dutifully scribbled as Dr. Keene bent down over the body once more. He pried open eyelids, peered down the victim's throat, and cautiously sniffed the glass.

"Right," he said. "Victim's body additionally shows signs indicating poisoning."

"Yeah, that's what we've been tellin' you. Mather drank the same rotgut what killed two dozen other idiots last night," the redheaded officer said, leaning against the wall of the pub with a frown.

"Poisoning," Dr. Keene added, with a pointed look at me, "by foreign substance. Arsenic, perhaps, or maybe thallium. I'll need to take a look at that glass but my initial assessment is cause of death: homicide. Mather was murdered."

The officers jumped to attention as I froze, pencil tip pressed hard into the notebook. Shocked whispers came from the crowd waiting at the pub door, and one of the officers leapt for the stairs, slamming the door shut, as the other shoved a finger in Dr. Keene's face.

"Look here," he said. "This fella died from alcohol poisoning. Everyone agrees he was gulpin' 'em down like a fish the whole night. No mysteries here. This ain't no radio drama murder and you ain't Sherlock Holmes."

"And you don't pay attention to the facts," Dr. Keene said, slipping his glasses off his nose and back into his shirt pocket. "Good thing this...you—what's your name?"

"M-me, sir?"

"You."

"R-Rosewood. Guy Rosewood."

"Well, good thing we had Rosewood here paying attention."

Grinning, he clapped a hand on my shoulder, and a strange, beautiful, unfamiliar feeling ballooned inside me. *Pride.*

I helped him.

I helped Dr. Keene.

A smile spread across my face as Dr. Keene gathered his things and collected my notes before heading back up the stairs, but when I moved to follow him I found my path blocked by the two officers.

"Couldn't keep your mouth *shut,* huh?" one said, and the other narrowed his eyes at me.

"What'd you say your name was, joker? Rosewood?"

I gulped. "I—um, no, I—"

Police. I can't get in trouble with the police.

"I'll just, um, head back to the morgue with Dr. Keene…" I said, edging around them, and I almost tripped running up the stairs. By the time I made it out through the crowd and to the street, Dr. Keene's black car was long gone.

I watched the road for a moment, my stomach in my shoes, before I felt someone tug at my sleeve. I jumped, ready for the cops, but instead saw a young woman with a worn but clean pram and her hair tied up in a scarf.

"'Scuse me," she said, pushing closer. "Katherine Jessop, I live in the neighborhood. You was in there? Frank Mather's dead? Murdered?"

"I, um, don't think I should, um, say any—"

"I knew it," she said, shaking her head. "I *knew* it was gonna happen."

"Oh. I'm…sorry for your loss?"

"My loss!" She let out an indignant laugh. "Frank Mather was a bum and good riddance. Nah, we all knew he was gonna get himself murdered sooner or later, and I know who done it, too. Tried telling the cops, but—"

Just at that moment I looked up to see the two police officers standing in the doorway, glaring at me with the kind of look that said *What in the hell do you think you're doing* now?

"Well, that's very nice," I said to the woman, "but I should really be getting back to work."

"Hey, where d'you think you're—*hey!*" she shouted.

It was too late. I could already feel adrenaline pumping through my bloodstream, the classic chemical response to threat: *fight or flight.* Only it wasn't really any question for me.

I ran.

I couldn't get in trouble with the police. I couldn't, I couldn't, if they found me, if they put everything together—

train whistle

shouting

crash

My breaths came out so fast I had to pull off to a side alleyway, clutching the walls and squeezing my eyes tight. I could feel my mask slipping, Guy Rosewood falling to pieces, and I spun around, pressed my forehead to the bricks, and forced myself to *slow down*.

In.

And out.

In.

And out.

Gradually, my heart slowed, my skin stopped vibrating. But the moment I thought about those cops again, something in my throat clenched tight and hard.

Be careful, boy. My father's words returning to me, tumbling over the dusty, abandoned miles of my brain. *Whatever you sow today, you reap for all the days following.*

What the hell had I sowed just now?

SEVEN
RUBY

Picking out the right dress proved nearly as tricky as picking out the right poison.

Nothing too frumpy—that wouldn't get *anywhere* with the men—but nothing too vampy, which would earn me sniffs of disapproval from the wives. Nothing too plain, because I needed to catch some eyes, but nothing too glamorous, as befitting the daughter of a thrifty public servant. By the end of my trip I had the poor shopgirl in tears.

At last, I decided: we were going into battle, and I needed armor.

Gold, to be precise. A delicate web of chain that swung down from shoulders to waist, gathering in swoops and waterfalls and dripping down my thighs to end in an explosion of foamy tulle. Under all this, emerald-green velvet, cut with a dip in front just deep enough to distinguish me from the married ladies but not so deep as to raise those married ladies' eyebrows. The shopgirl, bless her, found me a pair of cunning heels that strapped tight to my feet like boots—perfect for running in, and the burnished gold color of a sunset.

On the night of the gala, dressed, armed, and heeled, I looked smart, sophisticated, serious—but not too serious. The kind of girl you said things to, which just happened to be the kind of girl I needed to be.

And if the dress didn't work, I had my fallback plan: a hollow hairpin filled with concentrated arsenic and hidden in a small pouch inside my jeweled handbag.

"Listen, ladybug," Papa said as we stepped into a cream-colored hired car on our way to the gala. "If there's any sign of trouble, you are to leave, immediately. Get somewhere secure."

Poor Papa. He'd been a wreck all week, dashing between the office and home, bursting through the door every night to ask if we were safe. And of course we were. Albert's goons, annoying but reliable, rolled up every day to the graystone's curb to sit and watch and keep Mrs. Ritter running in and out of the house with cups of coffee.

I slid my arm around his.

"Everything will be fine," I said, and he patted my hand, his mind a hornets' nest of worry. I was touched to see that most of his worries had to do with protecting my scrawny hide, but he didn't know what I could do, or how I handled trouble.

The driver slowed as we reached the Drake Hotel, and a throng of reporters rushed for the curb. I felt the fears in Papa's mind settle into a steely focus, and I squeezed his hand.

"Ready?" he asked.

"Into the lions' den."

"Mr. Newhouse! Newhouse!"

Clicking cameras and shouts and shoving as Papa stepped from the car and reached back to help me out.

"Mr. Newhouse! Why so late? Trying to send the mayor a message?"

The nerve! It was hardly fifteen minutes past the hour—didn't these fellas know you never showed up for any shindig *on time*? I hopped out of the car and flashed the reporters a dazzling smile.

"Oh, hello!" I said. "Don't be mean to Papa, it's all my fault! Took me *ages* to get this look just right, but I'd say I aced it, wouldn't you?" I stepped in front of Papa and spun around, the gold chain on my dress swirling, and the moment I struck a pose the shutters clicked like mad again, all those minds completely focused on the pretty girl.

"That's enough, Ruby, let's not keep the mayor waiting any longer," Papa said, taking my arm to lead me inside, though the thoughts running through his mind were grateful.

I hadn't been to the Drake since Isadora Franco's debutante ball last summer, and I'd thought that took the seven-tiered cake for ostentatious displays, but *good golly*. The whole of the Gold Coast Ballroom was decked out! Real crystal on the tables, flowers stretching up to the chandeliers above, several dozen waiters mingling among several hundred guests…horsefeathers, what did this cost? The mayor might as well have hung a banner that read HAVE YOU TRIED THE CAVIAR? HERE'S HOW MUCH I LOVE JEREMIAH NEWHOUSE.

But underneath the silk tablecloths and oysters, I could feel a chill.

This party was supposed to be some kind of symbol of unity, but the shootout at our house had ruined that—never mind Papa's valiant efforts to keep the story out of the press. No one quite knew how to behave.

As soon as we stepped through the doors, I *felt,* rather than heard, the mayor coming, with all the subtlety of a freight train. Mayor Thomas "Tommy Gun" McGuire was massive. A body like a cannonball, huge and round and dense, with a smaller, rounder cannonball perched above his shoulders. Although six inches shorter than Papa, he loomed twice as large, announcing his presence with his lumbering steps and a voice that boomed so loud it gave me a headache—or maybe what gave me a headache was the tangled mess of bloated thoughts he called his mind.

"THERE HE IS!" Mayor McGuire pushed aside the crowd like Moses parting the Red Sea and strode toward Papa on thick legs. "Glad you could make it!" He grabbed Papa's hand and pumped it in what I could recognize, intellectually, as a handshake but what any good cop worth his salt would call a shakedown.

"Thank you," Papa said, and only someone who knew him well would detect the note of weariness in his voice. He gestured toward me. "Please allow me to introduce my daughter Ruby."

"You throw some shindig," I said, sticking out my hand with a smile. I didn't like Mayor McGuire, but I doubted he was at the top of Papa's list of suspects as the one running criminal activity out of City Hall. His brain was about as big as a pea, and in spite of tonight's party for Papa, he and Herman Coward were practically golfing buddies. Still, what else was I here for if not to run the minds of Chicago's civil servants through a fine-mesh sieve? While Papa and the mayor made small talk, I hunted for clues until I felt certain: Tommy Gun McGuire had a weakness for bribes and privately regarded Papa's reform efforts with suspicion, but he didn't want Papa dead.

"...now listen, I've got some people I want you to meet..."

I came back to reality to see the mayor throw his arm around Papa's shoulders. Papa paused just long enough to glance at me, the question on his face clear enough without me having to see into his head: *Will you be all right?*

Of course I would, especially with the mayor crossed off my list of suspects.

As Papa and the mayor headed for the proper, entirely-devoid-of-alcohol bar, I noticed a steely-eyed giant following hot on their heels, which got me worried for a moment until he gave a meaningful look to another man, prematurely balding with a pair of round gold spectacles just like Papa's. Albert Rollins, Papa's private secretary.

Sheesh, Albert looked happier'n a pig in mud, surrounded by all those powerful men, many of them throwing him pleasantries like tasty morsels to a friendly dog. When he saw me, he gave a little start of surprise. Did Papa not tell him I was coming? Or was he just shocked by my dress? I took great sport in shocking Albert, although to be honest, it didn't take much.

"Hullo, Bertie," I said, when I managed to beat my way through the crowd to him.

"Good evening, Miss Newhouse," he said, with a painful grimace of a smile. As an absolute nobody, I was taking up valuable real estate.

"Figured out yet who ordered that hit on our house?" I asked, and, hands flapping, he shushed me with so much enthusiasm, a few people turned to give curious stares.

"Are you mad, asking about that here?" he sputtered.

"No one's paying attention to us." I glanced around at the crowd. "Or at least they weren't before you started conducting."

"Really, Ruby," he whispered, "you don't know what you're talking about!"

I rolled my eyes. Turned out it was Albert who didn't know anything. While he chattered on at me, I took the liberty of poking through his mind. He agreed with Papa that someone powerful in City Hall was running a massive criminal organization, but he placed his bets on the mayor. Completely useless.

Much to his relief, I interrupted him to tell him I had to step off to the powder room. I was just scanning the crowd, searching for my next potential suspect, when I caught a whiff of a familiar, sharp, feminine mind...

"Oh, hello," I said, walking up to the reporter from the Gibsons' party. "How'd you manage to weasel your way in this time?"

The reporter, who'd been busy scribbling something in her notebook, looked up and, upon recognizing me, gave a world-class eye roll.

"I had an invitation," she said, but I saw her mind flash to a hasty bribe and a dark-haired waiter helping her in through the kitchens.

I crossed my arms over my chest. "I'll bet."

"Any comment on that shootout at your house?" she asked me, her pen poised over her notebook.

"Didn't you read the press release?" I snatched a vegetable pastry from a passing tray and popped it into my mouth. "New Year's revelers with bad aim."

"You know I don't believe that for a second."

"You're right." I dusted the crumbs from my fingertips. "It was an old beau of mine, driven mad because I didn't like the smell of his hair pomade. When the police tracked him down, he was still babbling about brilliantine."

The reporter crossed her arms and frowned.

"What?" I asked. "Don't you think I'm pretty enough to go to prison for?"

She stared me down for another moment and then burst out laughing. And what a surprise! Laughing, the reporter actually looked quite pleasant. It helped that she wore her own, kickier duds: a crisp lavender suit cut like a man's but tailored to her slim, tall frame.

"I like you better with a bit of acid," the reporter said, smiling, and I smiled back.

"Me too. You already know *my* name." I offered a hand, and she took it.

"Vivian Forbes."

"Sorry about that dress. How'd it make out?"

"Steamed it in the bath, like you said. It's wrinkly, but it'll recover." Vivian gave me a sly look. "You knew exactly what you were doing when you threw that drink at me, didn't you? Innocent as a damned milkmaid, Ruby Newhouse. Got me kicked off the Sunday Social News column."

"What a pity."

"Oh, you did me a favor. I've got a new beat. Politics," Vivian said, turning to the crowd with a satisfied smile. "Although it's not much different from the social pages. Secrets and scandals and everyone in bed with someone they're not supposed to be. They all want to sit on the throne, but there's not enough room for everyone and as soon as there's a new Caesar, the disgruntled senators get their knives out."

Her gaze lingered on Papa, stuck amid a swirling orbit of hangers-on, and regret twisted through her thoughts, as though she were watching a train wreck she was powerless to stop. I could tell she didn't know anything concrete about who might've ordered the attack on our house, but she guessed Papa had made a powerful enemy with his talks of reform. Phew, she was sharp—she *knew* people. I couldn't sift through every single mind in this ballroom, looking for who was after Papa, but maybe Vivian could give me a head start.

"Let's say…" I began, my voice casual, and Vivian's senses pricked up, "…there's something going on in City Hall. Some kind of criminal operation. And whoever's running it has got the police under their thumb and both my father *and* Coward on their enemies list."

"I'd say that's quite a theory," Vivian replied, focusing hard to keep from exploding with excitement.

"Who would you pin for the top? Hypothetically, of course."

"*Hypothetically.*" Vivian wasn't a dummy; she could see I was pumping her for information, and I held my breath as she made the calculation in her mind: How much was it worth to shoot the breeze with the state's attorney's daughter? "All right."

She looked out over the crowd, considering the faces. "It's not the mayor, that's for damned sure. He likes the attention he gets from your papa almost as much as the bribes from Coward." Her eyes rested on a red-faced man with a push-broom moustache and mop of long bangs. He stood in a corner, watching the crowd, holding a glass of something so desperately it made me think there was more in there than water. Police Commissioner Walsh. I glanced at Vivian, wondering what she thought of him, when she shook her head.

"I think you can cross Walsh off the list. He's greedy enough, but he's got bad nerves. Can't see him attempting something so bold." She frowned. "My guess? It's someone close to the mayor, but not that close. Start with the aldermen."

"The aldermen?" I didn't know much about them, fifty men elected to represent Chicago's fifty wards. Most operated their slices of the city as miniature fiefdoms, trading plum jobs and lenient policing for hefty bribes.

"They've got power and know-how," Vivian said. "You're gonna think it's someone dirty, but I'd take a closer look at the ones with good reputations and lots of connections." Her mind flipped through names before pausing on one that surprised me so much, I thought it had to be a mistake: a joyless stick-in-the-mud by the name of Dennis Ferry.

My knowledge of Ferry was pretty thin. He was on the older side and his wife wrote a popular newspaper column, *loathed* by my friends because she seemed to pin every vice in the city on jazz, bobbed hair, and rouged knees. She frequently dropped "pearls of wisdom from Mr. Ferry" into her articles, and they implied he was the type to keep to the straight and narrow—and remind you of that at every opportunity. He would be an odd sight at the top of a criminal organization, and a second later, Vivian seemed to agree, dismissing him with a single thought: *Other than that nasty stuff with his secretaries, he keeps his nose clean.*

Nasty stuff with his secretaries? The part of me that roamed the streets at night, armed with needles, perked up.

"Hold on." I nudged her and nodded to where Ferry stood, near Papa and the mayor but in his own small knot of admirers. Tall and gaunt-faced with a helmet of perfectly pin-straight snow-colored hair, he seemed to be droning on, one elbow stuck out in a chicken wing for his beady-eyed wife to cling to.

"What do you know about *him*?"

"He's a famous Dry," she said with a shrug. "Got a lot of attention swinging hard for Prohibition. Not that popular. I don't know, kid. He acts like the kind of person who follows all the rules."

"'Acts'?"

"Ran through three secretaries in less than a year. People talk."

"What does that mean?"

She looked at me carefully. "*Women* talk," she said, and behind the words, I could see it: Ferry's secretaries, young women, sharing stories, warnings, with other women. He was hard to work with, cold, cruel, demanding, demeaning, dangerous, and no one knew about it because no one listened to those women. Except Vivian.

A twang ran through my belly and I looked back at the man with the tidy haircut and dowdy wife, every inch of him the picture of perfect moral upstandingness.

I was here for Papa, to investigate the person who wanted to stop him, not chase down another bad man, but I couldn't help professional curiosity. I needed to know: *What kind of secrets are you hiding, Dennis Ferry?*

"I gotta go," I said, taking off, but Vivian caught my arm just above the elbow, squeezing so tight her half-moon-painted nails dug into my skin.

"This info didn't come free, you know. You owe me, and I always collect." With a final squeeze, she released me, smiling. "Good luck, kiddo. And be careful."

EIGHT
GUY

fter dumping another overflowing wastebasket into my trash cart, I paused to catch my breath and wipe a hand across my forehead. All week the morgue had hummed with activity, catching up on the glut of deaths from the start of the new year, and it didn't look like it would be slowing down anytime soon. Forget about visits to the autopsy room or medical library—I wanted a good meal and a hot bath.

Empty the wastebaskets, fill the trash cart, empty the trash cart out back, again and again, and then tidy the desks, wash the windows, mop the floors. I'd been going for hours. Finally, the air reeking of chemicals, I had closed the door to the second floor behind me and was making my way up to the third when the whole building jerked from a tremendous *crash*.

It sounded like it came from one of the doctors' offices upstairs. Had a cabinet collapsed? A bookshelf? Oh lord—not one of the lab experiments! I pushed open the stairwell door and rushed down the hall, running until I almost skidded on a splintered piece of chair.

I had picked it up with a frown when I heard another crash, followed by a bellowed string of unmentionable words, and looked through an open office door to see Dr. Keene, fists balled up on his desk.

"D-Dr. Keene?" I asked. "Are you all right?"

Sweating and scowling, Dr. Keene stood up and yanked a handkerchief from his pocket, which he used to mop his face.

"Denied—I'll give you denied when I'm through with you..." he muttered to himself, and then he kicked hard at the last shards of the chair so that I had to jump quickly out of the way, which caught his attention.

"What are *you* looking at!"

"I—I—I'm sorry, sir! I'll just—I'll—" I gulped and stooped down to pick up another piece of the chair, and Dr. Keene went back to ignoring me.

"*'Not in the public interest.'* My ass! Those idiots on the board wouldn't know 'public interest' if it popped out of a birthday cake singing 'Sweet Georgia Brown' and wearing nothing but a smile!"

I dropped to my hands and knees, brushing the splinters into a neat pile.

Eyes down.

Head down.

Say nothing.

Except...This was the first time I'd come face to face with him since I helped him at the bar...I swallowed hard again and then popped my head up.

"Is...Is there anything I...can do? Sir?"

He turned on me so fast I almost ducked down again, but then his expression shifted from outright murderousness to mere rage.

"It's *you*. Rookwood. Rockland."

"Rosewood, sir. Guy Rosewood."

He just waved a hand, as though my name hardly mattered. Which, honestly, I had to agree with.

"Rosewood, huh? Brilliant criminal investigator! This is all your fault, you know."

"M-m-me? M-m-my—"

"Look at this!" Dr. Keene picked up a piece of paper, a letter, emblazoned with the seal of the hospital at the top. "*Your grant proposal has been denied on the grounds that it does not serve the public interest. However, the board notes that you recently identified a homicide under unusual circumstances...* Do you get that? They heard about that nonsense at the bar!"

"...Oh." I still didn't quite follow.

"If you hadn't noticed that damned grit in the glass, I'd have signed off on death by alcohol poisoning and gone on my merry way. Instead, I had to do a proper autopsy, and there it was."

"Wh-what, sir?"

"ARSENIC! ARSENIC IN HIS ORGANS!"

"M-murder?"

"Well, he didn't swallow rat poison for fun, did he? My money's on one of those female companions, but anyway, who cares? It's not my problem anymore, is it?"

"Um. Is it?"

"Yes!" Dr. Keene shook the letter before dropping it on the desk like it'd bit him. "They want me to oversee more autopsies! Apparently there have been *concerns* that this morgue has been sloppy with their findings."

I thought briefly about Roger Carrell, the smelter diagnosed with pneumonia, the quick and casual way the coroner rubber-stamped death certificates with the most obvious causes of death. And sure, I knew as well as anyone that the morgue was short-staffed and hardly had the time to thoroughly autopsy every single body, but...well...I didn't disagree with the hospital board's complaints, either.

"Look here! *Somewhere lurks a murderer who would have gone unnoticed if not for your keen insight.* A murderer! It's one of the women, I'm sure. Probably the jealous type."

"Is that what the police think, sir?"

"What? The police? They won't quit harping about the liquor!" After a moment, Dr. Keene stopped shuffling papers and looked pointedly at me. "Well? Are you going to clean this up or should I get the broom myself?"

"I'm sorry, sir. Right away, sir," I said, disappearing back out into the hallway. As I rushed down to the basement to fetch the broom and wastebin, I thought about that woman who'd stopped me outside the bar. Katie? Katherine! Katherine Jessop, catching me by the sleeve to tell me she knew Francis Mather was going to be murdered *and* who did it. The way she said it.... It sounded almost like he wasn't the first...

I passed by the autopsy room and paused. Roger Carrell wasn't the only body I'd found with an official cause of death that didn't match the evidence. Just last month I'd come across a man who had supposedly died of asphyxiation, but his lungs lacked the telltale cherry red of carbon dioxide. Or what about Ernest W. Boyce, the famous philanthropist who'd supposedly killed himself two months ago? In that case, the death certificate got it right, the mercury in his stomach certainly caused his death, but I was less convinced it had been suicide. The newspapers had discovered that this "kindly old doctor" regularly duped desperate girls into giving him their newborns, which he'd turn around and sell to wealthy families. The papers and public seemed to agree it was guilt that made him kill himself, but a statement from the family disputed that. They said he never would have killed himself, that he'd disappeared on his way to meet one of those sad girls he'd betrayed...

When I returned to Dr. Keene's office, I stood in the doorway a moment, the broom in my hand.

Maybe I could dazzle him again with my brilliance.

Or maybe I could just prove myself a bigger fool.

"Sir?"

A long, weary silence, and then: "*Yes?*"

I set the broom against the doorframe. "Are homicidal poisonings common?"

"Not as a rule," Dr. Keene said, rolling his eyes.

"I was only wondering... It's curious, isn't it? Mather's death... and then there was that case with Ernest Boyce and his nephew thinking someone killed him."

"Insurance dog. Policy pays double in the event of murder."

"Well. Even so. It's strange to have two poisonings like that, isn't it?"

Dr. Keene gave me a flat-eyed stare. "Two poisonings. Months apart. In a city of, what, two and three-quarters million? Righto, call in Scotland Yard, we've got a humdinger of a case for them."

I winced and ducked my head, focusing on my sweeping.

"I only wonder, sir, if it isn't worth looking into?" I said, my eyes on the floor. "I just mean... well... that would be the kind of high-profile work the hospital cares about. Right? Work in the public interest? If you found evidence that this is one killer, if you caught him, you could—"

"If I caught a murderer like that, those bastards'd name a wing after me!" Dr. Keene said. "And if I found out the moon was made of green cheese, they'd probably build me a palace." He sniffed. "I am a scientist, Rookwood, not some rumor-chasing sensationalist. I deal in facts." Without another word, he snatched up his hat and jacket and sailed for the door, giving me a look that said: *I am where I am and you are where you are because of that.*

But...

What were the odds, really, that in the three months I'd been here, I would come across two mysterious deaths? Could there be more? And I couldn't stop thinking about Katherine Jessop...

"*We all knew he was gonna get himself murdered. I know who done it, too.*"

What did she know?

I finished sweeping up Dr. Keene's office, depositing the splinters in the wastebin and returning his papers to the desk. When I came across the hospital board letter, I paused. Even if this wasn't the work Dr. Keene wanted to be doing, this was the work the hospital thought him best suited for. And what had Dr. Keene himself told me?

Labs are expensive. Chemicals. Equipment. Assistants. Time to do the damn science you're trying to do. You only get money when someone with money cares about the work.

Identifying a series of murders would get Dr. Keene the kind of attention most researchers only dreamed of, and then he could do any work he wanted. He could even go back to work on tricoloroforms, his metamorphosis research that had been so quickly dismissed. And if I could help him…if I could present solid evidence of a killer working his way through the streets of Chicago…Well, the least he could do would be to offer to help me in my own research, right? Maybe I could find the answers I was looking for.

All I had to do was solve a string of impossible murders.

NINE
RUBY

Blood in the water, sharks all around.

I weaved my way through the crowd, and my heart raced but I felt steely-focused. What was Dennis Ferry getting away with?

Vivian's thoughts had a kind of razor-edged chill to them but no specifics—her sources hadn't given any details. If I could find out more, though, bundle it up and send it on, anonymously, to Papa...

While Ferry continued to hold sway over his group, I bent down to adjust the strap on my shoe and poked into his mind. I sensed idle thoughts about chitchat, the squeeze of a too-tight shirt collar, and then—glass.

Rahtz. Ferry had one of those slick, impenetrable minds, like Darwin, the Gibsons' butler. No surprise for a man who kept secrets. There was a whole side of him locked away in some dank cellar, and I wanted in.

Carefully, my hands busy fumbling with my shoes, I tested the surface of that thick wall, feeling for any cracks or crevices. I could sense *something* back there, flashes that disappeared the moment I tried to latch onto them, and I was close, I was close...

"Ruby!"

Like a damn bull in a china shop, Albert's voice shattered my focus, and I turned to give him a milk-curdling glare. I hadn't noticed he'd been chatting with Ferry, and apparently he assumed I was eavesdropping on account of *him*, the big-headed louse. I was about to squawk at him to never call attention to a lady adjusting her outfit when Ferry looked over his shoulder and spotted me.

A second to place my face, then it all slid into focus—*Jeremiah Newhouse's daughter*—and as Papa's name popped into his thoughts, it created a tiny, barely there crack in the wall of his mind and I slipped *in*!

Vaguely, I was aware of Albert hissing questions at me, making apologies to Ferry and his wife, but I had fallen too deep into Ferry's mind to really pay attention. It was like a cave of mirrors, cold and dark and slick and hard, as bad as any mind I'd ever encountered before and a flavor I recognized immediately.

Ferry wasn't a mild-mannered city employee. He wasn't even a hypocrite, railing on about good old-fashioned values while taking liberties with his fresh young secretaries. He was a monster. A cold-blooded, black-eyed devil—attacking women, breaking good men down, and Papa...*Papa*...

"*The state's attorney...is a...problem...*" Conversations like wisps of smoke, echoes and memories, Ferry speaking with someone...with Commissioner Walsh...

"*I want...up and running...no more competition...*"

"*Do...what you need...to do...*"

"Ruby, are you even listening?" A thousand miles away, a hand shook my shoulder, and I pulled myself, gasping, out of Ferry's evil brain. Blinking, I could see Albert staring at me—*Good lord, is she drunk?*—and Ferry's wife, her lips pinched into a frown—*No manners, these ridiculous flappers*—and Ferry himself—*Make sure she doesn't cause trouble after the funeral...*

"Wh-what?" I stuttered, not caring that, for the first time in my life, I'd failed to keep my poker face while reading someone's mind. Ferry frowned.

"Are you all right, my dear?" he asked with mild concern, but I could see his mind: Papa dead, me weeping, a city without its last protector, free rein to do whatever he wanted—it was him! It was Ferry! He was running the criminal organization, he ordered the attack on our house, he—he—he meant to see Papa *dead*!

I stumbled backward and might've fallen right off my heels but for a hand on my back, solid weight, and I turned and almost collapsed into a puddle of relief to see Papa, looking me over with alarm.

"Is everything all right?" he asked, glancing from me to Albert, who just threw his hands up in the air, thoroughly embarrassed to be associated with me.

"P-Papa—"

"There he is! Man of the hour! Take a seat, we're starting the speeches!" Mayor McGuire had burst through the crowd, ready to seize Papa, when he took in the whole scene: my white face, Papa's arms around my shoulders, Albert trying hard to shrink into nothing. "Something wrong?"

"Ruby, are you all right?" Papa's voice brought me to the present, and I reached for his hand and dug my nails in hard.

"Oh, Papa," I said, in my best imitation of Mama's airy breathlessness. "I don't feel at all well..."

She found something, Papa thought. *What did she learn? Who is it?*

"What's this?" Mayor McGuire crowded in close to me. "What's the matter with her?"

His booming voice brought a dozen pairs of eyes on us, and with them, a dozen minds, all of them crowding one another out. It was too much. I needed to tell Papa what I'd discovered and we needed to leave this party RIGHT NOW.

"Ruby, should you sit down?" he asked, holding tight to me, and I just kept my eyes wide, wishing he could see into *my* mind and the frantic, mad screaming going on there. But he got the picture and said, "Perhaps we should get you home..."

"Home? You're leaving?" Mayor McGuire's words lifted above the din of the crowd and then complete pandemonium broke out in the ballroom. Amid all the frenzy I locked eyes with Ferry, just for a second, and heard: *Don't let him get away don't let him go...*

A gasp went up as I swayed on my feet and fell into my father's arms. Eyes closed, I heard shouts for water and for a doctor—but that was too much commotion, would take too much time...I let my eyelashes flutter and said in a fetchingly weak voice, "Oh, Papa, did I fall? It's so stuffy in here..."

"Some fresh air is what the girl needs," a nearby voice said, and another agreed, and another. This time when Papa turned to the mayor and firmly thanked him for the evening but insisted he see to his daughter, not even Mayor McGuire could come up with a reason for him to stay.

"Quickly," Papa muttered, helping me through the ballroom. "Quickly."

I caught Mayor McGuire staring at us in shock, and there was

Commissioner Walsh, too far away for me to read his mind but with something on his face like disappointment, some plan disturbed, and there was Albert, rising to the occasion and calling for one of the body-guards...but where was Ferry? Where had that evil mind *gone*?

"What is it?" Papa whispered as we reached the door of the ball-room, and I bent my head near his.

"It's Ferry, Papa! He's the one—the person giving Walsh orders, the one who ordered that shooting—he's after you! He means to kill you before you can expose him!"

Papa's mind went electric with shock and his arm stiffened around me as we hurried through the lobby and out of the hotel, a mob of reporters and onlookers at our heels.

"Ferry," he said, *"Ferry..."* His thoughts were firing off faster than I could keep up with; it was as though my words had upset a flock of birds, and they flew past me before I could get more than a glance: *evidence...papers...club...Albert...Coward...*

We hit the street and Papa glanced around. "Where is our—oh damn, there it is." He nodded at the cream-colored car that had taken us to the gala, now parked half a block away. With one hand around my shoulders, Papa raised the other to hail the driver, but squinting down the block, I could see that—of course—he was asleep.

"Damn," Papa said again, and I almost didn't know what shocked me more—the events of the evening or that my papa had sworn in my presence, *twice.*

He yelled toward the car, but the crowd was ballooning around us, reporters knocking one another over to get photos, a hundred buzzing, burning minds. We needed to get out. I grabbed Papa tight around the arm and yanked him off the curb and down into the street.

"Get to the car," I said, my voice low. "We're getting you out of here, as far away as possible."

"Listen, Ruby," he said as we stumbled along down the street, camera shutters clicking behind us like a cloud of frenzied insects. "This is important—"

Ferry—Coward—Albert—the evidence

His thoughts swirled with fear and anxiety—or were those my own thoughts? I couldn't tell anymore. We made it to the car and Papa reached out to open the door for me. "It's not safe to talk around the driver, but the moment we get—Is he asleep?"

The door handle clicked open and at the exact same second, three things happened:

One: out of habit, I searched the dreaming mind of the driver, only to find it as blank, empty, and lifeless as a marble statue.

Two: a shout rang out from the crowd of people at the hotel, a man screaming "HERMAN COWARD SAYS HELLO!"

And three: Papa pulled open the door of the car, triggering a clever little pipe bomb, and blowing me, himself, sharp shards of car, and wet shards of driver all over the icy Chicago street.

TEN

GUY

Katherine Jessop's neighborhood smelled like motor oil and rotten garbage. I caught a glimpse of the latter, frozen into a pile at one end of the street, its stink not quite muffled by the cold, and readjusted the scarf around my neck.

I didn't wear my Guy Rosewood face. It was dangerous to rely on one set of features, and Guy Rosewood had already been in this neighborhood, investigating Francis Mather's death at the bar. I couldn't have the police knowing he was still at it.

I would have preferred to go as a woman...someone inconspicuous, unthreatening. But my abilities didn't extend to clothing and I didn't have the money for a dress. So, after leaving Dr. Keene's office, I put on the face of one of the clerks in the morgue, an older man with high cheekbones and hair so thin and white it looked like fishing line.

Early evening, and the sidewalks stood deserted, although I could see signs of the children who played there during the day: hopscotch drawn in charcoal, a sturdy stick leaning up against a stoop, the glitter of a stray jack in the gutter. I looked up at the apartment buildings, the windows bright with the warm light of dinnertime, and was wondering how in the hell I'd find Katherine Jessop, when a fellow standing outside one of the buildings gave me a long look.

"Lost, mister?" he asked, his eyes sweeping me up and down.

"I'm looking, ah, for a Jessop," I said, speaking in a fair replica of the clerk's airless voice. The fellow lifted an eyebrow but pointed at a building two doors down with a green stoop, and I continued on. The clerk's face itched awfully bad—something about wrinkles always did that—and I brought up a gloved hand to scratch around my mouth. I reached the building and saw JESSOP printed neatly next to the bell for the third floor. When I put out a finger to push it, I heard a voice from above.

"Doesn't work no more! Who you lookin' for!"

I stepped off the stoop and turned my face to the sky. There, in one of the upper windows, a woman in a house robe leaned out, a rumple-haired toddler at her side. I recognized her right away.

"Mrs. Jessop?"

"Ah, yah, that's me. Whaddya want? You wit' the city?"

"What? Oh. No. I…uh…I—"

"All right, all right." The face disappeared from the window and a series of bumps and thuds and bangs came from deep within the building, ending with a loud, metallic *click* and the swing of the front door.

"Yah?" Mrs. Katherine Jessop had the look of a young woman aged far ahead of her time. She'd traded the toddler for a baby over one shoulder and a flat-faced, sooty dog, which sniffed at my ugly shoes and growled.

"Oh, shut it, Buster," she said, pushing her slippered foot toward the dog. "Not you, bud. What's it ya want?"

"I c-came to ask you about…" I paused, glanced past her up the stairs. One of her neighbors had opened her apartment door and seemed just as interested in my business as she was. Mrs. Jessop followed my gaze, turning around and back again with a sigh before waving me in. "Come on. I got a kettle on. Mind ya don't step on that dog."

I followed her in as she climbed the stairs, the black dog bounding up after her like a shadow, and shooed the neighbor back inside. The sound of a radio grew louder as I reached Mrs. Jessop's apartment, and the music, combined with the high-pitched whistle of one of her children, set my ears drumming.

"Take off ya hat, stay awhile," Mrs. Jessop said, sailing into the kitchen and turning the radio down a hair. I pulled off my hat and stood with it between my hands, pinned under the twin suspicions of Mrs. Jessop's toddler and dog.

"Hello," I said to both of them, but neither looked convinced.

"Did you say your name?" Her voice brayed through the din of the radio and the clatter of the teapot.

"Mister, um…" I searched the apartment, looking for a suitable alias. Brasso? Borax? Hoover? My eyes landed on a pile of the toddler's discarded toys. "Mr. Cart…er. Carter."

"Mr. Carter. Huh." She reappeared with a cup in her hands. "Sit," she said, and both I and the black dog obeyed. "So, what's this for? Ya said ya ain't with the city?"

"My, um, employer sent me. From, um, the morgue."

"Ohhhh." Mrs. Jessop sat down at the table opposite me, her baby balanced in her lap. "Yeah, I was wonderin' if I might hear somethin' about that. Ya here about Frankie Mather, huh?"

"You…said you know who killed him."

"Sure," she said, shrugging. "Everyone knows. Ya could ask anybody on this block who killed 'im, they'll tell ya."

"Oh. Well…I'm asking."

Mrs. Jessop smiled. "It was our angel."

"Angel?"

"Yah. Comes to women in their time of need, and *whew* did Pauline Mather need some help. Ya know that bastard—eh, Sally, don't tell Pop you heard me use that word—he's the one been makin' her sick? Slippin' something in her evening tea, most like, for the last year. An' she's got a buncha little kids around. We used to tell her, Pauline, you gotta get outta that house or he'll kill you, but where she's gonna go? So, we did what we always did. We prayed to the angel to take her Frankie away, an' that's exactly what happened." Mrs. Jessop smiled at me like she was expecting a *thank you*.

"You…prayed. To an…angel?"

"Don't gotta say it like that. Listen, I'm a good Catholic girl, right, and I been lightin' candles my whole life over this kinda stuff. Fellow beats his wife? Someone's boy takes *liberties* with a pretty girl? Ya know, the priest says ya gotta forgive an' leave the judgment up to God but all those years I been prayin' ain't done squat for the good and ain't punished the bad. Then, 'bout two years ago, I hear from my cousin who lives out in Andersonville, her neighbor's little girl gets taken in the back of the candy shop an' don't come out the same. The men weren't no use 'cause that fellow's got some sorta political pull, but us mothers—we knew. That fellow were a bad seed. So, my cousin and her friends, they pray that somethin'll be done. Settle the scales, like. An' barely a week later, Mr. Nasty Candy Man's found dead. Police said he made himself a bad batch of candy, didn't clean out the mixer right and poisoned himself on metal cleaner, but my cousin and her friends knew. They had their prayers answered."

"Poisoned!" I scrambled in my pockets for a notebook. "You, you said Andersonville? A year ago? Do you know the fellow's name?"

"Ohh, *R* somethin'. Swedish, you know. Rasmus? Rasmussen? Somethin' or some sort." Mrs. Jessop smiled again and bounced the baby on her lap as I scrawled the name into my notebook.

I leaned forward, the notebook balanced on the edge of the table. "How many times would you say this has happened?"

"Well. There was Betty Price's boy—ooh he was a piece of work. Used to do all sorts of horrible things to dogs—sorry, Buster—and then there was whispers when he got older he moved on to women. And let's see...Oh! A year ago, last Christmas, there was this fellow, a Dr....Barnum, I think? He did, well, *special* operations?" She leaned in, eyebrows raised. "Ya know? The kind good girls don't get? Only he weren't much better'n a butcher. Killed two girls and got off scot-free, then turned 'round and killed a third. Well, he got his. Our angel saw to that."

"But, well, Mrs. Jessop...You see, the problem is...angels don't exist," I said, fumbling with my notes. "I came here hoping you could give me some information about Mr. Mather's killer, so we could bring him some justice."

"Bring *him* justice?" Mrs. Jessop laughed. "Ya heard anythin' I said? This ain't about him. This were justice for Pauline, and ladies like her. Ya know what I say now when my husband gives me lip? I say he better mind his p's and q's or I'm gonna tell my angel on him and she'll sort him right out."

"Yes, but you have to admit, murder is still—" I paused. Mrs.

Jessop's words rolled in my head for a moment. "She?" I blinked. "You said… 'she'? How do you know this murderer is a woman?"

And Mrs. Jessop gave me a look, the look that women give men from time to time: the exasperated, obvious, elucidating look that shows how little men understand about the things women, all women, know just by existing.

"'Course she's a *she*," Mrs. Jessop said, laughing a bit before giving her cooing baby a kiss on the nose. "Who else'd care about us?"

ELEVEN
RUBY

I just adored dreaming minds.

On nights when I couldn't sleep, I liked to sneak into my sisters' room. There was a rocking chair between their beds, and with the lights off and the curtains drawn and the sounds of their sweet, soft breaths, I'd watch the slow rise and fall of their chests and sail away into their bright and beautiful fantasies.

Everyone should be lucky enough to step into the dreamworlds of a pair of small girls. Together, we explored oceans and stars and heavens of huge pink clouds, palaces where they reigned as tiny, benevolent queens or warrior goddesses straight out of the stories I read to them. And if the dreams ever turned sour, I could just put out a hand, press it cool against their foreheads, whisper happy things that soothed away their fears.

When we got Papa to the hospital, I insisted someone pack up the rocking chair and set it up for me right in his room, no matter that it was past ten and I hadn't changed out of the emerald-green velvet dress. My armor was a bit dented, and bloody—but from me or Papa or the poor driver, I couldn't tell and didn't care. I refused to go home. Papa's doctor said they would know more about his condition in a few hours and so I waited, sitting in the rocking chair, trying to slip into Papa's mind and finding nothing but a sinking hole of darkness.

"Miss Newhouse?" The doctor, who had a mind sharper than his neat moustache, poked a head into the room. I jumped to my feet, setting the chair swinging.

"Will he recover?"

"I really should speak to your mother—"

"*No.* Please. For God's sake, please don't tell my mother anything without checking with me first." Mama had come and gone in a whirlwind so fierce I thought she might end up in her own hospital bed, after which I told Mrs. Ritter to take her home, dose her up with something sweet, and put her to bed.

"Please," I said again. "What's happened to him?"

The doctor sighed and spoke to me about probabilities and prognoses and how much he admired the "fight" in my papa, which didn't make sense, and anyway wasn't even true. I could see the truth right there in the doctor's mind.

It did not look good.

And it looked quite a bit worse than bad.

The bomb, which exploded the moment Papa pulled open the car door, had thrown both of us through the air like puppets and knocked Papa clean out. His body had blocked me from the worst of the damage. Other than my ruined dress, the only sign I'd been in a horrible explosion was the bandage wrapped around my left forearm and a trail of bruises down my rear and left leg. But Papa...In addition to the head injury, he'd gotten himself a broken leg and a few cracked ribs, not to mention a nasty burn on his right hand, now swaddled in several layers of evil-smelling gauze from his fingertips to his elbow.

We'd had one lucky break: the door of the cream-colored car had shielded us from some of the blast.

"Had your father not stepped aside to hold the door for you, had he been alone," the doctor said, "he would have been killed. You saved his life, Miss Newhouse."

Well. It was a sweet thing to say to the white-faced daughter of the state's attorney, but I felt sure it had even less truth to it than the doctor's empty assurances.

I had failed.

Horribly, terribly, and right when Papa needed me more than ever.

Failed to figure out the plan to attack him. Failed to realize until too late that the driver was dead. Failed to find out what exactly Papa had wanted to tell me, before that bomb closed his mind off.

What a miserably stupid girl I'd been, thinking I could protect Papa from harm, worrying more about getting a fancy new dress than how to keep sharp and focused. Sure, I'd discovered Ferry's nasty secret, but without Papa, how was I supposed to expose him? What was the point of reading minds if I just mangled it?

"Miss Newhouse, are you all right? You don't need to stay. We'll keep an eye on things here."

"Thank you," I said. "I'll stay." And I took my seat in the rocking chair, knitted my fingers together on my lap, and watched my father dream his darkness.

"Miss Newhouse! Miss Newhouse!"

I'd hardly realized I'd fallen asleep until I woke with a jolt, the banging on the door sending my heart up into my throat. Blinking, I jumped to my feet as the door to the room burst open, and I got a glimpse of a jostling crowd of man-eating reporters, all trying to elbow their way inside, while a bodyguard sent by Albert struggled to push them back.

"Over here!"

"Is he going to live?"

"What do you have to say to Coward?"

I ran to the door to try to shove it closed and winced as flash powder exploded in my face.

"Miss Newhouse!"

"Miss Newhouse!"

"Ruby."

Squinting through my outspread fingers, I saw, who else? Vivian Forbes, cool as a glass of water in her lavender suit. She looked over the chaos of the crowd, a raised eyebrow with a meaning as clear as her thoughts: *You owe me.*

"Get 'em out of here," I said to the bodyguard, pushing the last reporter away from the door. "Except for the woman in lavender. Bring her back in a minute."

I disappeared into my father's room and pulled the curtains around his bed. Chummy or not, Vivian didn't have the right to gawk at my sick papa.

Not five seconds later the door swung open again and Vivian appeared, a camera slung over one shoulder.

"Horsefeathers, are you mad?" I hissed. *"That* stays outside."

Vivian rolled her eyes but pulled the camera from her neck and handed it to Albert's fellow out in the hallway.

She waited until the door clicked carefully closed and then she let loose.

"How is he? What happened? Are you hurt? Did you see anything?" She didn't bother with a notebook, but it didn't matter; her mind was sharp and clear. I crossed my arms over my chest.

"This is off the record."

"Having a social chat, are we, kitten?"

"If you don't like it, you can go out with the rest of them."

Vivian's eyes narrowed as she thought all sorts of nasty things about me, but she smiled. "What did you bring me in here for, then?"

I raised my chin. I didn't want her—or anyone—to know that the span of time from when Papa stepped forward to open the car door to when we arrived at the hospital was nothing but a great, black chasm to me. Every time I tried to remember, I felt woozy and drunk.

"Tell me what you saw," I said.

"Hold on. No information without an interview. Front page." She took a closer look at me, the stained dress and the pitiful bandage on my arm, her eyes glowing. "With pictures."

Oh gosh—I knew exactly the kind of treacly pictures she had in mind: me, draped over my father's hospital bed, with gorgeous tears running down my face, underneath the headline WEEPING DAUGHTER OF DYING STATE'S ATTORNEY REVEALS ALL. I sighed.

"Fine. What did I miss?"

Vivian dropped into my rocking chair. "I got out there just before the explosion, in time to see you and your pop leaving, and I was off to the side of the crowd when that madman shouted out. Some eight-foot-tall mountain wrestled him to the ground. One of yours, I'm guessing?"

Albert's hired bodyguard. I felt a pang of guilt for thinking such mean things about Albert—irritating little toe-rag that he was. He'd leapt into action immediately, setting up the man out in the hallway and sending a pair over to the graystone to keep an eye on Mama and the girls.

"How could you tell?"

"Looked to be hired. And he obviously wasn't police," she added.

"Why do you say that?"

"Because he threw a fit when he had to hand the fellow over to Commissioner Walsh's men. Kept saying he was acting under orders from the state's attorney's office to hold on to him, but the police didn't care. They slapped the bracelets on their man and tossed him in a paddy wagon. The whole time, the fellow's laughing fit to burst."

"Laughing?"

Vivian rolled her eyes and I dug deeper into her mind, pulling out the memory: a sallow-skinned man with heavy circles under his eyes and slick, thin hair, dressed in the kind of clothes that wouldn't look out of place in a church donation bin, his eyes wild and his laugh a jerky series of high-pitched explosions.

Drunk, I'd guess. Not the kind of cold, focused killer Coward usually employed.

"You think someone's trying to set Coward up," I said.

Vivian shrugged. "The shootout at your house was fishy enough; paying some drunk to shout Coward's name tonight just confirmed my doubts. But word is, when they booked that man, he sang Coward's name like a nightingale."

"Oh, you don't believe Coward was *really* involved."

"Well, I'm suspicious by nature. And sense. And experience."

I chewed on my fingernail, and Vivian, her own nails shiny and neat with varnish, internally winced. No doubt Ferry had arranged for that fellow to shout Coward's name. How did I prove it?

"Can you get me into the jail where they're holding him?" I asked. "I want to talk to him myself."

"I could, but if you want to see him, you can just skedaddle across the yard outside."

"He's in the hospital?" I didn't understand.

"The morgue."

"He's *dead*?"

"Found conveniently strung up in the holding cell. Company line is it was a suicide, but if I were more cynical, I'd say it had all the markings of a police cover-up." She lifted an eyebrow. "This wouldn't have anything to do with that hypothetical criminal organization you mentioned, would it?"

I crossed my arms, wondering just how much to let on. "We're still off the record, aren't we? Anything I tell you, you can't print?"

"Not just can't," Vivian said, with a laugh, "wouldn't. I can quote you saying anything you like, but I'm not going to write a story like this—not to mention calling the police commissioner someone's lackey—without some actual proof."

Proof. Damn.

She wasn't wrong, either. Let's say she printed me up in the paper tomorrow morning, crowing on about political conspiracy and criminal activity. Let's say I claimed there was a plot to kill my father and pin the murder on Chicago's most notorious mob boss, and the mastermind behind the whole thing was dopey, dreary Dennis Ferry. What would be the response? PARTY GIRL RUBY NEWHOUSE MAKES WILD

ACCUSATIONS AGAINST RESPECTED CITY OFFICIAL, SCIENTISTS BLAME BATHTUB GIN. There wasn't a single soul who would believe me, and I didn't blame them. I could hardly believe it myself.

I needed something concrete. I *had* to take a look at that body.

"Listen," I said, "I've gotta check in with the doc before heading home, so—"

"Oh no you don't. You owe me those pictures." Vivian reached out to twitch aside the curtains around Papa's bed, and I smacked her hand away.

"One picture. And only me, no Papa."

"Hey! That's not—"

"No one cares about a sick old man in bed! I didn't take you for some sob sister writing sentimental fluff," I said, and rearranged my curls before slipping the strap of my dress down just enough to expose my bare left shoulder, delicately blushed from my run-in with the Chicago pavement. "I know just what your readers want, and I won't disappoint them."

Fifteen minutes later, Vivian disappeared out of the hospital as I watched from the window, wiping red lipstick and artfully placed tearstains from my face. She'd have to move her rear to make the morning edition—dawn was just a shimmy away.

Bending down to kiss Papa's cheek, I took one more glimpse into his mind. Still nothing but tumbling blackness.

"Good night, Papa. I'll figure out what's going on, I promise."

I grabbed my coat and slipped out the door, nodding to the fellow in the empty hall.

"Don't disappoint me, Jack," I said to him. "Goin' home for a bit."

He nodded back and watched me head for the stairwell, but when I reached the lobby and walked through the main door, I kept right on going, across the deserted hospital campus to a small building shaped unnervingly like a tombstone.

COOK COUNTY MORGUE, read the sign over the door. Locked, of course, but when I circled around the back, I found a row of dark windows, one of which had a broken sash. I gently pried the window open and slipped right on in.

Dark shadows. Silent as, well, a morgue. The polished wood floor creaking under my feet sounded loud as a gunshot, and I winced, but there were no nearby minds, no thoughts, nothing I could hear.

I was in an office or file room—hard to tell in the dark—and stepped out into the hall. Squinting at the tiny placards on each door, I walked slowly past offices and the records room. Where on earth did they keep the *bodies*? I wondered, and then I heard something down by the end of the hall: a noise, faint, like faraway music.

A mind.

Not just a mind, but a *machine*, fizzing and whirring and sucking in information so fast it took my breath away, and then giving it a name and shape and structure and spitting it all back out again in clear, precise thoughts. *Signs of hematoma in brain stem, bloody lungs indicate high saturation of carbon dioxide.*

Damn.

Frowning, I peered through one of the small windows set into the last door in the hall and could just make out a white-coated man sitting in front of a table piled high with papers, a notebook balanced on a rolling tray beside him.

Damn, *again.*

Who was this busybody dynamo getting work done this side of midnight?

I shot his back a nasty look and turned around—too fast, stupid me, as my heel caught on a nail in the floor, sending me careening for balance and raising a ruckus like a tap-dancing elephant. Oh, *rahtz!* I thought, as the exact same panic hit the fellow inside the room.

Well, well. One peek through the window settled it: the man hustled to toss those papers into one giant pile, his clear and methodical thoughts now scattershot with fear.

So, he wasn't allowed to be there, either—and *that* I could use.

I waited till he had his back to me at one of the basins across the room, pinched my cheeks a good bright red, and then burst through the door.

"Oh!" I said, as the fellow spun around, looking for all the world like a kid with his hand in the cookie jar, and I felt a funny jolt of surprise. He didn't look anything like I'd expected from his mind: a man in his middle age, tidy black moustache, sharp nose, staring at me with wide eyes. But his mind felt…younger? Somehow?

"Gol-*lee,* I'm sorry! Didn't think I'd bother anyone this late!"

His thoughts pos-i-lute-ly scrambled, like a collection of clowns in a burning house: *Who is that what is she doing down here got to run got to leave I'm dead I'm dead.*

"Um. *Am* I bothering you? Only, I think you might be just the person to give me a hand." I took a careful step closer, tilting my face so that the light overhead caught my rosy cheeks just so. Thank goodness I'd styled my hair for Vivian and still had the green dress on, although I had to hide the worst of the bloodstains with my coat. Turned out I did enough, because that whir inside the fellow's head caught, just for a second, to wonder at my big blue eyes.

Obligingly, I batted my lashes, peering up at him. *LOOK HOW WEAK AND HARMLESS I AM,* I practically spelled out in Morse code. *DON'T YOU WANT TO HELP ME?*

I could feel his thoughts go soft and slow—good grief, men made it too easy—when I pushed my luck, took another step, and his mind clamped down with fear.

Get her out of here

"Y-you aren't supposed to be here," he said, and again, his voice didn't sound a thing like his thoughts. One of the papers slipped from his hands down to the floor, and as he bent, quick, to snatch it up, I noticed that his shoes were cheap, old, and in need of a good polish. What doctor, even in the county morgue, couldn't afford a nice pair of shoes?

"You n-need to leave."

"But I can't go now!" I pulled my shoulders in, clasping my hands together the same way Genevieve did whenever she wanted to wheedle an extra half hour before the Victrola. Only Genevieve didn't have this dress.

"Please—it's my uncle. I only just got word..." A tremble filled my voice and I lowered my lashes to hide invisible tears. "I was too late to say a proper goodbye."

Leave out the details and let them fill in the gaps. I could see this fella putting it together: a young girl out at a party, tragic news, a rushed cab ride, but too late, too late!

"They tell me...he's here." I lowered my voice to a whisper, so that he had to lean forward to hear me properly. "Do...Do you think you could help me find him?"

She needs to go she needs help she's awfully pretty you need to go you'll be caught there'll be trouble—

"Please," I whispered. "I would be so...*grateful.*"

And that did it. Honestly, it was too easy.

"All right," he said, letting out a quick breath. "All right, just for a moment. What's his name?"

His name?

His *name*?

I FORGOT TO ASK VIVIAN HIS NAME.

"He came in, oh, not long ago. A, um, suicide. So terrible."

The man, halfway to the long row of cabinets that apparently held *bodies,* turned to give me an odd look, and before he could follow that odd look down to any unwelcome thoughts, I snapped my heels across the floor.

"Can you find him that way? Only, well, this might sound strange but I never knew my uncle's Christian name. We called him Uncle Speedy on account of he used to race horses out West—have you ever been out West? I've never gone past the Mississippi myself, but someday I think I'd like to see it, wouldn't you?" Gadzooks, what on earth was I even saying? My tongue prattled on with a mind of its own as I scanned a clipboard resting on a nearby table helpfully titled MORGUE ADMISSIONS. Hand-scrawled names and dates and other details marched down the list and my eyes went right to the entries for that evening. One was a woman, two were men, and beside the one listed as *Johansen, Louis,* under the *Admitted By* column, someone had written *George P. Wein, Sgt.*

"Anyway, Uncle Speedy was what we always called him, as I said, but his last name's Johansen."

"Johansen?" The fellow gave me another curious glance and then turned back to the row of cabinets with a frown. He paused before one and threw it open almost with a flourish.

"Here it is!" He had a look on his face like a pleased puppy, but it turned uncertain once he considered that Louis Johansen's pretty niece might not be thrilled to see her uncle's lifeless body.

He was gray and bare, Louis, but someone had covered him collarbone to toes with a stiff cotton sheet. A scruffy face, sandy hair, the kind of hard look a fellow takes on after too many liquid meals and not enough regular bathing. Across his throat, a pale, pinkish bruise stretched like a collar. Guess that was from the belt. Maybe it really had been a suicide...

Huh, came a curious thought from the doctor. *Wonder why that ligature mark isn't darker?*

I spun around, and he backed up quickly, almost tripping over his own shabby shoes.

"I'm s-s-sorry," he stuttered. "I'll give you a mo—"

"You know, the police said it was suicide, but I don't believe that for a second. My uncle would never kill himself! Not good ole Uncle Speedy. Could they have gotten it wrong?"

"I—I d-don't know. If that's what they said..."

"Well, you're a doctor, aren't you? What do you think?"

I'm not a doctor, the fellow thought, which almost made me laugh. Not a doctor! So, what was he then? Some kind of middle-aged medical student? An amateur autopsist? No wonder he didn't want to get caught!

"That's really…" He trailed off. "I mean I don't…"

Oh bother. Time to play wounded deer once again.

"Please," I said, touching a hand to my heart, which had the one-two-punch of making me look extra sympathetic and drawing attention to my décolletage.

He noticed. After another moment, he nodded and leaned toward the body.

Faint ligature marks with minimal bruising. Broken hyroid bone indicates body was hanged. Eyes… As quick as his thoughts, a hand reached out to flick up one of Louis Johansen's eyelids. *No sign of subconjunctival hemorrhage but some yellowing present.*

And wouldn't you know? This fellow had a gift.

Every now and then I had the pleasure of listening in on a mind *completely* in its element. Papa in the courtroom, Genevieve snuggled with a stack of books, Henrietta putting on a performance, Mama tending her garden. I couldn't put my finger on the mismatch between this man's outside and his inside, but the inside itself…

Smooth and confident and efficient, as neat and satisfying to watch as a stenographer's typing.

And a bit single-minded, apparently, because as he flipped back the sheet hiding Louis Johansen's unmentionables, he didn't even bother with the consideration that this was a naked man of relation to the pretty girl just at his elbow.

I gasped, I admit it. But not because I'd never seen a bare willy before.

"What happened to him?" I asked.

Bruises. Horrible, terrible, purple bruises, mottled like storm clouds and stretching from chest to hips. Of course, I knew what had happened. Someone had beat the ever-living stuffing out of him.

The man gave the body a careful look, his medical mind cataloguing each and every battered organ and smashed bone and tallying up the subsequent damage, and then he nodded. And smiled.

"Just what I thought! Those ligature marks and the broken hyroid bone—they indicate suicide by hanging, but just look at that throat! Hardly any serious bruising, and no sign of hemorrhaging in the eyes, so he couldn't have been alive when he was hanged! And then that trauma to the body! I'd have to cut him up to be sure, but I'd say he's got at least four broken ribs, massive internal bleeding, probably several ruptured organs, and you can't do *that* to yourself. No, this is a clear case of—"

His manners had finally caught up to the dazzling speed of his thoughts.

"Oh," he said. "Oh, I'm so sor—"

"Of what? A clear case *of what*?"

He blinked at me. "You...you want to hear?"

"Please. You explain it all so well!" And he had, truly. My extracurricular hobbies had given me an interest in biology, but none of the textbooks were even half as colorful.

A sort of dazed smile came across the fellow's face that made me think he wasn't often indulged like this.

"Blunt-force trauma," he said, almost dreamily. "Death by blunt-force trauma. Assault, I'd guess. Homicide."

"Homicide! He was *murdered*! Then it wasn't a suicide!"

"I guess you were right about Uncle Speedy," he said, with a genuine note of kindness. "Don't worry. As soon as the medical examiner performs the autopsy, he'll see what I've seen, and..." His words trailed off as he glanced at a tag tied to Louis Johansen's right big toe.

"Cause of death: suicide." The words filled his thoughts. *"Body to be cremated and disposed in potter's field."*

Uh-oh. Only fellows with no money and no relations went to potter's field.

"That's strange," he said. "It says—"

"Well, *thank you* so very much, I know my aunt will be absolutely stunned at the news, and I can't tell you how much of a comfort it will be to—" I went still as a mouse as the unmistakable noise of an opening door echoed down the hallway. Even without the benefit of sensing the *two* minds now coming closer, the fellow knew immediately what I did: we were no longer alone.

"You need to go!" he said to me in a furious whisper, shoving the body into its cabinet as he pushed me toward the door.

"Wait—"

But not even my décolletage could get me out of this one. His thoughts had burst into a million, frantic pieces, like a maddened, enraged beehive, driven only by the need to *get that girl out of here*. He seized my wrist and dragged me to the door, and we both paused just long enough to see two figures at the end of the hallway, one dressed in the unmistakable deep blue wool of the Chicago police...

My heart stopped, but the two men turned toward a side office, and the fellow behind me grabbed my elbow.

"Across the hall!" he said. "Go—now!" And he shoved me right out the door. Frowning, I scrambled to the door across the hall, grabbed the knob. Locked! Footsteps again—they were coming back. I had no choice but to dive back into the room with the dark-haired would-be doctor—except *he was gone*.

I blinked in surprise to see a young, thin man, his hair a faded ashy brown, his skin almost colorless, staring back at me with wide gray eyes.

"Who the hell—" But that was all I got out, because the man's thoughts unspooled rapidly, and they weren't nearly so unfamiliar as his face:

What is she doing back here? She needs to go! I need to go! She can't see me like this, she can't know, why is she looking at me like that—She needs to go, needs to go, needs to go...

TWELVE
GUY

What was she doing? Why was she back here? *Why was she staring at me?*

I was an idiot for getting rid of Dr. Chase's face and even dumber for putting on Guy Rosewood's, but what choice did I have? I recognized Dr. Napier out in the hallway, and he worked side by side with Dr. Chase every single day. He would know better than anyone that Dr. Chase wouldn't stay this late to work. Off with the white coat, off with Dr. Chase's face, grab a mop and start cleaning the floors, but then that girl had to go and ruin everything!

And, still, she didn't leave.

"You need to go," I said again, desperate, except the soft pretty thing from five minutes ago had also transformed, and now she stepped back from me, all steel and suspicion.

"Who are you?" she demanded, but judging by the footsteps making their way down the hall, we didn't have time for the most basic answer to that question, let alone the real one.

"I can't—You need—"

"Oh, *hold on*," the girl said, sounding annoyed. She spun around to face the door, threw a kerchief over her hair, and knotted it under her chin. I gulped, about to ask what she planned on doing, when she let out a horrible, high-pitched, skin-shivering scream.

"Wait! What—" But she shoved her way out the door, still screaming her head off.

"B-b-b-*bodies!*" she sobbed. "Th-there are *bodies* in there! Oh, oh!"

"What! Who—!"

I peeked out the doors enough to see Dr. Napier and the police officer staring dumbfounded at the girl, who threw herself into Dr. Napier's arms, wailing loudly.

"Good lord!" he said. "Who on earth are *you*? You're not supposed to be here!"

"I w-was j-just looking for the r-records room and m-my b-brother said to c-come down here, b-but I didn't realize there'd be b-b-*bodies!*"

Dr. Napier, judging from the gingerly way he tried to disentangle himself from the girl, seemed torn between pity and suspicion.

"This is the morgue," he said, and he glanced at the police officer for help, but the cop looked just as confused. "How did you get in here?"

"The front door was unlocked! I told you, my brother said—*oh!* I bet he wanted to play a prank on me! Oh, he's just *terrible!*" And she burst into a fresh round of tears. "I'm so glad you're here! Can't you please help me? I just want to g-g-go *home.*"

She was an actress! Or a sorceress. She'd used the same lines on me, and they worked just as well. Instead of scolding her or sending her marching, Dr. Napier melted like margarine, and together he and the cop led her to the stairs, the doctor's arm gently draped around her shoulders. As soon as they disappeared, I let out a breath and slid down the wall to the floor.

She saw me. She saw Guy Rosewood change.

Groaning, I dropped my face into my hands.

What had I done?

Thirty minutes later I was out on the sidewalk and rushing to the boardinghouse, having first returned the files I'd borrowed from the record room. I'd found those people Mrs. Jessop talked about, and a few more, besides. If there really was a killer out there, he—she—whoever—was remarkably prolific.

But none of that mattered anymore. After months of being careful, I'd ruined everything! I'd have to get back to the boardinghouse, quick, before that girl asked around about me. I had a bag kept packed in case something like this happened. I'd tuck the little dog inside and run... where?

I wanted to tear Guy Rosewood's hair out by the roots. I'd made such a mess of everything, and just when it started to look promising! How could I have—

"Hello!" The red-haired girl popped out from the shadows, cutting in front of me, and I almost, literally, jumped out of my skin, snatching quick for the edges of my disguise. She had her arms wrapped around herself as she stamped the ground with small, high-heeled feet. "Good of you to show up! It's freezing out here and *not to be too bold* but I'm not wearing any bloomers."

"Y-you!"

"*You're welcome* are the words you're looking for. Now. How the hell did you do what you did?"

Oh. What had happened to the oxygen in my lungs?

"D-d-do—"

"It's not a mask, is it?" The girl frowned. "No, look, you're six inches taller now. What are you, some kind of magician? Or a circus performer? How can you change like that?"

"Ch-ch-change?" I was playing dumb, I knew any second she'd figure it out.

Transformer

Demon

Shape-shifter

Her eyes went wide and her mouth dropped open. "But...How..." she started, and then she shook her head. "You...you can *change*. Your face! Everything! You can be different people! Show me!"

Show me. Do it. Do it now.

Oh lord. Just like before. I clutched the wall of a nearby building, my head spinning and my lungs horribly outpaced. *I think I'm going to be sick.*

My skin shivered, went hot and cold, and when I looked down at my hands, I saw that they flickered like the screen of a picture show.

No. Don't lose control!

But it didn't matter—everything was slipping away, my hands growing bigger, my feet growing smaller, so small I lost my balance, stumbled to the ground, tried to hide my face in my hands. Under my fingers, my features slipped and reshaped like soft clay, and I let out a sharp *ah!* of surprise, my heartbeat fast, my thoughts firing off in a thousand directions—*Stop stop stop it get control stop changing hold on hold on HOLD ON!*

"Golly, take a breath!"

A hand on my shoulder, small but firm, and when I looked up, I saw the girl staring at me with amused concern. I yanked Guy Rosewood back into place, but I could still feel my skin shiver, nervous as a kicked dog.

"Wh-what do you w-want?" I managed. "I can't—can't *be* anyone. For you. I mean, I'm terrible at it. I get nervous and then I lose control and it falls apart and—"

"Hush. I don't want you to be anybody."

"I...I have money. Some. I mean...I don't have much, but you can have it."

"I don't want your money, either," she said, letting out a laugh that probably would have sounded lovely and bell-like an hour ago but now made my blood go cold.

"B-but what do you w-want?"

She shrugged. "Nothing," she said, so kindly that the weight on my chest, the one that kept me pinned to the frozen Chicago streets, swooped into the air—

"Yet."

—only to come crashing back down.

"Come on, you. On your feet. You look pos-i-lute-ly spliffificated stretched out on the street like that." She bent down and helped me up, although I wasn't sure I had any control over my limbs just yet.

"Sp-spliffi...cated?" I asked, and she laughed as she led me over to a nearby bench.

"Drunk! Don't you know? You seem young enough to get the lingo, although...I guess you could be any age, huh? Gee, you could be a hundred! Are you? If I could change, I think I'd stay eighteen forever." She deposited me on the bench and then took the empty space beside me, looking absolutely eighteen with her bright, rosy cheeks and bobbed hair.

"Is this what you really look like?" she asked. "When you're not pretending?"

When am I not pretending? I wondered, but I just shook my head.

"Older? Or younger?"

Younger, I thought, because I couldn't speak, but that didn't bother the girl.

"Male or female?"

Male.

"Blond? Brunette? Or a copperhead like me?"

Dark hair. Dark eyes. A face started to swim into focus, but before its features could clear, I wrenched it hard from my thoughts. If I drew it in my mind, my Guy Rosewood mask might slip completely.

"Can you at least tell me your real name?"

My name? But that was twice as dangerous as my face.

"G-Guy. You can call me…Guy. Rosewood."

"Guy." She wrinkled her nose like she didn't like the taste of the name in her mouth, and she must have known I was lying. "I'm Ruby."

"Uncle Speedy's niece."

"Oh, *no!*" she said, laughing. "You didn't believe *that,* did you? No, I'd never even met that poor fellow before tonight. He confessed to trying to kill my papa on Herman Coward's behalf—before supposedly killing himself—but I don't buy that. Had to take a look for myself."

Coward? Attempted murder? I felt sure she was playing more games with me, so I took the safest route and just said nothing. She let out another laugh, softer this time.

"It's true," she said. "I promise." Pulling her collar tight to her throat, she stood up. The streetlight lit her from behind, so most of her fell in shadow except for the red halo of curls, and she turned slightly, letting the light hit her cheeks, her brow, her nose, her lips.

"Can I ask you one thing?"

I swallowed. *Here it comes.*

"That fellow…his autopsy…You said it was strange?"

"Oh." I blinked at her. "Well…His tag indicated the autopsy had already happened. Cause of death established and body to be disposed of. Only…"

"Yes?"

"A first-year medical student could have caught how he really died. And with an autopsy…well…there would be signs of…" How did I put this in a delicate way? Slicing and dicing? Removed organs? Missing pieces?

Ruby held up a hand. "I understand. So, a fake death certificate! That makes things tricky.… Think you could convince one of the doctors to do a new autopsy?"

"M-me…?" I trailed off, startled by what she was suggesting.

"Please." She'd done it again. The dewy eyes. The half-parted lips. The velvet-soft voice. It was a biological trick, those pieces of her whispering to my brain *I am young I am healthy I need you protect me care for me want me,* flooding my body with a cocktail of blissful chemicals as addictive as anything found down a seedy back alley. But just because I knew how it worked, that didn't make it any less powerful.

"I…I couldn't, even if I wanted to. It's too late."

"Too late!"

"Well, I mean, that cop, with Dr. Napier—he took the body away. To be cremated, I believe. In any case, it's gone."

"And you can't tell anyone what you saw? It's important! I mean, you work in the morgue, don't you? You must be a…what? You're sharp enough to be a doctor."

"Um. Janitor."

"Janitor!" she said, and she burst into laughter that made me feel about six inches tall. "Oh! Oh, I'm sorry! I'm not laughing at you! I'm just impressed, really!"

She smiled at me, but my cheeks burned, and I crossed my arms over my chest.

"Well. I can't help you."

Useless, I thought. *Useless and helpless and now she knows I'm practically nothing, she'll—*

Before I knew what was coming, she'd swooped over, taken Guy Rosewood's face between her gloved hands, and planted a kiss on his lips. It'd been so long since anyone had touched me that I didn't realize what had happened till it was over, and even then, if not for the perfume in my lungs and the burning on my mouth, I probably wouldn't have believed it.

What in the hell?

"Don't be sorry. Losing that body—well. That was rough. But it's not your fault, and you've been a doll and a half. That info about what happened to Johansen! Absolutely the berries! You're a whiz, you know, just brilliant. I really can't thank you enough," she said, and she leaned in again.

For half a second, I held my breath, wondering if she meant to kiss me a second time, and then she brought her lips to my ear, her curls tickling my cheek.

"And don't worry, Mr. Guy, the county morgue janitor," she whispered, and I couldn't tell what made the flush of heat rise in my chest: her words or her breath against my skin. "Your secret's safe with me."

"Wh-why?" I jerked back, confused.

"You're very helpful," she said, shrugging, and as she took a few steps backward out of the light, her voice lifted from the shadows with a laugh. "And I bet I'll need that help again."

THIRTEEN
RUBY

"Irises! In Chicago! In *January*! What an outrageous expense!" Mama reached for the flowers in my hands, which was when she noticed the vase. "That can't be real silver, can it?"

"Oh, Mama, don't be a goose. It's silver-plated, I think."

"Who could have sent something like that?" She reached out again, this time for the pale-pink card tucked among the blooms, but I spun away, heading up the stairs to Papa's study.

"One of Papa's old classmates," I called over my shoulder. "One of the rich ones!"

"Do they have a son? Send them a thank-you note!" Mama shouted back, and she returned to preening and pruning the veritable greenhouse that had appeared in our parlor overnight.

The card, as I discovered a moment later, had not been signed, but that hardly mattered. Only a handful of people in this city could have afforded the luxury of hothouse flowers in a Chicago winter, and only one would have included this message, neatly typed:

WASN'T ME.

Of course, Herman Coward could have been lying, but then why go to the trouble of sending flowers?

With a sigh, I tossed the card onto Papa's desk and turned to the warm stack of recently delivered newspapers. Half a dozen, and nearly every single one pos-i-lute-ly *screamed* with the news, now reported as fact: the state's attorney had almost been blown up by one of Coward's men, who had then been found dead by suicide. Reporters up and down Lake Michigan would be lighting candles in thanks for weeks: attempted murder, suicide, corruption, gangster violence. The Hollywood screenwriters couldn't've come up with a better story.

But Vivian did.

EYEWITNESS ACCOUNT: STATE'S ATTORNEY'S DAUGHTER TELLS ALL stretched above a photograph of me. Or someone who looked rather like me.

Eight inches by four inches and big as the sun, my photo had turned out even better than I'd hoped. Vivian had shot me from slightly above, so that I had to peek up through my long, dark eyelashes, as though watching from someplace secret and hidden. One shoulder, bare and beautifully bruised, crept up, giving a startling impression of nudity that was *just* eased by the slimmest hint of a neckline at the edge of the page. I'd left my lips parted, a Cupid's bow about to say something terribly important, while Vivian had painted on my cheek one tiny tear, shimmering like a jewel.

To be honest, I thought Mama would faint when she saw it. Instead she let out a sigh and said I looked exactly as she had when she was eighteen.

"It's the cheekbones," she'd said, touching a hand to my face.

Vivian filled her article with the treacly nonsense newspaper readers loved, and, true to her word, she'd kept my remarks about Ferry's criminal organization off the record. She also dropped in several juicy bits of speculation, along with a knockout of a quote from me: "It's important for the public—and the criminals—to know that any investigations Papa started won't end just because he's in a hospital bed, even if I have to get out there and do the investigating myself!"

I'd meant the line to come off like a snappy joke, but Vivian framed the whole story around it. I was a defiant daughter picking up the pieces of her battered father's honest work, and gol-*lee* it must've hit a note, because the 'phone hadn't shut up all morning. I had to tell Mrs. Ritter to just yank out the cable. I'd deal with that mess later.

Of course, clever lines played well to the public but they wouldn't mean a thing if I didn't actually keep Papa's investigation running. If only I'd managed to get any evidence from that body last night! I'd even wondered if I could convince the boy from the morgue to put up some kind of statement, but then I remembered the way he had literally fallen to pieces when I confronted him, and I knew he'd never make it.

He'd be a good fella to stick close to, though. Imagine being able to change your whole appearance in a finger snap! I could pull on Ferry's face, walk right up to the closest newspaper building, and say "Hullo! It's me, Dennis Ferry, and I'd like to confess that I'm up to some nasty business. Better send some federal agents after me—ta-ta!"

All the things a person could do with that ability, the ways someone could get richer or stronger or more powerful, and this boy chose to become a janitor at the Cook County Morgue. Why not a medical student? Why not a flipping *doctor*? He was brilliant enough, I could see that. But I could also see he had that rare thing: an honest mind. He wouldn't cheat, he hated to lie.

I let out a sigh. Maybe he wouldn't be such a good accomplice.

Since pulling on Ferry's face wasn't an option for me, I ransacked Papa's office as soon as I got home from the morgue, looking for any scrap of information related to the corruption in City Hall. I kept replaying the moment from last night when I told Papa it was Ferry, the shock and unease in his mind. His thoughts had flown too fast for me to make out the details but I knew he'd put some pieces together. Somewhere, he had evidence, clues about how to bring Ferry down. I just had to find it.

Two hours in and knee-deep in files, I had nothing. I doubted Papa'd be foolish enough to leave anything so sensitive at his office downtown, which meant my last hopes rested with Albert, who would be coming by any—

"Miss Ruby?" The door opened and Mrs. Ritter popped her head in. "You have a visitor," she said, sounding frazzled—by all the calls, I guessed, although her regular state had been pretty frazzled lately.

"Lovely," I said. "Tell Albert to come on in."

"It's Miss Stowe here to see you."

"Maggie? Oh, send her up!"

I tossed Herman Coward's card onto Papa's desk and a moment later felt the tornado of emotions that was Maggie Stowe. She burst through the doors of the study, obscured by bucketsful of fresh-cut flowers in a dizzying rainbow of color.

"Zounds, Maggie! You didn't have to desecrate your winter green-house for *us*. Did my mother see this? She'll have your head."

"Pish, pish." Maggie piled the flowers on the desk, letting out the most heavenly aroma. "The least I could do. How is he? How are *you*? Oh, kitten—it must have been ab-so-tive-ly *dreadful* for you! Damn, I should have brought over something from the kitchens—maybe those Christmas petit fours you like so much? I'll ask our cook to send some over. Does your papa need anything? A better doctor? Just say the word and I'll get Daddy to call his friends at Cook Medical."

Her mind whirled with so much genuine warmth and sympathy I could feel myself basking in it, a sweet spot of summer sunshine in a midwinter darkness. I let out a sigh.

"Could you really? Oh, Maggie, you're a *gem*. The fellow treating Papa now seems nice and all, but—"

"Put it right out of your mind, I've got it," Maggie said, and she went to take a seat opposite me but found it occupied by another recently riffled-through stack of files. After moving it delicately to the floor, she gestured around at the mess and asked, "Everything jake with your papa's work?"

I assumed she was just being polite. My sweet Maggie had a good heart but not much interest in the gritty details of Papa's lawyering, which she imagined involved lots of passionate shouting to juries and judges, while vastly underestimating the amount of paperwork. She'd never asked about one of Papa's investigations before, and I was surprised and more than a bit touched to peek into her mind and see it pink with embarrassment for neglecting to find out more, especially now it had nearly cost Papa his life.

"Take a seat, dear," I said, waving at the chaise. "This stays inside the room, of course—"

"Of course!" Maggie promised.

"Papa was in the middle of an investigation into corruption at City

Hall. Some kind of criminal organization, like Herman Coward's but worse. It's run by an alderman named Dennis Ferry, and the police commissioner is in on it."

Her eyebrows shot up her forehead. "But that's terrible! Ferry... where do I know that name from?"

Rolling my eyes, I tossed her one of the nearby newspapers, which I had opened to Mrs. Ferry's latest column.

"*I'll finish this week's note with words of wisdom from Mr. Ferry: Many of the evils of today's society can be directly traced back to this younger generation of women, who are more interested in bobbing their hair and showing up their future husbands in the classroom than in settling down to raise children and keep good, honest homes.* Oh bother! This idiot is running a criminal organization? Are you sure?"

"Ab-so-tive-ly. I found out last night at the party. I had just told Papa when he—" My voice caught and Maggie reached a hand over the flowers to grab my fingers and squeeze them tight.

"It will be all right, darling," she said. "Your papa's got a will of steel."

Before I could respond, a muffled *BrrrINGGG BrrrINGGG* came from beneath the fragrant pile on the desk, and I stared at it a moment before remembering Papa's private office 'phone.

"Hold on," I said, minding the thorns as I parted the flower stems in search of the telephone. "Hello?"

"Ruby? Ruby!" A tinny voice, with lots of hustle and bustle in the background, piped into my ear. "It's Albert! Rollins!"

"Yes, hello, I hear you," I said, not hiding my disappointment. How utterly frustrating to hear a voice unattached from its mind! All my beaux—not that there was an army, of course, but I did have a few—knew if they suggested a picture show or listening to the radio, I'd shut them down quicker than a basement speakeasy in a federal bureau. Even records grated at me. But worst of all was the 'phone, and even more so with Maggie here in the room, her thoughts clouding me up.

"Coming round soon?" I asked.

Maggie, in a bad stage whisper, asked, *"Who. Is. It?"* Silently, I mouthed *Albert,* and she made a face like she'd just licked a trolley pole.

"Too busy this morning," Albert was saying over the din of voices in the background. "With your father's...accident...the office is in disarray. I barely have the time to return your call."

"Well, you'll need to make the time. I've been digging through Papa's files looking for his investigation into City Hall, and I can't find a scrap. Did he leave it all with you?"

There was a long pause, and instinctively, I reached out to the place where Albert's thoughts should be, only to find it blank. Stupid telephone!

"Did...did your father tell you about that?" Albert asked, with a note of surprise I found insulting.

"Enough to know that's really why he got attacked last night, never mind Herman Coward."

Another pause. "Ruby, I...I think you..." He cleared his throat and I glared into the empty space in front of me. "I think maybe you have it confused."

"Confused!"

"I don't know what your father told you—"

"Well, I don't know what my father told *you,* but he uncovered a criminal organization inside City Hall, run by Dennis Ferry and protected by Commissioner Walsh."

"Ruby!" There was the hurried sound of a door closing, and the hubbub on the other end of the line quieted. When Albert came back on, it was with a whisper-hiss so guarded I had to press the receiver against my ear to hear him.

"You can't go around saying things like that! Commissioner Walsh is a very powerful person and Alderman Ferry—he's a respected member of the government!"

"Well, he's doing something nasty, and Papa must've been close to finding him out! I *need* Papa's files!" There was a tremendously long pause, during which I frowned at the 'phone and Maggie thought something like *Uh-oh.*

"Albert! Are you even listening to me?"

He let out a short, frustrated sigh. "You know, I saw your—ehm— photo in the paper today."

"What, that?" I said, ignoring the encyclopedia's worth of judgment in his voice. "Just a little interview."

"Well, I can tell you it did not make people happy over in City Hall. That business about you continuing your father's investigations—you can't say those things, Ruby!"

"Then why don't *you* say them? Aren't they your investigations, too?"

"Look—"

"You took an oath, Albert! It's your responsibility to bring criminals to justice, and I'm telling you, Dennis Ferry is a criminal!"

"I just—this is a very delicate situation!"

"No, Albert, a 'very delicate situation' is what you'll be in if you don't do your damn job."

"It's—It's—dangerous business, do you understand? You don't know what you're getting involved in!" Albert's voice filled with panic, and I couldn't figure out what he really meant. Was he trying to protect me? Or protect the investigation? Or protect the people involved?

"Are you listening?" he asked, and I made a sort of *hm* in the back of my throat. "You're wrong about City Hall, all right? There are no notes, no files, nothing. And as long as your father is out of commission, I feel it is my responsibility to step in and forbid you to do any further investigating. Honestly, Ruby, has all that moonshine permanently rotted your brain?"

"Probably the hot jazz and heavy petting," I said, rolling my eyes.

"This is serious, Ruby! You can't just—" And he was off, lecturing me like some monstrous governess. Whatever Papa might've thought of Albert, from now on I couldn't count on his help. I waved an arm to get Maggie's attention, flapping my hand like a chattering mouth, and after a moment she cottoned to what I was up to and shouted in a molasses-dipped Southern accent, "Ruby! Ruby! Can you come heah for a minute!"

"That's Mama, Albert, gotta run!" I dropped the receiver onto the 'phone like it was a foul bit of trash and leaned back in my chair. "Well, Albert's a bust. Whether or not he's got any information on Ferry or Walsh or Papa's investigation, he's not interested in being helpful."

"What will you do?"

My eyes drifted to the desk, Maggie's gorgeous flowers, and the rose-colored card. I reached out for it and turned it over and over between my fingers.

WASN'T ME.

"If Albert won't give me answers, I'll just have to find someone who will."

FOURTEEN
GUY

Deep breaths. In and out, old boy. I had my notes balanced on the sink in the men's lavatory, neatly typed up on one of the clerks' typewriters in the dead of night. Every time I felt another wave of nausea crest over me I glanced down at the official-looking report to steady myself.

"The facts don't lie," I whispered into the mirror, wondering if I could make Guy Rosewood's face look more confident. "Dr. Keene, I have something important I need to bring to your attention regarding—"

The door of the lav swung open, and I jumped, knocking my report to the floor. I was scrambling to gather the pages when a hand snatched one away.

"'Levels of toxicity,' 'patterns of injection sites'—what in the hell is this?"

Dr. Keene himself, standing in the doorway, waved the page in the air.

"S-sir! I—"

"Oh, it's you. Rookwood? Rockland?"

"R-Rosewood, sir."

He pushed the paper toward me. "Clean this up. Someone could trip."

"I, um, sir! That is, I wanted to s-speak with—"

"*Now?*" he asked, and the look he gave me might have caused me to shrink several inches.

"Well, not right this second, but—"

He'd already disappeared into one of the stalls, and I dropped down to the floor to get my report. The papers were all out of order, and my sweating, shaking hands offered no help. By the time Dr. Keene had reappeared and rinsed and dried his hands, I'd mostly succeeded in wrinkling the corners of my report so horribly that it looked indeed like something that belonged on the floor of a men's lav.

"S-sir! This—these—it's for you!" I thrust the papers out to him, and with a deep sigh, he plucked them from my fingers with one hand while opening the lavatory door with the other. Eyes on the pages, he strode down the hallway to his office with me on his heels, and when we made it to the door, he turned to give me a long, strange look.

"Sit." He pointed into his office, and I tripped over my feet, landing messily in a wooden chair against the wall. Dr. Keene set the report on his desk and stood over it, his eyes snapping across the pages with the efficiency of a Gatling gun. The only thing I could hear, aside from the efforts I made to quiet my own strangled breathing, was the clock on the wall, and as the minute hand orbited thirteen times, I wondered how I'd gotten myself here.

It was that girl's fault. Ruby. Ruby red, like her hair, her lips…Her face showed up in my dreams, but it was her words—*You're a whiz, you know, just brilliant*—that took root inside me like an exotic flower, filling everything with color.

The night we met, as soon as I got home, I started my report for Dr. Keene, and every time my nerves threatened to tip me over, I remembered her words, her certainty. I'd only known her for fifteen minutes but Ruby Newhouse struck me as a person who didn't say a thing she didn't believe.

Thud.

My thoughts broke apart as one of Dr. Keene's fists landed squarely in the middle of the report.

"Who wrote this?"

"I—I did, sir."

"Not typed it up, any ninny with a working index finger could do that. Who did the research?"

I swallowed. "That would be me, s-sir."

"There are autopsy reports in here," he said, picking up one of the papers. "Chemical analyses, experiments done on organs… You don't have access to any of that! What have you been doing—sneaking into the labs at night?"

Yes. For the past week, I'd put my autopsy lessons on hold to dig through months-old medical records and police reports, looking for patterns of suspicious deaths. I bought kidneys and livers and lungs from my local butcher and tested how organs responded to certain poisons applied in certain ways, matching them up with the results from the medical records.

"Don't you know that's a damned crime, not to mention the wasted lab resources! I could have you fired in about thirty seconds. I could have you arrested!" He tossed the papers down on his desk. "Did you think I'd read this report and, what, hire you? *Thank* you? I

THOUGHT I TOLD YOU TO DROP THIS MURDER NONSENSE! What made you think this would be a good idea!"

Vague, desperate noises emanated from somewhere inside me.

"Speak up, damn you! I can't make sense of that ridiculous squeaking!" he shouted.

"I—I—I s-said, sir, b-because I'm right."

For a moment, I wondered if time had stopped, with Dr. Keene hovering over me, the sad life of Guy Rosewood tight in his fists. Then I heard the clock ticking and realized Dr. Keene was actually *considering* what I'd said. He opened his mouth. Closed it. Shook his head. And burst out laughing.

"*Right?* You're *right?*" Another laugh, straight from the belly. "He says he's right! The janitor with anatomy for a hobby says he's right! Hoo-*hoo!* That's a good one!" He picked up the report, rolled it between his fingers like a flyswatter, and as he stalked around his desk toward me, I braced for a smack upside my head. He moved fast, and I winced, covered myself, then felt his arm drape across my shoulders.

"You know, now I consider it…I think you might be right, too."

"S-s-sir?"

"I like your stones, Rookwood. That's what's wrong in the profession today! Too many gentleman doctors more interested in yachting and golf than real, messy science! Yes! Break down the door to the lab! Steal some bodies! *Take risks!* Oh, Rockwood, you take me back…" Dr. Keene, smiling, lost in thought, paced around his office.

"You…you agree with my findings?"

"What? Well, it's juvenile. Solid, but juvenile. You've picked out five suspicious cases over two years. That's hardly proof of anything, but it's a start. You'll need to tie them all together, that's the trick! Now, I like your hypothesis: each of those men had something nasty in their pasts, something they had to atone for. And that statement from the tenement woman—an angel of justice! Oooh, it's good, Roseland, it's good."

"R-Rosewood, sir."

"What's that? We're talking about your report!" Dr. Keene turned to the chalkboard hanging on his wall, covered with a maze of indecipherable notes. "Now, if we look back through the years, what would we find?" He erased the board with one hand while the other scrawled out *SIGNS OF HOMICIDAL POISONINGS IN CHICAGO.* I stared at it.

"We? Y-you mean, *me*?"

"Sure, you. What—did you want to scrub bloodstains out of tile for the rest of your life? Don't you want a real job?"

"A—a—a job?"

"*Tracking down the killer!* Isn't that why you brought me this report? You're going to help me, aren't you?"

Was I? My vague plans regarding these deaths ended with the moment I handed over the report and Dr. Keene thanked me for the work, offering me access to his notes on tricoloroforms along with his gratitude. Catching a killer had never entered my mind.

"Sir, I thought, well...I don't know if I'm really suitable for that kind of—"

"Balderdash! I say you are. I thought this whole business was nonsense and *you* managed to convince me otherwise, you sly fox. You know, if I solve these murders, those stuffed heads on the hospital board will give me anything I want!"

"Um. Yes, sir."

"That means I need the best working on it! I am stunned to admit, that means you."

Dr. Keene smiled, a *real* smile, genuine and rare, to judge by the way his zygomatic muscle strained.

"What do you say, Rosewood? Want to catch a murderer?"

I hardly knew what had happened, but Dr. Keene had managed to remember my name, and I knew there was only one thing I could say.

"Of course, sir. Of course."

"Brilliant!" He turned back to the board. "Then you'd better wrap up your janitorial duties, right quick, and get on back here before I go home for the day."

"Yes, sir!" I managed, and I ran out of the room feeling like my heart was on fire. A job. With Dr. Keene at my side. I couldn't believe it! Good lord—what if there actually was a killer out there? And we caught him?

I pulled open the small janitorial closet, a grin stretched across my face. I had to push aside my jacket to reach the bucket and mop, but as I went to close the door, I noticed something sticking out from the pocket. A note.

For a few seconds, all the possibilities of an anonymous note ran through my mind.

I know Guy Rosewood is a fake

I know who you really are

I know what you did

You're going to pay…

I plucked at it with my fingertips, holding it like it might burn me, and when I opened it up, I saw a beautiful, sprawling line of words:

Field Museum. Tomorrow. Twelve o'clock. Or else!—R

FIFTEEN
RUBY

The snowy leopard stared into my face, reflected in the mirrors of its amber eyes. I stood so close, I could make out the wrinkles in its licorice-colored nose and every pale, tiny whisker, shimmering as though dusted by fairies.

My delighted sigh fogged up the glass between us, which I wiped clean with a swipe from my trench coat. What lucky ducks we were to have the Field Museum parked on the edge of the lake and overflowing with treasures! Ever since Papa had dragged me to the Predators Room with all its stuffed and sewn-up monsters—against my will, because I was an absolutely horrid twelve-year-old—I'd been in love.

Lynx rufus

Ursus americanus

Panthera tigris

Oh, even their names sounded like something out of a magic spell book, whisking me away from ho-hum Chicago to the plains of Africa or the mountains of the west or the deepest parts of the ocean!

Usually I brought Genevieve with me—Henny, now at her own

stage of twelve-year-old horrors, couldn't be bothered—and we would zoom right off to the library after the museum. I always returned home with a castle's battalion of illuminating books, plus a few of the latest trashy pulps as balm to my mother's worries that I would transform into *one of those lonely women with a deeply unattractive attachment to proving herself right.* Papa, at least, was more than happy to indulge my many curiosities. He delighted in my scientific inquiries, which he privately took credit for kicking off, and never questioned me when I requested subscriptions to scientific magazines—or when I lobbied for a tiny, well-stocked laboratory in a corner of my mother's greenhouse.

Today, the museum stood nearly deserted, thanks to the miserable sleeting weather outside, practically hand-designed by some god of galoshes, and I was able to enjoy my favorites in peace and quiet.

Outside in the main hall, a grand clock chimed noon, so I blew those darling monsters a kiss goodbye. My heels *clack-clack*ed on the marble floor as I made my way to wait on a granite bench tucked beside a collection of blue-and-white Chinese porcelain.

I hoped the fiver I'd slipped that morgue secretary helped my note get to Guy. Would that sweet face-changer show? Or would he be too nervous to come any closer? That boy had something to hide—aside from, you know, that he could transform his entire body. But I didn't care about whatever skeletons he had in his closet. I needed his help.

Albert was as useful as a Swiss cheese soup ladle. He'd refused my calls and ducked me when I showed up at Papa's downtown office, looking for evidence (a search which turned up nothing but cobwebs).

Vivian, meanwhile, kept my phone ringing, asking if I had anything new to pass on to her. Her article had made a splash, but it was up against the rushing tide of opinion that Herman Coward was the lone suspect in my father's attack.

"You need to find something solid," she'd told me last time she called. "And if we're going up against the cops *and* City Hall, it needs to be proof so big, no one'll be able to ignore it. Documents, written testimony, photographs. Something I can put in the paper. That's the only way you'll be able to bring down the man who went after your father. But you've got to move quick, kid, or there's nothing I can do to help you."

As for Coward himself, whether he knew Mayor McGuire would never dare arrest him, or just because he wanted to thumb his nose at everyone, he acted as though nothing had changed. Practically the whole city knew he had planned a lavish bash for his birthday this weekend, which seemed like an excellent opportunity for me to drop by and ask about that deal Papa offered him. Fingers crossed, he could point me in the right direction to find the evidence I needed.

The thing was, Coward ran with a dodgy crowd. I could use a second pair of eyes, preferably attached to several hundred pounds of muscle. I didn't trust Albert's goons any farther than I could throw 'em, and since my list of hired brawn was short...

Ah *ha!*—a black-haired young man I'd never seen before rushed past me, his mind a flurry of nervous thoughts.

"*There* you are!" I said, jumping to my feet with a grin, and the boy from the hospital morgue—two or three years younger-looking now and nicely filled out—spun around sputtering.

"I'm not—You're not—"

"You kept me waiting *ages*. That's pretty rude, Guy."

"How could—How did—"

"I know it was you?" I looped my arm around his and together we walked through the wide main hall. "How do you change?"

"I—I can't—I don't—"

"You have your secrets, and I have mine. Now who is this I'm talking to? Is this the *real* you?"

"What? No. It's—no. Just…another—Look, we shouldn't be talking like this out in the open."

"No one's paying attention to us," I said, grinning up at him. "I like this one! Much handsomer than the others. Do you practice making those lips so kissable?" Stupid and silly but I had to do *something* to keep him from jumping out of his skin. My words—combined with my arm around his and the way I batted my eyelashes—worked leaping miracles. As the thought of that last kiss filled his mind, I could feel him going mushy and warm.

Cheeks red, he swallowed hard. "Wh-what do you want from me?"

Oh, applesauce. Was his real form a mouse? Maybe it was a mistake, thinking he could help me.

"Have you ever been to the Field Museum?" I asked, giving his arm a squeeze. "I adore it. Here, come see my favorite part." I steered him back into the Predators Room, where the two dozen furred, ferocious animals watched us with button eyes.

"Isn't it *inspiring*? They're mostly females. See the lions? They've put the male snarling up on that cliff but it's the lioness that does the hunting. Same with hyenas. Did you know they're matriarchal? The alpha female even grows a false penis."

He made a strangled, shocked noise, and I gave his hand a comforting pat.

"It's just for looks," I said.

"You brought me here to tell me...that?"

"No. I brought you here to ask a favor." Just as I expected, the worries inside his mind took flight like a flock of panicked birds, and I slid my hand down his arm, weaving his fingers between mine. "Steady there, fella. You don't have to pretend to be anyone. Or...not anyone specific. Just someone bigger. Meaner. Tougher-looking. Can you do it?"

"Can I..." He gaped at me. Even the stuffed animals in their cases looked doubtful. "I already told you, I'm no good at that stuff. I can't... pretend."

"You're doing it right now, aren't you?"

"But I don't—You saw me the other night, I panic, and then I don't know what to do, or say, or—" He pulled his hand away as he took a few steps back, his eyes darting around the room before catching on the wide-open jaws of a pure-white arctic fox.

"Say! Good lord, I don't want you to *say* anything!" I laughed. "That would be a disaster. I just need a warm body with a mean mug. I have to be somewhere a little, well, dicey, and I could use some backup."

"But why me?"

"Oh, I don't know. I guess I trust you," I said, shrugging, and Guy tore his eyes from the fox and fixed them on my face.

"You do?" he said, his voice soft with wonder. He smiled, my words warming him over like a bowl of homemade soup on a blustery day.

I could see in his thoughts that no one had ever told him they trusted him before. Which made no sense, because this boy practically radiated honesty. Being inside Guy's head was an absolute *pleasure,* like stepping into a cozy, familiar home. But a person didn't have to be a mind reader to see that in him. I'd noticed it again today—maybe something in the eyes. They weren't even *his* eyes, but they had some quality that seemed to stay the same, even when he changed. Something sweet and wholesome and, oh gosh, *kind*. Forget about the Predators Room...He belonged in a place devoted to puppies and kittens and sweet newborn lambs.

"You know," I said with a laugh, "I think I actually do."

"But you don't even know me. You don't know my real name or face."

"Not yet." I grinned, and the fear inside him melted away into something shy. A corner of his mouth—and they really *were* kissable lips, honestly, I wasn't just being spunky—twitched up into a kind of slow smile. He looked so sweetly surprised, like I'd just given him the most amazing gift possible, and for half a moment my stomach did a nice kind of swoop and my heart beat faster and then I realized what that meant. This poor puppy dog of a boy actually made my insides flutter!

Ruby! Really? Mr. Mouse?? Gol-*lee*, I needed to find a fast-talking fellow with a big car and bad manners, and *quick*.

Guy glanced back at the fox behind its glass case, posed with a helpless creature, a mouse or a vole or something, pinned under a paw.

"All right," he said, as much to himself as to me. "I can do it. Where are we going?"

"Don't look shocked," I said, holding tight to his arm and walking him into the next room: Flora of Europe and North Africa. "I need you to come with me to Herman Coward's birthday party."

"You WHAT?"

"*Shh!* Oooh, oleanders! Aren't they beautiful? Every bit of it, from root to petal, is dangerous. I read once a whole military troop died after accidentally roasting their dinner on some oleander branches. Causes heart failure."

Guy, who still had a long list of questions about Coward, paused. "How do you know that?"

Whoops. I forgot I wasn't talking to some bored trust fund baby but a veritable scientific whiz kid.

"Oh, my mother's a gardener. Always going on about 'natural this' and 'natural that.' She'd probably turn me out into the cold if I couldn't name twelve uses for witch hazel. Anyway, I like learning this stuff. It's as though the whole world's full of magic, and when you find out something new, you're in on it. A wink from the universe."

I'd just been babbling, but Guy's mind filled with so much surprise, I had to laugh again.

"What?" I asked. "Shocked a flapper knows how to read?"

His cheeks flushed a darling pink. "No, no, not at all, I only…" He didn't know how to put it, but I saw it clear in his mind: an image of himself, surrounded by books, notes, research, trying to fill his brain with everything he could know about bodies, how they worked. *She understands it,* he thought, with a glow of kinship. Or was *I* feeling that? Oh, applesauce, my head was spinning…

"If you ever wanted to learn more," he said, shy, "about biology, I mean, I could—"

"Hold on," I said, to Guy—and myself. Could I *please* keep my head around this adorable boy? "Let's get back to the real topic here. Herman Coward's party."

"Oh. Right. Why do you want to go?"

"I've got questions about who was behind the attack on my father, and I'm betting Coward has answers."

"He'll tell you?" Guy asked.

"I can be very persuasive," I said, as Guy thought *I bet.* "But I'm not empty-headed enough to stroll in there without backup. And you did say you'd do it for me..."

"I did?"

"I guess *I* said that. But you will, won't you?"

I blinked up at him, and it made him think of the girl back at the morgue, the one who'd persuaded him to help and almost landed him in a heap of trouble. *What in the hell is she getting me into?* he wondered.

Worried I'd lose him, I slipped my hands around one of his. "Please," I said. "You're the only person who can."

He let out a sigh, but it was enough.

"Oh, thank you, *thank* you!" I said, throwing my arms around him. He frowned at me, but I could tell he didn't mean it.

"Will...will I need a gun?"

"Golly, no! Just show up as yourself. Or, not yourself, but, you know. Bigger."

He swallowed hard but nodded.

"You're going to be brilliant. I know it!" I rose up on my toes and even though I wouldn't have minded giving those new, delicious-looking lips a try, I steered myself sideways and kissed his cheek. He'd given himself a bit of stubble, and I felt a thrill at that roughness. Or maybe it was just the lightning bolt that went through *him.*

His hand went to his cheek, which was rosy red now, and he smiled.

"Eleven p.m., tomorrow night," I said, wrapping my scarf around my neck. "Meet me at the corner of Lawrence and Broadway. Wear something nice, but inconspicuous. For clothes, I mean. Less nice for the face. And take some time to wander around the museum!"

His adorably dazed expression turned to panic when he realized this meeting was strictly business—and *over.*

"W-wait, you're going? But—"

"Eleven! Don't be late like you were today!" I dashed out of the room before he could finish that sentence, but I peeked back to see him, surrounded by flowers, sweet and soft and flushed with a crush I could've recognized even without mind reading.

Oh dear.

It wouldn't do me any good to fall for this kind-souled boy with honest eyes, not now, with so much on the line. *GET HIM OUT OF YOUR HEAD, RUBY NEWHOUSE.*

Time to focus. Time to sharpen my claws.

Running down the steps of the museum, I tallied up my knives and poisons. Arsenic to slip into drinks and cyanide to inject right into the bloodstream and maybe even a small vial of chloroform to drench a handkerchief if necessary. They would keep me safe if I got in trouble, but it would be nice to have some more insurance, so I raced in the sleet for the uptown streetcar to meet my gal on the inside.

"Maggie," I said, dripping slush all over the entryway of her de luxe uptown mansion, "I need a dress."

Maggie let out a squeal and hopped over to me before throwing her arms around my shoulders.

"When?" she asked, beaming. "What kind?"

"The kind that oughta be illegal."

Her mind spinning with possibilities, she threaded her fingers through mine and dragged me upstairs to her bedroom. Maggie had a closet the size of a garage, and how she managed to find anything in there boggled the mind, but in less than a minute she reappeared, arms heavy with a bulging satin garment bag and her face lit up with a sly smile.

"When your mother murders you," she said, dropping the bag onto a flowered *chaise longue*, "I don't want to be named an accessory."

The bag opened with a *zip* and as Maggie drew out the dress, my eyes went wide. Quick, I shucked off my knitted jumper and pleated skirt, yanked the dress over my head, spun around to the mirror—and whistled.

"Hot damn, Maggie! Where d'you do your shopping?"

It was a crime. An absolute *scandal*. I had to hand it to her: Maggie knew how to pick a dress.

Black-and-gold-striped silk flowed over my curves, so slinky and sleek it looked painted on. The neckline dipped low between my breasts and was held up, barely, by a black-jeweled collar that winked in the light like snake scales and tinkled with hundreds of tiny coal-colored beads.

This frock didn't so much show off my figure as offer it up for public consumption, and while I wondered *how on earth* I was going to sneak it past my mother, Maggie dug into her closet and produced black velvet heels, studded with glittering gold sparkles, before pawing through her jewelry drawer.

"Maggie, I can't," I said, as she settled a gorgeous headpiece over my curls, a band of geometric shapes and a trio of delicate feathers, the whole thing picked out in jewels I was certain were *real* diamonds.

"You're crazy," I said, shaking my head, and a burst of rainbows danced through my hair.

"Hush," she said. "I expect it back. Ahh." She stepped aside to take in her handiwork. "Look at you. Who's the lucky fella?"

"Herman Coward," I said, pretty convincingly, to be honest, given that the first things to pop into my head were Guy's kind eyes.

SIXTEEN
GUY

My breath poured out in a hazy white fog, and I stamped hard to get some feeling back into my feet, which tingled either from the cold or from the fact that they were two sizes too big for my shoes.

Wear something nice, but inconspicuous, Ruby had told me. I was more nervous about the face. I'd practiced a dozen different disguises, and in the end, I decided to borrow both my next-door neighbor's form and his one good suit from where it'd hung, half frozen, on the line.

This was crazy.

The moment that girl figured me out, I should have grabbed my bag and the little white dog and left town. *She knew my secret, and she knew how to find me.*

But I couldn't abandon Guy Rosewood—the investigation had only just begun. Now Dr. Keene greeted me every morning with a broad smile, asking, "What brilliant thing do you have for me today?"

Plenty, it turned out. Dr. Keene had me combing through the full records of poisonings—whether listed as accidental or suicides—and pulling anything that looked suspicious. Deaths by common poisons, available at any pharmacy or hardware store; sudden heart failures in otherwise healthy people. We had a sizeable stack of possible victims, and the findings seemed to invigorate Dr. Keene, who just today had formally named me his assistant. How could I leave that behind?

That's it, I told myself. *That's the only reason why I'm here.*

Except...I reached up to touch my lips, and they burned with the memory of Ruby's kiss.

Stop that. Stop thinking about that kiss. That kiss doesn't belong to you, not really, and anyway, you broke your damn promise.

Two years ago, Ann Arbor, Michigan.

I used to be less careful when it came to borrowing faces—it made slipping into places easier. One such place was the University of Michigan, and the face was a first-year medical student whose friends and professors didn't realize he'd taken on a double course load.

One afternoon, I'd just stepped out of a lecture when a girl ran up to me, threw her arms around my neck, and planted one, right in front of everyone in the golden light of the first real warm day of spring. I remembered her nose pressed up against my cheek and her curls brushing against my skin and how light she felt, jumping into my arms. Her teeth knocked against mine and her tongue slipped between my lips, and I was so astonished—my first kiss! Hell, my first anything!—I started laughing. And then she broke it off and gave me a funny smile, like I'd tried to put one over on her, and that made all the pleasant feelings inside me go cold. Told her it was swell to see her but I had to find the lav, and then I ran.

At the sink, I turned on the faucet and breathed hard, slapping water against my cheeks. I looked up into the mirror—and remembered they weren't my cheeks. That kiss belonged to some other fellow.

That girl never would have kissed me, or talked to me, even, as myself.

Staring into the mirror, water dripping down the face that wasn't mine, I decided I would never kiss a person with a stranger's lips. I wouldn't trick someone into caring about me.

But that meant being honest, with my face, my name, with everything I'd done. The idea that anyone would want to kiss me after that? Impossible.

There was a reason I was only myself with the little white dog.

And then Ruby dropped into my life and broke my promises before I could stop her, and now what? I couldn't keep lying to her but I also couldn't show her who I really was. She'd go running for the hills—if not the police.

"Good! You're already here!"

I spun around and caught red curls, blue eyes, and then my mind went blank except for...*Ruby*...

She ran toward me, light as a deer on tiny heels, the front of her coat left open in spite of the cold, flashes of gold appearing with every step. I'd only seen her late at night, exhausted after her father's accident, and in the daylight of the Field Museum, but tonight...She'd done something to her hair, which curled underneath some kind of sparkly crown thing. Or maybe it was her eyes, smoke-rimmed and darkly lashed. Or was it her lips? For all my experience changing faces, I didn't think I could ever understand the magic girls did with paint. How did she get her eyes to glow and burn like two tiny, fierce fires, or her mouth... It was the fashion these days to paint lips so dark they looked almost black, but Ruby's were rosy pink and perfect—and I was an idiot, I was a goner, all my noble promises went right out the window because I would give anything in the world to know what it would feel like, rubbing my thumb over those lips, just once...

And now they were smiling...

They were moving...

"Wh-what was that?" I asked, and she smiled again.

"I said, right on time. You're learning."

She had a nice smile. So nice that I almost missed the fact that she'd recognized me again. How? Six and a half feet tall, muscles so large I had to walk through doorways shoulder-first, and a face like a stick of dynamite, I couldn't imagine anything less like Guy Rosewood.

But somehow, she saw right through it, and a shiver ran up my spine.

She slid her small arm around mine and we walked together for a block before she led me down a set of steep stairs, to an iron door in the side of a nondescript brick building.

"Chin up," she said, giving me another bright smile. "Oh no, darling, don't actually do it. I meant get ready." She held up a hand and knocked with a hollow boom. Half a second later, a peephole opened up in the door, revealing a pair of heavy brows nearly obscuring two suspicious eyes.

"Yes?" a muffled voice asked.

"Bluefly," she said cheerfully, and the eyes narrowed further as the peephole slammed shut. Ruby's smile dropped off.

"He knows who I am," she whispered. "Stay sharp."

The door swung open to nothing but darkness. I could make out a kind of holelike hallway, the walls narrow and the ceiling low, the faint odors of crumbly brick and stale garbage. My heartbeat picked up, speeding along like a nervous rabbit.

"Straight ahead," said the rumbly voice from behind the door. "Don't trip on the stairs."

"Thanks!" Ruby said, reaching for my hand, which was so big hers disappeared inside it. The walls of the hallway brushed up against us. This new body had to stoop and squeeze to get through, and I didn't like it, climbing down stairs like I was falling into a well, trapped and tight. No lights, no noise...Was this really a party? Maybe Ruby could tell how nervous I was and kept whispering, "It's all right. It's all right....Almost there now, I think."

"Almost wh—" I said, and then another door popped open, spilling out bright, flashy, noisy chaos.

A huge underground ballroom stretched out before us, lit by a pair of shiny brass chandeliers a mile wide and a thousand pounds heavy with lights and hanging beads and dripping crystals. The bowl-shaped room looked like it could have comfortably held two or three hundred people but appeared to be brimming with at least twice that number: men in tuxedos and women in silk and a few in nothing but artfully placed sequins and spangles, with two-foot-tall headdresses rising over the heads of the crowd like glittery, gaudy signposts. Across the room, a white-suited band played a song I didn't recognize, something low and smooth, led by the largest and most beautiful woman I'd ever seen, standing at the end of the stage in a dress covered with diamonds.

"Ohh, that's Lydia L'Amour!" Ruby said, rising on tippy-toes to shout into my ear.

"Where's Coward?" I shouted back.

"I'm sure he'll find us. Come on, let's raid the dessert table before he ruins our fun."

I didn't want to move. Actually, I wasn't sure I could move. I would have happily stayed put in the doorframe, my back to the gaping black stairwell, only my toes officially part of the party, but Ruby pulled me along behind her, eyes bright but shoulders square and determined.

She found a clerk to take her coat, slipping free like a fish through water, and as I took in the full outfit—striped like a glamorous dark bumblebee and cut to reveal, well, everything—my throat went so dry I nearly swallowed my tongue.

Ruby glanced over her—good lord—bare shoulder and grinned at me before stepping into the crowd, and she looked so exposed that I couldn't help but put an arm around her, jumping as my fingers touched the hot softness of her back. I thought I knew about science and physics and geometry but the shape of her dress defied logic. I couldn't even begin to make sense of how it held together, how it slinked around her body like water, the shine of the fabric and the glitter of her necklace throwing light into the air. My eyes kept running over all that *skin*—shoulders and neck and back, the shadows that lingered just beside her heart…

"Eyes front, soldier," Ruby muttered, a smile on her lips. "Use that height and tell me what you see."

Right, I was here to help. I sucked down a shaky breath and peered over the heads of the crowd.

"I don't see him anywhere."

"Look for a back table. A back room. Somewhere private."

Ruby stayed close to me as we weaved through the crowd, and I tried not to get distracted by Coward's many attractions, but even in my craziest dreams I couldn't have imagined this level of bedlam. A monkey on a thin golden leash leapt from one unsuspecting shoulder to another, chased by a man in a white robe who lobbed melodic insults at it. A fireball erupted just to our right, sending up a *whoosh* of heat and light that illuminated the center of the crowd. On one table, a woman—fully naked!—stretched out, head tipped up to the ceiling, back arched into the air, a hundred tiny, pastel-colored cakes balanced on her body. I gaped at her and then looked away quickly before Ruby could catch me staring.

And that only covered the hired entertainment. Then there were the guests themselves, most of whom were so drunk I doubted they knew where they were. Half hidden between two pillars near the curved wall of the ballroom, a woman tilted her head so her male companion had better access to the coppery expanse of her neck, while from behind, another woman in a neat white tuxedo ran her hands up the sides of the woman's thighs. The ones who weren't kissing were fighting. I only just managed to pull Ruby out of the way when a sudden, noisy scuffle erupted between two men, which ended when one of them smashed his whiskey over the head of the other, spraying the air with liquor and bits of glass.

"Are you all right?" I asked her, kicking the shards out of her way. She laughed and wiped a hand down her bare arm.

"Wild party, huh?"

"Maybe you should've picked a different companion." I reached into my pocket to tug my handkerchief free and passed it to Ruby while glancing over my shoulder. Half a dozen men had appeared, like magic, to haul away the man slumped on the floor. *Head trauma, scalp laceration, possible concussion.* I wondered if anyone knew how to help him, if I should say something, and then I looked back at Ruby, who held my handkerchief in her hand, an amused look on her face.

"Nope," she said with a laugh, and she leaned in to tuck my hand-kerchief into my jacket pocket. "I think I picked just fine."

Her hand rested against my chest. I was sure she could feel the *thump-thump-thump* of my heart. Suddenly, every single person in the entire ballroom completely disappeared.

"Let me ask you a question," Ruby started, her mouth pulling up into a smile, but something over her shoulder brought my attention back to the ballroom. A balcony, a group of people at the railing, their eyes on Ruby, a man in an expensive suit...

I didn't have to say a thing. Ruby whipped her head around and looked up at the balcony.

"Coward?" I asked.

"Bingo. Come on. Maybe we can get this over with and still have time for a dance." She threw a wink over her shoulder and slipped her hand into mine again, leading me across the ballroom to the balcony. A large man stood at the bottom of the balcony's spiral staircase, but he must've been expecting us because he stepped aside as Ruby approached.

"Charmed," Ruby said to him, and we climbed up the twist-ing stairs. Coward had disappeared, but the other people at the rail-ing turned to watch us. Two men and a woman, fashionably dressed and holding cocktails, sporting the look of people who spent a good amount of time making and spending ill-gained money.

"Miss Newhouse?" Another man stepped out onto the balcony from a shadowed hallway. "Mr. Coward would like to speak with you in his office." He nodded toward the hallway and then gave me a mild look. "Alone."

I'd dropped Ruby's hand when we walked up the stairs, but now I shuffled toward her.

"It's all right," she said, stopping me. "I'll be all right."

That was good to hear, but what about me? I was supposed to wait here...alone?

"Are, ehm, you...sure...?"

"Cheer up, kitten." The woman at the railing gave me a lazy look and dropped to a chair before resting her chin on her fists. "We don't bite. Have a drink."

"No, thanks, I don't drink," I said, the words tumbling out of me before I could realize how that made me sound. "I mean, um, not that there's anything wrong with drinking. Alcohol, I mean. I mean, that looks like a great, um, bar, and, um..."

Ruby winced, and the other woman raised an eyebrow.

"I mean—"

"He'll take a double bourbon on the rocks," Ruby interrupted. "Be back in two shakes." She rose up on her toes, making to kiss my cheek but whispering softly in my ear, "They think you're a cop. Stay sharp and don't say anything."

Another wink, a smile, and she was gone, following the man to Coward's office as one of the fellows wandered over to hand me my drink.

"Well, old man," he said, "what's your name? Where are you from?"

"Yes," the woman added, "tell us all about yourself!"

Don't panic.

Don't panic.

"I...um..." I stared back at them, stared at my drink, and then—*DON'T PANIC*—bolted it down in one.

SEVENTEEN
RUBY

"This way," Coward's weasel-faced lackey said, leading me down a dim hallway. I gave one last glance in Guy's direction. Oh dear. He stood with his hands in his pockets, staring at the outstretched glass of bourbon like it was going to take a bite out of him, his mind a buzzing hive of unruly thoughts.

Don't say anything stupid, I wanted to tell him. *Sip your bourbon and shut your mouth.*

Golly, I hoped he was in one piece when I got back. Although that assumed *I'd* stay in one piece, too.

What did you bring to a private meeting with America's most notorious gangster? Aside from the needles in my purse, I had arsenic hidden under the bezel of the ring on my left hand and a chloroform-soaked handkerchief tucked inside my makeup compact. My favorite deadly hollow hairpin hid under Maggie's gorgeous diamond headband, and just in case things got extra messy, I'd tucked a slim steel finger blade underneath the lacy edge of my garter.

I felt reasonably prepared in case Coward turned threatening—or frisky—but there was something about this party that had nagged at me from the minute I'd stepped into the crowd, some strange sentiment among the partygoers, among Coward's men. I couldn't put my finger on it, and I scowled at the back of the valet's head. I'd already found it completely impenetrable, with the same practiced blankness as the Gibson brothers' butler.

"Here we are, Miss Newhouse," the man said, stopping at a plain wooden door, and my heartbeat went *drum-thrum* as I braced myself for whatever opulent nonsense Coward had in his private office, when the valet stepped aside to reveal…

Hm.

A plain, quite cheap-looking room. Linoleum flooring, pine desk, single spare bulb hanging from the ceiling. Had Coward stepped out and sent me to meet his bookkeeper?

"Ruby Newhouse."

A man—*It's Herman Coward!* I couldn't help thinking, like a star-struck gal catching her favorite actor on the street—turned from where he stood at the window, a drink in his hand.

"Father Christmas!" Genevieve had said when she was younger, stumbling upon Coward's picture in the paper: rosy cheeks, twinkly eyes, button nose. Santa Claus thirty years younger, shaved, and psychopathic.

He wore a custom-made suit, which draped beautifully across his wide bulk and must have cost as much as our mortgage. Everything about him looked overstuffed, from the swell under his neck to his short, fat fingers, wrapped like sausages around his glass and responsible for no fewer than half a dozen murders. (Although that was small potatoes; I had eleven in my column.)

"Hullo," I said, as cheerily as I could given my heart had started tap-dancing. "Happy birthday."

"Did you bring me a present? Or maybe *you're* my present. *Ha ha ha.*"

Ugh, that voice. Somehow he managed to sound both nasal and gruff, like a tin whistle made out of sandpaper. And his mind was hazy, grimy, muddled mush. It took more than alcohol to get like that; Coward had so much dope in his system it was a wonder he wasn't floating, which made his thoughts as easy to read as wet newspaper.

Wonderful! I might as well have sent Guy in here to talk to him.

Since I couldn't make sense of his mind, I paid sharp attention to the rest of him. I'd heard plenty about Herman Coward's ice-cold demeanor, but in front of me, he moved with twitchy, nervous energy. That Father-Christmas roundness had shrunk away, leaving the sallow look of a man who'd had too many sleepless nights, and up close, I could see that the cuffs of that beautiful suit were frayed and the lapel bore the ghosts of several stains.

"Drink?" He raised his glass in the air too quickly and a little sloshed over the edge and onto the desk.

"Not for me. Call it a family quirk."

I wasn't even sure he'd heard me. He threw back his own drink and reached for the bottle again before he'd even swallowed. Sloppily, he dropped into a chair and then stared at me over the edge of his glass with unfocused eyes, while I tried to square the dangerous, deadly Herman Coward of the papers with the drunk mess in front of me.

"You throw some shindig," I said. "Business must be booming."

My words worked like a sharp poke into the fog of Coward's brain, and I felt a flare of emotions inside him: anger, fear, resentment.

Coward grinned at me, but it was like a cheap mask, badly made and falling apart.

"It's a party fit for a king, right?" he said, and as he let out a hollow laugh, I remembered what Papa had told me: Coward was vulnerable. A gangster didn't make a deal with the state's attorney unless he had nothing left. In an instant, I realized I'd miscalculated: that glitzy, gaudy party just on the other side of the door wasn't Coward thumbing his nose at the city; it was *desperation*.

Quickly, I dug into the corners of his brain, and through the haze, I could feel it: his empire whittled down by Ferry's actions, his closest allies turned betrayers, and his reputation in the sewers thanks to rumors he was working as an informant. Coward was scrambling to hold on to what little power he had left, but it was too late. *That* was the strange feeling I'd caught out in the party, like all those people weren't at a birthday celebration but a wake. Coward was done for, washed-up, a shell, and immediately, my heart began to pound like a drum.

What was more dangerous than Herman Coward? Herman Coward with nothing left to lose.

"So—whaddya want?"

"I wanted to—can I sit? If they didn't look so smashing, I'd *never* wear high heels. I wanted to say thanks for the flowers." I dropped into an empty chair, propping one elbow over the edge so that the arsenic-filled ring pointed right at Coward's rosy cheeks. "Mama went gaga for that vase."

"She shoulda." Coward sniffed. "London silverwork. Cost a penny. You get my note?"

"Sure, but I already knew it wasn't you. Commissioner Walsh set you up. He got that drunk idiot to shout your name and then had his cops take care of him afterward."

"You think that impresses me?" He threw back his drink again, wiping his mouth with the back of his hand. "Ain't tellin' me anythin' more than I already know, kid."

"I'm telling you I know. And I know why. Walsh found out you made a deal with my father to pass on information about him."

Sudden as a striking snake, Coward brought his empty glass down on the desk so hard I was shocked it didn't shatter.

"I'm no *RAT*," he spat, his mind hot with rage. "That's a lie, get it? There wasn't *no* deal!"

Oh, horsefeathers—I'd forgotten I was talking to a jumpy gangster who would sooner throttle me than let me spread the word that Herman Coward had turned stoolie. Careful, Ruby.

"My mistake," I said, working hard to keep the tremble out of my voice. "But anyhow, you want revenge, don't you? Me too. Help me get something solid on Walsh and the operation he's wrapped up in, and I'll help you."

Coward picked up a cigar from a cheap ashtray and rolled it between his fingers, fidgety, his mind all sharp prickles. "You get some promotion I didn't hear about? They let flighty vamps run the state's attorney's office?"

"It doesn't have to go through Papa's office. I know a reporter—"

"Ohh, a reporter!" More laughter, and I had to clench my teeth to keep them from setting on edge. "Sweetheart, if I wanted something in print, all I'd have to do is pick up the phone. Besides, we're talkin' revenge on Walsh.... He's in hiding right now, and you know why?

'Cause the second he shows his face, it's gonna be his last. Evidence takes too long. I'll just kill him an' get it over with."

It took me a second to remember to look horrified at the idea of murder.

"Killing Walsh won't mean a thing," I said. "He's not the one in charge."

I gave him a knowing glance, and *that* got his attention. Through the slimy muck of his mind, I could sense a burning question: Who had told Walsh to betray him? The Herman Coward of a year ago might've been able to worm out the truth, but now, stripped of most of his power and influence, his contacts cut off, he was operating in the dark.

"You know?" His eyes glittered and he practically drooled with anticipation. "Tell me."

"Give me evidence against Walsh, I'll give you a name."

An image shocked through Coward's mind like a lightning bolt: a fantasy of him leaping across the desk, hands like claws, wrapping around my throat, wringing the truth out of me. I kept my lips pressed tightly together but behind them, my teeth began to chatter with fear. Coward had nothing left, nothing, and no patience for a lippy girl dangling in front of him the last thing in the world he wanted.

"Didn't you hear me *say:* I'm. No. *Rat.*"

"I don't want you to turn on anyone," I said, looking down into my lap while smoothing out a wrinkle in my gorgeous frock, mostly to keep my hands from shaking. "What is Walsh a part of?"

A strangled noise made me look up quickly. Coward was *laughing.*

"Come on," he said, a dark, wicked smile on his face. "I can't talk about that kinda stuff in front of a dame." But he didn't have to talk about it . . . he only had to *think* about it: I pressed into his mind, sensing flashes of information struggling through the muck like lightning bugs in a foggy swamp. Moving fast, I darted after those thoughts, followed them to wispy memories, hazy images... Coward might not know who was running the criminal organization, but he could see the damage it left...

My skin went cold.

It seemed Ferry dabbled in the usual illegal fare—bootlegging, graft, well-placed bribes—but what snagged me like a thorn were the women. He found them, he traded them, he threw them away, he used them as bargaining chips or threats or temptations or bait for secrets, for blackmail, and the police let it happen. The girls disappeared, new girls took their place, and Ferry got rich and powerful. Without my father around, he was unstoppable.

Anyone in that role, without my father around, was unstoppable.

Ruby, you idiot. As soon as Papa landed himself in a hospital bed, Coward lost any motivation for going after Walsh the legal way. I could never negotiate with Coward. I wanted to stop Walsh and Ferry because they were rotting out the soul of the city I loved. Coward wanted to stop them so he could replace them.

Sweat beaded on the back of my neck, just below the clasp of my jeweled black collar.

"Guess I'm just wasting your time, then," I said, my voice as cheerful as I could make it. "Thanks again for that vase. I'll let you get back to your bash."

Moving quick, I made it around my chair to the door, feeling Coward's mind coil like a cornered snake, but I'd only just pulled it open when his hand slammed it shut, shaking it on its hinges.

"Hold on now," he said, his voice soft. "You owe me a name."

The second Coward heard Ferry's name, Ferry was a dead man, and my chance to tear his foul business to shreds was gone forever. My fingers twitched, twisting the arsenic-filled ring into position, but I kept my chin held high.

"And I need evidence. Whenever you want to talk," I said, "you let me know."

His eyes narrowed, and I scoured that murky mind of his. What a mess! How did he even find his shoes in the morning with a brain like that? I couldn't see what he meant to do, it shifted so quickly, and when he leaned in, all I could think was *Don't flinch, don't flinch, don't let him know you're scared*...

"I bet you've got no idea who's in charge," he said, narrowing his eyes at me.

I pressed the hand without the ring against my thigh, feeling for the shape of the steel knife under my dress. "Oh yeah? What makes you think that?"

"I think if you knew who he was, you wouldn't be here. You'd know what he can do. You'd know what'd happen if he found out the state's attorney's daughter was pokin' her button nose into his business."

I'd found my knife and held it tight against my leg. "I can handle myself."

"Yeah? What about the rest of your family? Your mama? Or those two little girls? Or your pops, alone in that hospital room?"

It was as though he'd dropped a frozen lump of lead right in my gut, and that horrible, murdering Father Christmas just *smiled*.

"That's what I thought," he said. "You act tough, doll, but you ain't got a clue what you're messin' around in."

I wanted to shout at myself. How could I have left Papa unprotected!

But Coward was still watching me with that stupid, smug look on his face, and I kept my chin high.

"It'll take more than that to scare me off," I said, still very aware that Coward's huge bulk kept the only door out of this room shut. For a moment, something flashed in Coward's brain—*I'll show her scared*—but before he could move I had my knife between us, and I saw Coward glance down at it, eyebrows lifted in surprise.

He let out another laugh, but when he looked back into my face, something in his head shifted. The daughter of the state's attorney wasn't some goody-goody after all, and after a moment, he stepped back, taking his hand off the door.

"Well, doll, looks like we got ourselves a horse race," he said, watching me like a half-dead rattlesnake that knows he can still bite. "Whatever you're trying to get from this mystery man, however you're tryin' to find him, you better pray you do it before I do."

I just wanted to *go*. Out the door, back to Guy, Coward's party a distant memory, but I couldn't help myself.

"Why?"

"Because"—Coward smiled—"when I get my hands on him, there won't be nothin' left."

EIGHTEEN
GUY

"So then I told him, no, *I'm* with the salami!"

I couldn't help it: all that bourbon I'd just swallowed almost shot out my nose. These people were hilarious! What was Ruby so worried about? One of them—Jake? Jack? Jackie boy?—slapped me on the back, which just made me laugh harder and choke worse, and that made the woman at the table there—now I *knew* her name was Lulu, or at least I was pretty sure—spit out a burst of giggles, and soon we were all gasping for air and I couldn't even remember what I was laughing about—what were we laughing about? Who cared? This was *fun*.

"Oh look, it's your little bird!" Lulu said, and she tried to take a drink of her Champagne but ended up snorting halfway through, setting off another round of giggles, and we were lost again.

"Ruby!" I said, spinning around to see her, which was a bad idea— not the seeing her part, that was always good, but the *spinning*. "You're back! Have a drink!"

"Yes!" Lulu said. "Your friend is so entertaining!"

Ruby appeared at my elbow, smiling, and I liked that. I put my arm around her, and I felt so warm and tingly and good and better now she was back here, especially watching her snuggle in close to me, put her hand on my arm, and—

"Tell your new chums we gotta skedoodle," she said, and it confused me because she had a pretty smile on her face and her eyes were bright and happy but her voice came through her teeth.

"Champagne? Scotch?" Jake/Jack/Jackie boy leaned forward, and I set my glass on the table.

"Going to, um, get some air, be right back," I said, the words stumbling against each other on their way out of my mouth, and then before I knew it, Ruby had me by the arm again, leading me back down the stairs to the ballroom.

"Wh-what happened?" I asked, and without stopping, she gave me a hard stare.

"Have you been drinking?"

"You told me not to talk."

"Right, sure, of course, and I guess you can't talk with a glass in your face, huh?"

This was no good. She was mad at me, and I couldn't understand why but I did know I didn't like it. I kept following her down the stairs, and when we reached the bottom I said, "I'm sorry, Ruby, I just—"

"Stop. Oh, *damn.*"

She'd gone suddenly white, her eyes wide, but just as quickly she slipped her arm around mine and leaned in close, so close I could see every eyelash and freckle and smell her perfume and *oh,* that was nice…

"Don't look around," she said, a smile on her lips. "Act normal. We're getting out of here."

"What? What do you—ouch!"

She kept that smile plastered to her face as she dug her fingernails into my arm, leading us straight for a swinging door where waiters appeared and disappeared. But this dumb big body wasn't meant for speed, and Ruby kept having to pause while I ducked around dancing arms and kicked-out feet and squeezed between tables. We'd just reached the edge of the crowd when a man in a dark suit and a hat appeared between us and the door, and Ruby stopped in her tracks.

Anxious.

Nervous.

Scared.

I didn't think a girl like Ruby could get scared.

It only lasted for a second, though. Quick, she jerked me in the opposite direction.

"Never mind. This way."

"What is it? Are you all right?"

"That man back there? The one in the dark suit? No—don't look! He's here to kill me. And you, too, I guess."

Man? *Kill?*

Ruby dragged me back through the crowd, the hand in mine cold and clammy, and her free one—what was she doing? She reached under her skirt as we walked, hiking up the hem to reveal several glorious inches of thigh and the sheer lacy top of her stockings, and although I appreciated the show I didn't think it was just for me, but I couldn't figure out—wait— what was that slim, silver thing she slid from under the silk?

Ruby had a knife?

"Is it Coward? Is he—"

"No. This one's sent by the man who tried to kill my papa."

My head buzzed, from the liquor or from the chase, I wasn't sure. We reached the edge of the stage, where Lydia L'Amour had been replaced by a pair of dancing girls in pale yellow sequins and nothing else. A yellow satin garter flew high over our heads as Ruby pulled me around behind the stage, dark and half hidden by a velvet curtain, heavy with dust.

"No gawkers," said a short fellow in a squat flat cap and faded overalls, lounging on a chair.

"Just lookin' for a private spot," Ruby said, and she curled up against me in a way that made my stomach flip.

"Look somewhere else. Scram."

"We're only tryin' to—"

"I said scram, or I'll toss you out myself."

"Well, you don't have to be rude," Ruby said, huffing a bit but pulling me back around the curtain—where she went stock-still.

"R-Ruby?"

"You're going to need to change," she said. "Right now."

"But that's not—I don't—" She didn't understand. Panic made me lose control, and if the transformation came out badly, people would notice, and then—

"Hey." She spun around and gripped my hands tightly. She stared into my face, into my eyes, and even though I still looked like my neighbor, for the first time I felt like she could actually see *me*.

"Hey," she repeated. "Do you trust me?"

I did. Of course I did.

"Then trust me now: *you can do this.*"

Her words seemed to flow through my veins, replacing the adrenaline with something closer to steel. I wasn't sure of myself, but I was sure of Ruby. I nodded once, and she nodded back before turning away. Her face went ashen and I followed her focus to the opposite side of the room, where the dark-suited silent man strode through the crowd, staring right at us.

"He's—"

"Come on!" Again, Ruby dragged me into the crowd, only this time instead of avoiding the most thickly choked parts of the floor, she dove right in. I couldn't go an inch without stepping on a foot or bumping an elbow. I tried to squeeze next to a couple and ended up knocking a drink to the floor, the liquor sloshing across my shoes. The man let out an offended "Wise guy!" Only it was so crowded he could barely turn around, and anyway, Ruby had yanked me forward once more.

"Keep your head low!" she shouted over the din of the crowd, and I tried, I really did, ducking down and coming up again to see that Ruby had somehow acquired a squashy top hat, which she held in the same hand as the knife. Another half second later and she'd pilfered some-one's white fur coat, abandoned on a nearby table, and slung it low over her elbow. She glanced at the stage, where the two spangled dancers— now decidedly less spangled—shimmied and grinned behind two oversized feathered fans while the music gathered to a crescendo.

I twisted around to see the dark-suited man shoving partygoers out of his way, his other hand reached deep into his jacket's breast pocket and his eyes locked on—oh hells—me.

"Ruby…" I said, my voice breaking in a nervous squeak, but Ruby was staring at the dancers.

"Not yet…" she muttered. "Just a second…"

A man ten feet away jerked off-balance as the dark-suited fellow shouldered him aside. Another woman shouted "Ex*cuse* me!" when he pushed past her, but he didn't slow, and now his hand emerged from his jacket...

"Ruby!" I shouted, just as:

the spangled dancers onstage dropped their fans and their last sparkles, revealing nothing but miles of bare skin and a pair of toothy white smiles,

the man in the dark suit jerked a silver, snub-nosed gun free from his jacket, aimed it squarely at my stolen face, and cocked the hammer,

and Ruby grabbed me by the shoulders, shoved me down to the ground, and shouted "Now!"

Thrown off-balance between knees and elbows, I groped blindly for another body, another face—any face—and before I even knew if I was successful, Ruby had dragged me, still half crouched, through the crowd. We knocked into legs and rear ends and arms, and by the time I stood up enough to run properly—my body now a more maneuverable size—I realized Ruby had settled the top hat over her red curls and thrown the coat around her shoulders.

Another shout told me that the dark-suited man still followed, searching for us, and Ruby threaded through the crowd, making for an unattended service exit. Or so I thought, because before we reached it, she yanked me free from the crowd and pushed me up against a wall.

"Kiss me," she said, throwing her arms around my shoulders. I wanted to stop her, tell her *Wait, hold on, not like this,* but then her face rushed toward mine, all flushed cheeks and half-closed blue eyes and pink mouth, just slightly open, and then,

and then,

and *then*—

We touched.

An electric bolt leapt down my chest, down my arms, into my legs, back again. What was happening to me? Her fingernails against the back of my neck, her knee warm and insistent and stocking-smooth slipping between my legs, and her small, hot tongue slipping into my mouth, turning me into some kind of liquid, and then I couldn't think anymore, not even about what was happening or what she was doing to me, because my mind could only concentrate on *kissing Ruby.*

I felt my hands slide up her back, tracing the bumps of her spine, and disappear somewhere under the coat's mass of white fur, the skin underneath warm and damp. I couldn't remember closing my eyes, but they were closed and I was falling, over and over and over again, even though my feet stayed planted on the ground.

What in the hell had I ever been worried about? Kissing was as natural as breathing, and at least ten times more fun. And yeah, sure, somewhere, someplace, a hundred miles away and a hundred years ago, an alarm bell went off—something about danger and a gun and a man in a dark suit—but who even cared? I had Ruby in my arms, right here, solid and warm. Everywhere she touched me, I *burned,* and every second she kissed me, I wanted *more.* I didn't care where we were, I just wanted to get her somewhere I could toss that coat to the ground and run my lips over every inch of her.

But then she pulled away—

And I opened my eyes—

And she said something, hissed it into my ear—

And…disappeared…

I came to my senses—sort of—swaying on my feet and my ears ringing, but I couldn't make it make sense.

Was I dreaming? A man in a dark suit tried to shoot me and then

I transformed in a room crowded with hundreds of people and then Ruby kissed me?

And what had she just said? Just now, before she disappeared? Did I kiss her wrong—

Wait…no…she said…something about…

Go. Two minutes.

Go. Side door.

Two minutes, then—

GO.

That was a problem, because I was pretty sure I'd been leaning against this wall, trying to put the world back together, for at least a few years.

I took a breath. I dragged a hand through hair that felt longish and shaggy and a few strands fell into my eyes—white-blond? Then I threw one last look at the crowd, one last look at Herman Coward's rollicking birthday party, before hurrying over to the unassuming service door at the side of the ballroom and shoving it open to the cold Chicago air.

Should've slapped some sense into me, that wind, except my fever burned like a sheltered torch. This was a dream—wasn't it? It couldn't have happened—right? Except I could still feel Ruby's touch on my skin, still smell her perfume on my clothes, and as I ran down the alley, I wouldn't've been surprised if I'd lifted right into the air, rising like a bubble up to the—

Bundle of dirty white fur on the ground.

Squashy black top hat, dented and discarded.

A hand…an arm…a body…a face…

The man in the dark suit, with the gun, stretched out in the dirty alley, eyes wide open but blank as stars.

The alley was dark, nothing except a faint glow from the lights on the street, but I could see scratches in the old snow on the ground, kicked-up chunks of ice amid Ruby's discarded disguise.

"Ruby?" I ran down the alley, searching for her, my heart in my throat. "Ruby!" I reached the street, which spilled out onto a busy intersection. No sign of her. She'd disappeared, and that meant—I let out a shaky breath of relief—she had gotten safely away.

The smart thing to do would have been to take off back to the boardinghouse, but there was something about that man in the alley that didn't feel right. I turned back around to the body.

Now that my eyes had adjusted to the light, I could see him more clearly. No blood. Ruby'd had a knife in her hand, but this man had died from...

Bending down closer, I saw, at the corner of his lips, a small dribble of pinkish foam.

Poison...?

A violent, horrible poisoning...

I pulled open the man's jacket, my fingers tracing the skin just above the collarbone, right at the throat, where I could make out the small, faint, but unmistakable mark of a needle.

I sat back on my heels, my head spinning.

A helpless woman.

A violent man.

A horrible death by poisoning.

The angel killer had struck again, and this time she'd saved Ruby's life.

NINETEEN
RUBY

"Just toss that in the trash. We've got plenty of flowers at home."

Maggie lifted the vase from the windowsill of Papa's hospital room and looked over at one of the nurses with a smile. "Why don't you take it?"

The nurse paused from folding up a blanket to coo at Maggie, while mentally wondering where *my* manners had disappeared to, but I didn't pay her any mind. The minute I'd gotten home from Coward's I'd focused on one thing: getting Papa out of that hospital. In the morning, I rang Maggie up and asked her to send over that crackerjack doctor she'd mentioned, and by breakfast, we'd all met at the hospital to begin the process of getting Papa home.

Good thing Maggie was here to lay on the charm and friendly smiles, because I was in no mood. Coward's little warning last night had given me the shivers, NOT TO MENTION that man with the gun!

His arm wrapped around my throat, his gun pressed up against my cheek, his mind absolutely black with clarity. He meant to see me dead. Stars popped in front of my eyes but I let my weight fall, and the moment he was off-balance, I jammed my heel into his foot, spun free, and had my hairpin out and into his neck before he even knew what hit him.

At least I'd learned several important things.

Ferry knew I was still investigating the truth.

He did not like that.

He would try again.

I'd managed to escape, but not before nearly blowing apart my secret identity. Ferry's man had barely hit the ground before I heard the door swing open and saw Guy come running out. Twenty seconds sooner and he'd have seen it all. As it was, he almost saw *me*. I heard him yelling my name as I ran down the street, freezing, my poor old pink velvet sacrificed to Coward's coatroom.

What would I have done without Guy last night? Golly, he'd really come through in a pinch! I hardly would've guessed he could transform in a crowd like that. Honestly, I thought it was even odds he'd end up in a puddle on the floor. Instead, he pulled himself together, literally, and made the perfect distraction.

His hands in my hair, his body warm against mine, his lips...

Talk about puddles on the floor—I felt my cheeks go pink at the memory. How did a kid so sweet manage to kiss like that? He could teach those trust fund babies a thing or two. Or maybe it had more to do with that mind of his, warm and kind and smart and gentle—and hiding.

Why? I'd wondered before but now I needed to know. Not just because I wanted to see what he really looked like, but because every time he changed, some real bits of him shone through. And those real bits... Well. They were lovely. Lovely like starlight. Like something precious and beautiful.

I wanted to kiss *that* boy, pull him up close to me, touch the skin that belonged to him…

My eyes drifted over to the window, which revealed the hospital's huge lawn, covered in snow and polka-dotted with trails of footsteps. Beyond it lay the squat, gray morgue. Was he there right now?

I didn't even realize I'd let out a sigh until Maggie interrupted my brooding.

"That's the *third* time this morning you've done that," she said, and quick, I rearranged my face into a neutral expression.

"Is it?" I dipped into her mind, nervous my very perceptive best friend might've figured out I was acting moony over a boy, but instead I found her thoughts tense with worry for me.

Glancing over at the nurses, she leaned in close. "You know, darling, that was a narrow escape last night," she said, her voice low. Her mind kept turning over what I'd told her about Coward's party, the man sent to kill me—I'd stayed as close to the truth as possible while leaving Guy, and my needles, out of it. "Maybe…Maybe you should just forget about it all."

I could tell she wanted nothing more than to bundle me up and stuff me somewhere safe, but I shook my head.

"I can't let it go on. How could I ever live with myself? Maggie, I have to stop him."

Her thoughts spiraled back to the details I'd shared about Ferry's business, the innocent women caught up in it, and a familiar spark of outrage and anger flared up inside her. But just as quick, she imagined visiting *me* in a hospital bed.

"Just be careful, dear." She reached out to squeeze my hand and dropped a folded blanket onto a chair. "I'll see if I can find us some tea, shall I? I need something to warm myself up."

I gave her a weak smile as she headed for the door, but she'd barely been gone a minute before she rushed back in, her cheeks flushed and her eyes bright.

"Ruby—it's him!" she said. "It's Ferry!"

"What?"

"There's a whole crowd! Government people, I think…"

My stomach sank as I looked over at the door. "Oh *no!* I bet he found out I was moving Papa!"

"But how?" Maggie asked, and I looked over her shoulder at the young nurse in the corner, now clutching two of Papa's get-well vases, her thoughts spiked with guilt.

So, Ferry had eyes inside Papa's hospital room, did he? *Rotten old biddy,* I thought, shooting her a look as she beat it out the door. *I hope those flowers give you hives.*

"Hold on," I said to Maggie. There was another nurse—older, a bit on the mean side, to be honest, but with a clear, pragmatic mind—watching our conversation closely, and I turned to her. "Can you make sure no one bothers my papa?"

That got some begrudging approval from the nurse, who apparently did not appreciate a crowd of people pestering her patient any more than I did. I smoothed my hands down my plain flannel dress.

"I can't believe he has the nerve to show up here!" Maggie glared at the closed door. She kept thinking back on what I'd told her about Ferry, her thoughts growing more indignant every second. "What are you going to do?"

"Talk to him," I said. "Look after Papa for me, will you?"

For half a moment, I worried she'd insist on coming out with me, but she kept her mouth shut. I gave her a nod, then headed out to face the man who wanted to see Papa—and me—dead.

"Miss Newhouse! Our apologies for taking so long to visit!" An older man, someone I didn't recognize, stood at the front of a tight knot of government employees, a handsome bouquet in his arms. There were half a dozen men with varying polite smiles, and, in the back, Dennis Ferry, gaunt as a ghost and wearing a look of mild geniality.

"We heard your papa's feeling better and thought, *Well, it's high time we paid him a visit!* And so, here we are! See—"

While the man in front chattered on and tried to push the flowers into my arms, I kept my focus on Ferry and his stupid-slick mind. There was that impenetrable glass wall again, and although I had a pretty good guess why he was here, I would've preferred to pick through his thoughts myself.

"What's that?" In a moment of quiet, I realized Mr. Whatever-His-Name had asked me a question.

"We were just curious, ah, what was…Lots of commotion going on here…" He tried to peer around me, and the mean nurse crossed her arms with a scowl, lodging herself in the doorway—and my heart. Unlike Ferry, this man's thoughts spilled freely. I learned that this band of well-wishers was split between men who wanted to know if Papa's departure from the hospital meant he was well enough to end up back in office and men who wanted to know if it meant he was on his deathbed. And then there was Ferry, still smiling at me, his mind only revealing wisps.…He was angry…furious.…He wanted me out of his business.…He wanted me *gone*.

"Papa's doing so much better," I said with a smile, pretending I didn't see some of those pasty faces fall. "His doctor decided he'd be more comfortable at home."

"Wonderful, wonderful!" one of the fellows in the crowd said. "What can we do to help?"

"A police escort, perhaps? Or round-the-clock security for the whole family?" That from Ferry, who played the part of unassuming grandfather type, but I cottoned to exactly what he was doing. He knew I didn't trust the police—I'd nearly said as much in my interview with Vivian—but he wanted to play with me.

All right, then. I could play.

"Golly, no thanks," I said, laughing. "I can't have a coupla bulls trailing behind me. I'd never get into the good parties! No, don't worry, I've recently acquired some new security: strictly off the books and highly effective." *Highly effective at doing away with your toe-rag hired gun,* I thought, beaming back at Ferry, whose expression didn't change but whose mind suddenly filled with darkness. He knew I knew. About him. About what he did. And through the wall of his mind, a tiny flashing wonder: *How does she know? How did she survive? Who's helping her?*

"Well, that's good, that's good!" Mr. With-the-Flowers said. "Maybe we could, ah, just step inside and visit before you head out?"

"Thank you, but my father isn't—"

"Oh, we'll just be a minute!" He headed toward the door as I wondered if I could tackle him, but it was the nurse who saved the day.

"Oh no you don't!" Her stout body didn't budge. "No one is to enter this room without permission!"

A moment later, the door swung open from the other side, and a pink-cheeked Maggie appeared.

"What's this noise!" she said, in her best heiress voice. "Excuse me, fellas, but we have *the* Dr. Meyer coming through any moment and I will not have him delayed!"

"Our apologies," said the man with the flowers, but she wasn't looking at him—her eyes had caught on Ferry's face. Her mind filled with the stories I'd told her, like some horrible moving picture show: all the cruelty and exploitation and abuse and evil he'd sown in our city. Nothing less than pure disgust bubbled up inside her as she imagined screaming at Ferry, telling him she knew everything and he would *not* get away with it. In an instant of panic, I remembered my best friend's most charming quirk: she said everything that popped into her mind.

"You've got some nerve," she said, her voice stripped of upper-class refinement, "showing up here, when you—"

"Maggie! Darling!" I threw my arms around her, only slightly hysterically.

"I'm sorry, do I know you?" Ferry asked Maggie, his voice chilly, his mind dark with suspicion.

"This is Margaret Stowe," one of the other men said. "The heiress to the Stowe shipping fortune."

At *heiress,* something like cold amusement filled Ferry's thoughts, and he glanced over at me before looking back at Maggie with interest. My stomach dropped.

"Pleasure to meet you," Ferry said to Maggie, who looked like she was trying hard to keep from spitting in his eye. I didn't like the way his gaze lingered on her, a spotlight on my sweet friend, and I clawed into his mind, trying to figure out what about her he found so fascinating. Did he think *Maggie* was the one helping me take him down?

"Thank you, gentlemen. I think you know the way out," the older nurse said from the door. The men nodded their goodbyes, but Ferry didn't move.

"Good luck to you, Miss Newhouse," he said as he put out a hand. "It must be very difficult for a young woman to shoulder so much responsibility. I hope it will all be over for you soon."

Maggie's mind snapped with fury, and, quick, I grabbed her hand— to keep her from going after him or to keep myself steady, I wasn't sure.

He wanted me scared. He wanted to threaten me, in front of his colleagues, in front of Maggie, steps from the hospital bed where my father fought for his life. Just to prove he could.

Carefully, I let go of Maggie's hand and took his, looking him right in the eyes.

"Thank you for your concern, Mr. Ferry," I said, my voice steady. "But you should know: just like my father, I can survive anything."

TWENTY
GUY

No more liquor. Never again. My head rang and I kept feeling like I'd made a bad transformation. Why else would my tongue be three times too big for my mouth? But I knew exactly why: the tiny chemical foot soldiers in ethyl alcohol had wreaked havoc through my body, rerouting water from my brain, slowing down my neurons, and leaving me with a general feeling of death.

I considered myself lucky, given how Ruby's night had ended. I couldn't stop thinking of her, how she'd gotten us out of Coward's party alive, and that kiss...

And, *oh*, everything started to spin again.

What had happened to my promise? I told myself I wouldn't ever kiss as a stranger, but then I'd never counted on a girl like Ruby.

You'll figure it out later, I told myself, wincing up at the hospital building in the bright morning light—photosensitivity, another after-effect. *Just get through the day, and pray it's a quiet one.*

"Fresh body! Just came in." Dr. Keene tossed me a notebook the moment I stepped inside the morgue, then breezed past me on his way to the basement autopsy lab. "Come on! I need you to take notes."

Sighing, I shucked off my coat and swallowed another bout of nausea as I followed him down the stairs. While I'd been busy pulling reports and researching data, Dr. Keene had spent his time spinning up funds for our research into the angel killer. We now had a dedicated corner in the morgue overrun with files, but there was only so much we could do without another body, which was why, when I caught up with Dr. Keene in the autopsy room, he practically tap-danced across the marble floor.

"Healthy, middle-aged man dead in an alley!" Dr. Keene sang, gesturing to the body stretched out on the slab, and *there he was*. The man from Herman Coward's party, the one who'd tried to kill me and Ruby, who I'd eventually left, half frozen in the slush. With his body stripped clean of clothes, the puncture wound in his neck stood out like an angry red sting.

"It's one of ours, Rosewood, I'm sure of it!" Dr. Keene rubbed his hands together, looking down at the corpse. "Now let's get in there and see what's gummed up his works."

Cyanide. Fast-acting, deadly cyanide. As soon as we opened him up, he spilled his secrets. Dark, purplish-black blood. The veins leading to the heart stretched wide and strained. Cyanide killed by slipping into the bloodstream and taking the place of oxygen. As the body searched desperately for air, the heart beat faster, faster, faster, which spread the poison through every tiny vein, every muscle, every organ. The victim died gasping for breath, suffocated from the inside.

"Have those typed up and on my desk by the end of the day," Dr. Keene said, nodding at the notes as he washed his hands. "She's getting bolder, Rosewood. We've got to alert the authorities. There's a monster loose in this city, and we're the ones to stop her!"

Even after reading the autopsy reports and police blotters, it hadn't felt real. It took a body, stretched out before me, shrunken and bruise-colored under the lights, for the truth to hit.

A killer, right here in Chicago. The thought made me woozy, and then I reminded myself of the things I'd done. If she was a monster, then so was I. Maybe even worse, because she hunted bad men, but the people I'd hurt...

"You can't go out, it's not safe—don't you understand? You'll lose control and then..."

"...hey...HEY...what are you doing—what are you—hey—"

"Stop! Stop! Peter, STOP!"

Train whistle—crash—screams—

I winced and the notes slipped out of my hands onto the floor. My head felt like it was about to split open—no—it *was* splitting open, shifting between faces. As Dr. Keene turned, I dropped to the floor and kept my back to him, gathering up the papers, my skin on fire.

"Rosewood? All right there? Don't let those notes get out of order."

Say something, do something, make it stop. I shivered, my fingers jerking so that the papers rustled in my hands, and any second I was going to lose control, just like I had that day, when everything went wrong, so *pull it together pull it together STAND UP AND WALK OUT OF THE ROOM RIGHT NOW.* I wrenched myself to my feet and ran for it. Dr. Keene said something, shouted something—oh no—did he see something? Couldn't think about that, just get out the back door, and into the cold, sparkling air of a January morning.

The chill soaked into me as I gulped down breaths. My body just wouldn't behave, my skin slipping over my bones like silk, and I closed my eyes, dropped my head down between my knees, breathed, breathed, hiccoughed, breathed—

"Guy?"

Up snapped my head, and I was ready to run or fight or just get away except—except—except—it was *her*.

"R-Ruby!"

Rosy-cheeked from the cold and dressed in a shade of blue so perfectly blue that her eyes stood out like great glass marbles, clear and bright.

"What are you doing here?" I asked, and then I took another breath. "I mean, I'm glad to see you, I just…"

"Oh! We're taking Papa back home to recuperate," she said, gesturing to the street on the far side of the lawn, where a boxy private ambulance idled. "I was hoping I'd see you!" She said it with so much delight that even though my skin still prickled, a smile came to my face. "You all right?"

She gestured vaguely at my shirt, soaked through with sweat and steaming a little in the cold air, and I swallowed and pushed myself up.

"Yeah, yes, I'm, um. I'm fine. Thanks. But you—I mean, how are you?"

She lifted an arm and pushed up the sleeve of her coat, showing a mottled pattern of bruises the length of her ulna bone.

"No more sleeveless gowns. He grabbed me but I managed to get away. What about you? He didn't hurt you, did he?"

I blinked at her. She didn't know? "Ruby. He was dead by the time I got out there."

"*Dead?*" Those blue eyes went wide. "But—I don't understand— how? I mean, good riddance, really, I don't think I'll waste any tears on him. I'm just—shocked!"

"You didn't see anyone else in the alley? You didn't see who killed him?"

She shook her head. "No, or, I don't know. I can't remember—it happened so fast! I went out that side door and he...he *attacked* me. I tried to shake him off but he just held me tighter, and I thought... I thought..." Her voice went wobbly for half a moment, but she took another breath and carried on. "Oh, Guy, I thought he was really going to kill me, right then and there...." Her shoulders hitched, like she was trying to hold herself together. I couldn't help it—I put out my arms and she collapsed against me, pressing her cheek against my neck.

"It's all right," I said. "You're all right."

"And you, too!" she said, looking up at me. *Oh*, she was very close. I could see the tiny specks of color in her eyes, framed by long, dark lashes. "You did brilliantly, by the way."

"Me? I didn't do anything!" I was sure she felt every *thump thump* of my heartbeat.

She rolled her eyes, grinning. "You managed to transform in the middle of a crowded ballroom."

"That wasn't me," I said, the words coming out in a puff of white air. "I mean, I've never been able to do something like that before. Usually, I have to practice and concentrate and I'd *never* try a face in public I hadn't worked out before. But you...You told me I could do it...so I did."

I felt strange and shy, saying that out loud, but she was still in my arms, and she grinned up at me.

"That was *quite* a face. Whoever that boy was, he kissed like a dynamo. Too much to hope that that was the real you?"

"Um, the real me?" The warm feelings that came with the memory of that kiss evaporated.

Right.

I'd broken my promise. I'd kissed a girl while wearing a mask. And now I was falling for her.

"You don't have to show me, you know," Ruby said, her voice gentle. "You've got your reasons. That's just fine. But I hope you know you can trust me. And besides," she added, her fingers reaching up to brush one of my cheeks, "I can already see the real you. Something in the eyes. You can't hide from me, Guy."

"Peter." It just slipped out. Five years I'd held it back, bricked up, and now my name fell out of me as easy as a breath.

"What?"

I saw her eyes go wide.

"Peter. It's my name. I...I want you to know. I should've told you right from the beginning." I didn't know what I was doing, except Ruby falling into my life felt like a gift, and when you get a gift you should try to give something back.

"Peter," she said, trying it out, and I felt light-headed. "Peter," she repeated, this time like she knew what it was, like I'd chipped off a piece of my soul and held it out to her. She smiled.

"I like it. Peter. It suits you. The you in there, I mean," she said, pressing a finger to my chest. "Much better than 'Guy, the janitor at the Cook County Morgue.'"

"Lab assistant," I said with a smile. "I got promoted."

"Really? Oh, that's swell! It's about time they realized the smartest one in there was mopping the floors!" The look she gave me—like she was proud of me—I was pretty sure I could live off that look alone. "What are you doing? Is it what you want to study? You *do* plan on being a doctor, don't you? You must be learning so much!"

"It's…" How did I put this? Was this whole thing a secret? "I'm helping with, well, a special investigation."

"Oooh, what's it about?"

"It's…It's not public," I said, and her eyebrows raised but she smiled and drew an X over her heart.

"All right," I said, laughing. "I had this idea, a few days ago, that there was, well, a killer loose in the city. A murderer. Someone wandering around the city poisoning people. I told one of the doctors here at the morgue, and he thought there was something to it, so we've been looking into it. And the man from last night…*He* was poisoned. Cyanide. An injection, right into the throat. We think he might be one of her victims."

Ruby didn't move. Didn't breathe. Then: *"Her?"*

"It's just a theory. We think she may be a woman…and she may kill in order to help other women…Like you, Ruby. I think she may have saved your life."

Two seconds went by…

Five…

Ten…

She had a look on her face like I'd just slapped her.

"Ruby? Are…you all right?"

Blinking fast, she shook her head and took a step back, out of my arms. "Sorry, I just…Golly, you're saying a murderer saved my life last night?"

"I don't know. Maybe. His death looks very similar to others. Are you sure you didn't see anything? It would help with the investigation."

"No…" she said, her voice soft and dazed. "No, I'm sorry."

Relief. Pure relief. The angel killer had to be stopped—arrested, sent off to Joliet or the hangman's noose—but this time, I was glad she'd gotten away.

"How many?"

"What?"

"How many people has she killed?"

"Oh. I don't know for sure. Counting the fellow from last night, we've got six possibilities over the last two years."

"Six! You've found six!" Her eyes were wide and her face pale. She looked *terrified*. I put out a hand, touched her arm.

"Don't worry, Ruby. We're going to find her. I'm going to find her. And she doesn't hurt people like you. She only goes after, well, bad people."

She didn't seem to hear the words I was saying, or if she did, she heard them at the end of a very long tunnel. I could feel her swaying, and I took her other arm, held her steady.

"I know it's a shock, but—"

"No, I'm fine," she interrupted. "I'm *fine*. I'm—oh damn, I haven't been paying any attention—oh hello! I'm over here! Yes, I'll just be a minute!" She hollered across the courtyard to a group of people standing beside the ambulance before looking back at me. "I'm so sorry, they're waiting for me."

"Oh. Of course. Maybe later, we could—"

"I'm sorry," she said again, but I couldn't figure out what she was apologizing for until she gently pulled her arm free from my hold.

"Oh."

I didn't understand what had happened, how I'd gone from laughing with this girl to watching her wrap her arms around herself, looking cold and miserable.

"It's not—Peter, it's nothing to do with—It's just—" She had a desperate look on her face, and she turned to glance back at the ambulance. "My father is ill, and my family needs me so much right now, and I really can't—You're wonderful, but, last night, I shouldn't have…"

Kissed me. Let me think that it was anything other than a distraction. Ruby looked half a step from tears, and I pulled on a smile as false as any transformation I'd ever made.

"Of course, Ruby. You should be with your family. Of course. I'm sorry." That kiss hadn't meant anything. Why would I think a girl like Ruby would ever—could ever—would ever want to—

My thoughts broke apart as she rushed up and threw her arms around me, pressing her cheek against my neck. I just wanted to tell her *Wait.* I wanted to tell her *Stop. Don't go. Don't go because you've burst into my life like a beautiful fire and for the first time I feel warm and alive and I don't want to put that fire out…*

And then she pulled away. She took a step back. Her face crumpled. And of all the ways I'd feared hearing my name over the years—*We found you Peter what did you do Peter you're under arrest Peter*—none were as terrible as this:

"Goodbye, Peter."

TWENTY-ONE
RUBY

Damn it all. He was hunting—*me*. *My* murders. I'd left enough clues for someone to put it all together and that someone was Guy—no, oh golly—*Peter!*

I ran across the snow, trying to shut out his sweet, whirring, wounded thoughts, because if I felt any more, I knew I'd never be able to leave.

How could I have been such a prize idiot? How could I have fallen for a boy who wanted to see me hanged?

I let out a tiny hiccough of a laugh just so I wouldn't sob.

By the time I made it across the lawn to the ambulance, Papa was already bundled up and tucked in, fussed over by Nurse Graves, the mean old nurse who'd impressed me so much I'd offered her private employment on the spot. Maggie, though, stood in the snow, watching me run over with a raised eyebrow. She'd seen me in Peter's arms and wanted nothing more than to pounce on me with questions.

"Ahem," she said. "Done visiting your *friend* at the morgue?"

But then she took a second look at my face and her smile vanished.

"Roo—are you all right?"

There was a lump in my throat the size of Texas and I could barely swing myself into the ambulance next to my father. A moment later, Maggie joined me, her mind buzzing.

"What happened?" she whispered as Nurse Graves pulled the bay doors shut. But even if I'd known how to explain it without exposing Peter's secret—or mine—I couldn't begin to answer that question. I just squeezed her hand.

"Boy troubles. I'll explain later."

Maggie went quiet, though her mind churned with curiosity and concern. *When does Ruby ever have boy troubles?*

She wasn't wrong. I had it figured out! Keep things light and easy, kisses in dark corners, handsome fellas to squire me to parties—boys weren't worth the trouble otherwise. I'd never met one who could keep up with me: the smart ones lorded it over you and the dumb ones resented you and it was easier to just be whoever they wanted me to be. Ruby the glam gal, the funny flapper, the little vamp who only cared about good parties and hot jazz and never bothered tying anyone down because she didn't want to be tied down, either.

But Peter was different. Smarter than me, yet he wanted to show me everything he knew. Sweeter than any boy who'd shown me a good time. More honest than I was—he changed his outsides, but his soul never budged.

Of all the people who could have stumbled onto my crimes, why did it have to be him?

I'd never given much thought to being found out. I was careful. No witnesses, lots of alibis. My poisons came either out of my mother's greenhouse or from products found in just about any corner drugstore in the country. Gol-*lee,* they put arsenic in complexion solution! In the hands of a police detective or a rogue medical examiner, an investigation wouldn't have been worth a sniffle, but I'd seen the inside of Peter's head. That quiet, perfect efficiency. He liked puzzles and he was good at them and the only thing keeping him from seeing the obvious, from solving the equation of Ruby + dead man = murderer, was—

Infatuation?

A crush?

Love?

I could feel every pinprick of his pain as I walked away from him, and I wished, more than anything, I could tell him, *You have a kind and dear heart but if we continue to see each other you're going to figure out I've murdered a bucketload of people, so let's just end things now, before anyone's heart gets broken.*

Oh golly, *before.* Who was I kidding? Hullo, it's me, Ruby Newhouse, owner of a broken heart.

This meant more than just goodbye to sweet Peter. Goodbye, too, to my vigilante justice. I couldn't drop any more clues, not now that I knew it was Peter who'd be snatching them up. And so, I was done. Hang up my needles, it'd been a good run.

Honestly, it was a lot to think about over the course of one ambulance ride downtown, hovering over my father's unconscious body, knee to knee with my worried best friend. When we finally rumbled to a stop outside the graystone on Dorchester Avenue, I felt like I'd gone over Niagara Falls in a barrel.

What are they doing outside? Maggie's thoughts pulled me to the present, and I hopped out of the ambulance to see my mother and sisters and even the housekeeper, assembled on the lawn with four identical expressions of unease.

And then...

BANG!

Hurricane Albert.

He exploded out the front door, his normally slicked-back patent leather hair looking like it'd been pulled out by the roots.

"Ruby? RUBY!"

I took a breath, pushed thoughts of Peter out of my head, and strode through the front gate to kiss my little sisters. "Hello, darlings, how are you?"

"He's been raving for ages," Hen whispered, and Genevieve nodded, eyes wide.

"Go on inside. You too, Mama." I ushered my family back into the house as behind me, Maggie and Nurse Graves skillfully conducted the unloading process. "Hullo, Albert."

"Ruby!" He squeezed past the girls, Mama, and Mrs. Ritter as he rushed down the front stairs. "What is this? You moved your father from the hospital?" *Without telling me?!*

"Hold on, do you think I can get Papa settled before you grill me?"

The nurse, bumping into Albert, gave him a look that could melt steel.

"*You* are in the *way*," she said.

And he jumped aside like an obedient bunny.

"You'd think he'd offer to help," Maggie said, huffing, as I returned to tuck Papa's blankets around him.

"Oh, he'd only tell us everything we're doing wrong." I stepped back to let the orderlies by. Getting Papa inside, up three flights of stairs, and comfy again in his and Mama's bedroom ate up so much time I thought for sure Hurricane Albert had blown itself out, but he'd only gotten started.

"Do you really think this is wise?" he asked, the second my heels touched the first floor. Behind me, Maggie's thoughts prickled with annoyance.

"It's been ten days since Papa's attack, and Dr. Meyers said he was out of the most dangerous period and would be more comfortable at home," I said. "Mrs. Ritter, would it cause an international incident to get me and Maggie a cup of tea? Maggie? Orange pekoe?"

"Lovely," Maggie said, sailing into the parlor, while Mrs. Ritter, who'd been loudly wondering if she'd ever get her morning break, disappeared into the kitchen. I walked right past Albert to join Maggie. I wanted the squashy armchair, a whole bucketful of hot tea, and some of Mrs. Ritter's lemon cookies, in that order. Mr. Hubert, our sweet brat of an orange cat, jumped into my lap the moment I dropped into the chair, mewing all his problems to me.

"But you didn't consult—" Like a bad cold, Albert followed me in a sputter. "You didn't check first to see—" He groaned and rubbed a hand across his forehead. *She can't make these decisions on her own— what's next?!* "I heard a group of city officials arrived at the hospital to offer their assistance and you threw them out!"

"Not quite," I said.

"But not entirely wrong," Maggie added.

"Ruby—you can't talk like that! Those men—" His mind had been like a pot of popcorn on a hot stove, hundreds of jumbled thoughts exploding, but in a sudden flash, the pale, gaunt-cheeked face of Dennis Ferry appeared like a vision, and I went still.

Why was Albert *here*? I wondered, and I glanced at Maggie, whose thoughts chugged along a refrain of *That no-good self-righteous stick-in-the-mud prig*. Much as I appreciated her emotional support, her thoughts rang out too loudly for me to see into Albert's mind, so I sighed and stood up.

"Come on, Albert, let's chat in Papa's office." I dropped Mr. Hubert onto Maggie's lap and headed back up the stairs, Albert's fuming mind at my heels.

"You need to let go of this obsession with your father's accident!" We'd barely made it inside the room before Albert tore into me. "You're going to get yourself in terrible trouble, not to mention jeopardize the case."

"*What* case?"

"With the confession from the man at your father's party, we have enough evidence to move on Coward and—"

I let out a groan and threw my hands in the air. "The *dead* man, you mean! Anyway, Coward had nothing to do with that bomb. Papa wasn't even investigating him. He wanted to work with him!" I didn't know what disgusted me more—Albert's words or his thoughts. He didn't believe Coward had ordered that bomb any more than I did. There was something twisting in his mind, some kind of desperation, and when I pushed, I could feel it. A memory, a voice: "*Get that girl under control!*"

My hands twitched, and I wished I had a few of my poisons on me. So much for loyalty! I guess now that Papa had outlived his usefulness, Albert had found someone better connected to give him orders! Well, I wasn't going to let this spineless amoeba out of here until I got some answers.

Albert made the exact noise I happened to be feeling as well and yanked at his long-suffering hair some more.

"Listen. To. Me. Ruby. What you are doing is dangerous. Whatever investigation you think your father was undergoing—"

"About that," I said, narrowing my eyes. "I *know* there's evidence out there that Papa collected, and I'd bet my best satin knickers he passed it to you for safekeeping. So I find it strange, you acting like you haven't got a clue."

"I'm not—That's just ridiculous, Ruby! There's nothing—no evidence—no case!" he sputtered, but it was lies, all lies, and I saw the flash of Dennis Ferry's face again, and underneath that:

A memory…

A conversation…

Something Albert wanted to hide, something he was ashamed of…

Ohhh, think about it, you bastard. Think about it *hard*.

"What did you do with it, Albert? Where are my father's files?"

But he had regained control. He straightened his tie and swiped at a lock of hair that had fallen over his forehead.

"Stay out of this, Ruby. You are messing around in things you wouldn't understand."

That RAT. What had he *done*? I had to dig deeper. The memories were looser now, each of them covered in a layer of guilt like muck three inches thick.

"…*can't have…the publicity…case closed…*"

"…*help each other…new state's attorney…a deal…*"

"…*you work…for me…now…understand?*"

And then, just for an instant, it came in clear:

A meeting, Ferry, his face cold and serious, and he was telling Albert…he was telling him…

"*Jeremiah Newhouse is as good as dead, and the only people who* know what he was investigating are standing in this room right now. *You want to be running the state's attorney's office, don't you? Get rid of those files, and it'll be done."*

"You're working with him!" I shouted. "You're working with Dennis Ferry! He's the one corrupting this whole damn city, and Papa had evidence, and you—what? Traded it for Papa's job? Destroyed it?"

"Y-you don't even know what you're talking about!" he said, but he had gone pale and his weaselly brain filled with justifications—*never could have convicted, all too dangerous, can't get myself killed, warned Jeb to call it off...* "The files aren't like anything you're thinking. Your father had only begun to gather information, and I kept telling him we couldn't move against the police commissioner without a better plan!"

"Oh, go to hell, Albert. He trusted you."

"Then he should've trusted my advice and resigned! Maybe then he wouldn't be upstairs dying!"

That sent my shoe flying across the room, where it missed Albert's dumb face by *a hair* before smacking against the wall. Albert ducked, spun, looked at me with wide eyes.

"You're hysterical! You don't even realize I'm trying to keep your family safe!"

"Gee, Albert, let me throw you a damned parade," I said. "And you can get those idiot goons off our front yard! I want them gone by teatime."

"Ruby! You're not in any position to be making these decisions. Pulling your father out of the hospital, sending away his bodyguards! It's madness!" There was something of desperation in his mind when I mentioned his hired muscle, a note of panic, because—

Oohhh, he was lucky I'd given up my murdering ways: HE USED

THOSE BODYGUARDS TO SPY ON ME! HE TOLD FERRY I'D BE AT COWARD'S PARTY! *HE WAS THE REASON THAT THUG NEARLY TOOK OUT ME AND PETER!!!*

"You're spying on me! Do you know what Ferry did with that tip you passed along about me visiting Coward's party? He *hired a gunman to murder me!*"

"I don't—I didn't know anything—!" He really didn't know, but it wasn't as though he thought Ferry would meet me at Coward's party with a birthday present. What a worthless rat! I'd always thought Albert tiresome but mostly reliable—I never would have imagined he'd be such an opportunistic toady that he'd throw in with a monster like Ferry!

"If you ever show your face around here again, I'll—" I started, but Albert somehow managed to pull together what tattered scraps of dignity remained to him and lifted his chin.

"You'll what, hm? Now—now listen, missy! Your father has indulged your antics for too long, but now I'm in charge—*ahh!*"

There went my other shoe. Albert jumped a mile before turning tail like the miserable rodent he was, his thoughts scattershot. *She doesn't understand doesn't see I'm protecting him trying to protect him she's mad she's crazy have to get out of here have to report to Ferry have to—*

I chased him out of the office and down the stairs in stocking feet, shouting, "You go and tell Ferry! Tell him anyone else he sends after me is going to end up the same way!" But he was gone, out the door and off my very short list of allies, and all I could do was pant at the landing, wishing very much I wore pointier shoes and had better aim.

TWENTY-TWO:
PETER

Goodbye, Peter.

     Goodbye, Peter.

Goodbye, Peter.

Everywhere I went, I could hear her words in my ears. Walking to work. Taking the little dog out. Even at the morgue, every time I tried to focus on my work, I'd see her smile slipping from her face, her mouth crumpling into a frown.

Goodbye, Peter.

It was the first time in five years I'd heard someone use my name, and it worked like a key, unlocking memories.

"All right, Peter? All right, my boy? Now, watch this!"

Honey-gold light from the fire, sleepy and sitting in a heap of blankets on the floor, the world outside the cabin cold and dark. Shadows on a sheet stretched over a line, shadows making pictures, and behind the sheet—

"Ah-ha!"

Sometimes it would be a top hat and a moustache, sometimes a corncob pipe and a pair of bushy eyebrows, sometimes a bandana and a bandit's mask. Every time a different face and a different story, but with props and costumes and makeup and mimicry. He was an actor, a famous one, or he was before his wife died in childbirth, leaving behind a quiet little boy.

"*What next, Dad?*"

I'd thought about what came next so many times, it felt like a story that had happened to someone else. The boy getting older, discovering a strange ability, scared of what he could do, how he couldn't control it, no matter how many times his father stood him in front of the mirror and told him, "Just breathe, Peter. Breathe and focus. You'll get it."

They hid away in a cabin in a tiny town in Indiana. The boy practiced, trying to change, making faces at the window, but he was spotted by the wrong people. He knew he was supposed to stay inside, stay hidden, and still he chased after them. And when those boys attacked him, called him *freak* and *monster* and *unnatural*, he didn't know what he was doing, but he knew he changed, got bigger, the boys tried to run but he could chase them down, he could fight them, he nearly killed one, until—

"*Peter! Peter, stop!*"

He ran. As he ran his body kept changing, skin stretching, bones popping. He ran across some train tracks and his foot got small and slipped under a tie and then it got big and pinned him in place, and he fell, he could hear his father shouting, he could feel a rumble growing.

"*Peter! Hold on, I'm coming!*"

Bright lights, so much noise, his body betraying him, his father pulling him, tugging him free, pushing him out of the way...

scream—screech—crash—crunch

His father died, and Peter disappeared, but his father's face didn't disappear. I saw it every time I pulled down the mask, every time I looked into a mirror as myself. I looked exactly like him, the famous actor, the one who died in a notorious train accident because his son lost control.

So, wasn't it a good thing, in the end, that Ruby had said goodbye? I couldn't control myself, and that put people in danger. I wanted Ruby to be safe.

"Excuse me!"

I didn't hear the voice until it was nearly behind me, and I paused on the stairs heading up to Dr. Keene's third-floor laboratory to see one of the morgue clerks, panting as he raced up after me.

"You can't go up there!"

Had he forgotten I'd been reassigned? Just as I opened my mouth to explain myself, Dr. Keene appeared at the top of the stairs, papers in hand, frowning at me and the clerk.

"Something wrong?" he asked, and the clerk pointed at me.

"He was headed up the stairs!"

A quick look up and down from Dr. Keene and then a brisk "Well, get him out of here."

"Dr. Keene?" The moment the words left my mouth, I realized what had happened. I felt the clerk's hand on my arm and looked down at my hands—*my* hands, *Peter's hands,* not Guy's spidery fingers. Everything tilted sideways, the air disappearing, all the sounds, the voices—the clerk loud and insisting and Dr. Keene annoyed—shrinking down to a high-pitched whine.

I ran.

Tripped, really, down the stairs, down past the main floor and down to the basement with the clerk on my heels. Thank goodness he was older and I was young, tall and strong and miles ahead of him when I burst through the basement washroom door and spun toward the mirror and saw my own face.

Peter Buchanan, eighteen years old, from Peakington, Indiana.

Frantic, I forced myself to shift, but the face didn't move—my face. I could hear footsteps outside the door, and any second that clerk was going to burst in, see me, *recognize me,* and—

The door flew open and I spun around ready to fight or curl up into a ball and there was the clerk, the anger on his face dissolving.

"Oh, it's you! Did you see a kid run through here?"

"K-k-kid?" The word stumbled out, and the voice belonged to Guy Rosewood.

"Never mind. Better get on. Keene's lookin' for you." He turned and the door swung shut behind him. I stared into the mirror, into the gray eyes and gray face of Guy Rosewood.

Damn it.

How had that happened?

What if this just got worse? What if I lost control again and next time I couldn't get away?

"Rosewood! You're late!" Dr. Keene said as I walked into his office.

"I'm sorry, sir," I said, feeling like my head was in one country and the rest of me somewhere else.

Dr. Keene gave me a funny look, and for half a moment I wondered if he was going to ask if I was all right, but then he shook his head. "Never mind, never mind. Take a seat! It's a celebration!"

I paused on my way to the chair.

"A celebration?"

Dr. Keene let out a bark of a laugh and set a large bottle of brandy on the desk with a heavy *thunk*. "Approved, Rosewood! Our grant!" He yanked the cork out with his teeth and produced two cut-crystal glasses from a desk drawer before filling them with a generous pour.

"You know what did it?" he asked, grinning as he handed me one of the glasses. "Your report! That fresh body, the one pumped with cyanide! I called up right away, said, 'Hey, we've got ourselves a matter of public interest now, and by gad we need to do something about it!' And it did just the trick! Fully funded! We're moving into a new lab this afternoon."

I blinked at him, my glass of brandy untouched. "I...Oh!"

Dr. Keene must have taken credit for my stunned expression, because he laughed again. "That's one of the things I mean to teach you, Rosewood! You need to know where to apply the right pressure. Who would care about a prolific killer? City Hall!"

"City Hall?"

"Half of scientific research is knowing how to clean your beakers, the other half is shaking the right tree to get the money! As it were, I was able to contact my city alderman—some stuffed shirt. He was very helpful, hmm, very helpful! Very interested to hear about the dead man from this morning! Wanted details, very interested in any theories I had about the killer."

"Do we have theories about the killer?"

"Theories? Of course not! But I told him about that interview you'd conducted with Mrs. What's-Her-Name regarding that first body in the bar, the bunk about an 'angel killer,' and by gad he ate it right up! I could hear him snapping his fingers to get word out to the press!"

"Is that good?"

"It's publicity, Rosewood! Attention means money and money means results. Remember that. It's one of the most important things I'm going to teach you." He lifted the glass in salute and had taken a deep drink before I realized what he'd said.

"You're...going to teach me?"

He gave me a sly look over the top of his glass. "You know, when I met you, I thought you were just about the least-impressive creature on this planet," he said. "Two weeks later, I've got a new lab, a better title, the recognition I deserve, and it's thanks to you. If we can pull this off, if we can actually catch this killer, it'll mean big things, Rosewood, big things, and"—he leaned over his desk—"I mean to take you with me."

I didn't know what to say. I could only stare at him, the silence ticking by, before choking out, "S-sir?"

Dr. Keene sat back in his chair, swirling the brandy in his glass. "Don't look so surprised, Rosewood. You've got a scientist's mind and a talent I haven't seen in ages! Better keep you for myself than lose you to those stuffed coats who call themselves professors. How does it sound?"

I knew he expected me to say yes, and why wouldn't he? Guy Rosewood was an uneducated janitor whose talent at biology was only matched by his skill at sticking his foot in his mouth. A mentorship with Dr. Keene would be life-changing.

But I didn't care about any of that. I didn't even care about the angel killer anymore. I'd lost control of my disguise, for the first time in years. That couldn't happen again.

"I'd like access to your research on tricoloroforms," I said, and Dr. Keene's eyebrows went up.

"That? You're still interested in—"

"Yes."

Dr. Keene looked like he wanted to ask me why, and if he did, I didn't know how I'd answer. I felt so worn out, I might've said the truth: I needed to know what I was.

But he just shrugged. "Sure, Rosewood. As soon as we find this killer, I'll give you anything you want."

I let out a sigh, then threw back my drink and set the glass down on the desk, feeling the liquor burn my throat. "Then I should get back to work."

TWENTY-THREE
RUBY

"Another cup, sweetheart?"

The coffee tasted like it came direct from the bottom of the Chicago River, but who cared? It was hot, and I was freezing. I held out my cup, but just then the door burst open, sending a blast of cold air through the diner. Spinning around, I saw Vivian—ab-so-tive-ly resplendent in dark tweed—narrow her purple-powder-rimmed eyes and stride in.

"Hullo, doll!" In one swift motion, she swept her coat from her shoulders and deposited it on the stool next to me. "Can't talk long. Got a new beat. Hey! Waiter!" She barked her order, coffee—black—and a bologna sandwich, her mind buzzing with a dozen different thoughts, from food to the newspaper to office politics to her cat back at home to me in my plain knit dress.

"What's the story, morning glory?" she asked, sliding into a seat. "You said you wanted to chitchat."

"This is off the record," I said, and when Vivian rolled her eyes and considered walking right back out again, I added, "For now."

This better be good, she thought. I took a deep breath and double-checked that the people around us had their attentions on their coffees.

"Dennis Ferry is running a criminal organization out of City Hall, sending vulnerable women into encounters with men for money and blackmail," I said, and something went *snap* inside Vivian's mind, like she had to restrain every atom of her being from reaching for her reporter's notebook to scribble this down. To her admirable credit, she didn't move a muscle.

"Hold on," I said. "There's more. The police set up that pipe bomb and arranged the shootout at my house under Ferry's orders. Papa had been digging into corruption within the police department and clearly got too close to the truth for Ferry's comfort."

"So, Commissioner Walsh is working for Ferry?" Vivian asked, her eyes wide.

"*Hold on.* There's more. My father's files on the City Hall investigation disappeared, and when I went hunting for them, I learned they had been destroyed by my father's secretary, Albert Rollins, in a deal with Ferry. Albert's running the state's attorney's office now."

There was a long pause, and Vivian stared at me before gently clearing her throat.

"I'm afraid to ask. Is there anything else?"

"Nope. Oh! My father was making a deal with Coward, information for leniency, but now that Papa's sick, Coward's decided that straight and narrow isn't the path for him. He's planning on bumping off Walsh, and Ferry, too, once he figures out he's the one in charge. Then he'll take the business over for himself."

Poor Vivian. I'd tossed a handful of sand into the smooth gears of her mind and all she could do was stare at me, beautifully-made-up eyes bugged out and unblinking, as she tried to put this together. *She's lying she's not she's making it up she's too smart for that she's crazy she's scared she's desperate.* Half a second later the journalist came back and she smoothed her hands down her skirt, regaining an air of professional unruffle.

"What proof do you have?"

I let out a laugh. "None, obviously, or this conversation wouldn't be off the record. Tried to get my hands on the body of the man who shouted out Coward's name—no suicide, he was murdered—but it was burned to ashes. Same with my father's files. And Coward's already claiming he never planned on ratting out anybody to anyone. So. That's where I'm at. I know Ferry has to be stopped, but I haven't got the faintest *how.*"

"Well," she said. "*Well.* A conspiracy, involving the police commissioner and the state's attorney's secretary and the blandest alderman in the city, plotting to murder the state's attorney? Exploiting girls to trap marks? Kiddo, if my editor ever hears I agreed to go off the record on this, he'll kill me." She called over the fellow behind the counter and raised her mug for a refill. "It's a great story, but without any evidence, what the hell do you expect me to do?"

"Can't you—I don't know—look into it? You're my best hope!"

"Look, this is knockout stuff, but what happens when I bring it to my editor with no proof and no sources? Hell, even if I told him I heard it all from the teenaged daughter of the man at the center of the plot? If I was lucky, he'd just fire me. For all I know, Ferry could have him in his pocket, too, and then I've gotta duck trigger men every time I step out my front door." She shook her head. "If you could bring me something, then maybe…"

"How?" I asked. "What would *you* do?"

Her thoughts started spilling out—*Ferry's careful, he's got information hidden somewhere, not in his office, not anywhere near his nosy wife, somewhere he feels in control*—but she stopped herself. *She's gonna get herself killed...*

"What're you after here?" she asked. "You told me all you cared about was keeping your family safe, right?"

"Yeah, and you told me if I found evidence, publishing it would keep them safe!"

Vivian frowned. "*If*, kiddo. If. I thought your pops probably had something stashed in his bedside table, not that there was a city-wide conspiracy hell-bent on burying this. You want my advice now? Take care of your pops, keep your head down, and get out of the city."

My chin snapped up.

"You're telling me to give up? After what he did? Are you *joking*?"

She wasn't. She pictured my body stretched out on a street corner, polka-dotted with bullet holes, as inevitable as the sunrise. "It's a lot to risk for revenge," she said with a shrug.

"I'm not talking about revenge. I know what he's doing now. How many people he's hurting. Not just my own family, but dozens, hundreds. I need to stop him..."

I trailed off, overwhelmed by the wave of pity flooding through Vivian as she listened to me.

"That's noble and all but...it's a lot for a kid like you to handle. I mean, think it through. You can't go to the police, you burned your bridges with City Hall, your father's own secretary betrayed him, and I wouldn't trust Coward to take care of a baby doll. Now, you're a capable gal and I'd sock anyone who said otherwise, but still, this is an awful lot to take on by yourself. Who do you have to help you if things get hairy?"

Peter, I thought, automatically, and then, *Oh, not anymore, huh? Maggie? Maybe…*

"What about you?" I asked, and Vivian let out a sigh.

"Honest?" Vivian said. "I wonder if I should've even published that first story. Didn't seem to do a thing except put a target on your back. But look, even if I wanted to write your story, I'm off the politics beat."

I made a noncommittal *hmm* and tried not to crumple onto the counter. "Of course," I said. "You switch beats more'n I switch dance partners. What is it now? Horses? Haberdashery?"

"Murder," she said, reaching into her bag to pull out a newspaper, and with all the pride of a new mama showing off her babe, she placed it in front of me.

There, two inches tall:

MURDERESS STRIKES FEAR INTO CITY

Oh dear.

Oh, oh, oh dear…

"Amazing, isn't it?" Vivian asked, and as she read the first few lines, I heard them echo in her mind: *In the run-down streets of Chicago, a killer lurks, an avenging angel who has dispatched no fewer than six… Ruby!*

She reached out, grabbing me as I swayed on my seat.

"You all right? I never thought you were one of those fading flower girls with no stomach for this stuff!"

Everything looked a bit blurry and I blinked at her.

"What…is this?"

"What is it? A gift to newspapers everywhere!" Vivian said,

laughing. The counterman brought her check and she flashed him a toothy smile. "She's called the *angel killer*. Been goin' on for years. Bad husbands, bad beaux, bad characters—mysteriously done away with under strange circumstances. Got to be so regular in some parts of town, folks in rough situations know to ask this angel to take away their tormentor. And she does."

Of course I did. I'd like to see anybody walk the streets in some of those neighborhoods, listening in on thoughts, and *not* wishing murder on certain unsavory characters.

… Please, I can stand him hurting me, but don't let him near the children …

… and he walks around bold as brass, like he never did those things to Mary Louise …

… take her, she's nothing, she's dirt, she's …

"How … how did you hear about it?" I asked, still confused. Wasn't Peter's investigation supposed to be secret?

"The fellows who put the pieces together—some doctor in the city morgue and his whiz-kid assistant—put out a call to City Hall. Wouldn't you know? Our fair mayor decided a murderer on the loose would be just the thing to distract from his state's attorney almost dying. Now this doctor's running the whole investigation, root to stem. They say nothin' goes past him and his boy wonder."

"But why are you writing about it?"

"Because," Vivian said, with a twinge of offense, "it's a sensational story, and *I'm* a sensational reporter. Had to practically break someone's arm to get it and I ain't giving it up. My editor says if I get the scoop on the killer's I.D., he'll give me five hundred smackers. A cool thousand if I beat the coppers, too."

She sounded confident, and she *felt* confident, and my stomach dropped a mile. It was bad enough to have Peter hunting me, let alone a sharp gal like Vivian! But when I pressed into her thoughts, I didn't find much. She'd published almost everything she knew, which wasn't any more than Peter.

"Well. Good luck, I guess."

"Oh, don't be sore, kiddo," Vivian said, folding up the paper with care and sliding it into her bag. "I'm sorry I can't be more help. This angel story's hot, hot, *hot*. Every second I waste is another second I could be scooped!" She laughed and gave me a playful shove. "Hey. You're a gal in trouble, maybe you should pray to the angel killer to take your baddie away!"

She threw on her coat while I felt my stomach writhe into knots. Forget the stuff about the angel killer—which was a ridiculous name, by the way—I'd just lost my best source of information.

I let out a glum sigh. "If I confess to the murders, will you help me find the evidence I need?" I asked, and Vivian barked a laugh.

"Sure—I'll even give you the thousand!" She laughed again and turned for the door. "You'll need it!"

No Vivian. No Peter. Not even Albert, whatever good he might've been. I had no idea how to take down Ferry. Vivian's guess, that Ferry had a secret stash of information somewhere, was probably spot-on, but how could I find it?

I walked home, my head aching so badly it took me a moment to catch a stream of thoughts, far away but focused on *me. Newhouse girl alone no sign of security…*

I whipped my head around and felt the thoughts break off in alarm as I spotted a derby-hatted man in a boxy black car across the street, which roared away before I could get a good look.

"Hey!" I shouted. Ferry was still spying on me! I wanted to run after the man, chase him down, stuff him full of poison—damn. No poisons, not anymore, not when Peter had his brilliant mind on every dead body in Chicago. How long before he'd put it together? How long before Ferry ran out of patience and sent someone else after me?

I stepped inside the house, my spirits somewhere around my shoe leather, expecting to argue with my cooped-up sisters—perfect hellions now that I'd banned them from all their favorite haunts—and was relieved to find Maggie fiddling with the rubber plant in the parlor.

"Oh, hello!" I said, unwinding my scarf from my neck. "What are you doing here?"

"I brought lunch," Maggie said. "For everyone."

"Really? Golly, you have good timing! My sisters are about ready to skin me alive and Mrs. Ritter's walking around like she's got a guillotine hanging over her head—honestly, I think she's about had it with our family, and I can't say I—" With my coat and galoshes tucked away, I could give Maggie a good once-over, and what I saw alarmed me. She looked thin, drawn, her mind elsewhere, and when I pried into her thoughts, all I could hear were stern instructions to *Pay attention! Smile! Look happy!*

"Oh, darling, that's just awful!" she said, while her mind chanted *Pull it together, don't cry, don't cry…* She smoothed a piece of blond hair behind her ear, and as she did, her hand came up without its usual blinding flash. Where was her engagement ring?

"What's the matter?" I asked.

"Wh-what? Oh! I'm perfectly fine!" *Pull it together, Maggie…*

I frowned and grabbed her hand, dragged her upstairs to my bedroom, and pushed her onto the bed.

"Sit. Spill. Did something happen with you and J.P.?"

"No, it's—it's nothing, I swear! It's—" But her words broke off in a sudden messy sob, her face crumpling as she dropped it into her hands. I went to her side in an instant, my arm around her as I tried to follow the frantic zip of her thoughts. *Money scandal photos outrage J.P. Daddy scandal scandal…*

"Maggie! What is it? What's wrong?"

She tried several times to speak, but I could see she just needed to *get it all out,* and I fetched her my handkerchief and held her till the worst passed. At last, hiccoughing, my lace handkerchief entirely in ruins, she tilted pink-rimmed eyes up to me.

"Oh, Ruby… You'll think I'm an idiot."

"Why? What happened?" A face swam to the front of her thoughts: a party… a man, dark and intense… "Oh dear, is it an affair? And someone's found out about it?"

"An affair? No, no! It's much worse than that," she sniffled, and I saw it all in an instant: *Maggie, beautiful and funny and flirty, two nights ago, a party at the Hotel Le Grand, laughing as a dark, intense man introduced himself, handed her his card, "I'm a photographer… an art photographer, and you have the look." J.P. off to play cards and Maggie alone, deep into the hotel's secret liquor stores, that photographer so charming, so magical, telling her about his pictures—"They're the thing in Paris now, society girls displaying themselves freely…"—then, somehow, she was alone again, alone in his room, and she had Champagne in her hands and pictures spread out before them and he was saying… he*

*was saying… "They're not half so beautiful as you…Don't you want…
to see…?"*

"I don't know how it happened," she whispered. "This man…
sauced me up and stripped me down and took some photos and, oh,
Ruby. I feel like such a fool! I don't know how I made it home but he
showed up at my door the next day with these…*pictures,* and they're
terrible, *terrible!"*

"Oh Maggie, oh *no.* Is that where your engagement ring went? He's
blackmailing you?"

Frowning, Maggie stretched out her fingers. "He says I have to keep
paying him or he'll send the photos off to every newspaper from here
to the Atlantic, with a special set just for my father and J.P."

I was so mad I could spit! What a *disgusting* snake, preying on
Maggie like that. And I would bet every one of Mama's old diamonds
that she wasn't the first. Those Parisian "society girls" were no doubt
girls just like Maggie, duped by a con artist into shedding their clothes
and their pennies.

"He needs to be stopped," I said, and I didn't realize I'd said it out
loud until Maggie glanced up over the edge of my handkerchief, a look
of awe on her face.

"B-but how?"

Arsenic, belladonna, chloroform, cyanide. Magical potions danced
in my head, happy to be slipped into that monster's bloodstream to put
an end to Maggie's suffering.

But I was retired. How does one handle a blackmailer without
killing him? The lawyers I knew were all men, and I could guess what
they'd make of an heiress getting herself drunk and alone with a man
of ill character. Probably they'd tell her to 'fess up to her father, beg

him to settle with the photographer, and hope to hell the photos never got out.

"Do you think you can make a deal with him?" I asked, chewing a fingernail. "Ask his price and pay him off?"

Maggie shook her head. "Daddy controls my trust fund and I only get so much allowance a month. Besides"—she shivered—"I don't think he's the kind who negotiates. I think he'd almost rather those photos get out... Maybe I should just come clean to Daddy and hope he doesn't ship me off to a convent!" She let out a hysterical giggle, but it wasn't really a joke. Stewart Andrew Stowe was not the kind of man to shrug away his daughter's indiscretions. He'd likely even feel it his duty to tell J.P. what she'd been up to. A gray and bleak and isolated future stretched out before my sunshiney friend, all because of one horrible moment and one terrible man. I couldn't stand it.

I wouldn't.

I couldn't kill him. But I could still do something.

"Listen to me." I grabbed Maggie's hands. "That monster can't get away with it."

"But—"

"No. Maggie. If he's done this to you, he's done this to other women. And even if your father pays him off, he'll just find another girl and do it again."

Her eyes had filled with tears. "I know. I know! It's horrible. But what can we do?"

I gave her a smile and squeezed her hands tight between mine. *"Stop him."*

TWENTY-FOUR
PETER

Amazing what a decent budget could do.

Better glassware. A wider range of chemicals for poison analysis. A fleet of eager researchers to wade through the acres of medical records and police reports. Two full-time detectives assigned to the case. Under city orders, Dr. Keene and I moved to a spacious laboratory on the seventh floor of the main hospital. It was an unoccupied dissection lab, beautiful with clean white tile and bright skylights. Dr. Keene whistled now while he worked and took to chuckling to himself as he walked from table to table, ordering around the assistants and clapping them on the back.

"We're doing it," he would say, rubbing his hands together. "We—are—doing—it!"

And we were.

The court orders to exhume suspicious bodies flowed across judges' desks like water, and soon enough we had all the bones, livers, brains, and hearts that we needed. Under Dr. Keene's instruction, I set in motion the delicate processes to extract whatever poisons might be present: cut out some tissue, use acid to break it into its chemical components, and make those atoms and bonds reveal themselves. It was better than magic. It was science.

Without Ruby to distract me, I threw myself into my work. Late nights, early mornings, coffee cups and sandwiches left forgotten on my desk, dashing to the boardinghouse to take the little dog out for air and then back to the lab again. When I was home, trying to sleep, I thought about her, and even with the dog snoozing on my chest I felt ragged and restless. On the worst nights, I would have to slide the dog onto the bed so I could roll to the floor, my disguises slipping fast until I ended up iced with sweat, wearing my own face. I reminded myself this would all be under control as soon as we wrapped up the investigation.

"Rosewood?"

My head snapped up, vision blurry after hours spent peering at tissue samples through a microscope. There was Dr. Keene, smiling at me with pride and benevolence, and a tall, suited gentleman behind him. Another tour, it seemed. Dr. Keene had taken to inviting various would-be benefactors to visit the lab, where they nodded politely at the experimental setups and interrupted my work.

"Oh, come on, we'll let you get back to it soon, Rosewood," Dr. Keene said. "I wanted to introduce you to the man who has made this all happen! The fellow from City Hall who approved our grant." He leaned in and muttered, "Make him happy, Rosewood, he controls the purse strings."

The gentleman smiled at me. "Please, don't let me slow you down, Doctor...ah...?"

"Mister," I said. "Rosewood."

"Mr. Rosewood. A delight. My name is Dennis Ferry." He put out a hand, which I shook. "Dr. Keene tells me you were essential in discovering this killer's methods. That body found in the alley outside Herman Coward's party… You're certain he's one of your victims?"

"That's what the signs indicate, sir," I answered, shuffling a few papers on my desk.

"And the woman who killed him—you did say you believe it's a woman, didn't you?"

Dr. Keene gave a good-natured laugh. "That's the working theory, at the moment."

"Then this woman who killed him," Ferry continued. "She's responsible for… how many deaths did you say?"

I glanced up at Mr. Ferry, suddenly and strangely uncomfortable. He had a look on his face I only recognized through years of practicing my own expressions in the mirror: he was trying very hard not to smile.

"Rosewood—did you hear Mr. Ferry?" Dr. Keene leaned over, eyeing me.

"We haven't proven anything conclusively yet. But I believe we can count on six… at least," I said, wary. I didn't like the way Mr. Ferry looked at me.

"Six!" Mr. Ferry rocked back on his heels. "We have a murderess who has killed half a dozen men! Remarkable!" His voice had gone so soft I felt a wave of goose pimples crest over the back of my neck, which hardly made any sense. Mr. Ferry was here to help us. But nonetheless, I didn't like him. I wanted him to go. I wanted to get back to work.

"Well, I suppose I should…" I said, tidying up the papers on my desk again, and Dr. Keene looked ready to hiss at me to be polite when Mr. Ferry stopped him.

"Yes, of course! Of course," he said. "We must do everything to support this investigation. Determining this woman's identity is City Hall's chief priority. Anything you want or need, just ask. We will spare nothing until we have her.

"Thank you," he added, and he put out a hand to me again. This time, I stared at it for a moment before I took it. Ferry's skin was dry, cold, his grip unnervingly strong. I felt my throat go tight as I looked up into his face, his eyes that seemed to bore right through me. "We never would have known about her if not for you."

TWENTY-FIVE
RUBY

Men were so damn predictable sometimes it was a wonder how they managed to stay at the top of the food chain.

I'd decided to take my mind off things—like Ferry's plots to kill me, being the target of a city-wide manhunt, oh, and Guy, Peter, Peter, Guy—by going after Maggie's creep. But he was such a pathetic two-bit crook, he hardly taxed my brainpower.

Rex Blanchot, thirty-five, with salt-and-pepper hair made more peppery by a generous helping of brilliantine and a ridiculous pencil line of a moustache on his upper lip. Currently occupying a knockout three-room suite at the Hotel Le Grand, thanks to Maggie, of course.

Over the five nights I spent spying on him, I managed to learn a whole slew of unsurprising facts.

He preferred blondes (too bad for me, my blond wig looked a fright).

He loved cards.

He'd caused no fewer than half a dozen suicides.

And, most importantly, he had a bad mind, cold, violent, cruel.

He would have been an excellent candidate for my list, except, of course, I was retired. *No more bodies.* Especially now. Over a week spent reading ladies' magazines and newspaper columns in the hotel lobby, I'd had plenty of time to catch up on the city's latest colorful character. MIGHT OF CITY HALL BEHIND ANGEL KILLER HUNT! She was second in popularity only to Peter's boss, Dr. Gregory C. Keene, who made it clear that he was running this whole operation.

"I'm talking about every speck of dust! It goes to my eyes first!" His quotes filled the articles, but I could see through them. Peter was the brains behind the bravado, and he wouldn't miss a trick.

So, no murder, no matter how much Maggie's scummy con man deserved it. Get to Rex Blanchot and steal Maggie's photos and get out again, with everyone's hearts still beating.

On the night of, my little silver purse held everything a glam gal needed: lipstick, powder, handkerchief, and nothing else. No poison, no knives, not even a pair of sewing scissors.

As for the dress, once again Maggie delivered a knockout. Low-cut and flaming red, it was the kinda dress that would've looked down-right cheap if it weren't so expensive. Three inches of rich, dark mink fur trimmed the hem, while the skirt glittered with a dozen huge, intricate snowflakes picked out in pearls. Maggie had even provided a coat—which I promised would return home with me—of luxurious black velvet with a gorgeous cream collar of fluffy ermine.

Thanks to her clothes and her generous hand at the makeup vanity, I practically wore a billboard that said *Hullo, look at me! Wouldn't I be lovely to rob?* And good thing, too, because I only had about twenty seconds—the time it took Blanchot to leave the card room in the back of the hotel and wander through the dining room into the lobby—for him to notice me.

Eight twenty-eight, a glass of soda water in my hand, I took my place at the bar.

Prey

Bait

Quarry

That was how women looked to men like Blanchot, those wretched creatures. I wished I could tell them it *never* made me feel pathetic or small to hear those things. It made me feel powerful.

Think I'm weak? That's whizzing! I'll love it when you realize how wrong you are.

There was nothing that felt better than that perfect, glorious moment. The sudden shock a man felt watching this kitten transform into a damn tiger.

The clock struck half past eight and two minutes later Blanchot walked in, nose out of joint thinking of the dough he'd lost, and saw me sitting there. It was a little like looking into a fun-fair mirror of myself, seeing his impression of me reflected in his thoughts: a beautiful, fresh, wealthy, fragile girl, laid out perfectly. Why wouldn't he get a taste?

"Good evening, miss," he said, and off—we—*went!*

He was charming, funny, kind, mysterious, just like Maggie had said. He wheedled my name (*I'm Thelma Abellard*) and my story out of me in seconds, welcomed me to Chicago when I told him I was visiting, and offered the requisite sympathy when I said my ex-fiancé had taken off with the makeup girl at Marshall Field's. He managed to get real drinks from the bartender, which he quickly doctored up with a few pours from a flask in his pocket—just whiskey but of course I didn't drink any—and then when we were both pretending to be silly and soppy, he began dropping hints like bread crumbs: *photographer, Paris, art.*

And wouldn't you know? I looked uncannily like his favorite, most popular model.

And wouldn't you know? He had some of her photos upstairs if I'd like to see them.

Honestly, I almost felt bad for fellows like this.

He had a plan, too, which I cottoned to as he led me, giggling, to the best suite in the hotel. Champagne, portfolio, sneak out his camera, sneak the girl out of her clothes, then sneak her out of his room. I figured my best bet to snatch Maggie's pictures was after the portfolios but before the stripping down, when poor Thelma Abellard would get a nasty case of the spins, and Rex Blanchot would learn you shouldn't mix zozzled gals and de luxe hotel carpeting.

"Here we are!" Blanchot pushed open the door to reveal a room so large and ostentatious that it had to've come from a dozen Maggies. I wanted to gawk at the marble tables and velvet curtains inches thick and crystal dripping from the ceiling like stars and everything that didn't move covered in gold leaf, but to Thelma Abellard, this was old stuffing. I took one look at the jewel box of a room and yawned.

"Cute," I said, dropping my purse onto a small table, and Blanchot smiled like a cat in a creamery.

"Take a seat, doll. When we look at Parisian art, we have to drink Parisian Champagne."

I made my eyes heavy, my limbs boneless, and I sank into a high-backed chair. The second he ducked into the bedroom, I scoured the room for his hiding place, but other than a few cameras on a table, I saw nothing unusual.

I closed my eyes and moved my senses sideways, into Blanchot's brain. His thoughts were crowded with plans for me, locating the

Champagne, when one jumped out: *Better put that away.* I pushed in deeper, pulling free an image of a battered steamer trunk, shoved into a corner of the bedroom and spilling over with dirty clothes—and files.

In a second, I had it figured out: fake a tummy ache and rush, embarrassed and crying, into the bedroom. Slam the door shut, run the water in the bathroom, grab Maggie's pictures, hide them under my flimsy dress, and then wait for Blanchot to coax me out. He'd realize the photo opportunity was over for the night, but I could make another date—or say anything, so long as I got out the door with those pictures.

"Bubbly, and art," Blanchot announced, returning to the sitting room, a portfolio tucked under one arm.

Quick, I dropped my eyelids into a kittenish sleepy smile and purred, "Ohh, Champagne! My favorite!" And Blanchot, laughing, handed me a glass. I wondered if he'd sit in the chair opposite me, but of course that prat took a knee right at my feet, resting the portfolio in my lap and giving himself a spectacular view of my décolletage.

As I *ooh*ed and *aahh*ed and pretended sips of Champagne, I turned page after page of bright young things smiling gamely at the camera, until I came to a gorgeous dark-haired woman stretched out on a couch, not a stitch on her. I reacted just the way Blanchot hoped: a sharp gasp followed by a burst of giggles.

"I'm terribly sorry! You weren't supposed to see those," he said, but he didn't close the book.

"She's not *wearing* anything!" I said, covering my smile with my hands, and then I took another peek.

"I feel like such a cad. Those are some photos from a special exhibit—forgot they were in there."

"There're *more*?"

"Only a few. I don't work with many models talented enough for that kind of art. It is art, you see, in places like Paris where they understand those things. I'm sorry, I should have known a girl like you wouldn't be interested. We'll just get this out of the—"

"Wait! I mean—she's real pretty…"

"A professional," Blanchot said, and *ooohhh* that was a lie! This girl was the daughter of a well-off British businessman, who'd had to funnel several hundred pounds into Blanchot's pocket just to get him to go away. "But she isn't nearly as beautiful as you."

Ugh. Gag. Maybe I wouldn't have to fake the vomit.

"Really?"

"Really," Blanchot said, reaching for a camera just as his other hand came up to slip one of my straps off my shoulder. I closed my eyes, pretending to swoon, Blanchot's hand as squirmy as a fat, pale spider on my skin, his mind full of all the wonderful possibilities going on under my red dress, when a burst of light and the sizzle of flash powder exploded before me. My eyes popped open just in time to see Blanchot, gazing at me like a wolf, reach down for a handful of my chest, which was when I decided this had gone on quite long enough.

I slapped one hand over my mouth, eyes wide, and retched.

The Champagne spilled from the glass just at the right moment for Blanchot to think I'd thrown up on him, which made him sit back fast on his heels. I took my chance and ran, straight for the bedroom, and slammed the door. Damn!—no lock. One of Blanchot's shoes—thick and with a heavy sole—rested nearby, and I kicked it under the door, wedging it closed. As Blanchot shouted from the other room, I kept retching while I tore open the steamer trunk to find—

It was a pile, a mountain, an evil hoarder's nest of pure, sabotaging filth. A hundred different files, at least, labeled with different names. Men, women, old, young, most caught *in flagrante* or nude or otherwise engaged in activities that made my cheeks flush.

But no time to gawk. Blanchot pounded on the door and I needed to find Maggie's file, which I discovered near the top of the pile and shoved underneath my skirt, safely secured by a waistband I'd worn for just that purpose.

"Thelma? Thelma!"

I had time to get to the bathroom, run the water, splash some on my face, when another label caught my eye.

D. FERRY

D. Ferry?

What in the hell was *Ferry's* name doing here?

"Darling, I can't open the door! What's wrong!" Blanchot shouted, while his mind raced. *Why is the door jammed is she getting sick how do I get this back on the rails?*

I grabbed the file, only it was five times thicker than Maggie's, and I knew I'd never get it up the back of my skirt—but I couldn't *leave* it there! What if this was the evidence I needed?

I looked around, searching for a bag, a jacket, maybe I could pretend I threw up in something, take it out with me.

Another bang at the door. Damn it! I needed more time.

The washroom. Go!

I slammed the door behind me and sat on the cold white tile, Ferry's file in my hands, shaking as I imagined what a professional blackmailer might have on Dennis Ferry.

Was this it? Was this the missing piece to take him down?

I flipped open the file to see.

Commissioner Walsh, his shirt unbuttoned, a very young woman in the shadows behind him. Next photo: another city alderman, this one laughing with a pair of half-naked girls perched on his lap. My fingers trembled as I sifted through them, photos of girls, of politicians, of policemen. There was enough dirt in here to take down half of City Hall—including our fair mayor, featured in the front seat of his famous blue sports car next to a laughing Herman Coward—but absolutely nothing on Ferry, which was when I realized: this file wasn't about him, it was *for* him. The photographer was one of his tools…which meant Maggie…This wasn't some run-of-the-mill blackmail. Ferry had been looking for my allies, and Maggie stood up to him that day outside Papa's hospital room. He went after her because of me! It was all my fault!

BANG

BANG

SNAP!

The bedroom door burst open, and, panicked, I flipped the file closed and shoved it into a pile of towels on the floor before leaning over the toilet bowl, hugging it tight just as Blanchot pushed open the door, annoyed and breathing hard.

"*Uugghhh,*" I said in Thelma's silly voice. "Think I…had too much…"

Get her out of here, Blanchot thought, but as he reached down to take my arm, his eyes caught something resting on the floor just behind the toilet: the photo of Commissioner Walsh.

How did… he wondered, and then he kicked at the pile of towels, revealing Ferry's file. *What is this…*

I scrambled to my feet, trying to come up with a lie, but Blanchot was too sharp for that. The look on his face turned my blood cold, my eyes darting around the room for something to protect myself with.

Razor. Medicine bottle. Glass, stop her, pin her down, find out what she—I winced as my head burst with pain—stupid Blanchot's thoughts! But I couldn't dwell on that—he was coming for me—and I snatched a large crystal bottle of cologne from the floor near the tub and *smash!* Shards of glass skittered across the floor and the dense, stinging smell of perfume burned my eyes and lungs, but I had a jagged bludgeon in my hands.

"Come here, you little—" he snarled.

He reached for me and I swung the bottle, making him jump back, but the stupid thing was too heavy and the room too small and him too fast and when I lifted the bottle again, he snatched me by the wrist and twisted it back so hard I expected my bones to snap.

"Who told you to get that file!" he demanded. *"Who are you?"*

"I know you're working for Dennis Ferry!" I gasped. "I've got connections in the state's attorney's office. If you have evidence against Ferry, I can get you a deal!" It was a lie, obviously, and not one of my best ones, but he didn't need to believe me, he just needed to *think* about any dirt he might have on Ferry, and I gritted my teeth together, trying to follow the churning patterns of Blanchot's thoughts.

Evidence—clubhouse—receipts

Hand her to Ferry—no, he'll be angry

Gotta keep her quiet, keep her quiet for good

"Where is—" But before I could get another word out, he'd dragged me from the washroom, leaving behind the mess of glass and cologne.

Tie her up make her quiet get rid of her get rid of her

His thoughts were like fireworks, black and red and white, flashing, wild, hot, and I couldn't keep up. I hunted cold-blooded killers who hurt and destroyed because they liked it, and this passionate anger made me dizzy, breathless, or maybe it was just knowing that, cold-blooded or not, Blanchot intended to see me dead.

Curtain sash, belt, suspenders, around her neck, stop her stop her

He wrenched me so hard I heard a *pop* from my shoulder and felt an almighty riot of pain, but I couldn't think about that, I couldn't—

Ruby, you need to move or you will die.

Need something, need something, stop him stop him

What was that in his hands? Oh—a poker, a fire poker—he raised it up and I spun, rolled, felt the *thud* of the poker on the floor. My hands were wild, searching blindly for *sharp hard heavy*, and I saw him raise the poker again, his face like some kind of two-cent horror flick, and I didn't know *what* I found, but I threw it, and Blanchot had to duck. I scrambled back, knocking against his bedside table. Something clattered, and I turned to see a bottle and *oh lord hallelujah*, it was sweet, beautiful, toxic *mercury bichloride.*

POISON, the bottle read, EXTERNAL USE ONLY.

Mercury bichloride was a corrosive, a medical tonic prescribed for—*ugh,* of all things—syphilis sores; it worked by burning and was just about the last thing you'd want splashed in your face, as Rex Blanchot discovered.

He screamed, covering his blinded eyes and dropping the poker to the ground with a thud, but before his reaching hand could grab it again, I snatched it up and swung it, hard, landing a blow right on his left temple. Blanchot dropped to the floor, blood dripping from his skull, his eyes half closed and his mind muzzy. This was why I preferred poison! Was he dead? Was he *dying*? I didn't know if I wanted the answer to be yes or no, but I knew he had been shouting and pounding and this was a posh hotel that would notice those noises and so I needed to *leave.*

In the struggle, Maggie's photos had slipped out of my dress, and I raced to gather them up before running back to the bathroom for the rest of Ferry's file. When I returned, I held the photos over Blanchot's face, breathing hard.

"Where does Ferry keep his own records?" I demanded, leaning in close, but his eyes swam around in his head, rolling like marbles. "He's got someplace he thinks is safe—*where?*"

Can't speak can't breathe pain pain help pain, went the runaway train of his mind, and I hissed out a swear—I knew what those fuzzy-edged thoughts meant.

"You can't die yet, you monster! Dennis Ferry! You took photos for him! He must've paid you, you must have something—or know something!"

Blanchot blinked. He shivered. He turned unseeing eyes to my voice.

Can't talk can't talk can't talk so cold

"You don't need to say it out loud! Just think it!"

Can't talk…So cold…So…cold…

"Stay here!" I bent down and grabbed his collar. "Don't die!"

But he was slipping away, slipping through my fingers, no matter how hard I pulled at him, slapped his cheeks or shouted in his face. I couldn't stay inside a dying mind—it pulled like a whirlpool before it went out—so I let him go and his thoughts turned small and faraway and still.

"*Damn,*" I spat, just as the door sounded with a heavy knock.

"Mr. Blanchot? Hello?"

A hotel employee, sent to investigate the suspicious sound of arguing on the penthouse floor. Now he was wondering if he had the wrong room.

"Hello? Is everything all right?"

Leave it alone? Could be someone hurt in there? Maybe just get the key...

I heard his footsteps and his mind fade, but he would be back. I had minutes, maybe, to get out of here. Plenty of time, except...

I glanced over Blanchot's body to the steamer trunk, its catalogue of misery. When the police found him, they'd find *that*. What would happen when those pictures got out? Nothing anyone deserved...

Run, Ruby! part of me shouted. *Get out.*

But I couldn't. I set Maggie's and Ferry's files down, bundled everything from the trunk into my arms, carried it to the fireplace opposite the bed, and shoved it in. A set of matches sat on the mantelpiece, and I lit one and fed it to the photographs. They twitched and curled and caught, burning bright and fast. One by one, faces appeared and disappeared in the flames, arms and legs and torsos turned to black ash. I wished I could write to them, every one, tell them their nightmare was over...

But the hotel steward would be back in seconds, so I grabbed the two files and raced back through the sitting room to snatch up my purse and coat, flung open the door, shut it quietly behind me, and disappeared down the hall, just as footsteps rounded the corner.

I smoothed my hair, threw on the coat, and headed down the stairs to the lobby. The hotel employees would only remember a pretty girl in a flaming red dress. *Nothing more.*

The cool Chicago wind nipped at my flushed cheeks, filling me with wild, ridiculous relief so intoxicating that I didn't even remember I'd forgotten to destroy Blanchot's camera until the next morning.

TWENTY-SIX
PETER

I squinted down at the paper, trying to decipher the notes I'd recorded during Dr. Keene's latest autopsy.

"Signs of mercury burns across face," I muttered, and then my writing went blurry and I rubbed my eyes. Yawning, I glanced up at the clock on the wall. Past ten! How had it gotten so late? This day felt like it started three years ago.

Another dead body, this one blinded by mercury bichloride and with a sizeable dent in his skull. Just a homicide at first glance, except the victim had been chatting with a pretty girl the last time he was seen alive. That got us sent to the crime scene, but Dr. Keene didn't take over until the police identified the victim: he was an extortionist, a photographer who blackmailed his subjects.

"There's our 'bad fella' angle," Dr. Keene said, slapping my shoulder; then he barked to the officers, "All this evidence—everything—I want it back to my lab!"

It felt like the break we needed, and that was before I detected the faint odor of recently burned flash powder in the air and a camera discarded underneath the sitting room chair. It was real, concrete evidence, the kind that sent Dr. Keene buzzing back to the lab, eager to get the autopsy done.

"This is *it*, Rosewood—I can feel it!" he kept saying, but hours later, we weren't any closer to an answer. Dr. Keene had packed up around dinnertime, telling me to go home and get some rest, but I had a few experiments to mind, the autopsy notes to type up. It wasn't until I remembered the little dog, waiting for me—and his dinner—that I pushed back my chair with a sigh and snapped off my desk lamp.

Work. Eat. Walk the dog. Practice my transformations. Try to sleep. I felt perched on top of a bicycle that didn't move, no matter how fast I pedaled the wheels round and round. I needed to crack the case of the angel killer, so that Dr. Keene would work with me, so that I'd learn to control myself, so that I'd be safe…and then what? Before I'd met Ruby, that was as far as I'd dared to imagine. Then she'd shown up, believing in me, saying I'd make a brilliant doctor. She opened a door to a world I'd never imagined existing, and then she left, and it was as though that door shut tight again.

Out in the hall, the hospital was sleepy and quiet, and I made my way downstairs to the sound of my own footsteps, my mind racing with thoughts, and then I pushed open the doors to the main floor and found *her*.

I was seeing things, it didn't make any sense, I was just thinking about Ruby and my eyes played tricks on me, and then I watched her hand come up and brush a lock of hair behind her ear as she studied the notebook she held.

"Ruby?"

She startled, turned, and then she noticed me, her lips curling into a smile so sweet I felt it warm me down to my toes.

"Peter!"

It was strange. Everything I knew about science, about physics, about how the light fell on her face and why her cheeks flushed and the very nature of her voice, moving in waves from her lips to my ears... but I couldn't begin to explain why as soon as I saw her, I smiled.

"What are you doing here?" I asked, and she laughed.

"Well, it's nice to see you, too!" She held up her notebook. "Meeting with Papa's doctors. My family's got me run ragged and this was the first I could get away. I'm dead on my feet!" She looked it. She had pale-purple bruises under her eyes, which darted around like she was looking for something just over my shoulder, and there was a kind of breathlessness in her voice I hadn't heard before. But maybe I was imagining it, because a second later she gave me a broad, easy smile and asked calmly, "How are you?"

"I'm, um, I'm—" Not sleeping? Always thinking about her? Wondering how I could see her again? "Fine."

"You're here late. The new job got you keeping long hours?"

"Oh! No—I mean—yes. I mean—well, we found something."

I watched her eyes go wide, and she leaned in closer. "Really! That's swell! I've been reading all about you in the newspaper, you know. 'The wizard assistant'—when I saw that I just about burst with pride! I wanted to tell everyone *I knew him when he was mopping floors,* and now here you are, running a big lab!"

She'd done it again, pulled me out of whatever box I'd been happy to live in, and I didn't know whether to be mad or grateful but I knew that I couldn't let her walk out of my life, not again.

But...how? How did I get to spend another minute with her? Could I ask her out for coffee? Dinner? People ate food, didn't they?

"Um, I was just heading out, but—"

"I've been reading about your lab!" she said, and her voice was breathless and fast again. "I'd love to be able to work in a place like that. My papa set up a laboratory for me, you know, in the back of my mother's garden. Nothing special, just whatever you can buy out the back of a magazine. I've got a few beakers and pipettes and a burner that's *useless,* really. But to think, you get to work in one of the best-stocked labs in Chicago! Golly, it must be amazing."

She gazed past me at the stairs leading up to the lab, and I remembered our talk in the Field Museum, when she told me how much she loved science, and without thinking I blurted out, "Do you want to see the lab?"

I just needed an excuse to keep her around, just for another second, and at first I felt like I'd shoved my foot in my mouth but then her face lit up with excitement.

"Really? You mean really, truly? Oh, *Peter,* I'd love that! Are you sure you won't get in trouble?"

No, but she had a wicked smile on her face, like that only made it better, more exciting, and I pulled the keys from my pocket.

"It'll be fine. Everyone else has already gone home. No one will know."

We climbed the stairs to the top floor, down the dark hallway, and when we reached the door, my hands shook so badly the key kept slipping in the lock. But I got it open, and Ruby let out a gasp of surprise.

"Gol-*lee!* Look at all this!" She stepped inside, her eyes wide. I'd left the lights off, but moonlight streamed through the high glass ceiling, turning everything silver and blue and reflecting off the instruments.

"You know...you can't tell anyone about whatever you see in here."

She spun around. "I would never. Ooh, look at the size of that Florence flask!" Her eyes lit up as she pointed at a huge round-bottomed glass beaker, which simmered over the low orange-blue flame of a burner, while a coil of tubing rose like frozen steam from its mouth, collecting the vapor.

"We had to manufacture it special! See, the size of the standard flasks just wouldn't do for the kind of distillation I had in mind. We needed something large enough to..." I paused, because this was usually the moment when the eyes of whoever I was talking to glazed over, but she put out a hand, touched my arm.

"Enough to what?" She had that same bright, curious expression that I'd noticed the first night we met.

"Enough to, um..." All right, Peter. Get a grip. I took a step to the flask. "Well, this one is distilling, well, mercury—mercury bichloride—from the tissue of the latest victim."

I turned to see Ruby, illuminated by the flickering of the flame under the flask, her skin soft gold, her eyes glittering. My throat went dry, and I stepped over to my desk and fumbled with my notes.

"The typical method for mercury distillation involves several acid baths, and it can take days to work through properly. But I had this idea to—"

I glanced back over my shoulder to see that Ruby had moved to the evidence table, one of the photographer's cameras in her hands. She set it down—hard. The back of the camera, where the film should go, popped open.

"Oh *gosh,* Peter. I'm so sorry, I just picked it up—I wasn't thinking! Did I ruin it? Is it—is it something important?"

I crossed over to the table and picked up the camera, nervous for a second before I recognized it.

"No," I said, "don't worry, it's fine. See? There's no film in it. We sent it out to be developed hours ago. No harm done.... Ruby? Ruby!"

·TWENTY-SEVEN

RUBY

No film. *No film.*

"Ruby, are you all right?"

I was cooked.

"Yes." *What now? WHAT NOW, RUBY?* "I'm fine."

"Are you sure? Do you need to sit down?"

Somewhere far away, Peter was talking to me, but all I could think was what this meant: a photo existed of me in a murdered man's room.

She's pale, she's faint...

I blinked, looked up at Peter. "I'm so sorry. Must be more tired'n I thought. I...I should be getting home."

A cloud of *!!!* exploded in his mind, panic that I was leaving, but I couldn't think about that anymore, I couldn't think about *him* anymore. It was over, it was too late, any minute he'd learn the truth about me, and I was an idiot to think I could charm him to let me into his lab, distract him long enough to destroy the evidence...I was also an idiot to think coming here was only because of the photo and not because of this brilliant beautiful boy, who was looking at me with confusion and desperation but not—*yet*—complete betrayal.

"Do you want to sit? I can make you some coffee, or—"

"Gosh, I would, it's just so late, but this was aces, really! Good luck—with everything." Oh dear. Why did I feel like I was about to burst into tears? His sweet gray eyes went soft, his face crumpled, and there at the edges, I could see glimmers of the real boy—Peter—who could never hide because his kind soul shone through.

"Oh, Peter. Goodbye. Thank you. Don't forget me!" A laugh burst out of me, huge and desperate and almost a sob, because of course he wouldn't forget the girl who lied to him, but I hoped through it all he didn't forget *me*, Ruby. "I...Oh, golly. I'm so glad I met you."

Now, go, I commanded myself, but I just wanted one more second, and right when I felt my resolve harden, he took my hand and—poof!—he *changed*.

Oh.

My.

I knew it, even without his saying a word, that this was him, the real him, Peter, but his *face*—

Handsome. Not just good-looking or even movie-star cute but knock-you-sideways-with-a-frying-pan, what-happened-to-the-air-in-this-room *handsome*.

Sharp jaw and full lips and narrow nose and dark eyebrows framing the most smoldering brown eyes I'd ever seen. Gorgeously messy curls falling over his forehead with such a deep richness, I wanted to rake my fingers through them. Taller, younger, every inch of his body in such perfect proportion that even though he still wore his shabby, out-of-style Guy clothes, they suddenly hung like a fashion plate.

And then *that look* on his face.

Like he'd just thrown off his clothes in one beautiful blaze of stupidity or bravery, it all rested on how I reacted.

"Is this—*you*?" I looked down at the hand in mine—how did he manage to reshape his bones? The texture of his skin?

"Yes?"

"But—" I looked back up at him and *bam!* He could stop traffic! He could stop *rockets*. "You're handsome. You're—you're a picture star!" I laughed. "What on earth are you doing sweeping floors? Go to Hollywood! Why wouldn't you choose to look like this all the time?"

Because I hate it, he thought, and gently pulled his hand away. *Because I don't want to be Peter. Because every time I see this face I think of my father and I can't stand it.*

"I didn't mean anything by that," I said quickly. "Just—I... like it. You. This face."

"Because it's handsome?"

"Actually—no," I answered, and I felt a nervous *swoop* in my belly. How could I put it? "Remember I said how I always recognized you?" I reached up to touch his cheek. "Something in your eyes... Only now it's not just your eyes, it's all over, and it's... You're beautiful, Peter. Inside and out."

The room felt very still. I could feel my heart thrumming in my chest like a strummed guitar string, and I wondered if Peter had cottoned to what I meant, that for the first time, I was seeing the whole him, nothing hidden, and it just looked *right*.

But his mind tossed like a storm. *Doesn't she see does she recognize...* A newspaper appeared, a photo across the front page. It was Peter's face but older, a middle-aged man with smile marks around his eyes, and wouldn't you know? It did ring a bell...*Had I seen it before?*

"Hang on," I said, frowning. "Why do you look familiar?" The second the words came out of my mouth, it popped into both our minds. A horrible train accident, a death, and on the front page: BELOVED ACTOR KILLED IN TRAIN DERAILMENT. I could see the glamor shot now, could remember the lights dimmed in the theater district, his poster in the window of every playhouse downtown.

But I couldn't figure how that involved Peter, until it flickered through his head.

The man, his *father,* telling him to stay in, hide, and Peter going out, getting in trouble, boys, fighting, his transformations beyond control, running, running, shouting, train tracks, a stuck foot, the rumble of a train engine, bright bright blinding light, shouting, heavy weight, shove, tumble, and then—*screech, scream, crunch, crash.*

Guilt.

Guilt blame crushing weight.

He thought it was his fault his father was dead?

The *shame* burned me like a wall of heat, and I winced. I wasn't supposed to be seeing this, it was private, and I pulled back.

"I'm sorry. Maybe I'm mistaken," I said quickly, but Peter shook his head.

"No. No, I don't think so. This person—me—I'm supposed to be dead. I...lost control, and...bad things happened." He looked up, around the lab. "That's what I'm doing here. The doctor who runs this laboratory, Dr. Keene, he's done research into, well, people like me. At least, he has some ideas about how a person *could* change. I got a job in the morgue because I need his help, to learn how to control...

this." He put out a hand, and for a moment I thought it was a trick of the flickering light of the burners before I realized he was changing, skin and bones and size and shape, quick as falling water. "He promised me, if I helped him with this case, he'd show me his research. I've got to make sure it doesn't happen again, someone hurt because of me."

"That's crazy," I said, and he blinked, gave me a funny look. I just wanted to grab him by his shirtfront and shout right into his perfect face that he was *mad* to hate himself. Didn't he know there were real monsters out there? I'd consider myself something of an expert when it came to recognizing souls, and his was so pure it made me feel better about this whole damn disaster of a world.

"Crazy to want to keep people safe from me?" he asked, and this time I did grab him, his wrists tight in my hands.

"Crazy to think anyone would need protecting from you! To think you're anything but good and kind and sweet and honest and brave and—damn it, Peter!" I closed my eyes and went up on my toes and landed a kiss right on that beautiful, perfect mouth.

Just for a second, but shoot, I lost track of time, the feel of his mouth scrambling my insides, and then his free hand came up and climbed the back of my neck and tangled in my hair and I knew if I didn't push him away that second I'd melt on the floor.

"Sorry!" What had he done to the air in this room! "I just—sorry!"

But the kiss had worked: he'd stopped thinking about his father and whatever horrible thing he thought he'd done. All he wanted *now* was to do what we'd been doing two seconds ago.

Damn. I'd never get out of here alive.

"No, I—I've wanted—" He caught my eyes, then he caught his

breath, and when he talked again, he was steady: "I've never met anyone like you before. I didn't even really think there *was* anyone like you."

Careful, Ruby.

"Golly!" A nervous laugh erupted from me, and I slipped my hand from his. "Head down to any bar on the North Side and you'll find a dozen vamps just like me! You know flappers—we're worse than rats!"

"That's not true," Peter said, "even if you pretend like it is."

You could've knocked me sideways with a feather. Who was this? The Guy I knew would never. But then, this wasn't Guy.

"All right," I said, shaky. "So who am I?"

"Smart," he said without thinking. "Curious. You like asking questions and learning things. You let people underestimate you. You keep your real self at a distance. You wear masks, just like me." He reached out and touched a finger to my cheek and I felt a shiver roll from my spine to my toes, which would probably stay rooted to this floor for the rest of my life.

"Am I right?" he asked, with the kind of smile that turned my insides to goo.

"You dope," I said, trying not to smile back. "You already know you are. Too bad. Being just a party girl sounds like a lot of fun."

"Ruby Newhouse is meant for a lot more than parties," he said, so sincerely that I got an ache in my chest, because Ruby Newhouse was headed for prison. But he was waiting for me to say more, his mind open and curious and even though there was a voice in my head positively screaming *GET OUT AND LEAVE THIS POOR BOY ALONE*, I just couldn't help it. My minutes of freedom were numbered and I wanted to spend them talking dreams with a sweet-souled boy. Sue me.

"I want to go to law school. I want to be a lawyer. And I know, a woman lawyer, but it's not as ridiculous an idea as you might—"

"It's not ridiculous," he said, and he meant it. Actually, he thought it sounded brilliant. "Your father's a lawyer, after all. Is that what you want to do? Become state's attorney?"

"State's attorney!" I laughed, and then I saw his face. "Oh! You're serious?"

"Why not? You're smarter than any lawyer I've ever seen. Tougher, too. If not the state's attorney then what?"

"Well, I'd like to help people. My father taught me to respect the law. He says that in a perfect society, all men and women are equal. But just look around! We hardly live in a perfect society. Every day, I see people treated differently based on who they are or what they look like. And they don't know their rights! Or they do, but they're scared. Or their rights have been taken away by people in power. A good lawyer—the kind of lawyer I'll be—can ensure that the law is respected and upheld, and that means you've gotta protect the weak and punish the wicked."

"What kind of wicked?" he asked.

I laughed. "Are you joking? Corruption, graft, crime, and that's just what makes the evening papers. I just…I have to *do something*. To help. To stop it or at least…People who do bad things need to see that they can be stopped. Women need to know their rights will be respected. I've lived it, being treated as small or weak or unimportant or dumb just because I'm a girl. I want to show everyone what a girl—a woman—can do. It's all I've ever wanted."

As soon as I said the words, I felt like a complete idiot. None of this mattered. I'd been caught, it was over, and I'd never be a lawyer. Those wicked men would walk free.

"Look," I said quickly. "I know I get carried away, and I know most people don't care—"

"I care," he said, looking into my face with steady eyes. "I understand exactly what you mean."

It sounded like just a line at first, and then his mind opened up like a beautiful flower and I saw it. To stay hidden, he'd stepped into other bodies, other lives, for years. Men, women, all ages, sizes, colors. They were temporary disguises, but he saw how the world shifted around him with every change, the scales tipping one way or another, the people who thought they had a right to ignore him or hate him or hurt him, just because of how he looked.

And then he saw me. He saw me wanting to make sure that didn't happen to anyone, and his whole heart just about burst open with pride. He couldn't imagine anything better. He couldn't imagine a better person to try.

Oh, what was he doing?

What had I done?

TWENTY-EIGHT
PETER

Ruby stared at me in the dancing light of the burners, her face like a question.

I felt stripped open, bare, but I recognized that same feeling in the way she stood looking at me. Like for the first time in either of our lives, someone had *seen* us.

I took a step forward, then another, until we were so close she had to look up to catch my eyes. The quiet gurgles of my experiments filled the air, the soft, hushing *hiss* of vapor releasing. I could see Ruby's pulse kicking at her throat, and I bent down and touched my mouth to that spot. Everything seemed to slow down. My lips traveled up her neck, to her jaw, her cheek, her ear, her temple. I felt like I was standing at the edge of a cliff, my whole body shaky, but I wasn't scared. Actually, I couldn't remember ever feeling this unafraid.

When I pulled away to look into her face again, I saw that her eyes had closed. The edges of her lashes glittered—was she crying? And then her eyes snapped open, and she was reaching for me, rising up on her toes slowly, carefully, graceful as a dancer, to brush her lips against mine.

It started out slow, Ruby's skin warm and soft and gentle. Every time we'd kissed before, I'd worn disguises, the world around us chaotic and messy. Now we were alone, in the twinkling light of the lab, and these were my lips she was kissing. I felt every touch, every sensation, every tremble, and it was so overwhelming—like we'd discovered fire, right there, together.

My fingers tangled into her hair, her hat tumbling off her head, and I reached around with my other hand, pressed her closer to me, hips to hips. The kiss had turned into something essential, insatiable, I didn't want to stop. Her hands were reaching for me, too, one slipping up under my shirt, another at the back of my neck, her fingernails scraping me so gently that I couldn't keep in a small moan.

I yanked off my coat and let it drop to the floor, put my arms back around her, and lifted her onto the edge of the table. I ran one of my hands down her side, down her silk stocking. I just wanted *her*. Every inch of her. But I didn't know how to say that or ask for that or even where to begin, and then she whispered to me, "*Yes.*"

She had her eyes closed, head tipped back, and I touched my lips to her throat so I could feel the vibrations her words made, "*Yes, yes, ye—*"

"What in the hell is happening here?!"

The lights snapped on and *jump—pull away—door—Dr. Keene— Dr. Keene—standing in the doorway—my face, I'm not wearing my Guy Rosewood disguise!! What do we do what do we do what do we—*

"You *cad*!" Ruby hopped off the table and gave me a sharp slap on the cheek, and before I knew what was happening, she burst into tears.

"I *told* you I *didn't* want to *neck*! How *could* you!"

What? I thought frantically.

"What?" Dr. Keene said, and Ruby rushed toward him.

"Oh, *thank you* for getting me away from that monster! He said he just wanted to go for a walk, go somewhere quiet. If you hadn't come in—" She interrupted herself with a fresh round of sobs, as Dr. Keene, bewildered, tried to figure out if he was furious at finding two strangers in his precious lab or if he should comfort the pretty girl calling him a hero. Eventually, duty won out.

"You're not supposed to be in here! How did you get in?"

"How did we get in? The door was unlocked!"

"Unlocked! *Rosewood!*"

Dr. Keene scowled.

"Don't be mad, we'll leave and—"

"Now hold on," Dr. Keene started to say, when Ruby began crying again.

"Oh no—*please* no! If my parents find out, they'll flay me! Please, we'll just go! We didn't mean to come in here! We didn't know this room was anything special!"

At last, Dr. Keene seemed to notice Ruby's very blue eyes, and I could see him melt. "Oh, fine," he said, a fond smile on his face. "Get out of here—and don't ever let me catch you sneaking around again!"

Ruby let out a squeal of delight and gave him a quick kiss on his cheek, which glowed pink, and then pulled me toward the door.

"Hold on, Slick. Not you." Dr. Keene frowned at me with something like recognition. Ruby looked over, eyes wide with panic, but she didn't understand—she needed to go! She couldn't do anything for me, and she'd only get in more trouble if she stayed. SHE NEEDED TO GO! With one last, desperate look into my eyes, she wrenched herself away.

Dr. Keene didn't bother watching her leave. He tossed a few files on a nearby desk, eyeing me as he did.

"Sit," he said, pointing at one of the chairs. "I know you."

"No, you don't."

"*Sit*. You were at the morgue a few days ago. I remember you. You disappeared, and now here you are." He spread out his hands. "What are you doing here?"

"I didn't—I'm not—" *Attack him*

Knock him out

But I didn't know how to knock anyone out.

Change

Disappear

Change into *who*? And *how*? He wouldn't let me out of his sight!

Okay then. Panic. Seemed like the only option left. My body took care of that, my hands shaking and my vision blurry and a sheen of sweat appearing on my forehead. I raised a hand to my face, running my fingers over my cheeks. My cheeks. Mine. Me.

Deep breath

Panic was what Guy Rosewood did.

I'm Peter, and I'm going to get out of this mess

"Look, you caught me," I said, and if I didn't sound as smooth as Ruby, at least I didn't stammer. "I work for the *Tribune*. They gave me a sawbuck to sneak into your lab."

But Dr. Keene rolled his eyes. "Come on—a reporter? You're just a kid. And a bad liar." He stood up and walked over to the telephone.

"Wait!" I yelped. "I just—Everyone in the city is talking about you! I had to see for myself!"

"You tried to get into my lab *before* we made our findings public,"

Dr. Keene said, brandishing the receiver at me like a club. "And I don't have time for this." He picked up the phone. "Hello, operator? Yes, this is Dr. Keene. Get me Detective Parcell."

Wincing, I dropped my head into my hands, like I could knead a plan into my skull. How long before Dr. Keene recognized me, same as Ruby had done, and figured out who I really was?

"Hullo, Parcell, it's Keene. I'm at the lab. Look." He turned his back toward me, hunching over the receiver. "I've got this kid here, he broke in. Seems harmless but I don't have the patience for him right now. Think you could—Right. That'd be swell."

Change. Disappear. Run.

And then what?

"No, don't send someone. You'd better come yourself. The photograph came back," Dr. Keene said in a low voice, and I lifted my head out of my hands. "I think it's going to be *her*! The fellow at the photography lab called me as soon as it developed, and put it right into my hands....No, I haven't opened it yet....I was hoping my assistant would be here...wanted him to take a look with me, but he's left and—All right. I'll see you then."

The receiver made a *clatter-click* as he set it down, while my heartbeat thudded in my chest.

"Police coming soon. They'll sort you out."

I couldn't help it. I leaned forward in my seat. "Did you say...you got a photograph? Of the angel killer?"

For half a second, Dr. Keene gave me a look that would curdle milk, and then he let out a laugh. "Maybe we did, maybe we didn't."

"But if you did, if you caught her, you'd be the most famous scientist in the country! In the world!" *You'd get your lab,* I thought. *And I'd get access to your research!*

I couldn't lose Guy Rosewood—not now!

Dr. Keene let out another laugh. "Well, I guess you're right! If this is really her, and *if* she can be identified." He pulled the envelope from his jacket pocket and gazed at it with a fond, dewy expression. "You know, my science tied this all together!"

It was, technically, *my* science, but I didn't care. Dr. Keene could take all the credit he wanted, so long as he kept his end of our deal. He ran his fingers along the edge of the envelope, as though about to open it, then gave me a sly look.

"You can see it on the front page," he said, and he tossed it onto the desk before taking a seat and letting out a sigh.

Get out of here

Run

GO

I squeezed my eyes tight for a moment to clear my head. I'd watched Dr. Keene for months; I knew he didn't care about some kid sneaking into his lab, but he sure as hell wouldn't let an opportunity for fame and respect slip through his fingers.

"You're wasting your evening sitting here with me?" I asked, glancing at the clock, and Dr. Keene, who'd propped his feet up on the desk and closed his eyes, just grunted. "I mean, if you've broken your case, don't you need to move fast? That girl—if you did manage to get a photo of her—must know she's been caught, right? She's probably skipping town right now, while you're busy minding me. Do you care more about making sure I get a slap on the wrist for trespassing than solving the case that could define your career?"

He'd opened his eyes and dropped his feet back to the floor, and I watched as his gaze slid sideways to the envelope.

Open it, I thought. *And get so excited you forget all about me and run right out the damn door.*

"Aren't you going crazy not knowing? If you caught her?"

Dr. Keene gave me a dry look. "You think I don't know what you're doing, kid? You want to see, too, don't you?" Honestly, right at that minute I couldn't care less about the identity of the angel killer, I just wanted to *leave,* but I broke into a grin, the kind that said *Hey, you got me, but could you fault a fellow for trying?*

And wouldn't you know? No, he could not.

Laughing, Dr. Keene reached around to one of the dissection trays and retrieved a scalpel. "Guess I should tell you to keep your mouth shut, but on account of you're going straight from here to jail, we'll not worry about that."

With one neat slice, he opened the envelope, then reached in and slowly, *slowly* pulled the photo free...

He blinked, a strange look on his face.

"Well, well..." he said, his voice soft.

My heart started pounding. *What are you still doing sitting there?* I wanted to shout at him. *GET OUT OF HERE.*

But Dr. Keene hadn't moved. His mouth pulled into a frown, and I couldn't help it, I glanced down out of pure curiosity.

Soft, blurry profile

Full, dark lips

Two fringes of eyelashes, cast down, brushing the tops of her cheeks

She was in motion, her body like a dozen different ghosts placed on top of each other: hands balled into fists and resting on the arms of a plush chair, crossed ankles tucked underneath her. And her face...her *face...*

It was Ruby.

I stopped breathing.

No, it wasn't Ruby.

It couldn't be her.

I only thought so because I'd just seen her and because she filled up my brain and my heart and my body, and it couldn't be her.

But it was.

Blurred. Indistinct. I could see why Dr. Keene squinted with a frown, why he hadn't put together the shadowy girl in the photo with the vibrant one in the lab, but I knew. With every cell in my body, I *knew*.

It was Ruby. She had come here tonight to steal that damn photo because she murdered Rex Blanchot and half a dozen other unfortunates, too.

Well.

What had happened to the floor to make it tilt so violently sideways like that?

"Gosh, there she is," Dr. Keene said. "A little hard to make out, but no matter. Once she's on the front page, someone will know the girl!"

Front page. Ruby's face in every newspaper.

They'd find her, arrest her, *hang* her.

"Kid? You look a little...pale?"

The buzzing started in my hands and got faster and faster, my control over my body slipping away. Then my arms went jerky, wild, my bones and skin and hair, every inch of me on fire—*DON'T CHANGE, NOT IN FRONT OF DR. KEENE, DON'T DO IT, KEEP CONTROL*—and every time I closed my eyes and saw her, it hit me like a wave of water. *Ruby's a killer Ruby's a murderer Ruby's a liar Ruby's dead.*

I jumped to my feet, but before I could catch my balance, they swelled and shrank, so fast I stumbled to the ground, and even though I squeezed my eyes shut, I knew I was changing. I felt my hair stretch, curl, disappear, felt my bones pop, heard the rips in my shirt and Dr. Keene's confused shouting.

"What are you—*How* are you—*Rosewood?*"

Oh *no!* I glanced up, feeling my Guy Rosewood mask fall into place, and saw the look of horror on Dr. Keene's face before another face took over, then another, another...

"You can change!"

No...*no*...

Gotta get out—gotta go!

My legs spasmed and sputtered but I wrenched myself up. Everything tilted and spun so badly I could barely see anything, but there, in Dr. Keene's hand, the photograph, the envelope...

I didn't think. I dragged myself forward and snatched the photograph from his hand—when he grabbed me, I changed into someone *big* and gave him a shove that knocked him backward into a table full of glassware, which smashed to the ground with a thousand sharp clatters. I winced, I didn't want to hurt him, but there was no time. All I could do was hold tight to the photo, gather up my coat, and *run,* out the door, through the hall, down the stairs, willing myself to *stop changing stop changing,* but every time I tried to gain control it slipped away again.

"Stop! Security! Stop him!"

Dr. Keene's voice, the sound of my footsteps, my head woozy and spinning, I hit the first-floor landing and thought *Someone young, someone small, someone no one will notice.* My arms and legs shrank, my clothes growing huge around me and my feet flopping in shoes several sizes too big, but it worked. When I walked through the lobby, breathing hard but still able to keep my mask in place, I got a few curious glances from doctors and nurses and patients in the waiting area and nothing more. By that time, Dr. Keene had appeared, shouting about a man, tall, dark hair, and I just sailed through the front door, my breath coming out in frosty, pale clouds, the photograph still clutched in my hand.

Where to go? Where to go?

I didn't want to run, but I had no choice.

Pound-pound-pound-pound

Down the front steps, out to the sidewalk, and with every footstep, another thought jolted through me like a lightning bolt.

Ruby is the angel killer

Dr. Keene knows what I am

He knows what Guy Rosewood is

Guy Rosewood—the boardinghouse—the dog! The little dog!

I'd bet every cent to my name that right this second Dr. Keene was looking up my address, and in ten minutes he'd call a police car straight to the boardinghouse. I couldn't let them throw the dog into the streets!

Before I could think to do it, my legs stretched long and muscular and perfect for running, and I made the forty-minute walk in fifteen, arriving at the front door with my lungs on fire.

Guy Rosewood slipped into place just as I pushed open the door to the sound of Mrs. Coyne's thumping phonograph.

"G'evening!" I said, walking quickly through the front parlor, and Mrs. Coyne jumped to her feet.

"Hello! There's supper ready—come on in before—"

"Sorry," I said, and I made for the stairs, "got to run to, um, washroom."

"All right, dearie, but you head back down soon's you—oh! There's the telephone, hold on!"

I froze, foot on the step, hand gripping the banister, as Mrs. Coyne hurried off to the big black telephone currently screaming in the corner.

"Hello? *Hello!* Wait! Wait—can't hear ya! Let me turn down this music!"

Go

But I couldn't move until Mrs. Coyne cut off the phonograph with a sharp *squeal* and returned to the 'phone.

"What's that you were sayin'? Oh, Rosewood? Yeah, he just came—"

I *ran*, up the stairs, down the hall, listening to Mrs. Coyne shout my name—first in her regular, friendly way, then with alarm, then with something like *fury*. Her footsteps followed mine, and I only just got my key in the door, only just got inside with the lock clicked closed as she arrived, pounding her fists and shouting, "Open up! What'd you do! POLICE LOOKIN' FOR YOU—OPEN UP!"

Dark in the room, but I didn't care. I ran right to the open closet, where the little white dog trembled in a corner.

"Shh…shhh…" I told him, gently pushing him off the bag on the floor, the one I kept packed with food and clothes and money. I pulled it onto my shoulder and slipped the photograph inside before reaching down for the dog. He was watching the door, behind which Mrs. Coyne still screamed, with a look on his face that said *There is no way I'm going out* there.

"It'll be all right," I whispered, and I scooped him up and dropped him into the bag next to the photograph, where he sat with his front paws and fuzzy head sticking out from the top.

"OPEN UP OR I'LL BREAK THIS DAMN DOOR DOWN MYSELF!" Mrs. Coyne shouted, and I didn't doubt her for a second. A rumbling, deeper voice asked her something—one of the other tenants—and when Mrs. Coyne answered, "The police are after 'im, is what! Help me get this door down!" the pounding on the door went deeper, stronger, the whole thing vibrating on cheap hinges.

The little dog gave a terrified yelp, and I put my hand on his back as I hurried over to the washroom to retrieve my notebook. Then to the window, wedged shut with decades of flaking paint, which hardly budged until I changed into someone ten times brawnier and my new muscles practically tore the damn sash right out of the wall.

Gusts of icy wind burst into the room, but I threw my legs over the sill, holding the bag and the dog close, and dropped down onto the fire escape. It shook and shivered under my weight, so I changed again, this time to a slim, reedy boy, swimming in Guy Rosewood's bigger clothes.

Behind me, I heard the door burst open, and I ducked down just as Mrs. Coyne scrambled into the room. My fingers burned on the icy metal of the fire escape, but my new body was light and strong and quick and by the time Mrs. Coyne stretched her head out the window, screeching Guy Rosewood's name, I'd made it to the street and instantly changed again: an older man with steely-gray hair, tall but bent with the weight of the bag.

"Rosewood! Hey, you!"

Squinting, I looked up. "Eh?"

"Seen a tall fella come through there?"

I put a trembling hand up to my ear. "Wha's that?"

"I said, did you SEE a MAN run through THERE?"

But I decided the old man, in addition to being hard of hearing, couldn't see very well, so after blinking up at Mrs. Coyne in a bewildered way, I gave a friendly wave and continued, stiff-legged, down the alley, reaching the street as a trio of black-topped cop cars screeched to a stop, sirens moaning.

Under my hand, the little dog ducked down into the bag, and I kept patting him, kept patting him, whispering to him in my wheezy old voice that everything was okay. As I pulled my coat tight against my throat, the police poured from their cars and ran into the boarding-house, searching for a man who didn't exist and a name they'd soon discover meant nothing. I turned my back and disappeared down the street, no one bothering to give me a second glance.

TWENTY-NINE
RUBY

I wasn't looking at the camera

Step, step, step—down the stairs.

I'd worn heavy makeup

Through the lobby, to the front door.

My red hair won't show

Out to the street, still running.

Peter's falling in love with me, he'll protect me

My stomach twisted so badly I almost lost my footing. I couldn't think about that, about him, about his arms around me and his lips on my skin and his shining *star* of a soul. I was such an idiot! I'd gotten him into a jam, and all I could think about was myself. Oh, *damn*, what had I done? I felt like an egg, cracked open, and my heart beat faster, and—

PUT HIM OUT OF YOUR HEAD, RUBY NEWHOUSE, HAVE YOU FORGOTTEN THE COLOSSAL MUCK OF TROUBLE YOU'RE IN??

The picture! The picture that was now being developed and would soon arrive back at the hospital and appear in every paper. But so what if they printed some blurry, dim picture of me? No one would think I had any reason to go off to the Hotel Le Grand at midnight, dressed in a costume worth twice my father's salary, to murder some scum of a man. No one would connect Ruby Newhouse with Rex Blanchot that evening.

Oh.

Except for Maggie.

DAMN it.

I was cooked.

An hour later I rang her bell and told her to get dressed and take me for a drive in her sports car. Lovely Maggie, she didn't even care that the clock said near midnight or that I'd never done anything like this before. She just cinched the waist of her dressing gown tighter and told her butler to make me a cup of tea while I waited, and then she reappeared, dressed like a sweet little soldier in a slate-colored suit and a pair of slim-legged pants—golly, I didn't even think she *owned* a pair of pants!—ready for anything.

"Let's go," she said, wriggling her fingers into mint-green leather gloves, her thoughts prepared for the worst—I'd failed to get the photos, Blanchot had duped me as well, he'd been tipped off that Maggie was after him and demanded an even bigger payment—while still fierce with love for me.

Something caught in my throat and I wanted to throw my arms around my friend and kiss her, but the butler was watching and the valet had brought the car round, and so I just nodded and followed her out to the drive.

"Where to?" she asked, and I told her anywhere. Somewhere quiet and private.

"Why, Ruby Newhouse, are you asking me to park with you?" she said, and the giggle that came out of her was slightly frantic, her hands shaking as she settled them on the steering wheel.

Something's wrong. What's wrong? she wondered. I touched her arm.

"Deep breaths, darling. You're safe, I promise."

She turned her big brown eyes to me. "And you?"

"Drive. I'll tell you the whole gruesome story when we get there." Wearing a tight smile, I gave her a squeeze.

The engine roared and the car leapt forward, and as Maggie navigated the road, her mind swam with possibilities, each worse than the last and every single one miles from the truth.

"Here we are," she said, fifteen minutes later, her voice shivering as she drew the car up to a rocky, secluded promontory overlooking the lake. Saturday night and this spot would be dotted with cars and couples like beetles on a log, but tonight we were alone. Nothing to hear but the crackle of tree limbs, soft bird sounds, and the soothing *whoosh* from the water.

"I know it's frozen but let's get out, shall we? It's absurdly dark in here," Maggie said, popping open the door. She left the headlamps on, and they shot their beams out over the lake like twin lighthouses, giving the front of the car an eerie glow, while everything else was coated silver in the moonlight. I slid next to her on the hood, still warm from the drive so the bite in the air felt more like a nibble, and after Maggie draped the driving blanket over our laps, tucking us in together, I felt almost snug.

"Ruby, I can't stand it anymore: tell me what happened."

Here we go. I swallowed, just once, and then I reached into my pocketbook and pulled out the file with her photos.

In the dim glow of the headlamps I saw her eyes go wide.

"Is it…"

"It's all there. Photos, negatives. No one will ever know."

A huge, rushing wave of relief filled Maggie's mind and heart—I could feel it sweep over her, lifting up the weight she'd carried and smashing it to pieces.

No matter what happens, I told myself, *I don't regret doing that for her—or the other people in Blanchot's steamer trunk.*

"Maggie, there's something important I have to tell you," I said, shifting sideways so I could look her right in the eye, and she went stiff again.

Did he hurt her? she wondered. *Did he do something to her?*

"Maggie. He's dead."

"Wh-what? Dead?" Her eyes went wide. "How?"

"I killed him."

A bomb seemed to explode in her mind, scattering all her thoughts to bits. Her mouth opened and shut while she tried to pull those fragments into some kind of sense. *Killed him? How? Why? What happened? Killed him?*

"I murdered him." Still looking into her face, I reached down and took her hands between mine. "I threw mercury bichloride in his face and when he was distracted, I knocked him sideways with a fire poker. Take a breath and listen to me carefully. He was a very bad man, and *I threw poison at him and then murdered him.*"

Poison? she thought, and she said, "Oh."

Ruby killed a bad man, she thought, and she said, "Oh."

Just like the…, she thought, and she said, *"Oh."*

"Yes."

"What?"

"What you're thinking. Yes. That."

Maggie blinked. "I—I'm not thinking anything!"

"Maggie. It's all right. The girl in the papers? That's me. I killed Blanchot, and he wasn't my first. He attacked me for stealing the photos, and I killed him."

She didn't want to believe me. She wondered if I was joking, and a hysterical giggle slipped out before she clapped a hand over her mouth. Then she thought, *He attacked her? Because of me?*

"It's not your fault," I said quickly, and she blinked at me.

"R-right." She took a breath. "Okay. Okay. Then…" *What now?* "We need to move the body, right?"

MOVE THE BODY? Now it was my turn to blink at her.

"We have the car. Do you think we can carry him out, the two of us? I could pull round the back of the hotel…" She trailed off, wondering how to get him out of there without anyone seeing. All I could do was stare at her. She wanted to help me move the damn *body*?

"Wh-what are you laughing about?" she asked me, and oh, I couldn't help it—I thought my ribs might burst apart.

"I just t-told you I'm a flipping murderess!" I gasped. "Why aren't you hauling me off to the cops!"

"Well, but, you're not a *mean* murderer, right? Those men who d-died—they weren't good people, were they? That's what the stories said. They were wretched criminals who just hadn't gotten caught, like that horrible Blanchot. You never killed anyone who didn't deserve it." She gave me a cautious look. "Right?"

I didn't know what to say. I couldn't tell her that I'd looked into the minds of the people I'd killed and searched for any scrap of decency or love or honor or regret—and found nothing. That I had killed those people and still slept spectacularly well. That the alternative—brushing up with minds of pure evil and leaving them be—would have eaten me up far quicker.

So I just nodded.

And she nodded back. "Of course."

"Of course?"

"Ruby, I don't know anyone with a bigger sense of justice than you. Look at this!" She lifted up the file. "How many people would risk their lives cleaning up someone else's mistake?"

"You didn't make a mistake. That monster took advantage of you."

"See!" She laughed. "That's just what I mean!"

"But I'm a *murderer*, Maggie."

"Well...You said he attacked you. He tried to kill you, didn't he?" Her voice went quiet. "He...he threatened me, you know, when I told him I wouldn't give him what he wanted...I'd believe if he saw someone steal from him, he'd try to kill them."

"Yes. He tried."

"See? Isn't that...what's it called? Self-defense! And given the choice between my best friend dead or my best friend a notorious murderess of evil people, I have no doubt which I'd prefer." She nodded once, briskly. "Right. So. The body."

"Too late with that. The police've already got it. And there's more. I don't think it was any accident that Blanchot went after you, Maggie. I think he was working under Dennis Ferry. Ferry must've figured you were helping me and thought he'd distract *and* discredit you with a nasty little scandal."

"Ooh, what a rat!" Maggie said, mad enough to spit. "Ruby, we have to get rid of him!"

"Not so quick," I said, with a grimace. "Blanchot managed to snap a picture of me, just before it went topsy-turvy. It's only a matter of time before someone pins me as the angel killer, and then I'll have bigger problems than Dennis Ferry. It's over, Maggie." The car had gone cold, and even the blanket felt thin against the breeze. Wrapping my arms around myself, I shivered. "I just wanted you to know, first."

"But...But...You can't—I know! We'll get you out of the country! I've been planning that trip to Paris for ages. No one'd bat an eyelash if I took you with me! We can leave tonight, right now!"

I shook my head. "My family. My father. I can't leave. Who knows what Ferry would do to them?"

"Oh..." She frowned down at her lap, then snapped her fingers. "Then we'll get you a lawyer! A good one, the best that money can buy! And we'll make sure everyone knows just how evil this Blanchot fellow was. I'll even testify. I'll tell them everything, hang those stupid photographs! You saved your life—and mine, too—and I'm not going to let anyone haul you off to prison!"

She'd drawn herself up on the hood of the car until she was like some proud little statue of justice, and my heart felt so full I thought it might burst. I threw my arms around her neck, kissed her cheek.

"You're a doll, you know that?" I said, and she grinned and poked me in the ribs.

"Kisses? You *did* want to park with me, you wicked girl."

It felt so good to laugh.

"What are you hoping to find in all that filth?" Maggie asked, wandering over to where I sat at her dining table surrounded by all the papers and photographs from Ferry's file. "There weren't any photos of Ferry in there."

"No. There wouldn't be." I sat back in the dining chair and stretched my arms. We'd been up all night, me sifting for any clues, Maggie offering increasingly more ridiculous ideas to save me, kidnap me, smuggle me across the border.

"This is his blackmail," I continued, "but I'm certain these are copies Blanchot made for himself, probably without Ferry even knowing. The originals are out there, somewhere. But where?" I spread out a handful of photos in a line. "Some of these rooms look similar... Could they have been taken in the same place?"

I picked up another photo and pored over its details, ignoring the pinch behind my eyes. Outside, I could hear the birdsong of early morning. I'd left a message with Mrs. Ritter, of course, about where I was. The last thing I wanted was for anyone to be worried. But I also didn't want them to see me led away in handcuffs for a baker's dozen of murders...

"Roo?"

Blinking, I realized I'd completely missed something Maggie had said. "What's that?"

"I said, what about bribery? To get your photo back. I've got plenty to pawn. That out-of-fashion fur from my grandmama...or remember the hideous brooch What's-His-Name got me? You know, the one shaped like a bug?"

"Oohh, no, it was a *beetle*! Ugh. Pawning's too good for it. That thing should be burned."

"I bet it would be enough, don't you think?"

Did I?

Could I sway Peter to destroy the photograph? Would he take a match to it, for me?

I felt it, last night. He was falling in love. If I went to him, if I asked him to, if I used my best wounded-deer tricks and dressed up in my most pathetic frock and cried crocodile tears, told him only he could save me...

He'd do it.

And I'd destroy the most truly decent soul I'd ever met.

What was it about this boy that made him so special? He was cute—more than cute, really—who would've thought that Guy Rosewood's pale, forgettable face hid a veritable MOVIE STAR—but so what? I'd kissed cute boys before. Smart, funny, witty boys. Boys with trust funds and sharp suits.

Boys who never left me feeling like I was flying.

For all the time I spent searching under rocks for slimy monsters and soulless killers, maybe I should've paid more attention to the people on the other side of the fence.

Peter would do the right thing. I couldn't let him do anything less.

"No bribery," I said, steadying myself. "But we should still *ab-so-tive-ly* burn that brooch."

"Couldn't you at least try to tell your side of the story? Contact that reporter, tell her you want to confess, get her to write about you as a hero. The public wouldn't judge you if they understood why you did it."

Vivian's cool eyes, ringed in violet powder, appeared in my mind. She could put out a crackerjack of a story, that was true. Although once she found out *I was the angel killer* and didn't tell her, she'd probably hang me herself. But in any case...

"It's not the public's opinion I'm worried about. The law doesn't leave a lot of wiggle when it comes to murder."

Her thoughts rose up like a sweet bubble. *Trust Ruby to risk her own life to help all those people...*

"Putting you away would be a crime," she sighed.

"Most people would say the real crime was the murders."

But even so... Maggie thought, just as the bell rang.

"Oh applesauce! That's J.P.! I completely forgot we're supposed to go riding today! Listen, Roo, why don't you come with us?" *She'll be harder to find...*

I shook my head and began gathering up the papers and photographs. "No, I should get back home. See Papa, the girls..." Even though Maggie couldn't read my mind, I knew she knew what I was thinking. *See them while I can...*

"Oh, Roo," she said, rushing toward me. She threw her arms around my neck and kissed my cheek. "It will be all right in the end. I'm sure of it." She gave me another kiss and ran out to fetch J.P., while I turned back to the papers with a sigh.

What a ridiculous tangle. Time was running out and *still* I had no idea how to pin Ferry for his crimes...

I'd swept the photos into a neat pile and slid the least-scandalous one on top, when Maggie reappeared with J.P., dressed in heavy tweed with a thin cigarette between his lips.

"Roo!" He removed the cigarette to kiss my cheek. "Where the hell have you been?"

"Watching over my sick papa."

"Right! That. How is the old man, anyhow?"

"The same. Thank you for the flowers, by the way."

"Flowers? Doesn't sound like me. Must've been my valet," he said, shrugging; and as he slipped the cigarette back between his lips and his eyes grazed the photos, a single, surprised thought—*the Bull and Owl?*—leapt through his mind before disappearing again.

"Maggie, kid," he said, "why don't you get a dress like Ruby's?"

Bull and Owl?

"That *is* my dress, darling. I lent it to her last night."

I glanced down at the topmost photo: a portrait of three drunk men posed in an ornate parlor, one of the rooms that had popped up in a dozen different photos.

"Really? I've never seen it before."

What the hell was the *Bull and Owl*?

"Oh, don't be an idiot, don't you remember—"

"Hold on," I said, putting out a hand. "J.P., I found this photo in my father's files, and I'm trying to figure out where it could have been taken. You don't have any idea, do you?"

"Not the foggiest," J.P. said casually, though his mind told a different story: a tony gentlemen's club, wild parties. But there was an unease to the thoughts that made me dig deeper.

Rumors…Warnings…J.P. had been invited to a party there, had a good and fairly innocent time, planned to go back another night but a friend stopped him. *They offer a lot…but in exchange for a lot…Too many girls…Too many temptations…Secret photographs…Blackmail…*

"Are you sure?" I asked, pushing the photo under his nose, and Maggie gave me a look, wondering what was going on. "There was a note on the back of one of the photos. Something about a Bull and Owl?"

Not my best lie, but I was desperate. To my surprise, though, it was Maggie who turned on me.

"Oh, I know them!" she said. "They rent that brownstone on Schiller Street, not two blocks away—you can hear the parties from the garden! Mother has written the neighbors' association *three times* to try and shut them down but she never gets anywhere."

J.P. had a bored look on his face, but talking about the club was making him nervous.

"Sounds to me like they must have powerful members," I said to Maggie, but I kept my attention on J.P.'s thoughts. "You don't know who, do you?"

Maggie peered at me, confused, wondering what in the hell I was up to—*Why didn't she ask me about the Bull and Owl hours ago?*—but finally cottoned to my plan.

"Oh! Right, I think...I heard Dennis Ferry is a member. The alderman," she said; then she glanced at J.P. "You'd know, right, darling?"

J.P. simply shrugged. "Why would I?" he asked. "The car's running, Maggie, let's go." He paused to stub out his cigarette, fear lit up in his brain like fireworks at the mention of Ferry's name. Another memory emerged, hazy and blurred under several layers of alcohol. *J.P., stumbling around an expensive town house, looking for the washroom, trying to open a door, banging hard, yelling, and the door popping open to reveal Dennis Ferry, an office behind him...*

"Try that one more time," he said, his voice so cold it echoed, "and I'll have you dragged out to the lake and drowned."

"Hold on, darling," Maggie said. "I'm just going to walk Ruby to the door." She slipped her arm around mine and led me from the dining room.

"What was all *that* about?" she whispered. "How on earth did you figure out those photos are from the Bull and Owl Club?"

"Never mind that! If Ferry's a member, wouldn't that be an excellent place to hide his papers? All the evidence I need could be right there!"

"But who can search the building? Not the police!"

I raised an eyebrow at her.

"Oh, no, Ruby, you can't! It's too dangerous!"

"Not for me, it's not. Ferry would never guess I'd figured it out. Maybe I can sneak in, grab the evidence, and sneak out. Maggie, listen. If the police catch up to me before then…" I took her hands and squeezed. "Move Papa and Mama and the girls out of the city. Right away."

"Of course, darling, you know I wouldn't let a thing happen to them! But Ruby! I just keep thinking…if they're going to find out about you no matter what, there must be a way to show everyone you only meant to help people…" Her voice was soft but her mind spun. We made it to the door and she put out a hand to stop me.

"This isn't goodbye, is it?" she asked, and I gave her a kiss on the cheek.

"Don't worry. We'll see each other again before this is all over," I said, dearly glad—and not for the first time—that Maggie couldn't read my thoughts.

THIRTY
PETER

I sat in a small park with the little dog on my lap, across the street from Ruby's house, shivering and rubbing my eyes to stay awake and hoping I hadn't missed her.

I'd been there all night. Had she run? I might have, if I were her. I *did*.

And then there she was, hurrying down the block, her cheeks pink from the cold. I set the bag and dog down and stood, hoping she'd glance my way, hoping she'd remember the white-haired boy I'd transformed into at Herman Coward's party. Just as I thought she'd lost her touch, her head swung in my direction and a look of shock came over her—but not much shock. She'd been expecting something, if not me.

Carefully, she crossed the street, a smile on her face one second and then an uncertain frown.

She knew I knew.

"Sit?" I asked, gesturing to the bench, and Ruby made to take a seat when the little dog popped his head out of the bag and blinked at her with huge dark eyes.

"Oh!" she said, startled. "Well, hel-*lo*, handsome! What a big, strong pup you are!"

She reached down and nuzzled the dog behind his ears, taking a seat to coo at him and sending him into wagging wiggles of delight.

Traitor, I thought, but of course he fell in love with her in an instant. Hadn't I done the same thing?

"You have a dog! I didn't know that!" Ruby laughed as the dog stretched out on her lap belly up, pushing his nose into her hands like he couldn't get enough of her. "What's his name?"

"His name?" I frowned. "I...don't know."

"But isn't he yours?"

Was he? I'd found him on the streets, I'd taken him in and fed him and kept him safe. Did that make him mine?

"I guess I just never thought to name him," I said, shrugging, and I took a seat on the bench. When I looked up at Ruby the expression on her face was impossibly sad, just for a moment, and then she laughed again.

"Well, keep him away from my sister Henrietta. She insisted on naming our cat Mr. Hubert and I don't think he's ever forgiven us." She kept running her hands over the little dog, who'd closed his eyes and looked ready to take a long, luxurious nap.

And then. "I know why you're here. You saw it."

"I have it," I said.

She gave me a sharp look, but I just swallowed hard and pulled out the cardboard envelope, passing it over to her.

Her fingers trembled, and then in one motion, she pulled the photograph free.

I couldn't read her as she studied her own face. I couldn't even read myself. Was I angry she'd killed people? That she'd used me to get close to the investigation? Or was I just angry she hadn't told me the truth?

"That sonuvabitch didn't even get my angles right," she said, and she slid it back in and set the envelope down on the bench before burying her fingers in the dog's fur. "I'm sorry."

"For what? Lying? Using me?"

"Yes. All that."

I gripped hard to the edge of the bench. "From the moment we met, you used me. Did you always know I was hunting you? Even that first night?"

"Golly, have you been looking for me that long? No. I told the truth, sort of. I really had gone into the morgue to take a better look at that man. I didn't know what you'd been doing until you told me."

"Last night, you came to the hospital to steal this. And when you found out it was too late..." I closed my eyes, and the memory came back to me. She was in my arms, she was kissing me with all the passion and hunger and heat I felt for her...My eyes popped open and that same, stricken expression was on her face before she looked down quickly at the little dog.

"Did you think...what? For a couple of kisses, I'd steal the photo for you? Hide it? Destroy it?"

"*No.* Peter—listen—I—Last night wasn't an act. I really *did* want—I mean..." She shook her head. "I'm explaining this like an idiot, and I'm sorry. Maybe it started out that way...using you, I mean...but... The more I got to know you..."

"But you don't know me," I said, and gently, I took the little dog from her. "You don't even know why I'm not me."

She looked like she wanted to say something, but then just stared down at her empty lap, frowning.

"How are you?" she asked after a few moments. "You made it out last night?"

No, I thought. *No more Guy Rosewood.*

I nodded, and Ruby reached over—I thought she was going for the dog or I'd've moved; instead, she took my hand.

"Did you get in trouble?" she asked.

How did she always feel so warm, even in the middle of a Chicago winter?

"Dr. Keene saw me change. He knows that I'm Guy and that I lied to him about who and what I am. He called the police to my boarding-house. That's why I have all my things, and the dog."

"What are you going to do now?" She sounded like she cared, which made my stomach hurt. I had come so close to getting the answers I needed, the secret to learning who I was and how to control my trans-formations, and now it was gone.

"It's fine. It'll be fine."

I didn't even believe that myself. Of course I'd made a mistake. It was only what I deserved. I caused my father's death, I ran away like a coward. Why did I think Peter Buchanan deserved to be anything other than miserable?

"I can read minds."

I looked up, quickly, to see Ruby staring at me, the look on her face fierce.

"Wh-what?"

"Thoughts. Minds. Memories. I can see them. Hear them." The words—which made no sense to me—came out of her fast. "That's how

I always know who you are, even when you transform. I can hear your thoughts."

"But that—that doesn't make any—People can't do that."

"Just like people can't transform?"

I stared at her. Was this some kind of trick? Something to throw me off?

"Nope. No trick."

My mouth fell open. "How are you doing that?"

She shifted in her seat. "I don't really know, honestly. I just always could. It's like…a kind of hearing. I can't help what I hear when people are close."

When people are… But I'd just thought about…

"I'm sorry," she added quickly. "I'm sorry. I should have told you ages ago."

She could do this the *whole time* she knew me! When I looked at her and wanted to kiss her…When I felt myself falling for her…She knew. Just like she knew right now.

"Peter, I'm sorry." She looked miserable. "Do you want me to go? I can go."

"Can you—stop? Listening?"

"No. I mean, I'm trying to ignore it, but it's sort of like trying to ignore a beeping car horn. But there are…well…layers to a mind. Anything on the surface, anything you're thinking about right at that moment is hard to hide. But your memories, your secrets…I don't break anything open, Peter."

"But you can?" It gave me a jolt of fear.

"I mean, I could. I think. If I wanted to. But I don't," she added firmly. "It's not safe, pushing into a mind like that. Not safe for the mind, and not safe for me, either. I could go too deep and never come out…"

Another shudder rolled over me. Trapped inside someone else's mind?

"But even if it were easy, I wouldn't do it. It's wrong, pulling out people's secrets like that, especially the hidden ones. With you, I could feel them, those real memories of yours, hiding somewhere, but I didn't touch them."

But—I hadn't kept those memories hidden! Just seconds ago, I'd thought about them! I couldn't believe it—she knew the truth about me! She knew I was a killer, a monster, that I was the reason my father died—

"No, *no*." She grabbed my hand. "That's why I had to say something! I couldn't just sit and listen, because you're wrong, Peter. You need to know that! I know real killers. I know *real* monsters, and you— You're just about the furthest from a monster I've ever met. And it's not your fault your father's dead. It's his choice that you're alive. Don't you see? He chose to save you. And not so you could live a sad half life!"

"It's too late. If I try to go back to the lab, Dr. Keene will have me arrested."

"Maybe not…" She looked down at the envelope with the photograph. Picked it up. "I heard you thinking…Your doctor was the key to your understanding your abilities?"

"He's the only person I've found who's looked into cellular metamorphosis. He promised me, when we closed this case, he would help me, but—"

Ruby held the photo out. "Take it. Tell the doctor he can have it so long as he keeps your original bargain. I saw his mind. I'd bet he'll take the deal."

I stared at her. Was she serious? Did she understand that meant trading her freedom for mine?

"Of course I do," she said, sounding almost annoyed.

"But you'll—" *Hang? Die? Spend the rest of her life in prison? Get what she deserves?* Too late, I realized what I'd thought. My cheeks went pink, even though there was a part of me that remembered the horrible, choked bodies of her victims, the files, the fact that she was a murderer and didn't seem to feel any remorse...

"Because I don't feel any," she said, and I flinched. This was bizarre. "I understand no one should walk around with an executioner's ax on their shoulder, and if I knew of any better way to keep those people from destroying innocent lives, I would do it. But I've seen too many monsters slip away and I got tired of taking chances."

"I understand," I said, and she just scowled.

"You *don't.* Imagine you're sitting on the train and there's some well-dressed fellow next to you looking to all the world like a stock-broker reading the paper, but you can *hear* him, you can hear his thoughts and he's thinking the most awful, terrible, soulless things, terrible things he's done to people and even worse things he has planned... And even if you told the police, what if he got away? What if he got off? He's rich, he's smart, he probably has a thousand plans for escape, and then what? You'll have let some truly evil thing disappear back into the world...

"I did what I thought was best. I learned how to make poisons from common chemicals and plants. I put myself out as bait. I waited. And I acted. I don't regret that. Letting someone go, someone who would hurt an innocent person... *that* I couldn't bear. I would do it again. In a minute."

That was what she did with her ability. I used mine to hide and lie to people. She used hers to help people. I didn't think there was another person on the planet who'd discover they could hear other people's thoughts and wouldn't use it to cheat at cards or find out secrets. Only Ruby would think it was her personal responsibility to save the world from monsters.

"You're making too much of it." She shook her head. "You would've done the same thing in my shoes."

Would I? I wasn't sure of that. I let out a heavy sigh and looked at the photo. I didn't think I could hand it in to anyone now, knowing what I knew.

"I'm going to destroy it," I said, but before I could rip it to shreds, Ruby plucked it from my hands.

"No! That's your ticket to freedom!"

"It's your ticket to jail."

"So what!" She pushed it hard against my chest. "That's my decision to make, isn't it? I'm saving you, Peter Buchanan, whether you like it or not."

Just like Dad. What did they think they were saving?

"Something good," she said, her voice soft, and she smiled at me. "Maybe you should trust us. And not throw away what we're doing for you."

I didn't know what to say. But I slipped the photo back into my bag.

"I just have one favor, all right? Go to Dr. Keene, but tell him you'll give him the photo in twenty-four hours."

Twenty-four hours? Of course. She would run. Burn Ruby Newhouse and disappear.

"I am *not* going to run," she insisted. "But I have some things to take care of, before this mess gets messier."

"What things?"

"I know who's been after my family, and I know where he keeps his secrets. I'm going to get any evidence I can and make damn sure it gets published. And then, when the police come for me, well... I've seen what a ridiculous mess the legal system is... maybe I'll get off scot-free." She shrugged, like this was the easiest thing in the world, trading her life for mine, spending her last hours of freedom keeping the people she loved safe.

She would never run. Ruby Newhouse didn't run. She fought. And even if I couldn't make sense of the mess going on in my brain or my heart, I didn't think I'd ever seen anyone look stronger or more beautiful than she did, sitting on that bench with the winter sunlight on her face and her shoulders squared.

"You realize I can hear all that, right?" she asked, raising an eyebrow.

"I know. That's why I thought it."

Her eyes went wide, and she laughed. It was nice to know I could surprise a mind reader.

THIRTY-ONE
RUBY

ell him you need him to get into the Bull and Owl.

Shh.

Tell him you need him to change into Albert.

Oh, shut up.

"Don't forget. Twenty-four hours. Tomorrow afternoon."

Peter nodded. I wished I could see his real face, just one more time. Standing up, I put out my hand for that adorable squishy toy of a dog, and he hopped right over, wiggling and wagging so hard I thought he might fall off the bench.

"Take good care of him," I said to the dog, giving his cheeks such a good scratch that his eyes went blissfully closed. And then there was no little dog between me and Peter, just a goodbye, and how on Earth was that supposed to go? A hug? A kiss? A handshake? I didn't know, and neither did he, judging by his scrambled thoughts. Finally I leaned in and landed a kiss on his cheek, like the first time we met.

"I won't say goodbye," I said, "just good luck."

His mind went quiet, or maybe he'd already figured out how to hide what he was thinking, and he put a hand to his cheek. *Oh golly,* if he said anything to me right then I'd lose my nerve, so I smiled, I turned around, I crossed the street and left Peter Buchanan behind.

Ruby Newhouse, you fool. I should have jumped in his lap and covered him with kisses and taken up Maggie's offer to disappear to Paris, where Peter and I could stroll arm in arm with the little dog beside the Seine, all of us getting fat and happy on brioche.

Focus. You've got work to do, missy.

I slipped my key into the front door of the graystone, scanning my family's minds for anything out of the ordinary.

Mama: out in her greenhouse, cooing to her beloveds.

Genevieve: pinned under a giant book in the study.

Mrs. Ritter: worrying over tea and the sorry state of her shoes.

My darling favorite old nurse, Nurse Graves: fussing over Papa's blankets.

And...Papa?

I tossed my coat onto the rack and flew up the stairs, bursting into his room.

"Good heavens!" Nurse Graves gave me her most ruffled expression—which meant the flat line of her lips quirked a quarter inch into a frown—and continued tucking the blankets. "You could give someone a heart attack!"

"Is he doing better?" I asked, breathless. I already knew the answer: the horrible blackness of his mind had receded, just a bit, like the minutes before dawn when the sky shows the barest hints of color. "Has he woken up?"

"Does he look awake? Take those shoes off, missy, I didn't sweep this floor so I could count your footprints later."

With one hand on the wall, I yanked off my galoshes, studying Papa's quiet, still face. But inside...in his mind...

"What did the doctor say?"

"Improving but not much improved."

I crossed over to his bed and put a hand on his cool forehead. "Papa? Papa, can you hear me?"

And deep inside his mind, cutting through the darkness, a slim, golden shaft of light.

"Crying!" Nurse Graves peered at me. "What are those tears for?"

Sniffling, I let out a laugh. He was waking up, he was coming back! I kissed his forehead, pausing to whisper in his ear, "Just hold on a little longer. We're almost through..."

"If you're about done, I've got to wash these," Nurse Graves said, but she was touched, I could feel it, and I nearly kissed *her,* the wonderful old gargoyle.

"I'll take them," I said, pulling the sheets from her hands. "Don't leave him alone today, all right? Stay by his side."

Rushing from the room, blankets in my arms, I made it down to the kitchen in record time. I shoved the sheets into the laundry chute and was about to dash off to tell Mama to stay put for the rest of the day, when Mrs. Ritter, reading a newspaper in the kitchen, shouted out my name.

"Miss Ruby!" she yelled, with so much irritation dripping through her thoughts that I wondered if she was handing in her resignation. "You've had a message. I left it for you on the parlor table. And when you've got a moment—"

"Thanks!" I said, dashing out before she could say anything else. I couldn't handle staffing problems now. In the greenhouse, Mama gave me a kiss on the cheek, telling me, "Of course I'll be here, darling. Where else would I be?" Next was Genevieve, who seemed similarly content to stay home, but when I looked around for Henrietta, I realized for the first time she wasn't in the house.

"Genny—where's Hen?"

Genevieve readjusted her hold on the book and shrugged. "She went out this morning…" *She was supposed to be back before lunchtime…*

My skin went cold. Henrietta was *missing*?

I flew out of the study and made for the parlor. There, on the table just like Mrs. Ritter had said, I saw a plain, pale-blue envelope, *Ruby* written on the front in beautiful script. No return address, no name.

Damn.

I slit it open with my fingernail and stared in surprise as a bunch of fine golden thread fell out, twisting to the ground. No—not thread. Hair. *Hair.*

Inside, a single page, a single line.

You were warned.

THIRTY-TWO
PETER

Eyes up. Shoulders back. No one knows who you are.

It didn't seem right that the hospital should look the same when I walked through the doors, after leaving Ruby's house and hiding the dog in a new boardinghouse room. But, just like any other day, people crowded in looking for shelter from the cold, the receptionists sat at their long desk near the front door, the orderlies rolled stretchers and wheelchairs and helped patients out to the street.

I'd left the photograph back in the boarding room—I planned on giving Ruby all the time I could—but I wondered if I should've stayed put, too.

It's what Ruby wants, I reminded myself, climbing the stairs. *Her freedom for mine...*

What did it mean? Did she feel the same way I did?

"Last night wasn't an act."

Too bad I couldn't read her thoughts.

Sighing, I pushed open the door to the seventh floor and stepped into the hall. I'd changed clothes and faces, this time appearing as one of the hospital clerks assigned to the laboratory, a man named Darby who wasn't scheduled to work today. I planned to find Dr. Keene, get him alone in his office, and put forward the deal Ruby wanted. Her photograph for his research. But my stomach kept churning. This felt like a mistake.

I made it ten feet down the hall before I shook my head. There'd have to be another way. I couldn't let Ruby sacrifice herself for me. I'd just turned around when a door burst open and I heard a familiar voice boom out, "Darby! Get in here!"

Dr. Keene.

My skin went cold—*Don't change!*—but I remembered Ruby, how much she believed in me, and I closed my eyes, took a breath, and spun around.

"Good morning, Dr. Keene," I said, in Darby's cheerful chirp. Dr. Keene raised a hand, beckoning me, and I followed him in. The moment I'd passed through the door, Dr. Keene leaned in close.

"Any word?" he asked, his voice low. *"Did they find him?"*

I could guess who the "him" was.

"No, sir. Nothing."

"Damn!" Dr. Keene dropped his fist against his desk. "I had it! I had her! You know who will get the credit now? Those stuffed suits at City Hall!"

I stared at him. "Sir?"

He didn't hear me, or he didn't care, waving his hands in the air. "You've got to be the *first* to make the discovery to get the credit! I was almost there! I could have handed the negatives over to the newspapers along with some fine quotes, but now—"

Negatives. I'd stopped listening after that. There weren't any negatives in the envelope I'd given Ruby.

"What are you saying?" I asked, dropping Darby's friendly manner, and Dr. Keene gave me a *Who does he think he's talking to?* look. "I thought Rosewood stole the photograph of the killer."

"The photograph, yes," Dr. Keene said, his voice sharp with irritation. "But someone in City Hall got the negatives. They caught wind of what was going on, went around my back, had the developer send them directly. You know who it was? That snake of an alderman, Dennis Ferry. The one who approved my grant in the first place! He called me himself, told me he's presenting it to the press tonight. Going to be some big, splashy thing with whatever dope's running the state's attorney's office on hand. I'm not even invited! Can you believe it?"

His words swam around me, slowing everything down. *They had another photograph. They were GOING TO EXPOSE her, tonight!*

"Listen, see if you can get Detective Parcell on the line. He's been dodging my calls all day. Darby? Darby!"

But I was already gone, out of his office and down the hall, taking the stairs two at a time.

I had to warn Ruby, I had to tell her what I learned, I had to go *now*, and as I ran down the stairs, I pulled on the white-blond boy's disguise before bursting through the hospital's front doors. Thirty agonizing minutes later, I spilled out of a taxicab and pushed through the gate to Ruby's house. I ran up the steps and arrived at the front door, breathless, reaching for the doorbell, pounding on the door, ringing the bell again.

"Ruby! *Ruby! RU—*" The door opened so suddenly I almost spilled inside, but the girl standing in front of me—blond bob, expensive clothes, scowling—wasn't Ruby.

"Who in the heavens are you?" she asked.

"I need to speak with Ruby!"

"That wasn't what I asked."

"Please, I—"

"See, if I had asked 'What in the heavens are you doing here?' or even 'What's something you absolutely cannot do at this moment?' maybe your answer would have fit." Still frowning, she crossed her arms over her chest. "But I asked: 'Who in the heavens are you?'"

What could I say?

Guy?

Peter?

"I'm...a friend."

"A *friend*."

"Please. It's important. I need to speak with her."

For a moment, the girl's expression softened, and she glanced inside the house. I could hear the quiet sounds of someone crying. The hard look on the girl's face came back and she pushed me aside so she could stand on the stoop with me before closing the door behind her.

"Listen, I wasn't just being difficult. You really *can't* talk with Ruby."

"But—"

"No one can!"

"Oh...no...They got her...She's been arrested..."

The girl gave me a wide-eyed stare. "How do you know about *that*?"

"*You* know? Who are you?"

"Who are *you*? You still haven't answered me!" She let out an exasperated sigh and tossed her hands into the air. "This conversation is going around in circles! But if you know about Ruby's...activities... maybe you are a friend. And any friend of hers is a friend of mine. Margaret Stowe, at your service." She put out a hand and, gingerly, I took it.

"Here's where you give me *your* name, fella," she said, raising an eyebrow.

"It's, um…complicated."

Miss Stowe's frown reappeared, more suspicious than before. "I will reserve judgment only because I'm concerned about Ruby. She's missing. Not arrested, I don't think. But her little sister's been gone for hours, and then this card arrived. The housekeeper said not long after Ruby read it, she ran off!"

Miss Stowe pulled a folded piece of paper from her pocket and gave it to me to read.

"It's not signed," I pointed out, and Miss Stowe shook her head.

"Not with a name, but the last thing I heard from Ruby, she was going after the man behind the attacks on her family. And by *going after,* I mean…" She trailed off but gave me a look, the kind of look that said *possibly murder by extremely painful means.* My stomach dropped.

"They took her sister?"

"I don't know—maybe! As a warning, or, or—I don't know! I only just arrived. I had this idea, see, of how to help people understand what it was she really did. I know she's *guilty* but she's such a good gal, she at least deserves an honest shake, don't you agree? I hoped I could find her here, but I was too late. Now, I think you really need to tell me who you are and what you're doing here, because I'm actually very worried my best friend's life might depend on it."

I steadied myself.

"The last victim was a photographer," I began, "and he—"

"Yes, I know about that! Ruby said there was a photo of her."

"Two. One is safe. But there was another print made, one Ruby doesn't know about. It got sent to City Hall, and a man there, a Mr. Ferry, is going to release it to the press—tonight."

Miss Stowe let out a gasp and clapped a hand to her cheek. "But that's who she's after! He's the man behind the attacks on her family. Oh, he's *horrible*! How did he possibly find out about the photograph?"

"Ferry was funding the investigation to find the angel killer, ever since... That was his hired gun who turned up poisoned after Coward's party! He knew Ruby had survived, he knew the angel killer was responsible for the murder... He must have put it together." I felt sick. It was my fault he suspected Ruby...

"All he needed was proof!" Miss Stowe said with a gasp.

"There's going to be someone from the state's attorney's office at tonight's event, ready to announce charges."

"Ooohhh, I bet it's that rat Albert!"

I shook my head. "I didn't hear a name, just 'the dope running the state's attorney's office.'"

Miss Stowe rolled her eyes. "That's Albert. Ugh, he must be working for Ferry! And Ruby figured it out, so they kidnapped her sister! Probably wanted to make sure Ruby wouldn't run for it. But she doesn't know he's got her photograph, she doesn't realize—oh *no*, she's walking right into a trap! Wait, where do you think you're going!?"

I was already halfway to the street. "Going after her, of course!"

"You idiot boy! You don't even know where to go!" She ducked inside the house, reappearing a second later with a coat over her shoulders, while I realized *Oh, she's right.* "Don't think I'm going to let you dash off and do something stupid. That's *my* best friend out there, and I'm going to make sure she's safe! Now, you can help me, or you can get out of my way, or my name isn't Margaret Elizabeth Isabella Stowe!"

My mouth hung open before she snapped her fingers in front of my face and marched over to a beautiful cherry-red car.

"Coming?" she said, yanking the door open, and I followed behind this tiny force of nature, dumbstruck and awed and convinced I could trust her with my life.

"My name's Peter," I said, climbing into the seat beside her. "And listen, if we're going to rescue Ruby together, there's something about me you should know…"

THIRTY-THREE
RUBY

Now, when about to confront someone who desperately wants you dead, it is important to stay calm. I credited a good portion of my success as a murderess to my skills as a planner, and so before I dashed off to the Bull and Owl Club to rescue my sister, rid the city of an evil plague, and possibly kill a man, I made a quick stop at my bedroom to change into my sturdiest, rough-and-tumbliest clothes and dig into the secret hidey-hole I kept in the back of my bedroom closet.

Ahhh, how I missed my beautiful friends.

Arsenic and cyanide and strychnine, loaded into needles slipped into a leather sheath, which went under my blouse. Thallium hidden in the pendant of the bracelet around my wrist. Belladonna in the belly of the bird brooch to hold back my curls. I had needles and powders and chloroform-infused kerchiefs and I gathered up the whole lot, with my knife strapped to my thigh, just in case. We'd reached the finale, folks. Might as well go for drama.

As I made my way uptown to the Gold Coast neighborhood, I considered the rest of the plan. There was no point in sneaking inside the

Bull and Owl Club. Ferry would expect me to figure out where he was and come charging after Henny. So much so that I was sure it was a trap with my sister as bait. Fine by me. I needed to get into the Bull and Owl and I needed Ferry there, so I could look into his disgusting filthy mind and figure out where he hid his secrets.

I would trade myself for Henny—that was what he wanted, anyhow—and once she had made it out safely, I'd show him the *real* Ruby.

Then all I had to do was retrieve the evidence, pass the bundle off to Vivian with my hugs and kisses, and hopefully make it home in time to give Papa a proper goodbye before the police arrived.

Not so hard, was it?

In the light of the sunset, the brownstone meetinghouse of the Bull and Owl Club glowed like an ember, one block from the lake, on a quiet corner in the Gold Coast neighborhood. It had a turret at the top of its third story overlooking an alley down below and a manicured yard the size of a postage stamp. I'd bet anything that they had a door round the side or back meant for servants or deliveries, and as much as I would have loved to come crashing through a side window swinging a sword, I reminded myself that I was here for *Henny* and *the evidence* first. And so, since they were expecting me, I just unlatched the gate, closed it behind me, and climbed the steps to ring the bell.

I could sense minds inside, moving around. Maybe six? Seven? The thoughts were hard to read, thanks to those sturdy brick walls, but I felt pretty sure a few belonged to servants. The others could have been members of the club or bodyguards or even stinking Ferry himself, but no way to tell from out here, shivering on the stoop.

Time to get this mess over with. Hen needed me.

They had one of those charming pull-string bells, and when I gave it a good yank, I heard a *clang* from inside the house. A moment of nothing, and then, *Ruby Newhouse.*

The door swung open, soundless, revealing a pitch-black entryway so ridiculously dramatic that I almost laughed.

"Turn the lights on," I said. "What kind of idiot do you think I am?"

No voices, but I could hear minds: two men, at least, wary and hiding. They meant to ambush me the second I stepped foot inside the house. One had an ether-soaked rag in his hands, which told me I was dealing with amateurs: ether took ages to knock someone out and might leave their lungs raw and scarred. I'd like to avoid it, please and thank you.

A moment later, the lights came on, showing me an empty entryway. Straight ahead, I could see a hallway, maybe the stairs. Shadows on either side of the entryway suggested darkened rooms. As I slipped my knife out of its sheath and into my right hand, I reached into the two minds, searching for clues about their locations, and when I was certain I'd found the fellow with the ether, I *sprang.*

He'd been half hidden in a statue niche to my right, and I spun around, put my knife to his throat, and twisted the rag out of his hands before he knew what had happened. The other man was behind me, and he jumped forward, no poison on him but he had at least a foot and a hundred pounds on me. He ran for me, hands out, but I ducked free, pulling my hairpin from my curls and moving backward deeper into the house, eyes glittering, feeling the confusion of the two men in front of me and nothing behind me.

"You'll want to use chloroform, next time," I said, breathing hard, laughing, still backing up. "Ether's too slow to—"

A wall. I'd hit a wall, not with my body, but with my mind, and I knew what—*who*—it was. I spun around, my knife raised, but it was too late: Ferry grabbed my wrist and twisted it harder than I would have expected from a man of his age. The knife clattered to the floor while I searched his mind, but I could only feel blackness inside him, blackness that chilled me, distracted me so I didn't even notice that the two men had recovered and come for me. I wrenched free from Ferry and lunged at one of the men, burying my hairpin in his thigh. He let out a scream, dropping to the floor, and I'd just twisted open the arsenic in my ring, swung it blindly at the other man's face, but he was too fast, too strong. He grabbed me, I felt his arms wrap around my chest, my shoulders, my neck. My feet lifted off the floor and my eyes went wide as my throat closed off under the man's hand. I gasped, kicked, clawed, but the edges of my vision went blurry, dark, and I could feel myself falling into tumbling darkness when a face swam before me.

"Well, that was quicker than ether," Ferry said, his mild smile the last thing I saw before everything went black.

…head…

   …heavy…

   …ache…

   …have to…open…eyes…

"Are you awake?"

   …no…

   …eyes…burning…rub…hands? Wrists?!

"Don't move. You'll knock yourself to the floor."

Floor—arms—*rope*—everything was black at the edges, foggy and blurry, and I couldn't make sense of much but I did know this:

I was sitting in a chair

My hands were behind me, tied with rope

I had no idea how long I'd been knocked out

Blearily, I lifted my head, squinted into the dim light, and there Ferry was, sitting in a plain wooden chair, watching me with a neutral expression, flat-eyed like a snake, mind like solid ice. My focus shifted behind him, to the room. We looked to be in a cellar, stone-floored, rough walls, dank air. A row of tiny windows sat close to the ceiling, showing a glimpse of the world outside.

Dark. *How long have I been out?*

"How do you feel?" he asked.

"Why don't you untie my hands and you can find out?" My mouth had gone dry. "Where's my sister?"

"Having her supper, I believe. It's a quarter to seven."

A quarter to seven! That put my blackout at somewhere around *two hours*. So much for my brilliant plan. I needed to get Hen and get out.

Carefully, I picked at the rope holding my hands together, feeling for weak spots.

"Why did you take her?"

Ferry folded his hands together and looked at me coolly. "You."

"You thought if my sister was in trouble, I'd stop looking for dirt on you." I shifted in my seat, hoping it would hide how hard I was pulling at the ropes around my wrists.

"No. I wanted the chance to talk. I assumed you'd follow your sister anywhere."

"And what makes you think you're going to like anything I have to say?"

Ferry picked at a stray bit of lint on his pants. "Oh, I think you'll cooperate, as long as there's a family member's life in the balance."

It took every ounce of my strength to keep from leaping out of that chair, ropes or no. "You're threatening little girls now?" I asked in a snarl, but Ferry shook his head.

"Not her. Your father."

"My father?" Another tug at the ropes. "He's safe at home, he's—" A flash from deep inside Ferry, a feeling of satisfaction, of certainty.

I froze. I reached into his mind, hit the wall, but this time I clawed at it, harder and fiercer than I'd ever tried before. It was like trying to dig into rough and jagged rock, and then finally, *finally,* the tiniest, hairline crack. *A woman, my father, a pillow . . .* And the crack sealed up tight again and left me on the other side, dizzy and breathless.

"You didn't get his nurse, she wouldn't turn for anything, you're wasting your—" And I gasped. Not Nurse Graves, of course.

Mrs. Ritter. Our housekeeper. Troubled by money problems and *me* too busy to notice. Ferry got to her.

A wild, kicking *anger* sprang through me and I yanked at the ropes, bucked at the chair, spat and *screamed.* "You stupid monster! You leave him alone! You leave him alone or *I'll kill you!*"

"About that," Ferry said, in the same detached manner. He pushed himself to his feet and crossed over to a small table, which held a single lamp and a glass half full of amber-colored liquid. Pulling open a drawer, he took out an envelope. Small. Rectangular. Familiar.

"Where—" My words broke off. It wasn't Peter's copy; Ferry had his own.

"It doesn't look much like you," he said, his voice soft as he slid the photograph free. "But it will stand up in court. Ruby Newhouse, you're a murderer."

"You can bet your damn ass on that one," I said through gritted teeth, and I felt one of my fingernails hook into the knots at my wrists.

"It was a surprise to me." Ferry propped up the photograph against the base of the lamp, facing me so it felt like I was staring into a mirror, another me, also pinned in a chair and trapped. "I never would have imagined Jeremiah Newhouse's daughter would be any kind of threat. You put out that article, and I assumed you were just hysterical, making trouble. It wasn't until you asked Albert Rollins for help that I realized you meant to actually continue your father's work."

"Mean," I corrected. *"Am.* It's not over yet. And you better believe Albert is going to regret throwing in with you."

Ferry just smiled. "When Albert told me you were going to Coward's party, I thought it would be easy. I sent my henchman after you and figured the papers would report that Ruby Newhouse had been killed at Herman Coward's birthday festivities." He spread out his hands. "Instead, I hear you're alive and well and moving your father home, while my man is dead. I thought you had a lucky escape, Miss Newhouse, until I arrived back at my office to a phone call from the county morgue. A man had been murdered outside Herman Coward's party, and they believed he was the latest victim of a highly prolific, likely female, murderer.

"Still," he continued. "I could hardly believe you made a habit of killing men. I thought for certain your wealthy friend was assisting you, so I arranged for her to be cut off from her inheritance. And then what should happen? Rex Blanchot becomes the angel killer's latest victim, only he manages to snap a photo of his killer before his death. You are bold, Miss Newhouse, but not very careful..."

His fingertips brushed the surface of the photo, and I clamped my lips tight together.

"That photo doesn't mean a thing," I said. I slipped a finger into the knot. The rope was prickly, thick, but I could feel it loosen... "All it proves is I was in a room with him at some point. It doesn't prove I *killed* him."

"That's true." Ferry raised a finger and walked over to the door. "How very fortunate that I will witness your next crime."

Witness?

Next crime?

He disappeared out the door, and I heard footsteps, then the sound of several feet on stairs, one man, at least, holding what sounded like a large and angry cat. Only, it wasn't a cat, it was—

"Henrietta! Let her go!" The rope stretched against my hands, but not quite enough, and I could only watch as my sister, bound and gagged and red-eyed, was dragged into the room by none other than Commissioner Walsh.

"You! Finally crawled out of your little hole?" I spat, and through the police commissioner's terrified mind, I saw I wasn't entirely wrong. Coward had let it be known that Walsh was a dead man walking, so Walsh had spent the last few weeks hidden in a secret government apartment before Ferry called him to the Bull and Owl. His mind kept replaying the journey out to the brownstone, who might've spotted him, if Coward might've found him, and he was so nervous, jumpy as a caterpillar in a henhouse, convinced any second Herman Coward and his remaining goons would come swinging through a window.

Ferry closed the door behind them and smiled at Henrietta like a distant relation. "How are you, dear? Did you eat well?"

"*Mmphh-emm-PHHM!*" Henrietta said, and I was delighted to find that her thoughts, unlike hard-as-ice Ferry's or sludgy, slimy Walsh's, flowed into me as easy as ever, translating her muffled words into a stream of curses that would make a sailor blush.

What a *damn* good girl.

"Set her down," Ferry said, and a moment later Henrietta dropped to the ground with a crash so hard I felt my hands curl into claws in anticipation of *tearing them all to pieces.*

"Thank you, Commissioner." Ferry gestured to the chair. "Take a seat. Calm down."

Walsh, sweaty and pale, stumbled to sit, where he looked at Ferry's drink like a man marooned in the desert.

"Now," Ferry continued, "we're going to go over what has happened here. Miss Ruby, you have been obsessed with me since your father's accident and, operating under the delusion that I kidnapped your sister, you decided to come to my private clubhouse and attack me."

"*Mm-AHCT-mu?!*" Hen said, and I felt one of my ropes give a little.

"Unfortunately, you had fallen into such deep hysteria that you were quite unaware of your surroundings, and tragedy befell."

"Oh *really?*" I said, giving one final *yank* on the rope, which fell, miraculously, to ribbons on the floor just as I jumped to my feet, reached into my blouse, and felt—nothing.

"You're looking for these." Ferry put a hand in his own pocket and removed the leather sheath with my needles, along with the knife and all my jewelry. My skin crawled, picturing him pawing at me while I sat, unconscious and bound.

"No one, *no one*, would believe I'd kill my sister," I said, my mind unspooling, searching for weapons.

"You're right," Ferry said, and his voice went soft. "Exactly right."

He glanced over his shoulder, where Walsh sat, still shivery with fear, Ferry's drained glass in his hands. Ferry's glass—*Ferry's* glass. But Ferry famously didn't drink alcohol...

"No!" I shouted, just as Walsh grabbed his throat and let out a horrible gurgle. If Ferry had deposited any of my poisons in that drink, it was already too late: Walsh would be dead inside a minute.

I still rushed to his side, trying to catch him as he lurched to the floor, his body's cells tricked by the poison to turn against him, his mind spinning and whirling with thoughts, questions, the same in every dying man. *Why* and *what* and *how can this be?* plus a burning, raging, incandescent fury that he'd fallen for Ferry's trap.

The contract..., he thought through spasms of pain, *I signed— that—contract!*

Contract!

"*Is it here?*" I hissed, leaning down close to him so Ferry couldn't hear. "Your contract! Where does he keep his *files?*"

...dim...rage...why...rat...safe...office...upstairs...papers...

I could feel his mind slipping, sucking at me like a whirlpool, and I knew if I held on any longer, his dying thoughts would pull me down with him. I pushed him away just as his last sparks of life gasped into nothing.

Breathing hard, I looked up at Ferry. "You're killing your allies now?"

"He was unreliable," Ferry said, calm. "He knew too much. And I needed a body."

"*MFFMMHH! NNHH MMPH!*" Henrietta could only growl from

the floor, but I didn't have to be a mind reader to translate her muffled shouts. *I'm going to tell* everyone *what you did!*

Ferry gave her a flat look. "Do you think I'm going to send you off with a stern warning? You, my dear, are never going home. Just another young girl, lost somewhere in this city." He bent down and touched a fingertip to her pink cheek. "I am very good at making girls like you… *disappear.*"

Henrietta stared up at me, her blue eyes wide, her mind screaming *WHAT DO WE DO WHAT DO WE DO?*

This couldn't be it. This *couldn't* be the end. I still had air in my lungs. I still had claws. I was a bloody *killer* and I could take this paper-cutout, *pathetic* slug.

"Stand up, my dear." Ferry pulled Henrietta to her feet, and she struggled like a wildcat before suddenly going stock-still, her thoughts directed like a spotlight to a pinprick of pain at the base of her neck. Then I saw it, in his hand: a needle, the point just under the skin but the plunger not released. Yet.

"If you hurt her, I *SWEAR*—"

"Please," Ferry said in his quiet voice. "Not another word. This is a delicate operation. Now, Henrietta, I am going to take a step backward, just to the corner of the room, and you will come with me or I will push this needle right into your spine."

For a moment I was worried she was so frozen with fear she wouldn't—couldn't—move, but then that brave, wonderful girl took a shallow breath, and like a duet in some terrible dance, moved backward with Ferry to the far wall, where a boxy black telephone hung.

"Hello?… Yes, this is Alderman Ferry. May I speak to the captain on duty, please?"

I'd let her down. I'd failed Henny and my family—all of them. Papa dead, Henny eaten alive, Mama and Genny left on their own… And Peter, even Peter. His photo wouldn't buy him the freedom he deserved…

Henrietta stood motionless except for the tears rolling down her cheeks, and I wished I could hold her in my arms and coo away her nightmares…

"I would like to report something rather shocking. Ruby Newhouse has murdered the police commissioner."

Henrietta let out a small whimper.

"Look at me, darling," I said softly. "It will be all right. There you are, brave girl. It will all be all right."

"It happened not five minutes ago…. Yes, I saw it myself."

"Hen, I love you, darling. I love you very, very much."

"What do you *mean*?" The sound that came out of Ferry's mouth was so unlike him that I tore my eyes from Henrietta's face and stared at him in surprise. He'd gone red, his hand gripping the 'phone tightly, his eyes bulging from his face.

"*No!*" he shouted. "NO! That's—It's impossible!…I don't care— *You're* the ones making a mistake!…But how can that be! What do you *mean, 'Ruby Newhouse is already in jail'?*"

Somewhere in a distant room, I heard the chime of a clock on the hour, *bum-bum-bum-bummm, bum-bum-BUM-bummm,* but before it could finish its song there was a terrific crackle-*CRASH* of glass shattering under an almighty hailstorm of bullets.

THIRTY-FOUR
PETER

"Stop fidgeting, you look smashing. Let me just fix your lipstick." Miss Stowe—Maggie, as in "You *have* to call me Maggie"—leaned in, placed one hand under my chin, and dabbed at my lips before sitting back to admire her work.

"Gosh, you could fool her own mother. You could fool me!" She grinned and patted my hand. Well. Not *my* hand.

"You sure it's all right?" I said. I startled as Ruby's voice poured out from my lips.

"You *keep* asking that. You're fine! Anyway, hard part's done, isn't it?" She stretched out her hand, gesturing at the view. Concrete, rust stains, one filthy cot, and a row of metal bars, behind which I could see half a dozen police officers pushing paperwork and answering phone calls.

Who knew getting arrested could be so *tough*? A stumbling bum could wind up inside a paddy wagon before he said jackrabbit, but put two beautiful young society girls drunk and dancing in the middle of a swanky hotel during the dinner rush, and we could have asked for the moon. It took Maggie pulling me into the fountain in the hotel lobby, flinging off her shoes and stockings and slipping down the sleeve of her dress, before someone put a stop to it.

Now I sat waiting with Maggie in jail, my ankles soggy, wearing the face of a girl I wasn't sure if I loved or hated but hoped to hell I had saved.

"Do you think it worked?" I asked, looking out through the bars at the police officers. Maggie shrugged.

"I don't know. She's got an alibi now, whatever happens. The city's biggest mouths saw us tonight, and anyone who doesn't hear it from them will read it in the papers tomorrow."

It was Maggie's idea. She had me 'phone up half a dozen reporters—using a different voice with each one—to promise a smashing scandal of a story involving Margaret Stowe, heiress, and her lively friend. She even made sure to pick a hotel in the same neighborhood as the Bull and Owl's headquarters, which meant the jail we sat in was only a handful of blocks from Ruby...

"We're getting out before tomorrow, though, right?" I asked, and Maggie patted my knee.

"Of course, darling, don't worry. They know it's not worth the trouble to keep someone like me locked up."

"You seem remarkably calm for someone who just had her name dragged through the dirt," I said, but Maggie just laughed.

"Every heiress needs a disgrace or two. Father will probably threaten to take away my inheritance and my fiancé will probably threaten to cancel the wedding, but a dip in a hotel fountain isn't the kind of thing that brings dishonor on a family *forever*. Besides, I'd walk barefoot on flaming, broken glass if it meant keeping my Ruby safe.

I don't think anyone else in the world loves her as much as I do—except maybe you."

"*Me?*"

"Oh, don't act like I'm crazy. You *do* love her, don't you? Isn't that why you almost tripped over your own feet running to the Bull and Owl Club? You love her."

I looked down at my hands. Ruby's hands. "I don't know. . . . She lied to me."

Maggie made a noise like an offended elephant. "Oh pish. She trusted you with her biggest secret! Don't you realize what that means?" A smile spread across her face like a butterfly's wings. "She loves *you,* too!"

My stomach gave a leap and before I could reply, an officer banged on the bars of our cell with his billy club.

"Visitor!" He stepped aside to reveal a slim woman in her twenties or thirties, a notebook in her hand and a shrewd look etched onto her face. I didn't recognize her, but Maggie jumped to her feet, delighted.

"You must be Vivian Forbes! I just *love* your articles!"

A reporter? Vivian crossed her arms over her chest and rolled her eyes.

"I'll bet you do. Hullo, Ruby—ruining more dresses, huh?"

"Um," I said. "Yes?"

Maggie, a slightly panicked look on her face, let out a nervous giggle and stepped in front of me. "I called you here for a reason, Miss Forbes."

"Well, if it's to chronicle your turn as the Rainbow House's latest swimming enthusiast, I'm afraid you're out of luck. That mealy-mouthed Leon Zinn got the call and is already writing up his take, along with half the reporters in Chicago." She leaned around Maggie and gave me an icy look. "Thanks so much for the tip, kid."

"Oh, we've got a better story for you than *that*! How would you like the scoop of a lifetime?"

The arms stayed crossed but one eyebrow quirked up. "I'm listening."

Maggie clapped her hands together and leaned closer to the bars. "It's about the angel killer."

A jolt of surprise went through me and I started to get up. "Um, Maggie?"

"*Shh,*" she said, waving me away. "I've been reading your story, and you have it all wrong."

Vivian looked bored. "Oh yeah?"

"You keep writing about how the city needs to *stop* the angel killer."

"Yes," Vivian replied dryly. "One usually does want to stop a multiple murderer."

"Oh, but the angel killer isn't some Jack the Ripper monster. You're forgetting how she got her name. You're forgetting the *real* victims."

"Not the dead men?"

"No, no. See? *They're* the monsters."

Vivian made a kind of wet-cat hiss and slipped her notebook into the bag on her shoulder. "Miss Stowe, you're lucky you're rich and beautiful or I think you'd probably find life pretty tough. And Ruby? I'd suggest you find better friends. So long, ladies."

"Wait!" I jumped to my feet, and Vivian paused. I had no idea what Maggie had planned—frankly, I thought she sounded loony, too—but I trusted her. "Just…could you listen to her? Please?"

Vivian glanced from me to Maggie and threw up her arms. "*Five* minutes—and only because it's cold out there and I just got warmed up!"

Maggie grinned and gripped the bars. "Fabulous! Now listen. What I was *trying* to say is that you haven't paid nearly enough attention to the kinds of people the angel killer's victims were. The things they've done, the people they've hurt. The angel killer has *saved* lives, too."

Narrowing her eyes, Vivian glared at Maggie, but I saw her hand twitch toward her notebook. Maggie's grin stretched wider.

"I spent some time today asking around about those men, and d'you know what I found? They were bad people, Miss Forbes. Terrible people. Francis Mather was slowly poisoning his wife and most everyone in the neighborhood figured it was only a matter of time before they'd be at her funeral. Now? Sure, she's got five kids to take care of, but she's alive. Those kids are alive. And instead of grieving their mama they're lighting candles for their angel."

As she listened, Vivian's hands pulled out the notebook and jotted down some notes, moving smoothly as though they operated entirely separate from the rest of her.

"You go into those neighborhoods and you won't find a single wife, mother, or daughter saying a bad word about the angel killer. But they've got *plenty* to say about the city hunting her down."

"She's *murdering* people," Vivian said.

"She's *protecting* people! Innocent people! Women and children, people who can't go to the police or the law! The weakest and most vulnerable of this city! *She's* doing what no one else will. What the city and the police refuse to do! Don't you see? They don't want her stopped! And they're *furious* about it!"

"Look, it's a good angle, I'll give you that. But a dozen nagging wives—"

"A dozen?" Maggie laughed. "Try hundreds. *Thousands*. They're angry, and they're marching on City Hall"—she glanced up at the clock hanging on the opposite wall, which showed a few minutes to seven in the evening—"just about *now*. They want the mayor to decree the angel killer safe from any prosecution and create a city department to address the needs of the very people the angel killer is trying to protect."

Vivian leaned in closer to Maggie. "Is that true? There's a march on City Hall *right now,* thousands of people supporting the *killer*?"

"You can bet your bottom dollar," Maggie said with a smirk, and Vivian scowled.

"What the hell'm I doing here? Why didn't you just tell me to go to City Hall?"

"Wait! All those other articles are going to be about the march, but you—you get an interview with one of the people the angel killer helped."

"Oh yeah? Who?" Vivian asked, sliding her eyes toward me, and I shifted on the bench. But Maggie cleared her throat.

"Me."

"*You?*"

"That photographer, the one found dead two days ago. He had a habit of taking advantage of innocent girls. I got caught up in his con and he made my life miserable. He blackmailed me and knew if I ever tried to go to a lawyer, I'd just hear how it was my fault."

Vivian glanced up from her notebook to give Maggie a frustrated snort of solidarity. "Of course."

"I thought I'd have to live with that monster forever until the angel killer—whoever she is—stepped in and did something about it."

"Well. It's a good story. I want details."

"You'll get them, as soon as you agree to include three things: first, a demand that the city call off its hunt for the angel killer. Second, a request that the mayor do something to address the needs of the vulnerable in this city. And *third*"—here, Maggie drew herself up to her full, if not terribly imposing, height—"an announcement, that I, Margaret Stowe, will *personally* fund the creation of an organization dedicated to this cause."

Vivian stopped writing and my mouth fell open. A march on City Hall, an interview with an heiress—that made for a good story, at least. But money, especially the kind of money the Stowe family enjoyed, meant real action. No one would be able to ignore that.

After another few seconds of stunned silence, Vivian barked out a laugh and stuck out her hand.

"Miss Stowe," she said, smiling, "you have got yourself a *story.*"

Maggie smiled back and had just reached out to shake when a police officer stumbled through the door outside our cell.

"Shooting! A big one! Schiller Street! All officers to respond immediately!"

He might as well have set off a bomb. Everyone jumped to their feet, shouting, grabbing coats and hats, pushing for the door. Without another word, Vivian flipped her notebook closed and chased after them, ignoring the protests from Maggie. I got to my feet, too, racing to join her at the bars.

"*Wait!* Come back!" Maggie shouted, reaching through the bars, and I grabbed her arm and shook her.

"Didn't you hear what they said? Schiller Street—that's where the Bull and Owl is!"

Maggie gasped, one hand at her cheek. "But Ruby's there, Henny… We have to help them! We have to get out of here!" She started banging on the bars, a horrible, loud clanging that everyone else in the room ignored.

"Let us out!" she screamed. "*Let us out!*"

THIRTY-FIVE
RUBY

Henrietta…Photograph…Ferry…Proof…

I dropped to the ground, my cheek pressed to the floor, arms wrapped over my head as the *BLANG-TAT* of bullets erupted around me. I heard windows, doors, furniture crack and splinter. I heard shouts from above, and footsteps, and more screaming.

But all I could think was:

Henrietta

Photograph

Ferry

Proof

I'd shouted for Henrietta to get down before dropping to the floor, but had she? Was she all right?

I felt glass under my knees, bullets going *whizz-zzip* past me, and then one must have found the lamp because the room plunged into darkness. As sudden as a summer squall, it stopped, everything going quiet except for the footsteps above, heavy and running, and I shuffled forward on my knees until I reached something warm, something soft. My throat closed with a sob and I couldn't stop shaking until Henrietta pushed herself up, still bound and gagged, but her thoughts burning vibrantly, violently *alive*.

Gasping, I leaned forward to kiss her cheek and then froze.

"The needle!" I said. Her teeth chattered too hard for her to speak, but I could hear inside her mind: Ferry had dropped it, leaving her arms bound. "Hold on, darling, just hold on…"

I felt around in the darkness and my fingers tripped over a cigarette lighter—Ferry's maybe, or Walsh's—and the leather sheath of needles, both of which I stuffed inside my shirt, before resting on my little silver knife.

"Hold on," I whispered to Henrietta, and I wished I could see her face because her thoughts had gone completely incoherent with fear, stuttering and half formed as she tried to make sense of what had just happened..

Ruby! she thought. *Bullets—needle—Mr. Ferry…*

"Steady, sweet girl," I murmured, concentrating on her ropes. "One house fire at a time."

I slid the knife between the rope and her skin, sawing like mad until I felt her bindings fall into pieces. *Hen, check. Now… light.*

Was it safe to use the lighter? I could still hear sounds of the shootout upstairs, a dozen minds tangled together in rage and fear. I glanced up at the broken windows, but they were too high for me to see anything but the faint glow from the streetlights.

Flash went the little light—but we were alone. No Ferry, no shooters, and no photograph…

I hissed out a swear and turned back toward Henrietta, white as a department store mannequin as she stared down at Commissioner Walsh's body.

Dead dead he's dead he's dead he's poisoned he's dead

Golly, I had to do something.

Still holding the lighter, I grabbed Henrietta with my free hand and shook her.

"Hen. *Henrietta!* Look at me!"

I knew she could hear me. When she didn't move, I gave her a hard pinch on the arm.

"Listen!" *That* got her attention, the stinging pain cutting through her thoughts like a bolt of lightning, but at least her eyes were on *me*. "I'm going to get you out of here, and that means we are going to *move*. Understand? Nod so I know you understand."

She shuddered, then nodded, and I grabbed her hand.

Quick, I looked around the room for a way out. My first choice would be a window, but even if they weren't now shattered and jagged around the edges, they were too small and too high for us to get through.

There was only the one door, closed. A few dark splashes of liquid trailed a path out of the room. Blood, of course, and Ferry's most likely. He was wounded, hopefully badly enough that he hadn't gotten far.

"Hold on to my hand," I said, reaching back for Henny. "Stay low." I had the lighter and my knife held together in my right hand and my sister clinging to my left, and we crawled in a kind of half crouch across the floor, pausing at the door until I made sure there were no minds waiting for us.

I pushed it open and saw a dim stairwell, the stairs streaked with blood. My heart sank, imagining dragging Henny through a bloodbath and out the front door to safety, when I caught a glimpse of a heavy metal door tucked just behind the stairs. I ran across the room and pushed it open a crack, a cold gust of fresh air filling my lungs, and I looked out onto a blessedly empty and very dark alley. Quietly, I closed the door and turned back to Henrietta, but she stood as still as a marble pillar.

"Darling, we have to go."

"I—I—I—" *I'm scared.*

"I know." I squeezed her hand. "It'll be all right."

"R-R-Ruby…Wh-what-t-t *happened?*"

"Oh, baby…I wish I had the time to explain it," I said, as her thoughts scattered like buckshot—*Mr. Ferry a murderer, police commissioner dead, Ruby framed…*

"Right now, all I care about is getting you out in one piece. Do you understand? As soon as you get out that door, I want you to *go. Run.* Don't let anyone stop you, especially the police. Here—take this." I reached over to a dusty shelf and pulled out a man's long, brown overcoat. Draped over Henrietta's shoulders, it made her look even younger, big-eyed and scared. "If someone grabs you, do you remember what I taught you? About where to hurt a man?"

"Aren't you coming with me?" she asked, her voice so small it slipped like a dagger into my heart.

"I've got to take care of Ferry, or we'll never be safe."

"But—" She looked at me, looked at the door, thought about the bullets flying, the men who'd grabbed her, tied her up, and she shrank deeper into the coat.

"Listen to me." I set down the knife and took her by the hands. "You can do this, my darling. I want you to repeat after me: I am strong, and I am going to fight back."

"But, I…I…"

"I am *strong*."

"I…I am…st-strong," she whispered. "And I…"

"Am going to fight back. Reach down deep. Say it."

She took a breath, my dear sister, and I could feel her swimming against an ocean of fear, kicking her body, getting warmer, and finally *bursting* through the surface. She looked into my eyes, held my hand tight.

"I am strong," she said. No quaver in her voice. "And I am going to *fight back*."

I wanted to throw my arms around her neck and kiss her, but she wasn't a baby anymore, so I gave her a quick nod, led her over to the door, and pushed it open. The cold air felt delicious against my cheeks, but…

A contract…the safe…an office upstairs…

Commissioner Walsh's final thoughts had proven to me that the evidence I needed existed here, in this house. I wasn't going to leave without it.

"Are you ready? Hop in the first taxi you see and *get home*. Find Nurse Graves and tell her Mrs. Ritter is trying to kill Papa."

"*What?*"

A loud crash from the first floor made us both jump, and while Henrietta was distracted, I gave her a good push out the door.

"*Go*," I said, and she had tears in her eyes and a lump in her throat but she ran down the steps of the brownstone and out to the street, the tails of the woolen coat streaming behind her.

And now…

Photograph

Ferry

Proof

Cursing myself for bringing a sheath of needles to a gunfight, I climbed the basement stairs, crouching down low as soon as my eyes were level with the floor above. It was empty, a hallway, the walls dotted with bullet holes and the floor gritty with broken glass and plaster dust and *blood*.

From above, another crash, another round of gunfire—what was *happening*?

I closed my eyes and searched the entire building, trying to find and place the minds there…

To my right, a kitchen, but the single mind inside was gripped with so much fear and confusion it was probably just the cook.

To my left, the parlor and a mind screaming with pain—no! Gasping, I pulled away at the last second before the mind slipped away forever, nearly taking me with it.

That put another round of shivers into me, and when I took my search upstairs, it was with a little more care.

I felt the shape of fear-maddened minds, trying to fight, to hide, to defend themselves, and minds white-hot with bloodlust. It was too chaotic to make much sense until I hit two that were familiar:

Icy, impenetrable, flashing with pain. Ferry.

And another one, fierce, furious, triumphant. *Herman Coward.*

What the hell was he doing here?

But of course. He'd told me himself what he had planned.

"The second he shows his face," Coward had said, *"it's gonna be his last,"* and here he was, making good on that promise.

Damn. Herman Coward, doped up and wild and armed with a gun, complicated things, but I didn't have much choice.

Coward's mind, violent and red-hot, felt closer than Ferry's. I'd have to get through him first.

Adjusting my grip on my knife, I swung myself onto the landing and continued up the stairs. I sensed a man—one of Coward's—coming down and barely saw his eyes widen with surprise, his mind shouting *Girl!* before I leapt forward and got him with one of my needles. He yelped and crumpled in on himself, tumbling down the stairs, but it wasn't a fatal dose, just enough to knock him on his heels.

Another *blatter-tat-tat-tat* rang out just beyond on the second story, where Coward's thoughts blazed with determination and two more minds suddenly disappeared from my senses.

Just go up the stairs, I told myself, squeezing my eyes tight. *Quick, before he sees you—*Now!

I jumped and ran up the stairs, not even glancing down the second-story hallway and not stopping until I reached the deserted third floor. How long before Coward climbed those stairs, too? How long before the police arrived and stormed the whole place? I felt the seconds tick-tick-tick by and I *flew* down the hall, making for a closed door and the closed mind behind it.

BANG—I rammed the door open with my shoulder and stumbled to catch my balance, looking up just in time to see Ferry click shut the heavy metal handle of a large black safe.

"Open it," I said, pulling one of my needles free, and Ferry, bleeding from the shoulder but otherwise annoyingly unruffled, lifted a gun.

"Miss Newhouse," he said, his voice not quite as weak as I would have hoped, "you really do need to modernize."

"Herman Coward is downstairs. It's over."

"Is it? For you, maybe," he said. *There,* at the edges of his mind, between flashes of pain from his wound, was a teensy crack. "No matter what happens, if I live or die: you will go to prison and your father will be killed. Perhaps your whole family, if your sisters inherit your stubborn streak. If not tonight, then tomorrow or next week or next month. The organization I have built...That will live on..."

"I am going to kill you. And then I'm going to open that safe."

He laughed, the sound hitching in his lungs. "Do you have a stick of dynamite under that dress? Besides, if you're here looking for your photograph, it's much too late for that."

And through that teeny, tiny crack, I discovered a teeny, tiny memory. *Side door, trade-off, a face, a figure, a friend...*

Albert.

Albert Rollins had my photograph.

"At this moment," Ferry said, with the slightest gasp of pain, "your photograph is on its way to every newspaper editor in the city."

That was it, then.

It was over. I was going to hang.

And the funniest thing happened: a lovely kind of clarity settled down over me like a cool fog.

I pushed a tangle of sweaty curls from off my forehead, fluffed them back in place. Lifted my chin.

"That makes things easier," I said. "Now I don't need to worry about getting myself out alive, huh? I just need to get that safe open."

"There's only one place in the world the combination exists." And he touched a pale finger to his temple.

"Well," I said, narrowing my eyes at him. "That sounds like a *challenge.*"

Before he could respond, I attacked—not with my needles or my knife, but with my mind. I'd always been so careful, picking my way through people's thoughts, making sure I wasn't detected, but now, I didn't care what damage I did. I threw all my ability at him, ripping savagely at the wall around his mind, feeling it peel apart in chunks, and for the first time, I felt a mind shrink away in surprise.

"What—" Ferry cringed, his mind rattling, the hand at his temple curling into a fist. "What is—*How are*—"

"How am I doing this?" It took all my focus to keep at it, one slip and I knew my progress would disappear, but I couldn't help a smile. "How *indeed*. I'm just a girl, isn't that right, Mr. Ferry? Just another *girl,* just like the others you've tumbled up and tossed aside."

A groan spilled out from his lips, the gun in his hand forgotten as he squeezed his eyes shut tight. As hard as I fought, his mind fought back, walls springing up behind walls, layers, whole hidden worlds and black holes. I didn't stop, pushing and tearing at every new obstacle, and I could feel it now, his mind reacted more slowly, fumbling for footing, until I smashed through another barrier and felt the unmistakable tang of *panic.*

"I want you to think about everything you built, Mr. Ferry. Every horrible thing you've done." I felt it, that fear opening wide, crumbling those walls, all his memories and thoughts and secrets out in front of me. I looked into his face. "And I want you to know: it was a girl that tore it all down."

BAM!

I screamed and jumped and my whole body spasmed, searching for the gun in Ferry's hand, waiting for the fireworks of pain—but they never came. Instead, I watched as Ferry wheezed, his mouth dropping open before he crumpled to the floor.

The gun had fallen, spinning away from Ferry across the floor, and I stared at it for a second, confused, when I sensed the mind behind me, blazing like a fire. I spun around, and there, in the doorway, splattered with blood and laughing laughing *laughing* like a demon, stood Herman Coward.

"WHEW!" he screamed. "RUBY NEWHOUSE!" He burst into more laughter—his mind absolutely scrambled—and turned his gun on me. "What the hell you doing here?"

He was mad, utterly crackers, something had broken in him. I didn't know how many people he'd already killed—and neither did he. He'd come here for Walsh, but he planned on taking everyone else down, too.

Including me.

"*Roo*-bee Newhouse! Look at this! I just SAVED your LIFE!" He stumbled into the room, his gun swinging around in the air.

"You killed him!" I couldn't stop the words from tumbling out of my mouth, but the second they did, I knew I'd made a mistake. A wave of pure anger wrapped around Coward, the wild grin on his face drooping.

"I think"—there was the sharp *crack* of a spent casing exiting the chamber of his gun—"what you mean"—he took a step forward, his mind like a roiling vat of hot tar—"is *thank you.*"

Another click of the hammer but this time I was ready, ducking down before the *BLAM*, rolling on the floor while *BAM-BAM-BAM!* Dust and wood and splinters sprayed around me, making me dizzy, and then I heard *click-click-click-click*—out of bullets, he'd have to reload, and without another second's thought I pushed myself to my feet, yanked out as many needles as I could hold, and stabbed them into Coward's chest.

His mouth dropped into an O of surprise. He swiped at the needles, confused, delirious, then took a stumbling step and dropped the gun to the ground. The moment it hit the floor, I kicked it away and had a shiver of panic when Coward lurched forward—*how??* I'd given him enough to level an elephant—but then my beautiful poisons finally kicked in, and he fell with a crash that I felt from my boot soles to my shoulder blades.

"Uggnnhh…"

Ferry!

I spun around to see him slumped on the floor, clutching his chest. I didn't know much about bullets, but I did know fatal wounds, the way they seared and tore someone up from inside out, and Ferry didn't have much time left.

"Hold on, you horrible bastard!" I said, reaching down and grabbing him by the front of his shirt. *"You can't die yet!"*

But he only laughed, the laughter more like breathless choking. Already I could hear sirens screaming down the street. The police would be here in seconds, and as soon as they found me…

"Tell me!" I shouted the words, and when he didn't budge, I closed my eyes and plunged into his mind. It was a world I didn't recognize anymore: those walls broken into jagged shards, into mirrors, into mazes. I could feel his memories surface like gigantic, underwater, prehistoric creatures, all long teeth and scaly skin. *An older woman with a mouth like a knife's edge, the frozen surface of the lake in winter, a girl thin and crying…*

Be careful, I reminded myself. *Be…care…ful…*

I could feel my own mind fading, I was falling in too deep, pulled into those hidden pools inside his head, and *how* would I ever find the combination? How would I escape?

I could feel darkness licking the edges of his brain like cold fire, and I pushed back. *Tell…me…*

Tell me…the…combination…

It was like wading through icy slush. But there, ahead, a spark, and I chased it and caught it before it blinked out into the darkness forever.

Ferry, bent over the safe, his hands rotating the dial, the numbers chanting in his mind:

24

21

5

It disappeared like an ember lifting into the air to become ash, but it didn't matter. I had it, and now I had to *go*.

A wall. I hit a wall.

This one wasn't keeping me out, but keeping me in, and I felt Ferry's mind wrap around me, a million snakes, thick like oil, pulling me down and fading fast…

What would happen if I stayed trapped in a dying mind?

I'd never see my sisters again…

I'd never see my parents again…

I'd miss Papa waking up…

I'd miss Maggie's wedding…

I'd never tell Peter…how I felt about him…

And that

was

unacceptable.

I felt myself grow big, grow strong. I felt all the *Ruby* bits inside me glow white-hot against the fading light of Ferry's mind. I felt the love inside me grow into a thousand-foot sword, and I *attacked*.

SMASH. I hit the wall and shock rolled through me, but I thought of Peter's face and threw the sword straight back into the wall and this time *broke through*. Immediately, my body collapsed, and when my hands and knees hit the floor, I wrenched myself free. Ferry let out a long, choking breath, and went still.

Sirens. Footsteps. No time.

I sprang to my feet and spun the knob on the safe with shaking hands. Twenty-four, twenty-one, five. A stack of files sat inside and I grabbed the lot, holding it tight to my chest. Downstairs, I could hear an almighty crash followed by more gunshots—all right, I needed to find another way out. I looked around the room for half a second before making for the window on the back side of the building and shoving up the sash. A thin layer of frost and ice clung to the fire escape outside and the wind cut through me, but out I went, clinging to the papers, shivering and swearing and trying not to slip down the ladder.

I reached the second floor just as a window exploded into bits of glass, barely missing me.

"Police! Hands up, Coward, we've got you!"

They didn't know he was dead, but it didn't matter. As I spun down the next ladder, I heard more gunshots, screaming, and Coward's men spitting white-hot-bright thoughts.

Just a few more feet, and then a quick six-foot drop that did a number on my ankles, but I managed to keep a hand on the files. Like a rabbit loose from a trap I was *off*, not toward the front of the house and the police and the shooting, but back down the same alleyway I'd sent Henny to, running, running, running so fast I didn't see the person stopping me but felt his arm grab me around the ribs.

I shrieked, twisting just enough to see that *snake*, that *rat*, Albert

Rollins, in possession of my photograph and probably hoping to steal back these files.

"Let go! *Let go!*" I yelled, bucking and kicking and trying to grab a weapon without losing my grip.

"Wait! *Shh!*"

"I'm going to kill you, let me go!"

"Ruby—RUBY!" He had his hands all over me, and I remembered the advice I'd given my baby sisters and gave his instep a good stomp with my sturdy little boots before throwing my elbow into his stomach.

"Oof!" Albert said, doubling over in pain, and I spun free, my feet stumbling over something large. I looked down, and *there was Albert,* stretched out on the ground, a lump on his forehead, wearing—good golly, practically nothing!

I looked up, and *there was another Albert,* gasping for air. The Albert standing in front of me blinked, caught my gaze, and then it was a dream, a fairy tale, the frog transforming into the prince, because Albert said my name, only he wasn't Albert, he wasn't, that horrible face melted away and *in its place…*

THIRTY-SIX
PETER

"Peter!"

She hopped over the real Albert Rollins and threw her arms around me, laughing.

"Oh, is it really you? Are you all right? I'm so sorry, I thought you were him! Golly! Is he *dead*?"

"Just—knocked—out," I wheezed, and then she spun around again.

"Gosh, I'm sorry! Did I hurt you?" She had her hands on my shoulders, and my body felt like it'd been knocked over by an elephant, but I looked into her face and even in the shadows I could see her glowing like a cheerful candle flame. Wouldn't you know it? My aches and pains just melted away.

"You're alive!" I breathed. "You're safe." She looked at me with amazement, her hand on my cheek and her body warm against mine, and then I didn't care about anything else: I closed my eyes, tilted my face down, and kissed the hell out of her.

Nothing else, I didn't want to do anything else with my life except kiss Ruby Newhouse and thank everything good in the world that she was safe. I didn't care about her mind reading or her murders. I didn't care about my past or bad memories. She was here and alive and had made it out of that house and back into my arms and I felt sure I wouldn't ever let her go.

"*Ahem.*"

Ruby and I both jumped, Ruby's face full of alarm, before we looked down the alley to see Maggie, still in her peacock party dress and watching us with a satisfied smile.

"Maggie! What are you doing here? What are you *both* doing here?!"

"Saving your life, darling. Where's Henny?"

"Escaped," Ruby said, with a grin. "She should have made it home by now."

Maggie's smile glowed. "Wonderful! And Peter? Have you got it?"

"Oh!" I reached into my jacket—Albert's jacket—and pulled out the cardboard envelope containing Ruby's photograph and negatives.

"My photo!" Ruby said, and I handed it over to her as Maggie clapped her hands together.

"Brilliant! I was hoping he'd have it! We'd just pulled up from jail when we saw that rat scurrying off from a side door, and I told Peter to take his face—and his clothes—but *I* was the lucky one to knock him out!"

Ruby spun, back and forth, between me and Maggie. "Wait, you know about Peter? And you were in *jail*?"

"You were, too, darling," Maggie said, "and escaping cost me my favorite diamond bracelet—thank heavens the coppers here haven't got a shred of decency. But listen, I really think we should *move this conversation* before things get hairy...er."

She nodded back to the house, where smoke now poured from the second-floor windows. As another wail of sirens approached, Ruby squeezed my hand and together we ran after Maggie back down the alley to her waiting red coupe. We'd barely tumbled into the front seat when the car roared off like a horse getting the spurs.

Ruby ended up on my lap, her arms around my neck, a stack of files in a mess on the dash, and Maggie spun the steering wheel like a champion driver, zipping past the commotion at the Bull and Owl and making for Lake Shore Drive, all the while tossing us knowing glances.

"You two idiots," she said happily. "I told you she loved you."

Ruby went beautifully pink. "Enough about *that*. How on earth did you two find each other?! What's going on?"

"Oh no," Maggie said. "You first, from the beginning, and this time no secrets."

Ruby and I exchanged a glance, and then she turned to Maggie.

"All right, but listen, there's just one *teensy* thing I have to mention to you first."

We arrived at Ruby's house just as she finished up her story and revealed her secret, which Maggie took amazingly well, all things considered.

"Mind reading! But—oh lord—the Duchamps' party last summer! I thought just horrible things about your new bob, and you could hear me the whole time! I feel like such a perfect idiot!"

"Well, that bob was a disaster, you weren't wrong. Darling, I never cared about that stuff and anyway, you were always one of the good ones."

Before the car even stopped, one of Ruby's sisters had run from the front door. Ruby slid off my lap and rushed over to her, taking her sister by the shoulders.

"Hen! Oh, thank heavens you made it home! And Papa—?"

The little girl burst into tears and Maggie, coming round the other side of the car, clutched my arm, but Ruby started laughing, kissing her sister's cheeks, and turned around to us.

"He's awake! He's finally awake!"

And lucky. As his gruff and formidable nurse explained to us, she'd had to fight off his attempted murder at the hands of the housekeeper, who'd fled the house with a very stern warning that she had better run if she didn't want to spend the rest of her life in prison.

After Ruby had seen him, tucked her sisters into bed, and sent her mother off to her bedroom with a kiss and a sleeping tonic, she joined us in her father's library upstairs, pushing aside several thick law tomes on the shelf to reveal a large, dusty bottle of liquor.

"In the state's attorney's own library?" Maggie gasped, fanning herself with her hand.

"Oh, shut up," Ruby said, grinning. "I almost died an *alarming* number of times tonight—I'm having some Scotch. Now talk."

I let Maggie take over, and between generous swigs from the bottle, she paced the floor of the library, explaining her whole day in dizzying detail. She began with the dozens of people she'd talked to about the angel killer, then our dip in the hotel fountain, continuing through to organizing the march on City Hall and her interview with Vivian, and finishing with our dashing escape from jail, courtesy of her diamond bracelet and a junior police officer open to bribes.

"We headed to the to-do at the Bull and Owl and thought there was no way we'd ever get in, and then I spotted that miserable rat, Albert! Ooh, he looked so *smug* I just knew he'd have your photo on him! I gave him a good sock with the tire iron and Peter stripped him down to his union suit—I hope frostbite takes care of his most favorite parts. Now, what's in there?"

With a deep breath, Ruby turned to the stack of files on the desk.

"Straight from Ferry's private safe." She looked nervous as she picked it up, but I knew she'd done it, she'd found the evidence she needed, and she flashed me a small smile.

"You don't know anything yet," she said to me.

"Well," I replied, "open it."

Her fingers shook as she riffled through the papers, but slowly, the expression on her face hardened into something like relief, if relief could also look queasy.

"It's all in here," she said, her eyes on the files. "Contracts, receipts, blackmail on every major player in City Hall—minus Papa, thank goodness. Lists of corrupt cops, details about bribes, financial statements. Gosh, it's a prosecutor's dream! No one involved in this mess is going to walk away."

"Brilliant!" Maggie said, her eyes shining. "That takes care of Ferry's evidence. And as for yours…"

She plucked the photo from its envelope and studied it for a moment before crossing over to the fire in the grate and dropping the whole thing in.

"Oops." She grinned and looked back at Ruby. "That's that, then. Peter will destroy his copy, Ferry's is ashes, and between my money and those angry women marching on City Hall, I'm going to make sure everyone in this city sees the angel killer as a hero."

"But Peter's investigation, and the mayor—" Ruby started, and Maggie wagged her finger to cut her off.

"You let me handle the mayor. There's some dirt on him in there, right?"

"Sure. But I don't think he was involved in any of the really mucky stuff."

Maggie gave a brisk nod. "Pretty soon the city is going to wake up to the news that one of its respected aldermen was running a criminal organization inside City Hall, along with half the police force and Chicago's civil servants, and Mayor McGuire is going to have to decide if he wants to be leading the cleanup or caught up in the middle of it. He's going to need as much good press as he can get his hands on, and I bet an organization for mistreated girls, helpless mothers, and adorable orphans will do the trick. I'll give Tommy Gun a choice: give up the chase for the angel killer and throw the weight of City Hall behind reform, or, when we send that package off to Vivian, we stick the mayor's photos right on top."

For a moment, Ruby could only blink at her in amazement, and then she started laughing.

"Maggie—you're a wizard! Where'd you get this nerve?" she asked, and Maggie blew her a kiss.

"Where else? From you, of course."

It took a few more hours to hammer out the details and get our stories straight, but by the time Maggie gave Ruby a sleepy hug, we knew that Ruby's secret would be safe. No prison, no noose, no more hunting her down.

"Need a ride, handsome?" Maggie asked me, but Ruby reached out and took my hand.

"Nope," she said, smiling. Maggie's eyebrows lifted but her grin only grew, and she disappeared down to her car with a wave.

Alone on the front steps of the house, Ruby and I watched her drive off, and then Ruby tugged at my hand.

"Do you fancy a walk? I sure as hell do."

The streets were cold, but the sky overhead bloomed with dawn, a beautiful, pale pink, the color of summer and seashells. Ruby kept her hand in mine as we walked down the empty sidewalk, our breaths pouring out in soft white clouds.

"Thank you," she said at last.

"For what?"

She snorted out a laugh. "'For what?' For everything. For saving me. For trusting Maggie. For keeping that photograph. For forgiving me."

"You can see that, can you?"

"Well..." A small smile crept onto her lips. "I sort of hoped."

"It's strange. You reading my thoughts. I keep trying to push away certain things but they just—"

"Become impossible *not* to think about?" She squeezed my hand. "You'll get better at it. And until then, I promise to tell you what *I'm* thinking. All right? And right now I'm thinking...I'm so glad you're here. But I'm also thinking, what will happen to you? You can't go back to Guy Rosewood."

"Ah, well...Good thing I have experience hiding."

"Peter..." She pulled me to a stop and put a hand to my cheek. "I know you don't want that."

Her skin felt so warm, but I shrugged away from her touch. "I don't have much choice. Dr. Keene will be furious that the mayor's ending the angel investigation. Anyway, he saw me change. He'll figure it out. He'll find Peter Buchanan and what I did—"

"Peter! You were just a boy!"

"I killed my father. And not just him. Three people died when that train derailed. If I had listened to him...they all would still be alive..."

She reached out and gripped both my arms, squeezing hard. "Peter, listen! You made a mistake, and now you have two choices: you can live forever with that mistake or you can *do something* about it! I can see you, do you understand? I see every single inch of you and you deserve more than masks and running. You have a brilliant mind and a beautiful heart and if you don't do something with those gifts—"

"Ruby, it's a good story, but Dr. Keene was my only hope." I took a deep breath. Maybe she already knew this, but I wanted her to hear it from me. "I…can't control it. My abilities. When I get shocked or scared, I lose control. That's what happened to me that night my father died, and I know it'll happen again. What if I hurt someone else I care about? What if it's you? I'm not going to take that risk."

"And what about me? What about what I'm willing to risk? If it meant giving you the kind of life you deserve, I'd take that chance any day of the week! Do you hear me, Peter Buchanan?"

"But—"

"No buts. You saved me, and I'm going to save you!" And before I could say another word, she rose up on her toes and kissed me breathless. When she pulled away, all I could do was stare at her.

"Say you trust me."

"I…I trust you," I said, and even though I wasn't sure, and even though I knew Ruby knew that, she smiled.

"Good. And Peter—*no more masks. This* is the only face I want to kiss." Just to make her point, she did it again.

One week later, Ruby strode into Dr. Keene's office with me, the real me, trying to catch up.

"Hello!" she said brightly, and when Dr. Keene started to ask her who we were, she was off: "My name is Ruby Newhouse. Yes, the daughter of Jeremiah Newhouse. Yes, he's doing much better, thank you, expected to recover. Now, listen. You know this fellow, don't you?"

Dr. Keene blinked and then shot to his feet.

"You! Rosewood? Or—who—*what* are you—"

"Hold on," Ruby said, cutting him off with a wave of her hand. "I know you might be a little sour to see him right now, given he ran off with that key piece of evidence you needed…and then the mayor pulled your funding…But look. You know what he can do, don't you?" She glanced at me, and even though I felt pretty sure my heart was trying to climb up out of my throat in protest, I switched to Guy Rosewood and back again.

The color drained from Dr. Keene's cheeks and a hand clutched at his chest.

"This is what you study, isn't it? Or you *did*? Here's what's going to happen." Ruby reached into a briefcase and pulled out a neatly typed document. "Peter is going to apply for medical school this fall and will be accepted, thanks to a glowing letter of recommendation from you. In between his studies, Peter will assist you here, helping you learn more about those tri-tri—what are they again?"

"T-tricoloroforms," Dr. Keene said, still looking very white.

"Right! I've already secured a private sponsor for your research. You can publish your findings, so long as you credit Peter as an anonymous subject. And don't pester him. He's going to be studying very hard."

It took Dr. Keene a second to realize she'd finished, and the silence was so deafening even I could almost hear his thoughts. Without the glow of publicity from the investigation, he'd lost his lab and ended up back in his dingy office in the morgue. This could be his ticket out again.

He glanced over at me, studying my face.

"Rosewood?" he asked.

I just replied, "It's Buchanan, sir. Peter Buchanan."

Ruby smiled and handed him the document.

"What the hell is this?"

"A contract," she said. "Legally binding. You agree to the terms I just laid out and you will receive your first payment to fund your research. Should you ever break the terms, you'll be subject to severe financial penalties."

Dr. Keene gave her the kind of look you might give a small dog that had just delivered a stern lecture, and gave me the kind of look that said *Can you believe this nonsense?*

Ruby snapped her fingers to get his attention back. "Hello! There you are. If you don't like this deal, we're happy to walk away. I'm sure there are plenty of other scientists who would pos-i-lute-ly *jump* at the chance—"

"Now hold on!" Dr. Keene held up a hand. "Leave me the papers. I'll let you know."

But Ruby gave me such a huge grin, I knew the answer was yes.

"Brilliant!" she said, putting out her hand, and Dr. Keene, slightly more awed, stared at it before shaking it.

"You've got some bulldog here, Buchanan."

"She's not a bulldog, sir. She's my lawyer."

"Same difference," Dr. Keene muttered, sinking back into his chair. Ruby linked her arm around mine and led me to the door.

"I'll expect your response at the 'phone number listed there by one p.m. sharp," she said, and just before we stepped outside she glanced over her shoulder. "And if you do a good job with Peter, we *might* know a mind reader you can take a crack at, too."

EPILOGUE
RUBY

"**R**uby. We have to go."

"Right, right, almost done. Five more minutes."

"You said that fifteen minutes ago. We're going to be late."

"Oh, you know these things never start on time, especially—" I glanced up from the Himalayas of books and papers surrounding me and realized I'd already lost my audience. Jumping to my feet, I only just managed to catch sight of the door of the reading room swinging shut.

"Hey!" I shouted, setting off a chorus of "*Shhh!*" as I threw the books into a pile.

My heavy bag *tha-thump*ed against my back as I dashed out of the reading room, down the stairs, and out the door of the public library, blinking from a combination of the bright summer sunshine—and *him*. One hand in his pocket and the other held out for my things, with a smile on his face that made me weak in the knees in the best way.

"That's a mean trick," I said, giving him a poke in the ribs, and he just laughed.

"If I let you miss this, you'd never forgive me."

He had a point there. What had we been working for all these months if not this moment? And maybe I'd forgive him someday, but *Maggie* would murder me.

Thirty minutes, two streetcars, and a long, hot walk later, we arrived in front of a beautiful building just north of the city, a refurbished white-stone miniature mansion with an expansive yard, which gasped a little from the heat but still glowed green.

We stood on the front steps for a moment, taking it in, and then I straightened Peter's tie and he tucked a stray curl behind my ear and we headed inside together.

Maggie, with her good party hostess sense, had moved the event to the backyard, shaded by draping elm trees and fragrant with the work of two full-time gardeners. Everyone wore their summer thinnest, men in linen and women in lace, and I felt out of place in my wilted georgette blouse, my college girl's pleated skirt, until I glanced over at Peter and, with a smile, he released a thought as delicate and beautiful as a fine piece of dandelion fluff.

"You're getting so good at that," I said, my cheeks flushed, and not from the heat. These days, I couldn't read Peter's mind. Oh, I could if I *really* wanted to, like I had with Ferry's; I could claw and fight and pull down his defenses and probably get inside. But I wouldn't. I liked having a bit of mystery.

"Look." He nodded at a small stage erected at the end of the yard. "They're about to start."

Wearing a pale-pink dress dotted with huge, hand-painted bunches of hydrangeas, Maggie climbed onto the stage and beamed at her assembled guests. She'd aged about fifteen years in the last six months, and only in the best ways, but if the crowd thought they'd be getting .

Madame Stowe, Proper Heiress and Benefactress, they were dead wrong.

"Hullo, folks!" she said into a microphone perched on top of a podium. "Welcome to our shindig! So glad you're here. I've sprung for cold *everything* for lunch, and I don't want it to go to waste, so I'll be quick, but I've got to say a few words to mark the occasion."

She smiled out at the crowd, a mix of our friends and the older philanthropist set and at least a dozen women, standing together in twos and threes or minding small children, nervous but beautiful and decked out in what looked to be custom duds from Maggie's favorite dressmaker.

"A few months ago, I learned we had a problem in our city," she began. "Women, children, the most vulnerable citizens we have, were being hurt and taken advantage of. And no one seemed to care. *I* didn't care, either, actually, until I became one of those victims. The life I loved was as good as over, and then *she* stepped in and saved me, just like she saved so many people here today."

Maggie grinned at a few of the women in the crowd.

"Since then, I've been working to create a place where people can get the help they deserve. I am tickled to pieces to officially open the Stowe House for Women, Children, and Families, which will provide legal and medical support to those in need. And I've really got to thank a few people now.

"First, Mayor McGuire, for agreeing to stop that witch hunt and publicly vowing to make our city safer for all citizens."

Tommy Gun, a glass of ice water in his hand and at least thirty pounds skinnier than he was six months ago, wearily turned and waved to a polite smattering of applause. He hadn't weathered the months of newspaper articles and public inquiries and resulting scandals with anything approaching grace, but he looked happy enough to be basking in the one positive thing his administration had helped create.

"Next, we would be completely lost without the skillful assistance of the head of our legal department, Jeremiah Newhouse, who—" *Much* louder applause here, and even Maggie paused to clap her hands together as Papa pushed himself up from a chair near the stage and nodded slowly. "Yes, he's done a *smashing* job, and we're thrilled he's joining us permanently. Under his guidance, we'll have the *best* damn lawyers— oops, I mean, the best darn lawyers working on behalf of our clients."

More applause, and although I joined in, I couldn't help but feel a stab of sadness. Papa had recovered, remarkably, but not enough to take on the task of the state's attorney's office. That role had gone, *much* to my displeasure, to Albert Rollins, who had *somehow* managed to weasel free of the stink of the Bull and Owl Club and hold on to his interim position. The only thing that kept me from tearing him apart was the rumor that Albert had discovered that dreaming about being state's attorney and *actually being* state's attorney were as different as a horse and a horsefly. Last I'd seen of him he was a walking definition of *in over his head* and most people were betting he'd finish the year in a sanatorium.

"And before I let you loose on the caviar and *crème fraîche*, I've got to thank one more person." Maggie's hands settled on either side of the podium, graceful as butterflies, and she stared into the crowd until her eyes caught mine and her face lit up. "To our angel, wherever you are. We are here today because of you. Many of us are *alive* today because of you. Maybe your methods were a little messy, but your intentions were always to protect the forgotten and save the lost. Thank you, for showing us who to fight for. I hope we can live up to your example."

One of the women Maggie had invited began to clap, then another, then another, and soon the applause rose up like a wave. I could *feel* the women I'd helped, and it didn't feel like they'd been rescued. It felt like they'd been listened to. They'd been believed. I could feel their hearts and hopes and bruises. I could feel their strength and confidence. I could hear them.

Thank you

Bless you

For me, for my family

I won't let this happen to anyone else

A beautiful little army, finding their weapons.

"And with that," Maggie said, "let's celebrate!"

A cheer rose up from the crowd and I recognized a few of our rowdier friends rushing for the appetizers, led by Maggie's fiancé, J.P. Thanks to Maggie's indomitable charm and considerable influence, social work had become the newest fad among the yacht-and-cocktails set. I'd been to half a dozen fund-raising galas supporting causes from women's rights to anti–animal cruelty leagues, and even J.P. had helped bankroll a croquet club for some local youths. It seemed like if the angel killer had been the first pebble, Maggie was the hill, helping everyone else to roll merrily along.

"Lemonade?" Peter asked as I fanned myself.

"*Please.*" The moment he disappeared I felt a familiar sharp mind approach.

"Any comments for the paper?" Vivian asked, pen poised over her open notebook.

"Nope, sorry."

"You're never interesting anymore." She snapped her notebook closed and rolled her eyes before yanking at the throat of her crisp white blouse. "I'm hot and bored. Let's chat off the record."

"Off the record?" I glanced at her with a raised eyebrow, but she was serious. She knew this was nothing but a society party, a pleasant human interest story, and she already had her quotes. And she had all the notoriety she needed, after a series of scathing articles dissecting everything wrong with City Hall—and how to fix it. Frankly, I couldn't believe she'd accepted such a piddling assignment as the opening of the Stowe House, and when I peeked into her mind, I got another surprise: she'd done it because she wanted to talk to me.

"How's your pops?" she asked, collapsing into the nearest garden chair and fanning herself with her notebook. "Really, I mean."

I sat down beside her and glanced over at Papa, who'd managed to sweep Peter away into what was almost certainly a boring conversation they both would thoroughly enjoy.

"Off the record? He'll never see the inside of a courtroom again. That attack roughed him up good. Don't get the wrong idea—he's still sharper than any of us—but it makes him nervous, I think. Sometimes he gets confused or forgetful. Still, Maggie was smart to snatch him up. He'll do good work here. Brilliant work."

"Until his precocious daughter takes over for him. Heard you're the youngest summer intern at Wollinsky and Wright, then it's off to the University of Chicago next month. Two years and straight on to law school? Clerking for the city's best judges? What's your goal? President of the world?"

"I'll settle for a degree and a good job," I said, feeling a funny kick in my gut. This lawyering business was *hard,* even with Papa spoon-feeding me appellate briefings from babyhood. Twelve-hour days at the law firm, then holing up all weekend at the library to get a jump on my classes. And *that* was just the stuffing-my-head bit, never mind the charming welcomes from the fellas in the firm. Half of them thought I only got the position because Mr. Wollinsky felt sorry for Papa and the other half thought it was because Mr. Wollinsky liked the shape of my stockings. I glanced over at Vivian, sharp and smooth in her tailored outfit, and leaned in.

"From one career gal to another: Any advice?"

"Really?" She looked surprised. "All right. Keep your head down. Work ten times harder. Be better than them every chance you get, and don't expect anyone to notice. You'll have to be smart and charming and humble and confident and everything all the time, all at once. Remember that other gals aren't your competition, they're your allies. Stick to them like glue, support them—you're stronger together. And don't pay any attention to the bastards dragging you down. Believe me, there will be plenty. None of them are smarter than you, even the smart ones. But I've got to say, Miss Newhouse. I'd bet on your pony. You'll be running this city inside a decade. Someone's gotta," she said, turning to raise an eyebrow at Mayor McGuire, sweatily shaking hands.

"You know," she continued, "as persuasive as Miss Stowe is, I didn't expect her to convince the mayor to give up the angel killer. And I shouldn't be saying this here, but I gotta admit, I'm a little disappointed to never know who she is."

"Oh yeah?"

"Yeah. Especially since I'd heard some rumors... There was a photo floating around, but somehow it went missing..."

I took a sudden interest in my fingernail varnish. "Shame."

"And that's not all. I dug around at the hotel where that photographer died—the one who bothered Miss Stowe—and found a fellow who *swore* he saw a red-haired girl drinking with him that night."

I looked up and gave Vivian a deadpan stare. "Too bad there are so many girls with red hair in this city."

"Oh, it's a real tragedy," Vivian said, with a crooked smile and her thoughts slanted sideways. *I know it was you, Ruby Newhouse.*

Go still. Stay calm. Remember to breathe.

But I'll keep your secret.

"Anyway, if this angel killer ever wanted to tell *her* side of the story, I hope she knows I'm a sympathetic ear."

"Don't hold your breath. It looks to me like she's retired."

"Oh, I wouldn't say 'retired.'" Vivian gave me another sly grin as she rose to her feet. "Just moving on to bigger and better things." She put out a manicured hand and I took it. "Good luck, doll. I'll read about you in the papers. You get any tips about anything, you know where to find me."

"I wouldn't dream of contacting anyone else," I said, and she winked at me and headed back into the crowd to enjoy her free lunch.

I watched them all for a minute as I stretched out my legs. Papa looked better than he had in ages, despite Mama and the girls fussing over him.

Girls. Good grief, they had turned into little ladies overnight.

Whoever had arrived back at our home the night of the mess at the Bull and Owl, it wasn't my frivolous sister. Henrietta seemed to have left that girl behind in the basement of the brownstone. I kept dipping into her thoughts, worried her sunny stability masked some deeper fear, but she was made of strong stuff, my sister, as we'd both discovered.

As for Genevieve, she'd been happily distracted by Peter's arrival in our lives, finding him an excellent resource for her scientific inquiries and a soft touch when it came to borrowing lab equipment. They went on regular excursions together, after which Genny would return home laden with books and clanking like a tinker's cart; overjoyed to have inherited my laboratory, she'd already transformed it into a humming monument to discovery.

And Peter…He seemed so much happier these days, busy getting ready for school, which took a heap of studying and some well-intentioned finagling of his transcripts. What extra time he had, when he wasn't finding secluded spots with me, was spent in Dr. Keene's lab, learning more about his abilities. It helped, but…there was something else bothering him.

A few weeks ago, after thoroughly researching the situation, and on Papa's advice, I'd convinced Peter to write to the Peakington, Indiana, police, explaining who he was and offering any help in closing the case of the train derailment. We both got a surprise: a polite if perfunctory note stating the case had already been closed. An inquiry had found the conductor traveling at three times the recommended speed and halfway into a bottle of moonshine besides. He should have had plenty of time to safely stop the train. Only his reckless actions were to blame. As for the boys, either no one had believed they'd seen a mysterious, hidden child change his face and body, or the boys had decided it was too crazy to mention. The letter didn't even bring it up.

"That's smashing!" I told Peter when I heard the news, but he just nodded. He wouldn't say anything else, and he'd gotten too good at hiding things from me…

"All right?"

I looked up and there he was, appearing like the best kind of dream with a sweating glass of lemonade in his hand.

"All wonderful," I said.

"I saw you talking to Vivian."

"Yes, she—You know her?"

Peter took her seat and sipped from his own glass of punch. "Sure, but she doesn't know me. I met her that night Maggie and I ended up in jail. When I was..."

"Me? You know, something I've always wondered about that night... Maggie said you two were dressed to the nines."

"Sure. The nicest dress I'll ever wear."

"But you were *me*. And you had to *change clothes*." I leaned in a bit, in case any dowdy matrons were listening in. "Tell me honest: Did you peek?"

For half a second, his eyes went wide, his walls slipped, and I caught an image of myself, not a stitch on me, shy, tortured, eyes closed, eyes open, and then the walls came up fast again and Peter's cheeks turned a delicious shade of pink.

"I—um—I mean, I—"

"Don't worry," I said, giving him a poke in the ribs, and I leaned in even closer, so that I could make out every thread of gold in his big brown eyes. "But that means you *owe* me."

His eyebrows went up and I heard his breath catch in his throat and *oh* I would've slid onto his lap and covered him with kisses, hang those stupid old matrons, except—

"Happy!" A furiously cheerful white snowball tumbled out of the house and onto the grass, barking to get everyone's attention before careening over to us. "Hello, you ferocious beast! Keeping an eye on things?"

I pulled the little dog up on my lap and Peter reached over to scratch him behind the ears. It'd been Peter's idea—both the name and his new job as dog-in-chief of the Stowe House. Peter didn't have any place for him at medical school, and when Maggie'd complained that the Stowe House seemed too unwelcoming, especially for their littlest guests, Peter suggested a small white dog might be just the ticket to warm things up.

"How's work?" Peter asked, smiling at him, and Happy gave his hand a good wash. "What do you think—does he need a walk?"

He didn't fool me. He just wanted me to get out of there with him, but lucky him, that was what I wanted, too. Maggie wouldn't miss us for a few minutes, three-deep in admirers, so I dashed inside the house for Happy's leash before following Peter out across the lawn and down to the street: tree-lined and quiet and sleepy with summer haziness.

As we walked toward the lake, the sunshine fell on his cheeks. I didn't think I'd ever get tired of looking at him, the real him—beautiful inside and out. And because we had a rule that *I* had to tell *him* my thoughts, I did.

He smiled, a sort of polite, uncomfortable smile.

"What's the matter?" I asked. I still couldn't tell.

"It's…I'm glad. I'm glad you like this face. I mean, since it's mine, and I'm going to try to stop wearing masks. And I like not hiding any-more, but…" He sighed. "Every time I look into the mirror, I see him. And I don't care what that letter said. It's my fault he's dead."

Peter took my hand, but he kept his mind closed. What was going on in there? Maybe I wouldn't ever know, but not for the first time, I wished he could see inside me.

We reached the lake and let Happy off his leash to play in the waves, barking and biting at the water, and as Peter watched him, a smile pull-ing at that mouth, it felt like *time*.

"Peter." I reached into my handbag and pulled out a soft leather roll.

"What's that?"

I opened the roll, showing off my tiny, glittering needles, and felt shock race through his mind like a lightning bolt. Then the wall came up again.

"I don't regret it," I said. "I never wanted to kill anyone, but I told myself if I didn't do something, then it was my fault, and if that meant I had to become a killer in order to save a lot of people, then I'd do it." I weighed the needles for a moment in my hand, and with one swift gesture threw the bundle far, far, far into the lake, where it landed with a splash and then disappeared.

"What's changed?" Peter asked.

I looked down at Happy digging in the sand.

"I don't know. I thought I'd have to do it forever. I thought there would always be horrible people and a broken system to deal with them. But now…" Maggie, the women at the Stowe House, Vivian and her advice: *stick together, you're stronger as a group.* "I'm done with needles and poisons and listening in on secrets. I'm going to go to college, then I'm going to go to law school, then I'm going to go wherever I'm needed, and I'm not going to stop until I know that everyone has the protection and dignity they deserve. Maybe that means I won't ever be able to stop. But maybe I'll show enough people the way to go, and they'll take up the fight when I can't. And this time"—I took his hand and squeezed it—"I'm not alone. I've got some help, from a brilliantly talented, good-hearted boy."

When he made a face, I laughed. "You still don't get it. Every bit of you makes me happy. Mind and heart and—"

"Face?"

"Yes. I'm *glad* you look in the mirror and see your father, Peter.

It's a gift. Don't you realize? A bit of him living on. It should remind you, every day, how proud he would have been to see you exactly like *this*: warm and happy in the sunshine, with people who care about you. Look into the mirror and think about that."

He was quiet for a moment, and then he raised his hand. "What about this?" he asked, and the hand shifted shapes and colors so quick it took my breath away. Carefully, I threaded my fingers through his.

"You think this thing makes you strange. You think it's going to push people away. But it's just the opposite. It's made you the person you are. It's made you compassionate and smart and tough and kind. It made me fall for you! It's not an enemy."

He let out a long breath and closed his eyes. I could feel years of tension and anxiety and fear, and I felt him…push them away. To try to look at the thing inside him with the fondness I had. To look at it like a friend.

I let out a laugh as soon as I felt it. He finally saw what I saw. Just the first small step. But it was enough.

And since I'd promised him I'd always be honest with him, I had to say it. "Peter, I—"

"I love you," he said softly, and I laughed again. I leaned in and kissed him, threw my arms around his neck and kissed him till we were both breathless on the shore of Lake Michigan, warm and happy and laughing.

"You know," I said, "you read my mind."

He put out his hand, and I took it, and together we walked with Happy back toward the party. We'd worked so hard for this moment, and I sure as hell planned to enjoy it.

ACKNOWLEDGMENTS

This book might've just stayed something on my laptop that I pulled out every now and then to read, if not for these amazing people who helped get it out to the world and into your hands.

First, my incredible editor, Sally Morgridge. Working with her was a pleasure, from start to finish. Sally's thoughtful comments and questions (and cheering on both professionally and personally) truly made this book into something I am incredibly proud of.

My extraordinary agent, Sara Crowe, has believed in me and this book for longer than pretty much anybody. She found this book's perfect home, back when I wasn't sure if it would ever exist in the world, and she has always been there with encouragement, reassurance, and guidance. A special shout-out also to the entire Pippin Properties team! I feel so lucky to be a part of such a wonderful community of creators and champions.

Everyone at Holiday House has been as welcoming and passionate about books as an author could possibly hope for. Thank you for taking such good care of this book (and for catching all my anachronisms).

Writing is a lonely profession, or it would be if not for my lovely fellow writer friends, who are always there to commiserate, gossip, celebrate, and (every now and then) take a look at something I've written. Special thanks to the people I've successfully kidnapped away to a remote island to keep me company over the years: Erin Bowman, Annie Cardi, Camille DeAngelis, Annie Gaughen, and Emily Martin. And thank you to Claire Legrand and Lisa Maxwell, amazing writers and even better people who offered their much-appreciated words of support and encouragement.

Mackenzi Lee's friendship and frequent texts have carried me through the toughest and darkest moments of the last few years (by which I mean trying to figure out how they made a musical out of Spider-Man), and her love and encouragement have been nothing short of sustaining. I love you. Please move back to Boston.

I am proud to say I'm a working mom, and I could not have written this book without the dedicated childcare workers and teachers who cared for my children so that I could pursue my dreams. Thank you to every person who held my daughters' hands, made them feel safe and loved, and helped expand their worlds. A special thank you to the teachers who managed to do all that through a computer screen.

Most of this book was drafted in 1369 Coffeehouse in Cambridge, Massachusetts, where I sat typing away, fueled by tea au laits. Thank you for having the best iced chai in the city and for giving me the closest thing I have to an office. I can't wait to get back to creating there.

Where would I be without my fantastic family, the one I was born into and the one I was lucky enough to marry into? These people buy my books, push them onto their friends, drive for hours to my events, and are always there to cheer me on. Thank you especially to Mark and Anne Toniatti, for all your continued love and support.

Sloan and Gahyee, even though you're a world away, you both are such a special part of my life. I miss you, and I'm so grateful for our regular chats and your love, advice, and encouragement.

Mom and Dad: Thank you, for everything, but especially for being there when the world shut down. I couldn't have made this book what it was without your help and the many things you did to make sure my family was safe and supported. I hope I can be half the parent you both are.

Abby, the dog, can't read, but she deserves some acknowledgment for being my best-behaved and most-obedient child, as well as the cheapest therapist around.

Dave. I love you. You have always been there, from the first moment I thought about being a writer, through the highs and the lows, to celebrate, to comfort, to encourage, to reinforce. I am so lucky to go through this experience with a true partner, in every sense of the word.

And finally, Iris and Flora, my girls. How can I even begin to say how much you mean to me? I wrote and edited this book usually with at least one, and sometimes both, of you hanging onto me, sitting next to me, and hiding small toys in my hair. I wrote this book for you both, because I believe in girls, in all their strength, their girliness, their fierce love for their friends, their unwavering determination to do what's right. You two have crashed into my life like meteors of joy, and I'll never be the same. You're everything to me. I love you.